DRAGON EYRE ASHFALL

Christopher Mitchell is the author of the epic fantasy series The Magelands. He studied in Edinburgh before living for several years in the Middle East and Greece, where he taught English. He returned to study classics and Greek tragedy and lives in Fife, Scotland with his wife and their four children.

Brigdomin Books Ltd
First Edition, March 2022
ISBN 978-1-912879-72-4

For Conor

ACKNOWLEDGEMENTS

I would like to thank the following for all their support during the writing of the Magelands Eternal Siege - my wife, Lisa Mitchell, who read every chapter as soon as it was drafted and kept me going in the right direction; my parents for their unstinting support; Vicky Williams for reading the books in their early stages; James Aitken for his encouragement; and Grant and Gordon of the Film Club for their support.

Thanks also to my Advance Reader team, for all your help during the last few weeks before publication.

THE TWELVE REALMS OF DRAGON EYRE

The Twelve Realms of Dragon Eyre (in 5254, when *Dragon Eyre – Ashfall* takes place)

The archipelagos and island chains of Dragon Eyre were traditionally split into twelve ancient realms. Geographically, the realms were also separated into two 'Rims', denoting the eastern and western edges of the ring of archipelagos. The invasion of Dragon Eyre by Implacatus began in 5228 (twenty-four years before *Badblood* begins), and was completed by 5231, when the last rebel, Queen Blackrose of Ulna, was defeated.

The Western Rim

1. Alef – *80,000 natives; 40,000 settlers; 25,000 Banner forces.* Alef consists of hundreds of tiny islands, most of which are uninhabited. It has large oil reserves, which are administered and protected by Banner garrisons. 200 dragons remain, living on the remotest islands.

2. Olkis – *300,000 natives; zero settlers; 45,000 Banner forces.* The most unruly and chaotic of the Twelve Realms, Olkis is a haven for rebels, surviving dragons, and pirates, who roam the seas around Olkis. The Realm of Olkis used to include the semi-independent island of **Tankbar**, whose entire population was annihilated by Banner forces following an uprising in 5248. 2,500 dragons live in relative safety in the mountainous regions of the south-west.

3. Ectus – *50,000 natives; 150,000 settlers; 60,000 Banner forces.* Converted by the occupying forces into a vast complex of naval and army bases, with the main shipyards of Dragon Eyre located on the northern coast. Heavily-forested mountains provide the wood to construct the fleets of the Sea Banner. No dragons remain.

4. Gyle – *800,000 natives; 600,000 settlers; 40,000 Banner forces.* Traditionally, Gyle was the main island prior to the invasion, and remains the capital of Dragon Eyre. Its foremost city is the settler-built Port Edmond, named after the Blessed Second Ascendant. Includes the islands of **Mastino** and **Formo**. No dragons remain.

5. Na Sun Ka – *100,000 natives; 100,000 settlers; 30,000 Banner forces.* The former spiritual home of the dragon-worshipping tradition of the Unk Tannic. For administrative purposes, the outpost of **Yearning** is considered part of the realm of Na Sun Ka, despite its location in the Eastern Rim. No dragons remain.

Note – under Banner occupation, the group comprising **Ectus**, **Gyle** and **Na Sun Ka** are referred to among the settler population as the '**Home Islands**'. Despite the presence of rebel Unk Tannic cells, there are no dragons remaining on the Home Islands, meaning that they are relatively safe locations for the settlers to dwell.

The Eastern Rim

6. Haurn – *zero natives; zero settlers; zero Banner forces.* Occupied by greenhides following an uprising in the Eastern Rim in 5239. 500 dragons live in colonies on the southern cliffs, while a small number of natives live on the scattered islands to the north of Haurn.

7. Throscala – *100,000 natives; 80,000 settlers; 30,000 Banner forces.* The main Banner base of the Eastern Rim. 200 dragons hide in the mountain peaks on the east coast of the island.

8. Ulna – *70,000 natives; zero settlers; zero Banner forces.* The realm where **Blackrose** was Queen prior to the invasion. Devastated by greenhides following an uprising in the Eastern Rim in 5239. A few overcrowded colonies of refugee humans live on the southern isles of Serpens and Tunkatta, along with 200 dragons.

9. Enna – *60,000 natives; 20,000 settlers; 20,000 Banner forces.* Houses a large Sea Banner base, from where the Eastern Fleet patrol the seas between Geist and Throscala. Includes the smaller island of **Meena**. 400 dragons remain, mostly in the mountains of Meena.

10. Geist – *50,000 natives; 20,000 settlers; 13,000 Banner forces.* The borderlands of the occupation. Home to a large garrison of Banner forces, who defend the island from attacks by the dragons of Wyst. 1,000 dragons live on the islands between Geist and Wyst.

11. Wyst – *zero natives; zero settlers; zero Banner forces.* The only realm of Dragon Eyre where all attempts at colonisation or invasion have failed. Even prior to the invasion, Wyst remained aloof from the other realms, and has excluded any humans from living there for centuries. The 7000 surviving dragons of Wyst despise all humans, whether native or settler, and have successfully resisted the occupation.

Note – the distance between **Alef** in the Western Rim, and **Wyst** in the Eastern Rim, is further than the maximum flying range of any dragon. Consequently, Alef and Wyst can be seen as the two ends of a single, long chain of archipelagos.

Central Region

12. Rigga – *50,000 natives; zero settlers; 7,000 Banner forces.* Out of reach of any dragon, Rigga was traditionally the only human-dominated realm of Dragon Eyre. The resource-poor islands of Rigga are in the centre of the Inner Ocean, and can only be reached by ship. Prior to the invasion, it was considered by most dragons as exceptionally backward and primitive. A Banner garrison subdues the native population. No dragons have ever reached Rigga.

NOTE ON THE CALENDAR

Note on the Divine Calendar – Dragon Eyre

The Divine Calendar is used on every world ruled by Implacatus. As all inhabited worlds were created from the same template (and rotate around their sun every 365.25 days), each year is divided into the same seasons and months as that of Implacatus itself. Dragon Eyre differs from other worlds in not having four seasons – instead, the world has two distinct periods that share the same warm, sunny weather, but have alternating wind cycles.

In 'summer' (the first six months of the year), the wind blows anti-clockwise round the Inner Ocean.

In 'winter' (the last six months of the year), the wind blows clockwise round the Inner Ocean.

Each month (or 'inch') is named after one of the Twelve Ascendants (the original Gods of Implacatus). Through long years, the names have drifted some way from their originals, but each month retains its connection to the Ascendant it was named after.

In the Divine Calendar, each year begins on the 1st day of Beldinch.

Dragon Eyre Summer:

- Beldinch (January) – after Belinda, the Third Ascendant

- Summinch (February)– after Simon, the Tenth Ascendant

- Arginch (March) – after Arete, the Seventh Ascendant

- Nethinch (April)– after Nathaniel, the Fourth Ascendant

- Duninch (May) – after Edmond, the Second Ascendant

- Tradinch (June)– after Theodora, the First Ascendant

Dragon Eyre Winter:

- Abrinch (July) – after Albrada, the Eleventh Ascendant

- Lexinch (August) – after Leksandr, the Sixth Ascendant

- Tuminch (September) – after Tamid, the Eighth Ascendant

- Luddinch (October) – after Lloyd, the Twelfth Ascendant

- Kolinch (November)– after Kolai, the Fifth Ascendant

- Essinch (December) – after Esher, the Ninth Ascendant

DRAMATIS PERSONAE

In Ulna

Blackrose, Queen of Ulna

Maddie Jackdaw, Blackrose's Rider

Shadowblaze, Blackrose's Oldest Friend

Ahi'edo, Shadowblaze's Rider

Ashfall, Daughter of Deathfang

Greysteel, Blackrose's Uncle

Splendoursun, A Suitor from Gyle

Ata'nix, Leader of Unk Tannic (Eastern Rim)

Austin, Captured Demigod

In Haurn

Sable Holdfast, Witch

Badblood (Sanguino), Sable's Dragon

Deepblue, Tiny Dragon

Millen, Deepblue's Rider

Evensward, Dragon of Haurn

Boldspark, Dragon of Haurn

The Five Sisters

Ani'osso (Ann), Captain of the *Flight of Fancy*

Elli'osso (Ellie), Based in Olkis

Adina'osso (Dina), Based in Olkis

Atili'osso (Tilly), Captain of the *Little Sneak*

Alara'osso (Lara), Captain of the *Giddy Gull*

Olkian Pirates & Associates

Oto'pazzi (Topaz), Master of the *Giddy Gull*

Ari'anos (Ryan), Carpenter's Mate

Vizzini (Vitz), Seaman and Settler

Olo'osso, Legendary Pirate Patriarch

Udaxa'osso (Dax), Olo'osso's Nephew

Opina'osso, Olo'osso's Fourth Wife

Udo'rapano (Dora), Brothel-keeper

Dragons of Skythorn

Redblade, Dragon of Skythorn

Starbright, Leader of Skythorn

Leafscale, Dragon of Skythorn

The Colonial Gods

Horace, Governor of Dragon Eyre

Meader, Outlawed Demigod

Ydril, Commander of Throscala

Bastion, The Eldest Ancient

Dragon Eyre - Western Rim

N
W   E
S

Alef

Olkis

Tankbar

INNER
OCEAN

Rigga

Sabat City   Ectus

OUTER
OCEAN

Mastino

Formo

Port Edmond

Gyle

Sun Ta

Na Sun Ka

miles

0   100   200   300   400   500   600   700   800   900   1000

Dragon Eyre - Eastern Rim

N
W · E
S

Wyst

Geist

Enna

Meena

Ulna

Serpens

INNER
OCEAN

Throscala

OUTER
OCEAN

Yearning

Haurn

miles

0   100   200   300   400   500   600   700   800   900   1000

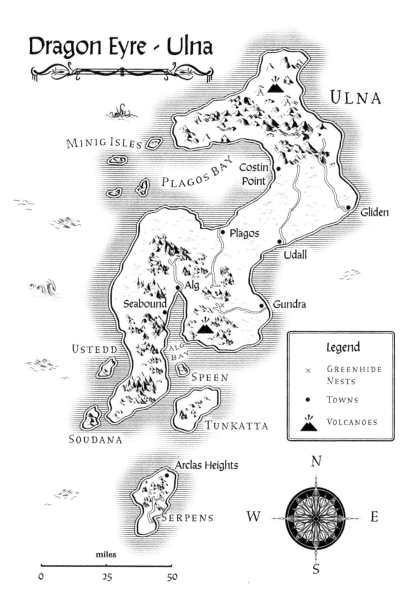

Dragon Eyre - Ulna

ULNA

MINIG ISLES

PLAGOS BAY

Costin
Point

Gliden

Plagos

Udall

Alg

Seabound

Gundra

USTEDD

ALG
BAY

SPEEN

TUNKATTA

SOUDANA

Arclas Heights

SERPENS

Legend

× GREENHIDE
NESTS

• TOWNS

▲ VOLCANOES

N

W   E

S

miles

0   25   50

Dragon Eyre - Olkis

OLBAN

FANSKA

QANA

TANROE

Cape
Endu

Yafra

Cape
Atar

Nankiss

THE KOLETI
ISLES

GARTMUN

Luckenbay

Aipura

MUCKLE
SKERRIE

The Skerries

Skythorn

Langbeg

Cape
Keru

Vipara

Pangba

OLKIS

Cape
Uneo

ONSAR

N

W   E

S

FELJIRA

NAGELI

0 10 20 30 40 50 60 70 80 90 100
miles

CHAPTER 1
OUTCASTS

Nan Po Tana, Haurn, Eastern Rim – 21st Luddinch 5254 (18th Gylean Year 5)

The small blue dragon soared up from the sparkling waters of the narrow bay, a huge fish clutched within her forelimbs. She extended her wings, sending cascades of water flying from them, and rose up to the height of the temple perched on the edge of the short cliff, as Sable watched from under the shade of an ancient olive tree. The dragon passed over Sable's head, taking her prize into the walled compound.

Sable shifted her position on the stone bench, her legs starting to ache. On the other side of the little bay, the small, abandoned village of Pot An was reflecting the glare of the sunshine. Its white-washed cottages had been neglected for twenty years, but remained bright enough to almost dazzle her eyes every morning. A mound of green-hide bones lay by one end of a rickety pier, the only evidence that the beasts had ever frequented the area, the dragons having chased them far from the vicinity of the temple where Sable lived with Millen, Badblood and Deepblue. A single-masted boat had berthed by the small jetty fifty yards to Sable's left, protected by the high walls of the temple compound. Millen was down there, speaking to the various merchants who sailed along that stretch of Haurn, linking the scattered communities of refugees. Next to Millen's feet was a large crate, filled with tanned leather, which he was using to barter with the merchants. Every ten days or so, the boat would stop at the temple's tiny jetty, and Millen would trade with them. Sable leaned on her walking stick, and hoped that they had some coffee to sell, or maybe some wine.

A fierce pain came from her left hand, and she rubbed the scar in the centre of her palm, her gaze on the stump where her little finger had once been. She had passed her thirtieth birthday, but felt much older. At least she could walk again, she told herself, though even that was a struggle, and she was usually exhausted by the time she had made it all the way from her room in the temple to the stone bench next to the little bay every morning.

No, she thought – do not feel sorry for yourself. You had your chance, and you blew it. Tough shit.

A peal of laughter came from the jetty, and she saw Millen shake hands with a few of the merchants. Sable frowned. Four merchants were on the jetty, when she was sure there had been five a few moments before. She was probably seeing things, or perhaps she was going mad.

The unmistakeable click of a crossbow being loaded came from behind her, and she moved without thinking, her battle-vision reflexes taking over. Her legs screamed in pain as she turned and threw herself to the ground. The crossbow bolt flew over her right shoulder as she hit the rocky path by the edge of the cliff.

'Stay still, bitch,' muttered a man, his hands reloading the bow.

Sable squinted up at him. 'Meader?'

The man's eyes narrowed. He lifted the bow, and aimed down its sights at Sable's head.

Sable started to laugh.

'You think this is funny?' Meader said. 'You took everything from me; you destroyed my life.'

'You've come for revenge?' she said. 'Do it.'

Meader remained motionless.

'Go on,' she said. 'I'm unarmed; defenceless. You can take my head to the gods on Gyle, and maybe they'll forgive you. Of course, that's if Badblood lets you leave Haurn alive, which I very much doubt.'

Sweat appeared on Meader's brow as he pointed the crossbow at her. 'Is this a trick? Are you in my head?'

'No tricks; I promise,' she said. 'Look at me. I can't fight you, Meader. If you want revenge, take it.'

His finger moved closer to the trigger.

'What are you waiting for?' she said. 'Do it.'

He cursed, and threw the crossbow to the ground, his eyes wild with anger. 'I'm not a murderer.' He sat on the bench. 'Despite what you made me do, I'm not a killer.'

'Are you going to leave me lying on the path?'

He stared at her. 'Get up.'

'I can't. Will you help me?'

A confused look passed over his eyes.

'Please,' she said.

He leaned forward, and took her hand. She groaned as he pulled her up, her back and legs burning in agony. She panted, and collapsed onto the bench.

'What's wrong with you?' he said.

'That's nice,' she said. 'You tried to kill me, and now you're enquiring into my health.'

'I should have killed you. You deserve to die for what you did, Sable.'

'Tell that to the thousands of natives on the Eastern Rim who are alive and free because of what I forced you to do. We saved them, Meader, you and I.'

'You made me an outcast; a renegade. I am wanted by the gods, as a traitor. I can never go back to Implacatus, or even Gyle – do you understand? The Banner are looking everywhere for me. You owe me, Sable.'

'Is that why you couldn't kill me?'

'That, and the thought of being ripped apart by your dragon.' He glanced around. 'Where is he?'

'He usually sleeps through the morning sunshine,' she said.

Millen appeared through an archway. 'Hey, Sable,' he said. 'I managed to get us some...' He frowned, his gaze going to the man sitting next to her on the bench. 'Who's this? Didn't I see you on the boat?'

'This is Meader,' she said. 'An old friend.'

Millen's eyes went to the crossbow lying on the ground by his feet.

'What did you manage to get us?' said Sable.

'What? Oh, some wine, along with the usual supplies. Will our guest be staying? The boat's about to leave.'

Sable glanced at Meader. 'Well? Are you staying?'

The demigod stared into the little bay. 'I have nowhere else to go.'

Millen nodded, though he looked far from happy. 'Have you got any luggage?'

Meader shook his head. 'I sold everything I had to get here.'

Millen picked up the crossbow. 'Not everything.'

'Keep it,' said Meader. 'I'm a lousy shot.'

'I'll get started on lunch,' said Millen. 'Deepblue caught a fish.'

'Thanks,' said Sable.

Millen lingered for another moment, then strode back through the archway into the temple.

Meader glanced at Sable. 'Boyfriend? Husband?'

'Neither,' said Sable. 'Millen is also an old friend. He looked after me when we got back from Ulna. He nursed me back to health; well, as healthy as I'll ever be.'

Meader said nothing.

'After I left you on the cliffs of Alg Bay,' she went on, 'I helped take care of Lady Seraph, and then, as a reward, the Unk Tannic shot me – once in the right thigh.' She lifted her left hand. 'And once here.'

'They shot off your finger?'

'No; a god cut that off a while back, in Lostwell. The bolt went right through my palm. Then, a dragon picked me up and threw me to the greenhides. I shattered my left leg, and then a greenhide ripped my back open. Deepblue saved me, though I don't remember it.'

'But that was a year and a half ago,' said Meader. 'How can you still be ill?'

Sable gave a grim laugh. 'I really am mortal, you know. I know everyone sometimes treats me as if I'm a god, like you, but I'm not. It took ten months before I could walk again, and I still need a stick to help me. I'll probably always need it. I got an infection from the wound in my back that's never really gone away.' She laughed again. 'And to think that I'd hidden some salve in among the Lostwell Hoard, for emergencies, and when I needed it, I had no way to get there.'

'What happened to the Quadrant?'

She raised her left hand again. 'I was holding it when they shot me. Blackrose has it now, I guess.'

Meader shook his head. 'And to think that I had imagined that you were living here like a queen.'

'How did you find me, Meader?'

'Luck,' he said. 'I've been on the run since... that day. I hid on Ulna for a while, then managed to get a boat to Throscala. That was where I learned that I was being held responsible for the earthquake that destroyed the fleet. Lady Ydril had detected my powers being used. I worked my way to Na Sun Ka, pretending to be a mortal settler, and hid there for nine months, but someone discovered who I was, and so I ran to Haurn. That was when I heard a rumour of a witch, living in a remote temple on the coast, from some of the fishermen on a tiny island to the north of here.' He glanced at her. 'My father has been arrested.'

She nodded.

'The blame for the destruction of the great fleet was placed squarely onto his shoulders. Have you heard of an Ancient by the name of Lord Bastion?

'I saw him once on Lostwell,' said Sable. 'He was with Edmond. Having said that, I don't know much about him.'

'He acts as Lord Edmond's right hand. If he gets involved in something, then you know things are serious. Anyway, he paid a visit to Gyle, took my father into custody, and appointed Lord Horace as the new Governor of Dragon Eyre. My father...' He paused for a moment, his eyes welling. 'My father has been disgraced; his career is in ruins, because of you, Sable. And now Bastion has him. Both of his sons are being treated as traitors.'

Sable frowned. 'Your brother, too?'

'Yes. Austin is still a prisoner in Ulna, but Lord Horace has decreed that he is a collaborator. He claimed that Austin is advising Blackrose, or some such nonsense. Horace always hated us, and now he has his chance for revenge.'

'What else did this Bastion do?'

Meader shrugged. 'He told Horace to consolidate the Western Rim, and await reinforcements. Then, he went back to Implacatus.'

'How do you know this if you've been on the run?'

'The news was being spoken about in every settler tavern on Na Sun Ka. I had to listen to people ridicule my father, night after night. Some even believe that he sent out the fleet with the deliberate intention of having me destroy it. He is a good man, Sable, and you brought him down.'

'He ordered the enslavement of every native in the Eastern Rim, as well as the deaths of every dragon. I'm not going to cry over his arrest.'

'Then, you don't understand what Horace will be like in his place. Horace intends to annihilate every native upon Dragon Eyre – it has long been his desire. He has already removed the legal protections over the slaves that my father instituted.'

'None of this makes me feel sorry for your father, Meader. We did what had to be done. I am sorry that you've suffered, but you should know that I would do it again.' Sable glanced out over the bay. The single-masted boat had left the jetty, and the men on board were guiding it back towards the open sea. 'Do you want to see where you'll be staying?'

'Before I climbed the steps up the cliff to see you,' he said, 'I had decided that I had two options – to kill you, or to persuade you to finish what you started. It turns out that I don't have the stomach for the first choice; and you're too ill for the second.' He sighed. 'What are we going to do?'

'Live, Meader; that's what. Help me stand.'

He got to his feet, and pulled her up. She gripped the walking stick, and grimaced from the pain in her legs. She led him through the stone archway, and they came into a large courtyard, surrounded on three sides by old white-washed buildings. On the open side, the fields and orchards of the compound stretched away into the distance.

'This is an old Unk Tannic temple,' she said; 'from back when the Unk Tannic were peaceful monks and priests. We have two hundred acres, all enclosed by high walls, which keep the greenhides out. We grow grapes, and tomatoes, and Millen has his tannery business, which is on the far side of the compound to keep the smell away.'

Two men of Haurn nodded to Sable from across the courtyard.

'And we have eight workers living with us,' she went on; 'volunteers from the neighbouring islands. One of them had a baby a few months ago, which is about as exciting as it gets around here.'

'No Banner?' said Meader.

'We haven't seen a single soldier here, nor any Sea Banner vessel. Their ships stay clear of Haurn these days.'

They walked on a little further, and saw Badblood, sprawled out under the shade of some tall cypress trees.

'You recognise my dragon, I'm sure,' said Sable. 'He's the only one, apart from me and you, who knows what truly happened that day in Alg Bay.'

'You haven't told the others?'

Sable shook her head.

'Did you know that most natives think it was the dragon spirits that caused the giant wave?' he said. 'Even after Governor Horace announced that I had done it. They don't believe him. The Unk Tannic are milking it for all it's worth.'

She shrugged. 'Not my problem.'

Badblood opened his good eye. 'Meader,' he said. 'I wondered if you would find your way here.'

'He's going to be staying with us for a while,' said Sable. 'He needs a safe place to hide.'

Badblood tilted his head. 'I am at your service, Meader. My rider might not like to admit it, but she feels an immense amount of shame for what she did to you. As do I.'

'I came here to kill her,' said Meader.

'And yet, I cannot help but notice that she remains alive.'

Meader frowned. 'I couldn't bring myself to do it.'

'I am very pleased to hear it,' said Badblood. 'Had you done so, then I would have ripped you to pieces and cast your head into the ocean.' He glanced back at Sable. 'How are you today, my rider?'

'The same as usual,' she said.

'My brother has healing powers,' said Meader. 'Have you considered flying to Ulna and asking for his help?'

Sable and Badblood both laughed.

'I cursed Blackrose before we left,' said Badblood. 'She allowed her new friends to throw Sable to the greenhides. We can never return to Ulna.'

'My leg's getting sore standing here,' said Sable, her right fist clutching the head of the walking stick. 'I was going to show Meader to his room.'

'You do that, rider,' said Badblood, 'then rest.'

Sable smiled at the dark red dragon, then escorted Meader to the left, where they entered the cool interior of a stone building. A few wooden chairs were arranged around a table, where a lamp stood next to a vase full of fresh flowers.

'This is where we have our meals,' she said, 'and sometimes sit in the evenings, if it's rainy. Above it are a few old bedrooms, where I imagine the priests used to sleep. You can take one.'

'Where do you sleep?' he said.

'In the next building along. Why?'

'Just curious. What about the natives?'

'There are cottages by the northern walls of the compound; they live there.'

'And Millen?'

'He sleeps in a little hut close to the jetty.'

Meader nodded.

Sable sighed. 'Was that your subtle way of trying to figure out if I'm sleeping with him? I already told you that he's not my boyfriend.'

'If I'm going to be living here, then I want to make sure I'm not getting in the way. The last thing I want is to piss Millen off.'

'If I were you, I'd worry more about upsetting Badblood. Go upstairs and pick a room, then come down for lunch. If you need to get washed, there's a water trough in the courtyard.'

'Are you not going to show me around?'

'No. That's why I sleep next door – no stairs.'

He glanced at her, then nodded, and made his way to the back of the room, where a stairwell began. She watched him leave, then limped back outside to where Badblood was gazing at her. She sat down on a bench next to him.

'Is this good or bad, rider?' the dragon said. 'Do you think he might try to kill you?'

'He had his chance,' said Sable. 'To be honest, I don't know why he didn't take it. He knows that you would have killed him, but I'm not sure he cares any more.'

'So, he has lost everything, and has nowhere else to go?'

'Yes.'

Badblood nuzzled her. 'Then, he'll fit right in with us.'

———

Meader raised an eyebrow at the large, full plates that Millen was laying on the table.

'This is more food than I've seen in a long time,' he said. 'Thank you, Millen.'

'It's no problem,' said Millen. 'It's not often we get guests, and Deepblue caught the fish this morning, so it's nice and fresh.' He sat opposite Sable and Meader. 'So, who are you, exactly?'

'Do you remember when I abducted a demigod from Gyle?' said Sable.

'Vaguely,' said Millen. He narrowed his eyes. 'Wait. Wasn't he the governor's son?'

'The former-governor's son,' said Sable. 'Meader's father has been arrested, and Meader himself is now wanted by the Banner authorities.'

Millen nodded. 'I see. Another renegade, come to join us. He doesn't have a Quadrant, does he?'

Meader smiled. 'Unfortunately not.'

'What powers do you have?'

'Stone.'

'Oh,' said Millen. 'That's a pity; I was hoping for something a little more useful; I mean, useful here in Nan Po Tana. Like clay powers, so we could repair some of the outer walls.'

'I can fix stone walls,' said Meader.

'Can you? Alright; let's put you to work tomorrow. The walls around the temple compound are old and crumbling, and I'm always worried that a greenhide might be able to break in.'

'I haven't seen any greenhides in this part of Haurn.'

'Yes,' said Millen, 'but that's only because Badblood and Deepblue scared them away when we first moved here. In fact, Evensward's entire colony helped out for a while, and chased all the greenhides away.'

'Evensward?' said Meader.

'She's the leader of the local dragon colony,' said Sable, pouring wine into an earthenware mug. 'They live about ten miles south of here. We stayed with them for a long time, but they complained about the smell coming from Millen's tannery, so we moved up here. Poor old Badblood and Deepblue just have to put up with it.'

'I can't smell anything,' said Meader.

Sable shrugged. 'You haven't got a dragon nose.'

They ate for a while, and Sable forgot about her injuries for a short moment as the hot food filled her stomach. When Meader finished, he sighed, and pushed his plate forwards.

'So,' he said, 'what are your plans?'

'You mean, beyond living here in peace?' said Sable.

'Yes.'

'None. That's it; we want to live here in peace.'

'But, you're the most powerful mortal on Dragon Eyre.'

'I was. Not any more. I lost the Quadrant, and can barely walk, let alone fight.'

'But... you still have vision powers?'

'Yes, of course. But I'm on Haurn. My range barely reaches Yearning to the west, and can't even go as far as Throscala to the north-east. I have no idea what's happening on Ulna, or in Port Edmond.'

'Did you not hear what I said about Bastion? He told Horace to await reinforcements – which means more Banner soldiers, and gods, will be coming. You must be ready.'

'Both sides hate me,' said Sable.

'Why are they sending more reinforcements?' said Millen. 'They lost dozens of ships and thousands of sailors and soldiers in the battle for Ulna. When will Implacatus learn?'

Meader shrugged. 'The Ascendants will never give up trying to take Dragon Eyre.'

'But why? Why do they want Dragon Eyre?'

'Good question,' said Sable. 'Well, Meader?'

'In truth, that is a great mystery to me,' said Meader. 'My father knew the reason, but he always refused to tell me.'

'Blackrose told me that it was because the gods hate dragons, and want to wipe them all out.'

'That's true,' said Meader, 'but it's a consequence of their invasion, not the cause. It's the same with the sub-created humans that live here. I don't think it was the gods' original intention to kill them all, but that course seems more likely with every passing year.'

Sable frowned. 'Explain that comment – what exactly is a sub-created human?'

'Well,' said Meader, 'the original humans come from Implacatus, and have been around for as long as the gods have. A sub-created human is one that was created by an Ascendant. So you, Sable, are sub-created, because all of the humans on your world were made by the Fourth Ascendant – Lord Nathaniel. Similarly, every native of Dragon

Eyre was created by the Tenth Ascendant – Lord Simon. Many of those on Implacatus believe sub-created humans to be inferior.'

Sable laughed. 'Hear that, Millen? We're inferior.'

'I'm not sub-created,' said Millen.

'You're not?' said Sable. 'But you're from Lostwell.'

'We never used the term "sub-created" on Lostwell, but I understand what it means. The only true natives on Lostwell were Fordians, also created by Lord Nathaniel. Everyone else: Torduans, Shinstrans, Kinellians, you name it – they all originally came from Implacatus as settlers, thousands of years ago. I'm descended from them.'

'Oh.'

'It's utter nonsense, of course,' said Meader. 'There's no difference whatsoever between original and sub-created humans – they are identical in every way.' He glanced at Sable. 'Well, maybe not in the case of the Holdfasts. However, many gods use this supposed difference to discriminate against those they consider to be inferior.'

'Don't the gods despise all mortal humans?' said Sable.

'Yes. Most do, in fact. That's what makes the difference even more stupid. Still, it's the rationale that Horace will follow, now that he's in charge. It gives him licence to dispose of the native population. If they aren't seen as "real" humans, then it's much easier to order the Banners to annihilate them.'

Millen frowned. 'There's nothing like the talk of annihilation to ruin a good lunch.'

'You must be prepared,' said Meader. 'The Ascendants have not forgotten Dragon Eyre, nor are they likely to.'

'You sound like a rebel,' said Millen.

Meader drained the wine from his mug. 'I guess I do. I have nothing left to lose, Millen. If the Banner soldiers catch me, I'll be taken to Gyle, and then spirited back to a dungeon on Implacatus, to join my father. On the other hand, if the rebels were to win, and drive the gods and Banners from this world, then I might be able to live in peace.'

'You're already living in peace,' said Sable. 'We're safe here.'

'For how long?' said Meader. 'The Sea Banner is pulling out of every base in the Eastern Rim, with the exception of Throscala, but they'll be back. Right now, the shipyards on Ectus are building a new fleet, to replace their losses, and Bastion's promise of reinforcements will be met. When they are ready, they will strike again, and roll up the Eastern Rim like a tornado. I had hopes that you might be able to stop them, but...'

'Now that you've seen the state I'm in,' said Sable, 'you realise that this is impossible?'

'What if I were to travel to Ulna alone?' he said. 'Tell me where the hoard you mentioned is kept. I could retrieve the salve, and bring it back.'

'The hoard will have been transported to Blackrose's palace in Ulna by now,' said Sable, 'and the salve will have been discovered. It'll be long gone.'

'I can't accept this,' said Meader. 'There must be something we can do. We cannot simply sit here and... and farm, as if nothing is happening.'

'I may be in constant pain,' said Sable, 'but I'm probably more at peace here, in Nan Po Tana, than I've been for years. Here, no one has any wild expectations of me; no one demands that I fix everything. I can just... live.'

Meader glared at her. 'Maybe you can, but I can't. I'm haunted by what happened. I've wept countless tears over what I did, and I will never be able to rid myself of the guilt.'

'Guilt?' said Millen. 'For what?'

Meader said nothing.

'We've all done things we're not proud of,' said Sable. 'The only thing we can do is look forward, not back. Try it out for a while, Meader. Help Millen fix the walls, and see what else you could do to make yourself useful. We have everything we need here – food, wine, sunshine, dragons, and a big wall to keep out the greenhides.'

Meader shook his head, then lifted his eyes to stare at Sable. 'How can you live with yourself?'

She shrugged. 'One day at a time.'

CHAPTER 2

THE FINER POINTS OF THEOLOGY

U dall, Ulna, Eastern Rim – 9th Kolinch 5254 (18th Gylean Year 5)
Blackrose soared along the warm air currents, the ocean
beneath her a dazzling blue, while the sun shone down from the cloud-
less heavens. To the east, there was nothing, just the endless sweep of
sky and sea, while, to the west, the coastline of central Ulna lay in a heat
haze of greens and browns. A wide river was flowing down from the
north, and, where it issued into the ocean, a city had been built – Udall,
the ancient capital of Ulna.

'Eighty thousand humans once lived in that place,' said Blackrose,
as she aimed towards the city, 'before the greenhides devoured
everything.'

'We still have a way to go, then,' said Maddie, sitting strapped into
the dragon's harness. She pointed down at a tall ship that had berthed
by the city's harbour. 'Look, more refugees from Serpens are arriving.'

'It will take many generations to re-populate the lowlands of Ulna,'
said Blackrose, 'but it pleases my heart that we have made a good start.
The over-crowded camps on Serpens and Tunkatta are emptying, and
my people are coming home.'

Maddie glanced down as they crossed the coastline. On either side
of the city, long, golden beaches stretched out for miles. Within the

boundaries of the ancient settlement, much was still lying derelict and abandoned, but new signs of life were rapidly appearing. The old centre of the city, and the harbour area, had been cleaned up, the streets and houses cleared of the filth left behind by the greenhides. Two hundreds yards from the harbour, an enormous bridge passed over the great river that split the city in two. Upon the colossal bridge sat the most beautiful dragon palace that Maddie had ever seen. Its white towers soared up into the sky, while workers were high up on the many domes, cleaning and repairing the ancient stonework.

'It's much nicer than Seabound,' she said.

'From a human point of view, maybe,' said Blackrose. 'Personally, I prefer Seabound, but I understand why you would like the bridge palace of Udall. I rarely stayed there before the invasion. I remained in Seabound each summer, and moved down to Plagos in the wintertime, but I felt that Udall would be a better choice to begin the resettlement of Ulna. The humans saw it as the best place to live, and I want my subjects to be happy.'

They flew over the palace and continued onwards, heading north-west. The populated parts of Udall petered out, and they passed large districts of the city that remained uninhabited. Beyond the city limits, the countryside opened up into farmland, and Maddie looked down at the many humans out working in the fields. Only a small proportion of the area around Udall had been cultivated, and much was lying unused. The signs of the greenhide occupation began to appear. Areas of nothing but churned mud and overgrown farmhouses ringed the city, along with heaps of greenhide bones. Twelve miles from the edge of Udall, a defensive perimeter had been set up, consisting of a series of tall, wooden watch-towers, from where dragons could look out over the lowlands. Blackrose banked, and headed for the largest tower. Two dragons were sitting upon the high platform that dominated the structure, and they moved aside to allow Blackrose to land.

'My Queen,' said Shadowblaze, bowing his head. 'You honour us with your presence.'

'Greetings,' said Blackrose. 'How goes the watch today?'

'There has been no sign of any movement for miles, my Queen,' said the grey and red dragon. 'Perhaps it is time to push the perimeter outwards a little.'

'Perhaps,' said Blackrose. 'Has a raiding party been sent out?'

'Yes, my Queen. A dozen dragons departed an hour ago, to sweep inland. I have no doubt that they will find what they seek. Large numbers of greenhides were reported to be on the move yesterday, crossing the lowlands from the direction of Plagos. Your plan appears to be working, your Majesty.'

Blackrose tilted her head in acknowledgement. Maddie caught Shadowblaze's rider frowning down at her from the grey and red dragon's shoulders, but she shrugged it off. Ahi'edo would never like her, but she no longer cared.

'Let me know how many greenhides are killed in the raid,' said Blackrose.

'I shall, your Majesty,' said Shadowblaze, 'once they have returned.'

Blackrose took off from the high platform, and turned back towards Udall.

'I have mixed feelings about this plan of yours,' said Maddie.

'I know that, rider,' the black dragon said.

'I mean, using humans as bait for greenhides? It's horrible when you think about it.'

'It is working, Maddie, and that is what matters. The surviving greenhides of Ulna are starving and desperate, and the presence of humans in Udall draws them like mudflies to a flame. Were it not for the resettlement, the greenhides would remain in the mountains, where they would linger for more years, devouring their way through the last remaining wildlife that exists upon this island.'

'I guess I'm used to the City, where we had the Great Walls to keep them out. Udall has nothing – just open fields.'

'But not a single human has been killed by the greenhides since we began living back in Udall. The perimeter towers see to that. Any that venture close to the inhabited areas are slaughtered. It is by far the quickest way to deplete their numbers. And, recall that the idea was not proposed by a dragon. It was Ata'nix of the Unk Tannic who came up with the scheme.'

Maddie frowned. 'Yes, I remember.'

'He has turned out to be a useful advisor, despite some of his more radical notions.'

'We might have to agree to disagree on that one.'

The dragon crossed back over the cultivated fields surrounding Udall, and aimed for the palace on the bridge. Several other dragons were circling over the huge structure, and others were taking off or landing from the many flat roofs that were interspersed among the domes and spires. The river was wide and sluggish beneath the strong, arched supports that held up the bridge, and a few boats were ferrying humans back and forth across it, while larger ones were setting out from the harbour to bring in the fish that accounted for half of the city's diet. Blackrose swooped down, and landed onto the central roof. It was formed of golden-coloured sandstone blocks, and had a low wall surrounding it, upon which trellises had been fixed, where vines and flowers thrived and bloomed. A ramp at one end led down into the shadows of the palace, and Maddie's apart-ment sat directly above the dark entrance. A solitary figure was waiting for them as Blackrose pulled in her wings and strode towards the ramp.

Blackrose halted. 'Shall I see you in an hour, rider, after you have bathed?'

'Sure.'

'Ask your servant to put your hair into a plait after she has washed it for you. Plaits get less tangled when we are flying.'

Maddie's face flushed. 'She's not my servant.'

'No? By what title should I call her?'

'Um... my assistant?'

Blackrose glanced at her. 'As you wish.'

Maddie scrambled down from the harness, and landed onto the smooth sandstone blocks. She watched Blackrose disappear down the ramp, then turned.

The young woman across from Maddie bowed. 'How can I help you, ma'am?'

'Blackrose says I need a bath,' said Maddie, 'and she also wants you to do my hair in a plait, but I'm going to ignore that piece of advice. I don't suit it.'

The young woman bowed again. 'Yes, ma'am.'

Maddie cringed a little as they walked to the side of the walled roof, where a short flight of steps led up to her apartment. The young woman had been assigned to her a few days before, after Ata'nix had suggested that the Queen's rider should not be without a servant to help her in her duties. The poor girl had been plucked from a camp in Serpens, cleaned up, and presented to Maddie before she had been given a chance to object.

Maddie unlocked the door to her apartment and entered, her servant following her inside. Maddie smiled. Her apartment was beautiful. Its central room had windows on both sides – one overlooked the Queen's platform to the south, and the other had an expansive view of the river and town to the north. There was no kitchen but, as Maddie was never expected to cook for herself, none was needed. She had a reception room, designed for entertaining guests, which had never been used, a private study, which had also never been used, and an enormous bedroom, next to her personal bathroom. It was sheer luxury. Her rooms at Seabound had been larger, but the spaces there felt cold, and too big, while the new apartment felt more human-sized. There was no running water, but servants brought some up from the river each day for her, along with her meals. The central room, where Maddie spent most of her time, had a wood stove, and her young assistant knelt down, and began preparing it to heat the water for a bath.

Maddie sat, and pulled her boots off. She watched the servant work for a moment, feeling a little awkward.

'Where are you from?' she said.

'Serpens, ma'am,' said the girl.

'I meant before that; where on Ulna?'

'I was born on Serpens, ma'am.'

Maddie nodded. Trying to get conversation out of the young native had been excruciating at times, but she was determined to keep trying.

'Do you have any brothers or sisters?'

'No, ma'am.'

'This might sound like a stupid question,' Maddie went on, 'but do you know anywhere I could get my hands on a sewing kit? I have a few things I need to fix.'

'I can repair any clothing for you, ma'am.'

'No offence, but I feel a little uncomfortable, you know, when I have to sit idle while you do all the work. It would give me something to do.'

The servant glanced over from the stove. 'Are you unhappy with the service I provide, ma'am?'

'No. No, of course not.'

The stove started burning, and the servant closed the grille. She stood, then walked over to Maddie and reached out and took hold of her tunic.

'What are you doing?' said Maddie.

'Helping you undress for your bath, ma'am.'

'Eh, no; I can manage that on my own.'

The servant looked away, embarrassed. She stood in front of Maddie, as if she didn't know what to do next.

'Sit down,' said Maddie. 'Talk to me.'

The young woman sat on a chair, her eyes lowered.

'So,' said Maddie. 'Why did you want to work in the palace?'

The servant gave a gentle shrug.

'Don't you want to tell me?' said Maddie. 'I can imagine that you've probably had a hard life, you know, living with the refugees on Serpens, and then we come along, and everything changes.'

The servant said nothing.

'Tell me something about yourself.'

'I was selected to be your servant, ma'am. You are a rider – the Queen's rider. It is a great honour to serve you. I was told that riders do not speak to their servants, ma'am, and that I should always remember my place.'

'Your place?' said Maddie, frowning. 'What does that mean? Who told you that?'

'Lord Ata'nix, ma'am.'

'I see,' said Maddie. 'Well, you work for me, not for him. I might have to have a little chat with Ata'nix.'

'Please don't, ma'am; I don't want to get into trouble.'

'Don't worry,' said Maddie. 'It'll be fine.'

Two hours later, Maddie was in a huge, cavernous reception hall within the bridge palace, standing next to Blackrose under an enormous dome, as a mixture of humans and dragons approached with their petitions and requests. Ata'nix, from the Unk Tannic, was present, as were several of his black-robed men, who were corralling the humans trying to reach Blackrose. Lord Greysteel was making a long speech to the gathered crowd, extolling the victories achieved by Queen Blackrose, while, in a far corner, a small group of dragon suitors was standing in a cluster, waiting patiently for an opportunity to approach the Queen.

Maddie waited for a lull, then approached Ata'nix.

The man bowed to her. 'Noble rider,' he said. 'How are you today?'

'Why did you tell my new... assistant not to speak to me?'

Ata'nix blinked. 'I'm sorry?'

'You told her to remember her place.'

'That's correct. You are the Queen's rider, whereas your servant is a mere peasant girl. She is exceptionally fortunate to have been plucked from the mass of humans to serve her betters.'

'But I want someone I can speak to.'

'She is not your friend, noble rider. Out of all humans, there are only two classes you should be associating with – priests of the Unk Tannic, and other riders. In other words, you have been chosen to serve the blessed dragons of Ulna, and, as such, you have been elevated above the mass of poor and illiterate peasants.'

Maddie's temper started to fray. 'They're only illiterate because the Unk Tannic refuse to open schools for them.'

'What use would schools be to humans such as them? They exist to farm the land, and fish the seas. We have spoken about this before, noble rider. Did you not listen to my earlier explanations about the divine ordinances of our holy religion?'

Maddie glared at him.

'All human life exists to serve the great dragon spirits,' Ata'nix went on. 'Each dragon, from the moment they crawl from their eggs, is endowed with an undying spirit that outlives their mortal forms. Our lives depend upon pleasing the great spirits, so that they intervene in our lives, just as they did when they destroyed the fleet of the occupiers. Riders exist to serve their individual dragons, and the Unk Tannic exists to ensure that the mass of humanity understands its place in this world. These are the only two classes of human entitled to privileged treatment. We bear a great responsibility; therefore the dragon spirits make allowances for the little luxuries we are permitted to enjoy.'

'What a load of crap.'

Ata'nix glared at her. 'I know that you remain unfamiliar with our traditions and customs, but there is no need to mock our religion. Dragons are divine; they are true gods, unlike the pretenders from Implacatus who have tried for so long to annihilate our way of life. I have been patient with you, noble rider, but a time will come when you will have to accept the faith of the Unk Tannic if you wish to prosper.'

'But it's nonsense! How can all dragons be gods? I've met a few who were downright evil; are they gods too?'

'Of course. Every single dragon shares the same immortal spirit. You saw what happened in Alg Bay – you were standing right next to me when the great wave smashed the enemy ships against the cliffs. How can you doubt the truth?'

'What about the explanation that it was a rebel god who did it? That's what the colonial government said caused the wave.'

'Would you prefer to believe the lies of our enemies, rather than accept the truth of your friends? The dragon spirits have the power to intervene in each of our lives. We pray to them, and sometimes our prayers are answered.'

'What about the times when your prayers aren't answered?'

'At those times, we must reflect upon the ways that we have displeased the dragon spirits. No one said it was easy, noble rider. Faith is hard. Were it easy, it would be worthless. One must pray with a pure spirit.'

'You have an answer for everything.'

Ata'nix smiled.

'That's what makes it even more stupid,' said Maddie. 'If your prayers are answered, you say that the dragon spirits did it. If they're not answered, then it must be the fault of the person doing the praying.'

Ata'nix paused, his eyes glancing around the huge chamber, and Maddie realised that everyone had been listening to their argument. The riders up on the low platform, as well as the numerous Unk Tannic stewards, were staring at her, while many of the dragons were tilting their heads as they listened.

'Please forgive the Queen's rider,' said Ata'nix. 'She is still learning. I'm sure she meant no disrespect.'

'You're out of your damn mind,' said Maddie, 'if you think I'll accept a religion that refuses to allow children to be taught how to read or write. Humans are not the slaves of dragons.'

'No one ever claimed that they were, noble rider,' said Ata'nix. 'What humans are, and what they should be, is grateful to the dragon spirits, for all of the benefits that they have brought us. True freedom comes from acceptance, and submission. We were created to worship and serve the dragons, and this is a noble calling far from the vile notion of slavery.'

'That's enough,' said Blackrose. 'This is a public meeting place, not an arena for theological debate.'

Ata'nix bowed low. 'Of course, your blessed Majesty. Please accept my humble apologies.'

Maddie narrowed her eyes, and said nothing.

'Let us return to the matter at hand,' Blackrose went on, her gaze going over the chamber.

'It has been brought to my attention, your Majesty,' said Lord Greysteel, 'that emissaries from Geist and Enna are present among us this day, bearing news from the northern realms.'

Blackrose raised her head. 'Please step forward.'

Two dragons moved closer to the platform.

'Queen of Ulna,' said one, 'I have journeyed from the ancient realm of Geist, while my colleague has flown from Enna, to report to you that the last of the occupation forces have been withdrawn from both realms, along with a large proportion of the settler population. Their sea vessels slipped away a few nights ago, under the cover of darkness.'

'This is wonderful news,' said Lord Greysteel, his scales shimmering like polished metal. 'That leaves only Throscala still occupied, out of the entire Eastern Rim.'

'Your Majesty,' said Ata'nix; 'I humbly request that cadres of Unk Tannic administrators and stewards of the people are immediately sent north to Enna and Geist, to facilitate the restoration of dragon rule over those places. For two long decades, they have suffered under the oppression of the foreign occupation. Please allow your faithful servants in the Unk Tannic to assist in the governance of the human population that remains there.'

Blackrose eyed the black-robed man.

'There is one complication, Queen of Ulna,' said the dragon emissary from Geist. 'On the morning after the departure of the Banner forces, dragons arrived from Wyst, to claim Geist and Enna as their own. They delivered an ultimatum, stating that all humans should be removed from both realms, and sent here, to Ulna. Otherwise, the Wyst dragons threatened to return in numbers to remove them forcibly. The dragons of Geist and Enna are split on this matter. Some feel bound to the human communities that live in the two realms, while others would be content to see the humans driven from our shores. However, we are not strong enough to oppose the dragons of Wyst, if they commence aggressive operations against us.'

Blackrose turned to Greysteel. 'Uncle,' she said; 'you have the most experience of Wyst and its traditions. Are these threats genuine?'

'I fear so, your Majesty,' said Greysteel. 'The Wyst dragons' hatred of humans is well known, as is their desire to expand out from their remote lands. They have long coveted Geist, in particular. I recall hearing many on Wyst who claimed that Geist used to belong to their realm in the past. I recommend that we open negotiations with them, to determine the extent of their ambitions.'

Blackrose turned back to the two emissaries. 'Thank you for bringing these tidings to Ulna. Stay with us this day, and rest, then return to your realms tomorrow, with the news that I, Queen Blackrose, will fly to Geist in the coming days to discuss these matters with the dragons of Wyst.' She glanced at the Unk Tannic leader. 'Any possible mission there will have to be delayed, until the negotiations with Wyst are completed.'

Ata'nix bowed low. 'As you wish, your Majesty.'

'The inner council will now withdraw for a short while,' said Blackrose, 'to discuss this development.'

A group of Unk Tannic stewards opened the tall doors to a smaller chamber, and Blackrose tilted her head to the crowd, then strode through the entrance. Lord Greysteel walked in after her, followed by Ashfall, Maddie, and Ata'nix.

Blackrose waited until the doors were closed, then she addressed her council. 'What are your views on this? I do not wish to go to war with Wyst, but I also do not wish to allow them to swallow up Geist and Enna.'

'We should support the humans,' said Maddie. 'Why don't we ask them what they want? Some of them might want to move to Ulna, but others might want to stay where they are.'

'What about a compromise?' said Greysteel. 'Allow Wyst to occupy Geist, in return for an oath that they will leave Enna alone, your Majesty? All humans in Geist could be relocated to Ulna, or Enna, whichever they prefer. That will allow us the time we need to build up our strength. If we give the dragons of Wyst nothing, then their fury could easily lead to the deaths of thousands among the human population, not to mention any dragons who oppose them.'

'It sounds like a test,' said Ashfall. 'The dragons of Wyst want to see how strong your will is, your Majesty. If you back down now, then they will demand more in the future. How many dragons could Wyst lead into battle?'

'Many hundreds,' said Greysteel, 'perhaps close to two thousand, if they drew on their reserves. They massively outnumber us, now that the occupiers have slaughtered so many dragons in the rest of the Eastern Rim. In the old days, Ashfall, we had the strength to resist the wilder demands made by Wyst, but now?'

Blackrose tilted her head. 'Ata'nix?'

The Unk Tannic leader bowed his head. 'This is dragon business, your blessed Majesty. Far be it from me to interfere.'

'Very well,' said Blackrose; 'I will take into consideration all of your advice, and think on it. I shall consult with Shadowblaze, and then depart for Geist within the next few days. Uncle, you shall assume full command in my absence. Unfortunately, Maddie, I will have to insist that you remain here in Ulna. The dragons of Wyst would refuse to negotiate if I brought a rider along. To my mind, their ways are backward, and unnecessarily isolationist, but such has always been the case when dealing with Wyst. Whatever happens, I will not abandon the humans of the two northern realms; such a course would be shameful. Now, I shall return to the reception hall, and hear the rest of today's petitions.'

Maddie glared at Ata'nix as they made their way back into the huge hall.

'Do you hate humans?' she said.

Ata'nix raised an eyebrow. 'You've lost me, noble rider.'

'Thousands might be killed by Wyst dragons, and you don't have an opinion?'

'I prefer to place my trust in the dragon spirits. What will happen, will happen.'

'Malik's ass, you're a right idiot,' Maddie yelled. 'You care more about your stupid religion than you do about the families on Enna and Geist. Do you think that dragons are incapable of making mistakes?'

Ata'nix paused, a faint smile on his lips. 'Dragons, by their very nature, are infallible. Only humans make mistakes, as you are doing now, most noble rider.'

'And then I punched him,' said Maddie, as she fell into a chair in her apartment.

Her servant said nothing, her eyes lowered.

'Unk Tannic asshole,' Maddie went on. 'It hurt my hand. After that, Blackrose said it would be better if I missed the rest of the meeting.'

Her servant remained silent.

'I've had enough of Ata'nix and his band of crazy black-robed fools,' Maddie went on. 'When Blackrose gets back from Geist, I'm going to tell her that it's them or me. A dragon could fart, and he'd sing a song of praise about the blessed smell. I'm sick of it. How dare he say that the humans are unworthy of being taught in school? Even Duke Marcus, asshole that he was, made sure we all had a decent education. Ata'nix's only aim is to make sure that he's one of the few humans not bound by his insane regulations.' She sighed. 'Sorry. I sometimes go on a bit, but I'm so angry. Blackrose thinks he's a good organiser, but she doesn't see the damage he's doing. What was the point of liberating Ulna, if the vast majority of humans still have to live like slaves? Are you going to say anything?'

'No, ma'am.'

'Why not?'

'It's not my place, ma'am.'

Maddie rolled her eyes, and resisted the urge to scream.

CHAPTER 3

FORGOTTEN

U dall, Ulna, Eastern Rim – 14th Kolinch 5254 (18th Gylean Year 5)

For over three hundred days and nights, Austin had listened to the sound of the river. There were no windows in his spacious cell, but light entered through four holes in the thick stone floor, through which he could see the waters of the slow-moving river flow beneath him. The noise made by the river wasn't deafening, but it was continuous; a never-ending companion of his imprisonment.

Blackrose and Greysteel had been true to their word. He hadn't been tortured, or harmed, and food arrived every day, at dawn and dusk; but he hadn't been able to leave the cell, and, with nothing to do or read, and no one to talk to, his stay in the dungeons of the palace of Udall had blended into one long meaningless haze.

Seabound had been different. There, his cell had been cold and cramped, but he had been able to speak to his guards through the thick door. In Udall, food arrived through a complicated trapdoor set into the wall of the cell, and he had spoken to no one since arriving. He had tried calling out to the men and women he saw in the boats that occasionally passed directly under his cell, but his voice had been drowned out by the constant low roar of the river. Sometimes, he had been tempted to use his flow powers to kill one of them, just to prove to

himself and the world that he still existed, but he feared the consequences, and knew from experience the horror of ending another
human's life. He would lie on the floor of the cell, his face pressed up
next to one of the gaps, and watch, hoping to catch a glimpse of life. On
the wall of the cell was a series of marks. When he had first arrived, he
had added a new mark for every day that passed, but he had long since
given up; the marks served only to remind him of the rude facts of his
confinement. He had shouted at the door to the cell, convinced occasionally that he could hear footsteps outside, but no one ever
responded. Once, after crying and yelling for hours, he had gone
hoarse, his voice nothing more than a croaked gasp, obliterated by the
dull rumble of the river.

The possibility that he had been forgotten haunted him. True, his
meals always arrived on time, but what if the dragons had set that in
motion, and then driven him from their minds? Perhaps he would be
interred for years, decades, or even centuries. He would have gone
insane by that point, his mind ruined by monotony, solitude, and the
inescapable sound of the river.

His father and brother would never forget him. Surely, the Banner
soldiers were searching for him; they were coming – it was only a
matter of time. He had been told in Seabound that the entire fleet
had been destroyed, but he had hardly believed it. Such a thing
seemed impossible. But, if it wasn't true, then why was he still a
prisoner?

At least his hands were free. In Seabound, he had been forced to
wear a pair of metal gauntlets, meant to protect the guards from his
flow powers, but in Udall they had been deemed unnecessary. No
dragon ever flew under his cell, and the stone walls were far too thick
for any powers to penetrate. Sometimes, he would play with his powers
– forming little eddies and whirlpools in the brown waters of the wide
river until he had exhausted himself, but mostly he just lay on the floor,
his eyes directed downwards, as his mind went round and round in
circles.

Tap, tap, tap.

Austin blinked. He glanced up from the floor. Was that a real sound he had heard, or was he finally starting to lose his mind?

Tap, tap, tap. 'Hello?'

Austin shot upright, his hands shaking.

Tap, tap, tap. 'Are you there?'

Austin opened his mouth, but he was so unused to speaking that nothing came out. The woman's voice was coming from the door of the cell. If he didn't respond, she might leave. He sprang to his feet and raced up the low steps to the door. He tried again to speak, but his voice seemed to have disappeared. He knocked on the thick wooden door instead, mirroring the same tap, tap, tap.

'Who's there?' he managed to gasp. 'Is someone there?'

'Yes. Do you want to talk?'

Austin almost burst into tears. 'Yes. Don't go; please.'

'Your name's Austin, isn't it?'

'Yes. Who are you?'

'Maddie Jackdaw.'

He tried to think, but the name wasn't familiar. It didn't sound like the name of a native of Dragon Eyre, though, so perhaps his rescuers had finally appeared.

'Are you here to release me?' he said.

'Eh, no. Sorry. I just wanted someone to talk to. I admit, and this sounds bad, but I'd forgotten that you were even down here.'

Disappointment clashed with a wave of relief that someone had come to visit him.

'Who are you?' he said. 'I mean, do I know you?'

'I'm Blackrose's rider. We met, very briefly, when you and Seraph broke into Seabound Palace. Sable sent you to sleep, then you healed Blackrose, after Seraph had tried to kill her.'

'Yes. I remember you now.'

'Are you dangerous?'

'What do you mean?'

'You would have killed Blackrose, wouldn't you, if you'd had the chance? I know you have healing powers, but someone told me that you also have flow powers, and that you can make people's heads explode. Is that true?'

'I do have flow powers,' he said.

'So, you are dangerous?'

'I don't know what to say to that. I've been your prisoner for... a while.'

'A year and nine months,' she said.

Austin sat by the door. 'That long?'

'Yes.'

'What's happening in the world?'

'Blackrose has gone to Geist, to speak to the wild dragons of Wyst about something or other...'

'I meant, about my father.'

There was silence for a moment. 'Your father? Who's that? I can't remember.'

'Governor Ferdinand.'

'Oh yes, that's right. Well, he's not the governor any more. He was arrested after the fleet was destroyed. Someone called Horace is in charge of the occupation now, but he hasn't done anything to try to re-conquer Ulna.'

Austin's last hopes faded. 'My father was arrested? Where is he now?'

'I don't know. All we hear are rumours.'

'And my brother?'

'You have a brother?'

'Yes. His name is Meader. He was with the invasion fleet. Did he survive?'

'Meader? Wait, that seems familiar. Where have I heard that name before? Oh, yes. Horace said that a demigod called Meader was responsible for creating the giant wave that wiped out the fleet, but the dragons here don't believe it. They all think that it was caused by the divine spirits, or something like that. The Unk Tannic have been filling their heads with all kinds of nonsense.'

'Go back a bit. Horace said that my brother caused the wave?'

'Yes. Does that seem realistic to you?'

'Yes. No. I don't know.'

'I certainly don't believe it was the great dragon spirits, but I've always been sceptical about that sort of thing. If there's a rational explanation, then why look for something supernatural?'

Austin bowed his head. His brother was being blamed for the slaughter of the Sea Banner? Meader's stone powers would have been capable of causing an earthquake, which could have created a giant wave, but why would he have done such a terrible thing?

'Sable,' he muttered.

'No,' she said. 'I told you; my name is Maddie Jackdaw, not Sable.'

'I meant, Sable was in my brother's head. She made him bark like a dog, or so he told me. Could she have made my brother destroy the fleet?'

'I never thought of that.'

'But, is it possible?'

'I suppose so. Malik's hairy ass; so it might have been Sable who saved Seabound? That won't please Blackrose.'

'Who's Malik?'

'Never mind. Damn it, that does make sense. Sable was in the palace, so she was obviously close by. She's in exile now; I'm not sure where, exactly. The dragons nearly killed her, so I don't imagine that she'll be coming back to Ulna any time soon. Anyway, your brother is wanted by the Banner forces, apparently. Horace said that they would hunt him down, no matter how long it took. Of course, as I said, the dragons here don't believe it was your brother who destroyed the fleet. They think that Horace is lying, because he doesn't want the natives to know that the dragon spirits are real.'

'You aren't a native, are you? Where are you from?'

'Another world. Have you heard of salve?'

'Of course.'

'Well, I'm from the world that makes it. Well, alright, we dig it up out of the ground; we don't actually make it. But, I'm from there.'

Austin frowned. Was it possible that the woman was telling the truth?

'You don't believe me, do you?' she said.

'I don't know what to believe.'

'I met Blackrose there. She had been sold to Lostwell, to fight, and then they moved her to my world.'

'Why?'

'Why what?'

'Why did they move her to your world?'

'We have a bit of a problem with greenhides on my world, and Blackrose was supposed to help us fight them. She didn't, which is why she was locked up, all alone, for ages. Her fate reminded me of yours, actually. I was thinking about how awful it was, to be locked up on your own, and then I remembered you.'

'Thank you,' he said. 'You're the first person I've spoken to since I got here.'

'The guards are under strict instructions not to go near you. In case, you know, you kill them. At least you're a god. A year and three-quarters isn't a long time for a god.'

'Which month is it?'

'Kolinch, which I think is Marcalis on my world, though that's hardly relevant. How old are you?'

'Well, if it's Kolinch, then that makes me twenty-three.'

There was a long silence.

'Are you still there?' he said.

'Yes. Wait. Are you saying that you're actually only twenty-three years old – not just that you look twenty-three years old?'

'That is exactly what I'm saying.'

'Oh. I've never met a young god before. I guess a year and two thirds is quite a long time for you.'

'Am I going to be locked up for a lot longer?'

'I don't know. To be honest, your value dropped a bit after your father was arrested, and I think that's why most of the dragons have kind of forgotten that you're still down here. Before, you were a useful hostage, but now? I remember that Blackrose had promised that you wouldn't be harmed, but there are no plans to let you go.'

'Maybe you could help me,' he said.

'Why would I want to do that?'

'It's inhuman, to keep me locked up like this.'

'Get a little perspective, Austin. Seraph and the fleet intended to slaughter us all, and you were with them. They were going to kill every dragon, and enslave the thousands of refugees. I think you got off quite lightly.'

'But...'

'But what?'

'Nothing. You're right. That's what we sailed to the Eastern Rim to do. Blackrose started an uprising, and we had to respond – what else could we do?'

'I don't know – how about leave Dragon Eyre alone? You invaded; you're the aggressor. The dragons are just defending themselves. Should they just roll over and accept defeat?'

'The Unk Tannic blow up taverns and schools. They're evil.'

'This may surprise you, Austin, but I'm not a big supporter of the Unk Tannic. In fact, I can't stand the lot of them. But, because they helped in the defence of Seabound, Blackrose feels that she owes them some loyalty. It's a mistake, in my opinion.'

'Are there guards out there with you?'

'No. I'm on my own.'

'Help me get out of here, Maddie. I promise I won't hurt anyone; you have my word. I'll get on a boat and never come back to Ulna.'

'Why should I trust you?'

'You seem kind.'

Maddie laughed. 'You don't even know me.'

'No, but you were kind enough to come down here to speak to me, and no one else has done that.'

'Talking is one thing – letting you go is a different matter altogether.'

'What about being let out of this cell now and again? I long to feel the sun on my face, even for an hour. You could put the gauntlets back on my hands, and shackle my ankles so that I couldn't run away. Please; otherwise, I think I might lose my mind in this cell. I'm not good on my own; I never have been. I've always needed other people around me, to talk to, to be with. I'm not strong, not like my brother. The moment I left school, I was sent here, my head filled with nothing but what I had been told about Dragon Eyre by my teachers, but now…'

'Now what?'

He lowered his voice, as his eyes welled. 'I want to see my mother. Meader told me that my father had sold her as a slave, and I want to go home to look for her.'

'Home? You mean Implacatus?'

'Yes.'

'Austin, what kind of father sells your mother into slavery?'

He lapsed into silence, as a tear rolled down his cheek.

'Is your mother a mortal?'

'Yes.'

'Damn gods,' muttered Maddie. 'Why are they all so bad?'

Austin had no answer.

'I'm going back up to my apartment,' she said.

'No, wait. Did I offend you?'

'No. I have things to do. I've enjoyed our little talk. Goodbye for now, Austin.'

He listened by the door, and heard a set of footsteps dwindle into the distance. He wiped his eyes, and leaned back against the wall, his mind going over every word that had passed between them. His father had been arrested, and Meader was on the run. In a strange way, that made him feel a little better – at least they hadn't willingly abandoned him. Still, he had trouble believing that his brother had been the cause of the great wave that had destroyed the fleet. His anger turned to Sable. Had she forced Meader to do it? But, at the same time, Maddie had been right – the fleet had intended to slaughter and enslave the entire Eastern Rim. Of course the natives and dragons would try to defend themselves. Who wouldn't?

The day passed slowly. Unlike the previous three hundred or so days he had spent in the cell, he spent every second re-living the conversation that had taken place with Maddie Jackdaw, his ears listening for any sound at the door. He nearly jumped a foot in the air when another noise came, but then he realised that it was time for his evening meal. The trapdoor set into the wall made its usual clanking sound, and he opened the hatch.

He frowned. Instead of his meal, a pair of metal gauntlets was sitting on the wooden tray, along with a note. He picked up the rough piece of paper. It had been made from reeds that grew by the banks of the river, and felt brittle in his fingers. On it were written three words.

Put these on.

He stared at the gauntlets, all thoughts of food disappearing from his mind.

A thump came from the door.

'Are you ready, prisoner?' barked a man's voice.

Austin glanced at the door.

'Have you put the gauntlets on?'

Austin frowned. 'I can't do them up on my own.'

'Just slip your hands inside, then remain sitting,' came the voice.

Austin leaned forward and picked up the heavy gauntlets. He pushed his left hand into one, then his right, but they sat loose, as if they would fall off if he pointed his hands down.

'I've done it,' he called out.

'If you're lying,' said the voice, 'then we will pepper you with crossbow bolts.'

'I'm not lying.'

'Stay clear of the door.'

A key sounded in the lock, and the door swung open, its hinges creaking from lack of use. Four men, dressed in black robes and armed with crossbows, peered inside. One of them stepped into the cell, and glanced down at the gauntlets on Austin's hands. He gestured to his

35

colleagues, and two followed him inside, while the third pointed his crossbow at the back of Austin's head. The two men leaned down, and fastened the straps on the gauntlets, securing them to his wrists.

'Come with us,' said their leader.

Austin stood. 'Where are we going?'

'You'll see. Quickly; come on.'

'What's the rush? I've been in here for months.'

'Stop arguing and get moving.'

They shoved Austin up the steps, and he left the cell. A slit window was on the right hand side of the long passageway, and Austin pressed his face to it, feeling the warm evening breeze against his skin. Hands pulled at his arms, and he was dragged away from the opening. They passed the doors of several other cells, then went up a spiral staircase. Despite the rough handling, Austin was unable to keep a smile from his face. Something was happening, at last.

They emerged from the stairwell into a large hallway, and the guards led Austin through a tall arched opening. Inside a hall, two dragons were waiting, along with several armed men in black robes. Beside them stood a young woman, who gave him a tiny nod as he entered.

Austin faced the two dragons. One was a large male, his scales like burnished steel, while the other was a slender grey female.

'Demigod,' said the large male; 'your services are required. Will you cooperate?'

Austin hesitated.

'Answer me, demigod,' said the dragon, 'or I shall put you back into your cell.'

'Cooperate with what?' he said.

'Maddie Jackdaw has reminded us that you possess healing powers,' said the dragon. 'Are you prepared to use them to help two injured dragons?'

'How were they injured?'

'They were mauled by a pack of greenhides that approached the perimeter. Will you help them?'

'Take me to them, and I'll see.'

'We cannot trust him,' said the slender female. 'The moment we remove the gauntlets, he will use his flow powers to kill us.'

'He healed Blackrose,' said the young woman, her voice confirming to Austin that she was Maddie.

'The two dragons will die if they are not healed,' said the larger dragon. 'I deem it worth the risk. If the demigod attempts to use his more deadly powers on us, I will incinerate him in a heartbeat.'

'I would like an introduction,' said Austin. 'To whom am I speaking?'

'This is Lord Greysteel,' said Maddie; 'Blackrose's uncle. He's in charge while she's away. And this is Ashfall, an old friend from Lostwell.'

'Princess Ashfall,' said one of the black-robed men.

Maddie rolled her eyes. 'Fine, Ata'nix. *Princess* Ashfall.'

Greysteel glared down at Austin for a moment. 'Let us take him to the injured dragons. Guards, keep your crossbows on him at all times. Follow me.'

Black-robed men opened a set of huge doors, and the dragons strode through, while the guards shoved Austin along. He caught Maddie's eye for a moment, but she looked away. He was led into another vast chamber, where two dragons were lying in pools of blood. Their wings were ripped, and both were covered in vicious-looking claw wounds. One of them was gazing out from green eyes, while the other seemed to be unconscious.

Greysteel turned to Austin. 'Heal them.'

Austin held his hands up.

'Remove the gauntlets,' said Greysteel.

Two guards came forward, and unstrapped the heavy metal gauntlets from Austin's hands. He stepped forwards, aware that at least a dozen crossbows were aimed at him, while sparks were flitting across Ashfall's jaws.

Austin felt out with his healing powers, sensing the injuries of the two dragons. He gauged that he had enough strength to heal them both.

'I have a price,' he said.

'You are in no position to bargain with us,' roared Greysteel.

'On the contrary,' said Austin; 'I think I am in the perfect position. I'm not asking to be released. All I want is to be allowed out of my cell for a few hours each day. Agree, and I will heal them.'

'This is outrageous!' cried Ashfall.

'I have been isolated in my cell for months,' said Austin. 'I think my request is reasonable.'

'So do I,' said Maddie. 'We could supervise him, and make sure he wears those things on his hands.'

Greysteel tilted his head. 'One hour, every three days.'

Austin frowned. 'One hour, every day.'

'Confined to the palace.'

'Alright.'

'You must swear not to harm anyone, or try to escape.'

Austin chewed his lip. 'Agreed.'

'Very well,' said Greysteel; 'you have my word. However, this is the last bargain you will strike. From now on, you will heal any injured dragon upon request. Do you agree to this condition?'

Austin nodded.

'So be it,' said Greysteel. 'Proceed.'

The others fell silent as Austin raised his right hand and concentrated. The bodies of the two injured dragons were vast, and he remembered how much power it had taken to heal Blackrose from the effects of Seraph's attack. He focussed on the first one, a huge, dark green dragon, and let his powers leave his hand in a torrent. Without waiting, he turned to the second dragon, and did the same. Both dragons convulsed, their limbs shuddering, then the rips in their wings healed, and the wounds on their flanks closed up. Austin took a step back, masking the fact that his efforts had almost exhausted him. To his left, the man Maddie had called Ata'nix was staring at him with a mixture of fear, awe, and outright hatred.

The two healed dragons raised their heads, their eyes glancing round the cavernous chamber.

'How do you feel?' said Greysteel.

'I feel wonderful,' said the dark green dragon. 'To whom do I owe my recovery?'

'To this demigod,' said Greysteel, 'the son of our enemy. However, you owe him nothing. I struck a deal with him to save your lives; you are under no obligation to him.'

The two dragons bowed their heads to Austin.

'Place the gauntlets back onto his hands,' said Greysteel, 'and then escort him to his cell.'

Austin held his hands out, and allowed the two black-robed men to re-attach the thick metal gauntlets.

'What about the practical arrangements, Lord Greysteel?' said Ashfall. 'You agreed that he should be confined to the palace, but I don't want him anywhere near my quarters.'

'We shall speak to the Queen upon her return,' said Greysteel. 'Until then, I command you, Ashfall, to supervise the demigod's daily outings. You shall escort him throughout the palace, along with a few of Ata'nix's men.'

'Me?' said Ashfall. 'I do not wish this task. I have no rider – what makes you think that I would be a suitable supervisor of this human?'

'It is precisely because you have no rider that I deem you suitable. You have no emotional stake, and are not bound to any human. You will be objective, and firm, but also, I think, fair.'

'I will do as you bid, my lord,' said the slender grey dragon, though her eyes burned with irritation.

Maddie strode over to Austin. 'You did good.'

'Thank you for remembering me,' he said. He turned to Ashfall. 'When will you come for me tomorrow, my beautiful dragon?'

'Do not refer to me as yours, human,' said Ashfall. 'I will obey the order given to me, but once Queen Blackrose returns from Geist, I will seek to relieve myself of this burden. I tell you now – I do not like humans, and I loathe gods, especially those who hail from Implacatus. If you cause me trouble, I will cause you pain.'

Austin stood his ground. 'You didn't answer my question.'

Ashfall glared at him. 'Dawn. Be ready.'

'I shall provide an escort of my best men,' said Ata'nix. 'They will ensure that the demigod's gauntlets are secure.'

'Thank you,' said Ashfall.

Ata'nix bowed. 'You are most welcome, princess.'

Ashfall turned for the main doors. 'I shall go for a short flight; I need to burn off my anger.'

The grey dragon strode through the entranceway without another word.

'She doesn't seem very friendly,' said Austin.

'Ashfall is a good friend of mine,' said Maddie. 'Treat her with respect, and I'm sure she won't eat you. Well, fairly sure.'

Austin smiled as the guards began to lead him away. 'Shall I see you tomorrow, Maddie Jackdaw?'

Maddie laughed. 'You can count on it.'

CHAPTER 4

THE GIDDY GULL

Off Pangba, Olkis, Western Rim – 15th Kolinch 5254 (18th Gylean Year 5)

A cold predawn mist shrouded the wetlands, enveloping the two ships that lay tied together. All lamps had been extinguished, and the sailors of both vessels were working in silence. On the smaller of the two vessels – a long, sleek brigantine – Topaz stood by the wheel, his eyes fixed on the spindly crane that was transferring goods onto the deck of the larger merchant vessel. To his left stood an officer from the merchant ship; and, on his right was Captain Lara, with heavy fur-lined robes over her shoulders to keep out the chill.

'We're almost done,' said the officer, his voice low, as he scanned the list on the scrap of reed-paper. 'Once again, Captain Lara, it's been a pleasure doing business with you.'

The captain said nothing, her eyes bleary from lack of sleep.

'Will you be docking at Pangba after this?' the officer said.

'What's it to you?' said Captain Lara.

The officer smiled, but his eyes betrayed his nervousness. 'We're sailing there, ma'am, as soon as the ship-to-ship transfer is complete. Perhaps it would be wise if you waited a while, so that we did not enter the town's harbour at the same time.'

Lara frowned. 'We know what we're doing. Where's my money?'

The officer gestured to a small group of merchant sailors, who were lingering by the bottom of the steps leading to the quarter deck, and two approached. One of them handed a large leather pouch to the officer, and he opened it.

'Two hundred for the oil,' he said, his hands inside the pouch as he counted, 'fifty for the cotton, thirty for the weapons, twenty-five for the assorted goods, and sixty for the scrap metal. That makes three-six-five.'

'We agreed two-fifty for the oil,' said Lara, her eyes narrowing.

'That was for unbranded barrels, ma'am,' the officer said. 'The oil we've transferred on board is marked with seals from the Alef refineries. We'll have to move it all into unbranded barrels in order to sell it on, and that costs time and money.'

'Bleeding thieves,' muttered Lara.

The officer raised an eyebrow. 'I am under orders from my captain, ma'am. Should I have the oil placed back onto your ship?'

Topaz glanced around as Lara fell silent for a moment. He gazed back up the waterway that they had sailed down the previous night, his eyes scanning for any sign of movement amid the thick sheets of mist. To the east, a grey light was growing, and a few of the marsh birds were waking up, their harsh cries echoing over the wetlands.

'Two-ten,' muttered Lara.

'Very well,' said the officer. He counted out another ten gold coins, and added them to a smaller pouch. He presented it to Lara. 'Three-seven-five. Do you wish to count it, ma'am?'

Lara shook her head as she took the pouch. 'If it's short, then I'll chase you down and kill you all.'

The merchant officer shrugged. 'We would never short-change the Five Sisters, ma'am.' He glanced up onto the higher deck of the merchant ship, and waved his hand in the air. An officer on the merchant ship returned the gesture, and the crane was pulled back, the last load transferred.

'Get off my ship,' said Lara, 'before you have a chance to rob us further.'

The officer inclined his head, then signalled to his men. 'Let's go.'

The merchant sailors left the quarter deck, and Topaz watched as they clambered up the net and back onto their own ship.

'Disengage,' said Topaz to a lurking midshipman.

The young officer saluted, and ran down to the main deck, where he began issuing orders to the sailors.

'Forty short,' muttered Lara. 'I should have stayed in bed.'

'Three hundred and seventy-five is a good haul, Captain,' said Topaz.

Lara eyed him. 'Do you have any idea how much those bastards will make when they sell that oil in the market at Pangba? Four times as much. We run all the risks, and we're the ones being squeezed. I still owe nearly three thousand for the *Giddy Gull*; I'm never going to pay it back at this rate.' She scowled for a moment, then turned for her cabin door. 'Wait half an hour, then take us back out into the open sea, Master. Wake me up when we get close to Pangba harbour.'

'Yes, Captain.'

Lara disappeared into her cabin and slammed the door behind her.

Topaz beckoned the midshipman. 'Tell the lads to have a break; we're leaving in thirty minutes. And fetch Vitz.'

'Yes, sir,' said the young officer.

Topaz lit a cigarette as the midshipman scurried away. He glanced around the deserted quarter deck. His quarter deck. Lara was a hands-off type of captain, who spent most of her time in her cabin, leaving Topaz to run the *Giddy Gull*. He watched as the merchant vessel slipped away through the mist, its anchor raised, and its sails billowing in the breeze.

A tall young sailor climbed the steps to the quarter deck, and saluted.

'Morning, Vitz,' said Topaz, offering him a cigarette.

The sailor took one. 'Thanks, boss. Are we going to Pangba after this?'

'We are indeed, and we'll have some gold in our pockets to spend.'

Vitz glanced at the back of the departing merchant vessel. 'Did we make a lot?'

'Enough,' said Topaz. 'Her ladyship feels a little hard done by, but that's what happens if we try to shift barrels of oil that have clearly been stolen from an Alef trader. I did try to tell her, but she doesn't listen to me.'

Vitz frowned. 'Boss, you're the only person she does listen to.'

'She didn't listen to me when I told her not to buy this ship.'

'I'm glad she ignored your advice, boss. The *Giddy Gull* is the best ship in the Western Rim. It's faster than anything the Sea Banner has sailing, and, well, it sounds stupid, but it's also the most beautiful ship I've ever seen.'

'That doesn't sound stupid, lad. You're right; everything you said is right. But beauty, speed and comfort come at a cost. Until she's managed to pay off the loans she took out to buy it, we lose half our takings with every ship we capture. Even so, it'll take us years before she owns it outright.'

'Sorry, boss, but I don't give a flying shit about any of that,' said Vitz. 'As long as we get paid, I'm more than happy to work on the *Giddy Gull*.'

Topaz smiled. 'More than happy, eh? I'm going to remember those words, the next time you're griping about working for the Five Sisters.'

Vitz cast his eyes down. 'What can I say, boss? Maybe I'm starting to resign myself to this life. I mean, there's no going back, is there? No one in the Sea Banner would believe that we were forced into it. We can never go back.'

Topaz took a draw on his cigarette. 'I used to think that about Olkis. I always thought that, if I ever returned here, then I would be lynched for having served in the Sea Banner. I mean, I spent seven long years working for them; but nobody gives a shit. As long as you do your job, then no one cares about your past.'

'It's different for you, boss,' said the young sailor. 'You're the best pilot in these waters. Every ship would pay a fortune to have you as their master. It's not the same for me. I have to hide my accent, and my real name, and pretend to be someone I'm not.'

'Just like me in the Sea Banner, lad. Anyway, Captain Lara likes you. You're safe, under my protection, and hers.'

'She doesn't like me, boss. She puts up with me, because of you. If she liked me, then she'd promote me to midshipman, or master's mate. I've done both of those jobs before, and yet she still has me up in the damn rigging every day. She doesn't trust me.'

'I think she's more worried that others will find out, and take the piss out of her for having the son of a settler landowner in her crew. Don't take it personally, lad.'

'You know who you sound like, boss?' said Vitz. 'You sound like the old master of the *Tranquillity*, trying to reassure you that, contrary to all evidence, you do actually fit in. I think I now understand how you used to feel.'

Topaz flicked his cigarette butt over the side of the quarter deck. 'We can continue this discussion later, over a few ales. It's time to go.'

Topaz thought about what Vitz had said to him as he guided the *Giddy Gull* through the waterways that wound through the wetlands. The mist was starting to clear as the sun rose above the horizon, and the sky above them turned blue. For twenty-one months, Topaz had served Captain Lara; first on the *Winsome* and then, when the old sloop had been scrapped, on the new, sleek brigantine. At first, he had worked for her under duress, but, as time had passed, and he had settled into his new role as master, he had found himself relishing his life once again. Were his loyalties so skin-deep? He had been faithful to the Sea Banner, and now he was faithful to the Five Sisters, despite the forced nature of his oaths to each. There was more to his switch of allegiance than that, he thought. Captain Lara had made him the master of her ship, something that the Sea Banner would never have done. Being a master at sea was the greatest feeling Topaz had ever experienced, and he found himself unable to hate the woman who had shown him so much trust.

The last of the mist had vanished by the time the *Giddy Gull* reached the open seas off the coast of south-eastern Olkis. There were still shifting sandbars to negotiate on the way to Pangba, but Topaz couldn't keep the grin from his face as he ordered the main sails to be raised. The breeze picked up, and he felt the wind against his face as the brigantine cut through the water, its long bow shearing the swell. Unlike the terrible state in which Lara had left the *Winsome*, the *Giddy Gull* had been kept in a near-pristine condition. It was the captain's pride and joy, and the sailors laboured each day to ensure that it looked its best. Her pride had been infectious, and the entire crew seemed to walk the decks with smiles on their faces, proud to work on such a vessel. A Sea Banner frigate had tried to chase them a few days before, but the *Giddy Gull* had lost its pursuer effortlessly, its speed leaving the frigate far behind, to raucous cheers from the crew of the brigantine.

Topaz guided the vessel between the sandbars, then swung the ship to the north-west, tacking towards the bay where the town of Pangba sat. The settlement had been built on one of the few stretches of solid ground on that part of the coast. To either side, marshes and wetlands spread for miles, the perfect place to conduct business of a less-than-legal nature.

Lara's first lieutenant came out onto the quarter deck, wrapped in a dressing-gown. He stretched his arms and yawned, a lit weedstick hanging from his lips. Topaz suppressed a scowl. No officer in the Sea Banner would have dressed as shabbily, or behaved as unprofessionally, as Lieutenant Dax.

'Morning, Master,' the lieutenant mumbled.

'Good morning, sir,' he said. 'Sleep well?'

Dax shrugged. 'My bleeding head is splitting.' He offered the weedstick to Topaz.

'No, thank you, sir. I still need to guide the *Gull* into the harbour at Pangba.'

'Whatever. How did the transfer go? We get our money?'

'Yes, sir.'

'How much?'

'Three hundred and seventy-five sovereigns, sir.'

'Shit. I was hoping for more. Is the captain still in her bed?'

'She was up for the transfer, sir, then returned to her cabin.'

The lieutenant stared at the door to Lara's cabin, his eyes narrow. He took a long draw on the weedstick, a hand resting on the hilt of his sword.

He muttered something under his breath.

'Sorry, sir?'

'Nothing,' said the lieutenant. 'Go back to work.'

Dax staggered down the steps onto the main deck, and disappeared among the busy crew.

Topaz gestured to the midshipman. 'Time to wake up the captain. Make sure you have coffee and a cigarette ready before you knock.'

'Yes, sir.'

Topaz turned back to the sea. The coastline of Olkis stretched away to their right, and he could see a headland that jutted out, marking the start of the bay where Pangba was located. A lighthouse was upon the high rocks of the headland, but it hadn't worked in years. Topaz issued some orders, and the *Giddy Gull* turned, passing the headland and entering the sheltered bay. The settlement of Pangba had once been far larger, before the invasion, and clusters of derelict houses lined the coast. A few were used as places to store illicit goods, or to hide fugitives from the Banner.

'Replace the standard,' Topaz shouted, then watched as a young sailor took down the flag of the Five Sisters from the top of the main mast, switching it for the plain, pale blue banner of the Olkian merchant fleet. The standard of the Five Sisters was carefully folded up and put away, and the new flag fluttered in its place. It was a ruse that fooled almost no one, but the corrupt customs officials in Pangba insisted upon it. For a suitable bribe, they would turn a blind eye to the presence of the Five Sisters' ships in their harbour, but only if they had deniability. If the Banner decided to search their ship, they were on their own.

Lara appeared next to him, dressed in her best captain's uniform, a mug of steaming coffee in her hands.

'Where's my asshole cousin?' she said.

'Lieutenant Dax went onto the main deck, Captain,' he said.

'I swear my father is trying to ruin me, forcing me to have that dipshit as an officer on the *Gull*. Did you tell him how much money we made?'

'Yes, ma'am. He asked.'

'Did you tell him the truth?'

'Yes, ma'am.'

Lara groaned. 'You're a good master, Topaz, but you're not the brightest, on occasion. Now, he'll be bitching to the crew about how I got ripped off by those bastards. He's spying on me, did you know that? Everything I do and say, he reports back to Ann and the others.' She lowered her voice. 'This situation will have to change soon; are you with me, Topaz?'

'You are the captain, ma'am.'

'We'll wait until we're back at sea. All kinds of accidents can happen at sea. Do the crew like him?'

Topaz paused for a moment, wondering if the life of the lieutenant was hanging in the balance.

'No, ma'am,' he said. 'The crew don't particularly like the lieutenant.'

'And what about me?' she said. 'What do they say about me?'

'The crew love you, ma'am.'

'Are you saying that because it's what I want to hear?'

'No ma'am; it's the truth. You always pay them on time, and you always share the takings. The *Giddy Gull* makes a big difference – the crew adore this ship.'

'My ship.'

'Yes, ma'am; your ship. However, if anything were to happen to the lieutenant, wouldn't your family get suspicious?'

'You leave that to me,' she said. She glanced at the approaching harbour walls. 'Take us in.'

Topaz shouted out his orders to the midshipman, and the *Giddy Gull* slowed as it passed a long breakwater. The main sail was lowered as they entered the calm waters of the harbour, and they inched along, threading their way between the crowded piers that jutted out from the main quay. They berthed in their usual place, at the far right hand side of the harbour, where it was quieter, and the ship was secured to the pier.

Lara assembled the crew. Topaz and a few of the other warrant and petty officers stood by her side, along with the lieutenant, who was still in his dressing-gown. She divided up the takings from the voyage, then each member of the crew stepped forward and took their share. The midshipman raised a cheer for the captain, then the crew dispersed.

'I want you back on board by noon tomorrow, Master,' said Lara, her eyes on the shabby harbour front. 'I want to plot out our new course for the coming days.'

'Back to Alef, ma'am?'

'Never you mind that for the moment, Topaz. I have a few ideas, and we'll discuss them tomorrow.'

'Are you also coming ashore, ma'am?'

'No. I'm staying on the *Gull*. You?'

'I'm meeting up with Ryan and Vitz, and heading to a safe house for the night.'

'Alright. Don't do anything stupid. The Banner soldiers aren't complete idiots – they know fine well that the Five Sisters occasionally dock here. Be careful.'

'Yes, ma'am.'

Topaz secured the wheel, then walked to his cabin, his arms and legs stiff after a long shift. He got cleaned up, and changed into civilian clothing. Back out on the deck, customs officials had gathered round Lara on the quarter deck, and Topaz noticed a small pouch change hands. Up on the pier, a handful of bored-looking Banner soldiers were patrolling. A few were glancing down at the *Giddy Gull*, but Topaz knew that they would never believe that such a vessel belonged to a crew of pirates, especially as Lara had all the correct legal documentation to prove it was hers. That wouldn't last for much longer, Topaz knew. The more ships they stole from, the sooner the Banner would realise that the brigantine was in the service of the Five Sisters. After that, they would have to move on from Pangba as quickly as possible.

Ryan and Vitz were waiting for him on the main deck, each with a bag slung over their shoulders.

The carpenter's mate grinned, and rubbed his hands together. 'Come on, Topaz; I'm nearly wetting myself with excitement.'

'You usually save that for the latter part of the evening, mate,' said Topaz.

Ryan frowned. 'That happened one time. One bleeding time, and you never let me forget it.'

Topaz shrugged. 'What are mates for?'

They strode up the gangplank, and squeezed past the group of Banner soldiers, Vitz keeping his head down. The lad had bulked out considerably since his days on the *Tranquillity*, and looked more than a match for most of the Banner soldiers. He was so strong in fact, that most of the crew presumed that he was the master's personal body-guard, assigned to protect him whenever they went ashore.

The three men walked to the end of the pier, and turned for the town centre. It was a shadow of its former self. In his youth, Topaz could remember how beautiful Pangba had been, with its wide boule-vards, flanked by swaying palm trees, and pretty squares with sparkling fountains. The war had changed all that. More than half of the town was in ruins, or abandoned and derelict, while the squat Banner fortress by the shore stuck out like a native in the Sea Banner. They passed a few filthy-looking taverns, where some of the crew from the *Giddy Gull* were already starting to get drunk, and walked by the old town hall, which had been a burnt-out shell for several years, destroyed by a bomb while the town council had been having a meeting.

A few locals nodded at Topaz as he walked, well aware of who he was. As the master of a Five Sisters vessel, he was respected by some, and feared by many. Despite his renown among the locals, Topaz knew that none of the Olkians would ever betray him to the Banner soldiers. The people of Pangba despised the pirates, but their hatred of the occu-pation forces far outweighed their other feelings.

They wandered down a narrow lane, out of sight of a nearby Banner patrol, and Ryan knocked on a sturdy, iron-framed door. A small slit opened, and a pair of eyes peered out. A moment later, Topaz heard the sound of several bolts being pulled aside, and the door opened. A man peered down the lane, then beckoned for the three sailors to enter. The man led them into a smoky room, where threadbare old couches lined the walls. A few young women were sitting there, and one jumped to her feet and ran towards Ryan.

'Baby,' she cried, 'you're back!'

Ryan grinned, and kissed her. 'Of course, darling. Do you think we'd sail to Pangba and not come here? Every night on board, I've dreamed of having you in my arms again.'

She smiled. 'Do you want a drink?'

'Soon,' he said, taking her hand. 'We've got more important business to take care of first.' He winked at Topaz. 'See you guys later.'

An older lady approached Topaz and Vitz as Ryan led the young woman away.

'Master Oto'pazzi,' said the older woman. 'A pleasure to see you here, as always.'

He passed her a bag of coins. 'The usual, please, Udo'rapano.'

'Call me Dora, please.'

'I will, if you call me Topaz.'

She smiled, then led them through a back door into a small, comfortable room. She lit a few candles.

'Take a seat. Your dinner will be in fifteen minutes. Ale?'

'Yes, please, and something decent to smoke.'

She snapped her fingers, and a young serving girl ran off.

'Everything will be with you soon,' Dora said, then bowed and left the room.

Topaz and Vitz sat.

'Right,' said Topaz. 'Out with it, lad. You have fifteen minutes to grumble, and then we're going to eat, smoke and drink, and after that, I won't care what you have to say.'

Vitz frowned. 'Call me by my proper name, boss; just once.'

'Fine,' said Topaz. 'Tell me your woes, Vizzini. And don't call me boss when we're off duty.'

'My life is over,' the young man said.

Topaz sighed. 'Don't be so bloody melodramatic, lad. You're not even twenty years old. Your life is just beginning.'

'I had a whole future mapped out for me,' Vitz said. 'I'm the eldest son of a man who owns thousands of acres on Gyle. I was supposed to become an officer in the Sea Banner, and then, after a glorious career, I was to take over the running of the estate. Now, I'll be hiding from the law for the rest of my life.'

'The Sea Banner got their asses handed to them in Alg Bay,' said Topaz. 'They're in no fit state to come looking for you. To be honest, they probably think you're dead. Your rich father probably thinks the same. In a way, you're free.'

'Oh yeah? Tell me; am I free to leave the service of Captain Lara?'

'Well, no, but that's the nature of the game. You sign onto a ship, and you stick with it, through good times and bad.'

'I don't understand you, Topaz. When you were in the Sea Banner, you hated pirates. Now, you're the master of a Five Sisters ship, and I've never seen you happier.'

'You know that I always wanted to be a master. That couldn't have happened in the Sea Banner.'

Vitz narrowed his eyes. 'So, am I meant to be grateful to the woman who slaughtered the crew of the *Winsome*? She kept me tied up for months; have you forgotten?'

'You were a hostage, to ensure that I behaved myself. But, look at us now – Captain Lara trusts us, and we have the finest damn ship in the Western Rim.'

Vitz lowered his voice. 'She's insane. You do know that, yes?'

'She's not insane. She just has four older sisters who are always breathing down her neck. She has a lot to live up to, a lot to prove. And, she's not as crazy as she used to be. That last ship we stopped – did she kill a single sailor on board?'

Vitz said nothing.

'Well, did she?'

'No.'

'Her style was to get herself a fearsome reputation. Now that she's got it, she can ease off a bit.'

Vitz stared at him. 'You actually like her, don't you? Despite everything she did to us – you're fond of her. I know she's pretty, but come on, Topaz; she's a sadistic bitch.'

'Hey,' Topaz said, raising a finger. 'She's the captain. I don't care that we're off duty; there's no badmouthing the captain in my company.'

'Dear gods,' Vitz groaned. 'I feel like a prisoner.'

'Are you thinking of deserting?'

'What's the point? If I ran away, I wouldn't even make it out of Pangba. Between the Banner forces and the damn Olkians, I wouldn't stand a chance. Captain Lara's got me by the balls.'

They paused their conversation as a serving girl walked into the room with a tray of ales, and a small pouch of weedsticks.

She smiled at Topaz and Vitz. 'Hello, lads. Where's Ryan?'

'He got distracted by Jena the moment we walked in,' said Topaz.

'I'll put a mug down for him anyway,' she said. 'He'll probably be thirsty after Jena's through with him. Anything else you need?'

'You got matches for those weedsticks?'

She set the tray down onto the table, then reached into a pocket and produced a packet of matches.

'Here you go, Topaz. You staying the night?'

'Yeah. Got to be back on board at noon tomorrow.'

She smiled again. 'You know where I sleep, if you're wanting any company.'

'Yeah, thanks. Maybe.'

'You always say that, Topaz, and yet you never come to my room.'

'You're a little too expensive for my budget.'

'I'll give you a discount. It's not every day we have the finest master in Olkian waters in our little tavern.'

She left the room, and Topaz picked up his ale and took a long drink.

'She called it a tavern,' Vitz muttered.

'So?'

'It's a damn brothel; that's what it is, mate.'

'It's friendly, and safe. I like the girls here, but I sure ain't paying for any.'

'Saving yourself for Captain Lara, are you?'

Topaz laughed. The lad was clueless sometimes.

'What about you?' he said 'You picking a girl tonight?'

Vitz's cheeks flushed.

Their food arrived, along with Ryan and Jena, who sat on his lap as they ate. When they had finished their meal, Dora appeared with a bottle of gin and a guitar.

'Play us a song,' said Jena.

Ryan took the guitar. 'Anything for you, darling. I'll play, and sing, and you can dance for us.'

She stood, and pulled a clasp from her hair so that it hung loose down her back. 'Alright.'

Ryan stared at her, his mouth open. Topaz got comfortable in his chair, and lit a weedstick.

'Dear gods,' said Ryan, as he started to play. 'This is the life, and no mistake.'

CHAPTER 5

GOLDEN SPLENDOUR

U dall, Ulna, Eastern Rim – 18th Kolinch 5254 (18th Gylean Year 5)
'I don't understand,' said Maddie. 'Are you saying that there isn't a single person on Ulna who knows how to forge iron?'

'That is exactly what I am saying, noble rider,' said Ata'nix. 'In fact, I would go so far as to state that there is no human in the entire Eastern Rim with such skills. Iron has always been in short supply, and this shortage has afflicted the Eastern Rim more than the islands of the Western Rim. A few may have possessed some knowledge of these arts before the invasion, but two decades of occupation and slaughter have reduced our numbers somewhat.'

'So,' Maddie went on, 'all of the iron in the hoard from Lostwell is sitting here, in Udall, gathering dust?'

'The pirates who dealt with Sable Holdfast obtained a small amount of the total,' said Ashfall, 'but they were more interested in the gold.'

'We need to entice some blacksmiths to Ulna,' said Maddie, 'or, we need to find someone else to trade with.'

'There were rumours of another pirate ship in the vicinity of Ulna,' said Greysteel. 'Should we approach them?'

Ata'nix frowned. 'Queen Blackrose forbade any contact with the Five Sisters, my lord.'

'Indeed, she did,' said Greysteel. 'My apologies.'

'Could we not equip our own ships?' said Maddie. 'We could fill a few with iron, and send them off to trade with the other islands.'

'They would never get past the Sea Banner vessels patrolling Throscala,' said Ashfall.

'And so we return to the topic of Throscala again,' said Greysteel. 'Until that outpost of the occupation surrenders, or is destroyed, Ulna is effectively cut off from the Western Rim. However, as of this moment, it is too strong for us to attack. They have at least three gods stationed there, under a certain Lady Ydril. Any assault would be disastrous.'

'Not if we place our faith in the great dragon spirits, my lord,' said Ata'nix. 'They came to our aid before – we should trust that they will do so again. The occupiers of Throscala will be annihilated, if the dragon spirits wish it so.'

'Regardless,' said Greysteel, 'we cannot attack while Queen Blackrose and Lord Shadowblaze are still in Geist negotiating with the dragons of Wyst. We must await her Majesty's return before such momentous decisions are taken.'

'What else is left of the Lostwell Hoard?' said Maddie.

'The grain has all been distributed,' said Ashfall, 'and the Unk Tannic have laid hands upon the weapons that we brought along with us.'

'With Queen Blackrose's permission,' said Ata'nix. 'Her Majesty authorised their use during the siege of Seabound.'

'Many of the other items have also been used up,' said Ashfall. 'The tobacco, for example – it too has been distributed among the human population. The bulk of what remains lies within the hundreds of sacks of iron.' The slender grey dragon paused for a moment. 'There is also a small flask of salve.'

Ata'nix's eyes widened. 'Salve? The famed rejuvenator of the false gods? We have some? Why did I not know this?'

'The flask was hidden away, inside a sack of iron,' said Ashfall. 'Its presence was not immediately obvious. It was only discovered when the last of the hoard was transferred to Udall.'

'If we had known of this,' said Greysteel, 'we could have used it to heal the injured dragons, and our deal with the demigod in the dungeons would have been unnecessary. However, a deal is a deal; we shall not renege on its terms.'

'I reluctantly concur,' said Ashfall. 'Supervising Austin's outings from his cell is a chore, but it is what we agreed. We must presume that Sable Holdfast deliberately hid the salve among the hoard for her own purposes.'

Ata'nix laughed. 'How she must have longed for it after the greenhides mauled her.'

'It's not funny,' said Maddie. 'She could have died.'

'I wish she had, noble rider. She deserved to die for her betrayal of Queen Blackrose.'

'That's quite enough, Ata'nix,' said Greysteel. 'It is unseemly to revel in another's pain, even that of an enemy.'

'She's not an enemy!' cried Maddie. 'Blackrose forgave her. She might be an exile, but she's not enemy.'

'My apologies, my lord,' said Ata'nix, bowing his head towards Greysteel. 'Now, if there's no other urgent business to discuss, I would like, with your permission, to introduce someone to the inner council.'

Greysteel tilted his head. 'Who?'

'A noble dragon of renowned lineage, my lord,' said Ata'nix. 'After fleeing the Western Rim at the beginning of the invasion, he had been living in a mountain sanctuary on Throscala, up until the last refuges there were destroyed by Lady Ydril. He has now come to Ulna.'

'A renowned lineage?' said Greysteel.

'Indeed, my lord. He is a cousin, a distant cousin, of the Gylean himself – possibly his last remaining relative. His entire family was wiped out by Governor Sabat, but he managed to escape the carnage.'

'I see. Does he wish to seek refuge upon Ulna?'

'He wishes more than that, my lord,' said Ata'nix. 'He would like to register as a suitor to the blessed Queen.'

'What is this dragon's name?' said Ashfall.

'Splendoursun, princess.'

'That's a fancy name,' said Maddie.

'Quite, noble rider.'

'Is he from Gyle?' said Ashfall. 'Why would he want to be a suitor to the Queen of Ulna?'

'As I stated, my lady, he is the last living relative of the Eighteenth Gylean. The occupiers believe that they were successful in wiping out that entire family, but he slipped through their net. It is true that he is not a close relation, but his claim is genuine. When the sacred Eighteenth Gylean dies, then Splendoursun will be next in line to inherit the throne of Gyle. Think how powerful a message it would be to unite the strongest dragon on this world with the only scion of the Gyleans! The two halves of Dragon Eyre would come together in a holy union. We could announce to the world that an heir to the Gylean throne has been found – one untainted by years of chains and captivity. The other suitors would give way, I am sure of it.'

'Can I ask a question?' said Maddie.

Ata'nix smiled. 'Of course, noble rider.'

'What's Splendoursun's opinion about the Unk Tannic? Does he believe that humans should be subservient, in the same way that you do?'

'Lord Splendoursun believes in the holy tenets of our faith, if that is what you mean.'

Maddie smiled. 'Right. If he mated with Blackrose, would he allow her to rule alone, or would he want to interfere?'

'Perhaps we should let him speak for himself?' said Ata'nix. 'He is waiting outside this chamber.'

'Protocol demands that he make his application to become a suitor in person,' said Greysteel. 'I have no objection to allowing him to address the inner council.'

Ata'nix bowed low, then hurried off. He slipped through a human-sized door built into the main entrance, then, moments later, the enormous doors slid open, and a dragon strode in, his head held high.

Maddie raised an eyebrow. The dragon's scales were streaked in gold, and his head was almost pure white.

Ata'nix bowed again. 'May I present Lord Splendoursun of Gyle?'

'Greetings,' said Greysteel. 'Welcome to Ulna. I believe that you have something you wish to say?'

'Yes,' said the gold and white dragon. 'I assume Ata'nix has informed you of my credentials. I am a member of the most noble family on Dragon Eyre. The last member, in fact, if we exclude my young cousin, the Eighteenth Gylean. My mother's father's sister was the Eighteenth Gylean's great grandmother. Lord Sabat, curse his name, was thorough, but he failed to exterminate all of my line. I have been forced to live in hiding these last two decades, but with Queen Blackrose's victory, I felt that the time had come to reveal myself.' He raised his head even higher. 'I intend to do three things. Firstly, I wish to apply as a suitor to the Queen. Secondly, as my claim far outweighs that of any other suitor, I shall force the others to withdraw their candidacies. And finally, I shall take Queen Blackrose as my mate, and together, we shall challenge the rule of the occupiers.'

'A little presumptuous, no?' said Maddie.

Splendoursun glanced down. 'Is this insect addressing me?'

'Maddie is Queen Blackrose's rider,' said Ashfall.

'Why is she present at a meeting of the Queen's inner council?'

'Queen Blackrose has placed her on the council, my lord,' said Greysteel.

Splendoursun laughed. 'I had heard rumours of the Queen's weakness towards her human subjects, but I would have scarcely believed this! An insect on the council? How droll. The Eastern Rim has always been a little lax in such matters, but this beggars belief.'

'Do you have a rider?' said Ashfall.

'I do not. My last rider was slain when we left Gyle, and I have not yet replaced him. Also, from now on, you will address me as "my lord" or not at all.'

'Princess Ashfall is not from Dragon Eyre, my blessed lord,' said Ata'nix, keeping his eyes lowered. 'Please forgive her ignorance.'

'Very well,' said Splendoursun. 'A princess, eh? Of what substance is her claim to royalty?'

'Her father was the ruling dragon of Lostwell, my blessed lord,' said Ata'nix. 'She has noble and royal blood.'

Ashfall's eyes burned. 'I have never claimed to be royal,' she said. 'Ata'nix has a tendency to get carried away at times.'

Splendoursun ignored her comment. 'Lord Greysteel – has my application been noted?'

'It has, my lord.'

'Excellent. I shall now begin the process of forcing the other suitors to abandon their claims. I have twenty dragons at my back; those who accompanied me from my refuge on Throscala. They will add weight to my words.'

He tilted his head a fraction, then strode from the chamber, Ata'nix hurrying after him.

Maddie glared at Greysteel. 'Aren't you going to stop him?'

'I cannot,' said Greysteel. 'The rules concerning a formal courtship make allowances for one suitor to attempt to intimidate the others into withdrawing. There is nothing I can do.'

'Blackrose isn't going to be happy about this.'

'I agree, young rider. I have long suspected that her Majesty plans to refuse the advances of every single one of the suitors, so their dismissal will be meaningless. However, it will be far harder for the Queen to refuse Splendoursun, especially if he is the only candidate. If she were to do so, the entire Western Rim would take it as a grievous insult.'

Maddie smiled. 'There's no way that she'll choose him.'

'I agree,' said Ashfall. 'His opinion of himself is far too high, and it's clear to me that he would try to govern Ulna, usurping the powers of the Queen.'

'The Queen might have no choice,' said Greysteel. 'If Splendoursun becomes the sole candidate, the pressure on her Majesty to accept him will be immense. A failure to do so could mean strife between the dragons of the Eastern and Western Rims. Our unity against the occupation will be irredeemably broken.'

'Ata'nix is behind this,' said Maddie. 'He'll be pushing for Splendoursun to be accepted, so that his ridiculous plans can become reality. How do we stop him?'

'I have one idea,' said Greysteel, 'but it must go no further, for the moment.' He lowered his voice. 'Shadowblaze.'

'What about him?' said Maddie.

'We should persuade Shadowblaze to register as a suitor. Think about it – he and the Queen have been friends since childhood, and he is utterly devoted to her. He would be a strong mate, and a good father, and he is loyal. If we could set him up as a candidate to rival Splendoursun, then the golden dragon's victory would become more elusive. Blackrose, once she is aware of our plan, would then choose Shadowblaze. The Western Rim and the Unk Tannic would be disappointed, but they would have to accept it.'

'A cunning ruse, you mean?' said Maddie.

Greysteel's eyes flashed across the chamber, and Maddie turned to see Ata'nix walk back in.

'One suitor has already withdrawn his claim,' the Unk Tannic leader said, a smile on his lips. 'The others won't be far behind. None of them can hope to compete with the noble lineage of Lord Splendoursun, not to mention the combined muscle of his retinue.'

'Such is the way of it, Ata'nix,' said Greysteel. 'Let us adjourn this meeting for now; we all have plenty to think about.'

'And then the golden dragon was like, "I'm so wonderful and mighty," and Ata'nix was like, "Oh yes, you truly are amazing, my most noblest and wonderfulest bestest dragon ever in all the world." Malik's ass, what a pair they make. Perhaps Splendour-idiot and Ata'nix should mate with each other.'

Maddie glanced up, but her servant remained silent, her eyes on the floor of the apartment.

'Anyway,' Maddie went on, 'that was how the meeting went, more or less.' She put her feet up onto the low table. 'Amalia's breath, I can't wait for Blackrose to get back. Why do dragon negotiations have to take so long? That was rhetorical, by the way – you don't have to answer. Not that you would have, but all the same.' She sighed. 'It would be great if you wanted to chip in to the conversation now and again; I feel like I'm talking to a wall.'

'Would you like a drink, ma'am?'

'Oh, alright. What do we have?'

The servant walked over to a cabinet by the window. 'There is some red wine, ma'am.'

Maddie pulled a face. 'Yeah? Go on, then; I'll have a glass.'

She yawned and stretched her arms as the servant filled a mug with red wine. She brought it over to Maddie.

'Thanks. Get some for yourself.'

'I don't drink while on duty, ma'am.'

Maddie took a sip. 'Yuck. It's so bitter.'

'It comes from a vineyard on Serpens, ma'am, where my family worked. I hoped you would like it.'

'Sorry,' said Maddie, feeling guilty. 'That was just my first impression; I'm sure it gets better after another sip.'

She forced herself to drain the mug, and tried to smile. 'Yes; it's very nice.'

A sharp pain formed in the pit of her stomach, and her eyesight went blurry. She blinked.

The expression on the servant's face changed. She walked to the rear window, waved to someone, and then returned to stare at Maddie.

'I don't feel so good,' said Maddie, clutching her waist.

'That's because I've just poisoned you, you stupid bitch,' said the servant. 'At last, I can finally tell you what I think of you. For days, I've had to listen to your crap; 'Yes, ma'am." "No, ma'am." "It's not my place, ma'am," while you went and on about your pathetic life. Lord Ata'nix told me it would be a challenging commission, but you've no idea how hard it's been not to scream; and the number of times I've wanted to slap you across the face...'

Maddie stared at her, unable to speak. She felt as if she were drifting off into unconsciousness; as if she were in a waking dream.

The front door of the apartment opened, and Ata'nix walked in, followed by four men in black robes.

The servant bowed her head. 'My lord.'

Ata'nix glanced down at Maddie, and smiled. 'The time has come, Miss Jackdaw. Unfortunately for you, you have become an obstacle in my path, one which has to be removed.'

'Can I slap her, my lord?' said the servant. 'As she once slapped you in the council chamber?'

'I will grant you this request,' he said, 'as a reward for having to endure the Jackdaw woman for so long. Go on.'

The servant grinned, then leaned over Maddie and looked her in the eye.

'I hope this hurts,' she said, then struck Maddie across the face with the back of her hand.

Maddie fell off the chair and onto the cold stone floor. She tried to move her arms and legs, but they felt like lead. Her head lowered, until her inflamed cheek was resting on the floor.

'Bind her wrists,' said Ata'nix; 'then hood her. A wagon is waiting for her at the gates of the palace.'

Maddie felt hands grab her, and she was dragged across the floor. She was rolled onto her front, and her arms were pulled behind her back, then her wrists were tied together. Ata'nix knelt down by her head. He grasped her hair in one hand, and lifted her face towards him.

'You foreign piece of trash,' he said. 'Queen Blackrose has always been too good for you. I will ensure that your replacement is someone... shall we say, more pliant? A believer, at any rate. Did you truly think you would be able to mock me and not pay for it? You don't belong here; Dragon Eyre is not your world, girl. It's a pity that you did not learn that lesson on your own, but so be it.' He glanced up at the other men. 'Get her out of here.'

A rough hood was pulled over her head, and a cord tied round her neck. She felt her shoulders and legs be lifted from the floor, then her strength ebbed, and she lost consciousness.

———

Maddie dreamt that she was flying on Blackrose, soaring high above the clouds. Her sister, Rosie, was strapped to the harness next to her, and both of the Jackdaws were grinning as the wind blew their hair into tangles. Below them, a volcano was spewing lava over the streets of the Bulwark, while greenhides were dancing on the battlements of the Great Wall.

Maddie frowned. 'Is this normal?' she said.

She opened her eyes. Darkness, and a strange motion. She gagged, and tried to move, but her wrists were bound behind her back. She felt nauseous, a fact not helped by the weird up and down motion beneath her. She moved her legs, and her boot caught something.

'Ow!' cried a man's voice. 'Shit on a stick. She's waking up. Get the captain.'

Maddie heard footsteps. 'Where am I?' she cried through the thick hood. 'Help!'

The man's voice laughed. 'That's right, little lady; we're here to help you. Now, quit writhing about before you kick me again.'

More footsteps approached.

'She's getting lively, Captain,' said the man.

'Take her hood off,' said a woman's voice. 'I want to see her face.'

'Right you are, Captain.'

Maddie felt fingers under her chin, then the hood came free, and was pulled from her head. She blinked in the dim light. A young woman was staring down at her, while three men stood around.

'Where am I?' gasped Maddie.

'You are on board the *Little Sneak*,' said the woman, 'which happens to be my ship. You are my prisoner.'

'What?' cried Maddie, trying to sit up. 'I'm on a damned boat?'

'A sloop, to be precise,' said the woman. 'My name is Captain Tilly, of the Five Sisters.' She frowned. 'You don't seem particularly valuable. Tell me, why do the Unk Tannic hate you so much that they paid me four thousand in gold to get rid of you, eh? What have you done?'

'The Five Sisters?' said Maddie. 'Do you know Sable? Are you taking me to Sable?'

'Who?'

'Sable Holdfast.'

'Never heard of her.'

'What? The entire Eastern Rim has heard of Sable.'

'Yeah? Well, I've been in the Western Rim. My sisters Ann and Lara got back last year, and told me that there was plenty for the taking out by Ulna. They weren't wrong; though I never expected the majority of the takings would come from a single prisoner.'

'Are we really on a ship?'

Tilly looked at her like she was mad.

'I've never been on a ship before. Where are you taking me?'

'Can you swim?'

Maddie shook her head.

'Bring her up onto the main deck, lads. Little Miss strange-accent is having some trouble believing that we're on a ship. Keep her wrists bound, though, just in case.'

Two men picked Maddie up by the shoulders and set her on her feet. She swayed with the motion. Captain Tilly left the room, and the two men followed, escorting Maddie. They went up a narrow flight of steps and Maddie gasped as the wind and sunlight hit her face. She glanced around at the sailors on the deck, then stared out into the vastness of the ocean.

'Turn her round,' said Tilly.

The men moved Maddie so that she was facing the other way, and she saw the shores of a large landmass in the distance.

'That's the northern coast of Ulna,' said Tilly. 'Do you believe me now?'

Maddie nodded, her fear ratcheting up a notch.

'What's your name?'

'Maddie Jackdaw.'

'Alright, Maddie Jackdaw; what did you do to piss off the Unk Tannic?'

'Nothing! Well, I punched one of them in the face, but that's not why they've done this to me. I'm Queen Blackrose's rider.'

Tilly's mouth fell open, and a few of the nearby sailors turned to stare.

'Holy shit,' muttered Tilly. 'No.'

'We can't have her on board, Captain!' cried a sailor. 'The dragon will come for us.'

'Chuck her over the side!' yelled another.

'Steady, lads,' said Tilly, raising her palms. 'We can't bleeding well kill her, can we? That would only make things a hundred times worse if Blackrose catches us.' She started to pace up and down the wooden boards of the deck. She eyed Maddie. 'Where is Blackrose?'

'On Geist.'

'Why?'

'She's meeting some dragons from Wyst. But, she'll be back in Ulna soon; I'm sure of it. You should take me back to Udall.'

Tilly snorted. 'What, and have to hand back the gold they gave me? No chance.' She pointed a finger in Maddie's face. 'You, Miss Jackdaw, have turned what was a pretty mediocre expedition into the bleeding pay-day of the decade. I ain't going back to Olkis empty-handed.' She rubbed her face.

'Are you taking me to Olkis?' said Maddie. 'Is it far?'

'What will we do, Captain?' said a sailor. 'As soon as Blackrose finds out that we've taken her rider, she'll be searching the ocean, all the way from Wyst to Haurn, maybe even further – you know how dragons are. She'll never give up.'

'Yeah?' said Tilly. 'Well, I ain't never given up neither. My sisters would laugh their asses off if I returned with nothing but a sorry tale about a prisoner we had to hand back. I ain't doing it. Come on; you're my lieutenant – think of something.'

The sailor scratched his head. 'Killing her is out, yeah?'

Tilly frowned. 'I don't know; what do you think?'

'I think you were right before, Captain. If the dragon finds us, and her rider is alive, then, well, she might just be persuaded to let us go. But, if she finds us, and we've killed her...' He made a cutting motion across his throat. 'We have to take her to Olkis.'

'I damn well know that, you dipshit!' shouted Tilly. 'How do we get there, that's what I'm asking...' She snapped her fingers. 'Got it.' She pointed towards the rear of the ship. 'Take her to the quarter deck.'

She strode off, and the two sailors hauled Maddie along after her. A large crowd of sailors followed, all trying to get a look at Maddie. They came to a flight of worn steps and ascended to a small deck.

Tilly halted in front of the wheel.

'Master,' she said.

'Yes, boss?' replied the man behind the wheel.

'You ever been to Rigga?'

'Yes, boss; a few years back.'

'Has the *Little Sneak* got what it takes to get there?'

The master frowned, and chewed his lip for a moment.

'Where's Rigga?' said Maddie.

'It's right in the damn centre of the Inner Ocean,' said one of the men holding her arms.

'Why would we go there?'

Tilly turned to her, a smile on her lips. 'Because, little lady, it's out of range of any bleeding dragon. Not a single one has ever managed to fly there, not never.'

The master nodded. 'It'll be rough going at times, Captain, but our little sloop can make it.'

Tilly grinned. 'Set a course for Rigga, Master.'

CHAPTER 6

SHAKING THE BRANCHES

Nan Po Tana, Haurn, Eastern Rim – 19th Kolinch 5254 (18th Gylean Year 5)

Sable watched the olive harvest from under the shade of a thickly-vined trellis. One of the natives from the Haurn isles was supervising the others as they worked, while Millen and Meader were lending a hand under the heat of the mid-morning sun. Millen had taken part in the previous year's harvest, and didn't need to be told what to do, but Meader was being guided as if he were a schoolboy. They laid out wide sheets of cloth around the bases of the trees, weighed them down with baskets, then shook the branches, the olives falling like rain. Sable reached up with her right hand, and pulled down a bunch of grapes from the trellis. She popped one into her mouth, her teeth bursting through the skin and releasing the sweet juices onto her tongue.

She smiled, only a small part of her jealous that she was unable to join in. Watching the others work relaxed her, and she pushed any regrets to the back of her mind. Her life might not have turned out the way she had expected, but there was nothing she could do about that. She was lucky, she told herself. She was alive. Her life was simple, but rewarding. She had friends, and, most importantly, she had Badblood. She glanced over at the dozing dragon. He seemed to spend half his day sleeping in the warmth of the sunshine, while Deepblue never missed an opportunity to fly. At that moment, she was flitting about overhead, watching her rider work alongside the others in the large olive grove. Meader paused, sweating, and pulled his tunic over his head, revealing a set of strong shoulders. Sable glanced at him. He was a good-looking young man, or appeared to be, despite the centuries he had spent alive. All the same, Sable had no interest in him other than as a friend. Still, he was nice to look at. She smiled as a young native lectured him on what he was supposed to be doing. He nodded, listening intently, which Sable found funny. There was Meader, a god, taking lessons from a teenage mortal on the art of shaking the branches of an olive tree. Millen joined them, and Sable watched them laughing together.

She grimaced, as the pain in her legs surged for a moment. She shifted her position on the bench, but she had been sitting still for too long, and knew that she needed to move about. She gripped her walking stick, and stood, swaying for a moment as her back ached. A dark cloud descended over her thoughts as she fought the pain. It had been a rough night, filled with discomfort, and she was still tired, despite the coffee they had made at dawn. She swore under her breath.

'Are you alright?'

She glanced up, and saw Millen by the bench, a water skin in his hand.

She shrugged.

'Go and lie down for a while,' he said.

'I like watching you work.'

Millen smiled, and took a drink. 'You mean you like watching Meader with his top off.'

Sable would have laughed at that comment, but the pain was too severe.

'It was a joke, Sable,' he said. 'You don't need to worry about me being jealous; not any more.'

'I know,' she said.

He frowned. 'Is it bad? It must be bad.' He put down the water skin and extended a hand. 'Here. I'll help you walk back to the temple.'

He linked his right arm with her left, and they turned from the grove.

'I'll be back soon,' Millen yelled to the others, then they set off.

'I feel so useless,' she said, as she struggled down the path.

'I know,' he said. 'We love you anyway.'

'I don't know what I did to deserve you, Millen.' Tears sprang from her eyes. 'If it weren't for you…'

'It must be bad,' he said. 'You usually need a few drinks before you start on that topic.'

'Don't make fun of me.'

'I'm not, Sable.'

They passed Badblood, who opened his good eye and glanced up at them.

'What's wrong?' the dark red dragon said.

'The pain's got a bit too much for her,' said Millen. 'I'm taking her back to the temple.'

'I wish there was something I could do,' said the dragon. 'Maybe we could fly later, my rider, if you are feeling better. Flying always cheers you up.'

She nodded, gritting her teeth, as the dragon gazed at her. They carried on, skirting the olive press and the orange grove, where the branches of the citrus trees hung heavy with fruit. They reached the temple courtyard, and Millen guided her into the tower. She sat down onto her low couch, her back screaming with pain.

Millen crouched down next to her. 'Is there anything I can get you?'

'A bottle of whisky and some dullweed,' she muttered.

'What's whisky? Meader has some dreamweed, but not even he touches dullweed. Shall I get you some?'

She nodded, and he hurried from the ground floor room. Sable lay down on the couch, the muscles in her legs matching the agony coming from her back. She panted, her eyes clenched shut, then heard Millen come back in.

'From Meader's stash,' he said, pushing a bundle of weedsticks into her hand. 'Is it getting worse?'

She opened her eyes. 'No. It just comes and goes.'

'It breaks my heart to see you in pain.'

'Shut up, Millen. Don't start with that.'

He nodded, then lit a weedstick for her. 'I'd better go back to the olive grove and help out. Will you be alright on your own?'

'I'm not a child.'

'I know. Sorry. See you later.'

Millen left the tower, and Sable took a long drag on the weedstick. She powered her battle-vision at the same time, and felt her pain ease a little. She began to regret snapping at Millen, but he had toughened up a lot since Lostwell, and she knew that he would be fine. She felt sorry for herself instead, and her eyes welled up as the dreamweed clouded her thoughts. She noticed the sound of a bird singing outside the tower, and focussed on it – anything to avoid self-pity. She glanced around her room. It was large, but almost empty, with just her bed, the couch, a table and some chairs, and a chest containing her clothes and other meagre possessions. The flowers in the vase on the table's surface were fresh, picked for her the previous day by one of the locals. She stared at them, their bright colours seeming out of place amid the misery of the pain coming from her broken body. She lay down on the couch, took another draw, and closed her eyes.

———

'You're going to set fire to the place if you're not careful,' said Meader.

Sable opened her eyes. 'What?'

'You fell asleep with a weedstick in your hand, again,' he said, frowning down at her. 'Use a damn ashtray.' He sat down next to her. 'How are you feeling?'

Sable groaned, and pushed herself into a sitting position. 'Who said you could come into my room?'

'Millen told me he'd given you my entire supply of dreamweed. I was just making sure you hadn't smoked it all. Did it help?'

'Not really,' she said. 'It might have helped me get to sleep, but I was already exhausted.' She passed him the bundle of weedsticks.

'Keep a few for yourself,' he said. 'You need them more than I do.'

'What time is it?'

'Late afternoon. You must have slept for half the day.'

She slipped a couple of weedsticks from the bundle, and tucked them into a pocket. 'The pain's lessened. That was the worst I've felt in a while.' She exhaled. 'Now, I'm back to the usual levels of aching. Annoying, but manageable. Could you get me something to eat?'

He nodded in the direction of the table. 'I brought dinner.'

'Thanks.'

'Do you need a hand getting to the table?'

She shook her head, then leaned over and picked up her walking stick from the stone floor. She gripped it, and got to her feet. Meader pulled out a chair for her, and she walked over to the table, and sat, her eyes on the bowl of fish and vegetables in front of her. She picked up a fork, and started to shovel the food into her mouth as Meader watched. He sat down next to her and removed the stopper from a flagon of wine.

'I didn't realise how hungry I was,' she said between mouthfuls. 'How did the olive harvest go?'

'Good,' he said, smiling. 'We filled over twenty baskets. Wine?'

She nodded. He filled two mugs.

'Millen's gone for a swim,' he went on, 'so it's just me and you for dinner this evening.'

She nodded again, then noticed a tightness in his eyes. 'What's up? Something on your mind?'

'My brother,' he said. 'I wish I knew how he was. The propaganda I heard in Na Sun Ka went on about how he was a traitor – collaborating with Blackrose and the rebels. But how do we know that it's true? What if he's languishing in a dungeon? Or worse.'

Sable said nothing, her thoughts on her dinner.

'I've been here for almost a month,' Meader went on. 'It's been like a dream. It's so beautiful, and life moves at a slow pace, but what if

Austin's been suffering this entire time? He might be suffering because of what I did.'

'You didn't do anything,' she said.

He frowned. 'I destroyed the entire Eastern Fleet.'

'No, that was me. You were merely the weapon I chose to do it. The sword in my right hand. You had no say in the matter.'

'I did have a say. If I had been braver, I would have taken the pain, but I didn't. I cracked, and placed my hands onto the rocks of the cliff. I knew what I was doing, but I couldn't stand the agony any longer. All you did was show me how weak I truly am.'

'Don't exaggerate,' she said, pushing the empty plate away. 'You lasted a lot longer than I thought you would. Some people buckle within seconds – you bore it for an hour.' She lowered her glance. 'I'm sorry.'

'Are you?'

'Yes. I would do it again, but yes. It was the only thing I could think of at the time; the only way to stop the fleet from destroying Seabound and ending the rebellion. It's on my conscience. All those deaths are down to me. Yet more to add to the long list.' She took a drink. 'I deserve this pain. I deserve to suffer. Not just for what I did to you, but for all of my previous acts. Still, I'm not going to sit here and dwell on how awful my life is – it's not. My sister has a crippled left arm, but she's never once complained about it, nor has she ever let it control her life.'

'Were you close to her?'

'No. I don't even know her, not really. Before I realised that I was related to her, one of my ambitions was to fight her, and beat her. I would have beaten her too. Not any more, but back then. I would have kicked her sorry arse for her.'

'You didn't know that you were related?'

'No. I was brought up by a different family, as an only child. The Blackholds. My adoptive parents couldn't have children, though I didn't know that at the time. I never met my birth parents; they both died ages ago. The Holdfasts were my enemies, until I discovered I was one of them.'

Meader smiled. 'That must have come as a shock.'

'It did, but it also saved my life. I would have been executed if I'd really been a Blackhold. Daphne saved me from the Empress's wrath, and then they sent me away to Lostwell. I doubt I'll ever see any of the Holdfasts again.'

'Would you want to?'

'I don't know. Yes, I suppose, though I wouldn't want them pitying me.' She smiled. 'Do you want to know how I'd feel if I ever saw Daphne again?'

'Tell me.'

'Guess.'

'Anger?'

'No.'

'Love?'

'Try again.'

'Hmm... I don't know.'

'Embarrassment.'

He laughed. 'Why?'

'Because,' she said, 'every time my life has been in danger recently; which has been a fair few times, to be honest; every time I think I'm going to die, I call on Daphne to help me.' She shook her head. 'I don't know why. I mean, it's ridiculous if you think about it. For one thing, she can't hear me, obviously, but why would I ask her for help? She probably loathes me. She saved me from the executioner, but that doesn't mean she likes me. I doubt she ever thinks of me. I probably haven't crossed her thoughts since I went to Lostwell. And yet, it's her that I cry out to for help, as if she were my mother, or something. It's pathetic.'

'What kind of woman is she?'

'Bloody-minded. Ruthless. She never gives up, no matter how impossible the odds seem. Nothing ever slows her down; not her crippled arm, nothing. If only I hadn't done what I did to Lennox. Then, they might be able to forgive me, but they never will.'

'Who was Lennox?'

'A soldier. I did the same thing to him that I did to you. Only worse.'

'How could it have been worse?'

'I made him burn down a hospital.'

Meader puffed out his cheeks, then refilled the mugs with wine.

'He then went on to meet my niece, and they fell in love and had twins. But, my niece always had conflicted feelings about him, because they didn't know that it was me who was responsible. Poor Lennox died thinking that he had burned down the hospital on his own. I told my niece the truth, just hours after he was killed. The look on her face will live with me until the day I die. No wonder she abandoned me on Lost-well. I think that's the difference between me and Daphne. She doesn't regret anything she's done; whereas I am full of regrets. I once killed a girl because she was talking too much. I cut her down in front of her friends, while Lennox stood by, disgusted, but powerless to stop me. Bracken, her name was. I still remember her. And then I killed Nyane, who was only trying to stop me abducting my other niece. I could have pushed her aside, but no – I killed her. And that's why the Empress will never forgive me.'

Meader kept his glance down. 'Why are you telling me all this?'

'Because you look at me as if you feel sorry for me, Meader. Don't feel sorry for me.'

'I can't help it,' he said. 'What you did to me was... bad, but I understand why you felt you had to do it. A small part of me is glad. That's sounds terrible. Not glad, exactly, more relieved. You're right about what would have happened if the fleet hadn't been destroyed. Right now, the Eastern Rim would be a very different place, if Seraph had succeeded. In my heart, I don't want to see the dragons destroyed, nor do I want the natives of Dragon Eyre to be exterminated. This month on Haurn has given me the time and space to think about my own life. I think... damn it, I think I'm becoming a rebel.'

Sable eyed him, but he wouldn't meet her gaze.

'Only,' he went on, 'now that I've come to this conclusion, I don't know what to do about it. I want to rescue Austin, but how? I want to oppose what Horace is doing, but it seems impossible. If I set foot on

Gyle, if I managed to find a ship to take me there, then I would be immediately arrested. Horace can detect the powers of the gods; he would sense me long before I reached the Winter Palace in Port Edmond. The same thing would happen if I went to Ulna to look for my brother. The dragons would incinerate me. I feel so helpless, that at times I want to scream. And then, the next day, I find myself content just to be here, picking olives, and tending the orchards, and working under the sun. Those things you told me when I arrived, that I might find peace here – you were right. Most of the time, I agree. It's just the other times I find hard to deal with. Whenever I think about Austin, for example. What right do I have to live here in peace, while he might be locked up in a cold, dark dungeon? Sorry. I'm rambling.'

'We have plenty of time to ramble,' she said, taking a drink. 'Light up one of your weedsticks, and we can ramble together.'

A few hours later, Sable was far drunker than she had planned to be. She reclined on the couch, with Meader sitting next to her. The pain in her back and legs had been dulled by the wine and the dreamweed, but she knew she would pay for it in the morning.

'So,' she said, struggling to keep her voice from slurring, 'you're telling me that the Eighteenth Gylean is locked up in a cage?'

'Yeah,' said Meader. 'It's shocking; terrible. I don't think he'll last much longer, to be honest.'

'Why don't they just kill him?'

'They need him. He gives the natives on the Home Islands hope, and it lends the colonial government an air of legitimacy. Technically speaking, the Eighteenth Gylean remains the sovereign ruler of Dragon Eyre.'

'Cruel bastards,' she muttered.

He gazed at her, then lifted a hand and moved it towards her face.

She swatted it away. 'Hey. What do you think you're doing?'

He blinked. 'You have a mark on your cheek. I think it's sauce from dinner.'

'Oh. For a moment there, I thought... never mind.'

'You thought I was going to try to kiss you?'

'Well, yeah.'

'You don't have to worry about that.'

'Why not? Is it because I'm ill? Do you not fancy me because I can barely walk any more?'

'It has nothing to do with that.'

'No? Then, why haven't you tried anything?'

'Do men usually try to come on to you?'

She shrugged. 'Not just men. I had a little fling with Captain Lara of the Five Sisters. Oops. I probably shouldn't have told you that. Keep it to yourself, yeah?'

'And Millen? You used to go out with him, didn't you?'

'No. I had one night with him; that's all.'

Meader raised an eyebrow. 'He's told me all about it.'

'That little shit. Has he been spreading lurid tales about me?'

'Not exactly. I mean, he didn't give me any details about... you know. I think he might have been trying to warn me off.'

'Did it work?'

He glanced at her. 'Do you want me to try something?'

'I don't know. I'm drunk enough, I guess.'

He shook his head. 'What would be the point? I admit that I think you're beautiful. I mean, of course you are; you're gorgeous. And I have an unfortunate habit of jumping into bed with any beautiful woman who'll have me. But, it would ruin everything. It'd be fun, but the next day would be awful. How would I ever be able to speak to Millen again, and me and you would probably fight and fall out.' He looked into her eyes. 'I'm very fond of you, Sable; I care about you, despite everything that's happened. You are my friend, and I don't want to spoil that.'

'Me neither,' she said. 'It took Millen months before he was my friend again. I'm not used to having friends. For most of my adult life, I've been using people, manipulating them. They think I'm their friend, right up until I betray them. It was part of my job, and I was damn good at it. If we exclude Badblood, then Maddie and Millen were probably the first real friends I've ever had.'

'You haven't slept with Maddie as well, have you?'

Sable laughed. 'No.'

'Can I ask you something?'

'You've already been asking me some rather personal questions, so go on.'

'That thing you did to my head…'

'Yes?'

'Is it… is it still there? I guess what I'm trying to say is – am I still under your control?'

Sable shrugged. 'I'm not sure.'

'How can you not know?'

'I'd have to go into your mind and take a look. I'm not as powerful as my niece. If she does something to your head, then that's it. My powers don't always last. Do you remember when I commanded you not to talk about me to anyone?'

'Yes.'

'How long did that work for?'

'A month? I eventually cracked, and told Austin.'

She smiled. 'I could go in, and put it back in place, if you want.'

'No, thank you. Could you check for me, though? I want to know.'

'Alright.'

She powered up her vision for the first time in many days, and entered Meader's mind. She searched for the block she had put there, the one that had been designed to cause him unbearable pain if he refused to carry out her orders. After a moment, she found it. It was weak, and frayed at the edges, but still there. She turned to his recent memories, and found that he had been telling the truth earlier. He really did care about her, despite his knowledge of what she had done.

She glanced away. 'It's still there.'

'Oh.'

'But, I reckon that you would be able to fight it. It's not as strong as it was.'

'Can you remove it?'

'Why? I could put it back whenever I wished.'

'It's the principle, Sable. I don't like knowing that you could make me bark like a dog whenever you feel like it.'

'There's nothing I can do about that. I can't make you immune to my powers. Only my niece could shield you from me, and she isn't here.'

Meader sighed. 'I think I need some fresh air.'

'I'll come with you. I could do with a little walk, maybe just to the jetty and back.'

She gripped her walking stick and pulled herself to her feet. The ache in her legs was still there, but was less than before.

Meader stood, and they walked out of the tower. A fire was burning by the far end of the courtyard, and the Haurn locals were gathered around it, sharing wine and food, while Millen was sitting with a baby on his knees, laughing with the others. Sable smiled, then she and Meader turned for the bay. The stars were out, and were shining down on the island, while the light from the fire lit their way. They walked through the stone archway, and came to the path that ran down the cliff to the temple's jetty. Sable halted, and took a deep breath, tasting the warm air, and smelling the scents of the island.

The water in the bay was rolling towards the shore, its surface reflecting the starlight.

'I love it here,' said Meader. 'I'm not sure which is more beautiful, the day or the night.'

They walked down to the jetty, then Sable sat on a bench as her legs began to get sore again.

'Shit,' muttered Meader, as he peered across the bay. 'Is that a greenhide?'

Sable peered into the distance, at the derelict village of Pot An. She noticed movement, then saw the ridged back of a greenhide, snuffling about on the ruined harbour opposite the temple.

'What's it doing?' said Meader.

'It can probably smell us,' said Sable. 'The dragons have chased most of them away, but they keep coming back. Don't worry, though; we're safe here.'

'It gives me the creeps,' he said.

Sable laughed. 'Try having one rip your back open.'

'Have you ever tried to read their minds?'

'No. Why would I want to do that? It's like asking if I've read the mind of a dog.'

Meader sat down next to her. 'They're not exactly like dogs, though, are they?'

'No. Dogs have more sense.'

'I am curious, though, to see if you could get into their minds.'

'Why?'

He glanced at her. 'You must be aware that they can be controlled by Ascendants?'

'What?'

'I can tell by the look on your face that this is news to you.'

'Wait. Ascendants can control greenhides?'

'That's what I said. No other god can do it. I think that when Lord Leksandr, the Sixth Ascendant, created them, he designed their minds in such a way that they could be manipulated, but only by other Ascendants.'

'What can they make them do?'

'Basic stuff. Attack, guard, stand still; march up that hill; attack him, but not them – that sort of thing. They can command hundreds of them at a time; whole armies of the green bastards. They can even control the queens.'

Sable frowned, her gaze on the beast standing on the other side of the bay. It was staring down at the water separating the village from the temple, its insect-eyes looking for a way to cross.

She took a breath. 'Alright. Give me a minute.'

She sent her vision out across the small bay, hesitated for a moment, then plunged her powers into the eyes of the greenhide. Instantly, she felt nausea almost overwhelm her. The mind of the beast was rotten, and vile, its corrupted thoughts of flesh and hunger as fetid as a decaying corpse left out in the sun. At once, she loathed it with a passion. Such a creature should not be allowed to live.

Drown yourself! she cried into its mind, then she broke the connection. She fell to her knees, cracking them against the hard ground, and vomited wine-coloured sick onto the gravel path. She clutched her stomach as it cramped, then heard a loud splash.

'Dear gods,' said Meader. 'Was that you?'

She glanced up, as Meader stood. He took a step forward, his eyes gazing down into the bay.

'It's... it's drowning,' Meader said. 'Those things hate water, yet, it jumped in. Sable, are you watching this?'

She groaned. 'My head is splitting.'

He laughed. 'You did it! Shit.'

'Help me up.'

He leaned over, and took a grip of her right hand. He pulled her to her feet, and she fell back onto the bench. She wiped the sick from her chin and looked down into the bay. The greenhide was flailing around in the water, but the rocks surrounding the bay were too steep for it to climb, and it slowly sank beneath the waves. A claw appeared above the surface of the water for a last time, then it went under again.

Meader sat back down, and turned to her. 'Do you realise what you just did? Do you have any conception of the power this gives you?'

'I feel terrible.'

'Sable Holdfast, you have the power of an Ascendant.'

'I don't care,' she groaned. 'And, I'm never doing it again.'

CHAPTER 7

SOMETHING ROTTEN

U dall, Ulna, Eastern Rim – 21st Tuminch 5254 (18th Gylean Year 5)
Austin paced the stone floor of his cell, anger and frustration combining in a sour mixture in the pit of his stomach. The dragons had lied to him. After five days of being allowed out into the palace, no one had come for him the day before, nor the day before that. Why would they treat him so badly? Were they so cruel, that they would show him a glimpse of freedom, only to snatch it away again?

His meals had continued to arrive, so they hadn't forgotten about him. He cursed Ashfall's name. She was responsible for supervising him; it was her fault that he had languished for two whole days without getting to see the sun.

He felt like crying. He knew it was a pathetic response to a mere two days of being stuck back in his cell, but his hopes had been raised, only to be dashed. It would have been better if Maddie hadn't come visiting – then, he wouldn't have had the chance to experience a tiny piece of freedom. He sank to his knees by a hole in the floor, and gazed down at the wide river. He was thirsty, but couldn't summon the will to lower his freshwater bucket down through the gap. He wondered how long it would take a demigod to die of thirst. Was it even possible? Would he linger for months as his body slowly wasted away from dehydration? He lay down by the gap, his mind going round and round the same thoughts of despair and bitterness. In the last year and a half, he had spent a total of five hours outside a cell, and those five hours seemed brighter and happier than any he had previously experienced.

Perhaps it was a test. Maybe the dragons were experimenting on him; pushing his sanity to its limits in order to break him down. A punishment seemed more likely. Yes, that was it. The whole thing had been a ruse to give him hope and then take it away. It wasn't a mere punishment – it was psychological torture.

The meal hatch rattled and clanged, and he jumped to his feet, his hands shaking. He ran to the wall by the door and pulled the hatch open, and his heart almost exploded with joy as he saw the pair of gauntlets lying there. He told himself to be calm – this could be part of the ruse. A cruel twist. He stared at the gauntlets for a moment, then pushed his hands inside, and waited.

The minutes passed. He sat by the door, his legs crossed under him, his eyes never leaving the entrance to his cell.

A key sounded in the lock, and the door opened.

'You bastards!' Austin shouted at the four armed men in the passageway outside.

One of the guards raised an eyebrow, then gestured to the others, who strode into the cell.

'Get his gauntlets secured,' said the lead guard.

'You left me here for two days,' Austin went on, his eyes wild with fury.

'Shut up,' muttered the guard.

Austin was so angry that he barely noticed the guards buckling the straps of his gauntlets.

'Right,' said their leader. 'Let's go.'

Austin was hauled up onto his feet, and dragged through the entrance.

'I can walk on my own!' he yelled.

'Shit,' muttered another of the guards. 'He's in a foul mood today.'

'Who cares?' said their leader. 'We've got slightly more important things to worry about than this idiot's temper.'

Austin stared out of a narrow window slit as the guards escorted him down the passageway, and he felt his anger start to lift. Maybe it had all been a simple mistake. He was led up a set of stairs and they emerged out into a large hall, where Ashfall was waiting in her usual place.

She glanced down at him. 'Demigod.'

He glared up at her. 'Dragon.'

'Keep a very close eye on him today,' Ashfall said to the guards. 'I need to report to Lord Greysteel, and I can't afford to be distracted by this demigod.'

'Yes, ma'am,' said their leader.

'Is that it?' cried Austin. 'No apologies? You leave me alone for two days, and then you act as if nothing has happened?'

Ashfall tilted her head.

'He shouted at us as soon as we opened his cell door, ma'am,' said one of the guards.

'You lied to me!' Austin yelled.

'I did not lie to you, demigod,' said Ashfall, 'and I am insulted that you think I did. I was unavoidably engaged elsewhere. There are matters of greater import than taking you out for a walk.'

'Yeah? Like what?'

'The Queen's rider has gone missing.'

Austin blinked. 'Maddie?'

'Yes. That is her name.'

'She's missing?'

Ashfall turned her head, not bothering to respond. 'This way,' she said, then strode off down the hall.

The guards pushed Austin along, and they followed the dragon through the vast hallways and chambers of the upper palace.

'What happened?' Austin said to the guards.

'Maddie Jackdaw has gone,' said one, his voice low and conspiratorial. 'Her servant was found murdered in her apartment, her throat cut. The dragons have been turning the city upside down looking for her.'

'I can hear you,' said Ashfall.

The guard's cheeks flushed, and he glanced away.

They reached an enormous hall, where several dragons were gathered. Lord Greysteel was holding court, standing on the low platform as other dragons talked in whispered voices.

'My lord,' said Ashfall, bowing her head at Greysteel. 'I have returned from the south, without success.'

Greysteel turned to her. 'How far did you go?'

'On the first day,' she said, 'I reached Throscala, and searched the sea lanes there. I saw many Sea Banner vessels, patrolling the waters of that island, but I could discern no sign of Maddie.'

'There have been no Sea Banner ships sighted near Ulna for many months,' said Greysteel.

'Indeed, my lord,' said Ashfall. 'On my second day, I scouted southwards of Throscala, but again, I saw nothing. Then I returned, as commanded.'

'This is dire news,' said Greysteel. 'Splendoursun has also returned, from searching the seas to the north and west of Ulna. He too, saw nothing.'

'My lord,' said a green dragon, 'we have no idea if the Queen's rider departed by ship. She may still be on Ulna. Or, a dragon may have carried her away, to the mountains, or back to Seabound.'

Greysteel's eyes burned. 'I have a dozen dragons searching Ulna. They have been to Seabound, Costin Point, and every place in between.'

'The rider might not want to be found,' said another dragon. 'Perhaps she murdered her servant, and fled in shame.'

'Maddie would never murder anyone,' said Ashfall.

'With all due respect,' said the other dragon, 'we do not know that for certain. She is a foreigner, with strange ways. Perhaps her servant insulted her, or struck her?'

'I also do not believe that Maddie would kill anyone,' said Ata'nix, standing next to a large gold and white dragon. 'And I knew that servant. The poor girl was a mere peasant, from Serpens.' He wiped a tear from his cheek. 'Her horrible death rips at my heart. Who could do such a thing?' He turned to Greysteel. 'With your permission, my lord, I will send agents to conduct enquiries at the harbour. Perhaps a more subtle, human, approach will yield the results we all desire?'

'Permission granted,' said Greysteel. 'Report back at once if your agents discover anything.'

Ata'nix bowed low. 'As you will it, my lord.'

Austin moved forward a few steps, sticking close to Ashfall's side, as Ata'nix hurried from the chamber.

'Why have you brought the demigod along to this meeting?' said Greysteel.

'We promised we would take him from his cell daily,' Ashfall said, 'and for two days, I have been unable to fulfil my obligations to him.'

'A promise made to a human can be disregarded,' said the gold and white dragon. 'They are without honour; therefore, no honour needs to be shown to them.'

'I disagree, Lord Splendoursun,' said Ashfall. 'When I give my word, I keep it. Did you see any ships on your search of the north?'

'We did not,' said Splendoursun. 'The ocean was empty. The winds of winter blow south along the Eastern Rim; therefore, logic would dictate that any ship would have gone in the direction of Throscala and Haurn. Are you sure, princess, that you saw nothing on your search?'

Ashfall's eyes burned. 'Are you questioning my honesty? I have already reported on that matter, in front of the entire chamber. Did you not hear me say that I saw nothing?'

'I heard you, Princess Ashfall, but your words gave me no comfort. You are opposed to the very notion of dragons having riders, are you not? It would not take a very large leap of the imagination to contemplate the notion that you also wish to deprive other dragons of their riders.'

'How dare you!' cried Ashfall. 'Maddie is my friend.'

'Silence, please,' said Greysteel. 'Bickering will get us nowhere. We need to consider the facts. Maddie Jackdaw was reported missing two days ago, on the morning of the nineteenth of this month. If she lives, she cannot have gotten far. The death of her servant points to two possibilities. Either Maddie was abducted, and her servant killed by those who carried Maddie away; or Maddie herself murdered her own servant, and fled.' He glanced around the chamber. 'I agree with Ashfall's judgement. I consider it highly unlikely that Maddie would kill anyone; she seems incapable of violence. Therefore, we must ask ourselves – who would stand to benefit from Maddie's abduction?'

'Ahi'edo loathes her, my lord,' said an orange dragon.

'That is so,' said Greysteel, 'but Ahi'edo has been with Shadowblaze in Geist, along with Queen Blackrose.'

'The Unk Tannic also hate her,' said another dragon.

'I can vouch for Ata'nix,' said Splendoursun. 'He was with me on the eighteenth and nineteenth of this month. We were discussing the withdrawal of several more suitors, and planning how to deal with the others. I have witnesses who saw him in my company, if you doubt my word.'

Greysteel gazed at the white and gold dragon, then tilted his head. 'The word of a dragon as noble as yourself need not be doubted, my lord.'

'What now, my lord?' said the green dragon. 'Queen Blackrose shall be returning to Udall soon. The messenger you sent to Geist would have arrived yesterday.'

'Surely the Queen would feel bound to continue the negotiations with the Wyst dragons?' said Splendoursun. 'Would her Majesty abandon such important talks for the sake of a human?'

'Maddie Jackdaw is her rider,' said Greysteel. 'Their bond is strong.'

'The nobler dragons of Gyle were more measured in their approach to riders,' said Splendoursun. 'We see a close bond as little more than a hindrance on our freedom of action, despite the traditions of the lesser isles.'

A few of the Ulnan dragons muttered at these words, their eyes burning.

'I meant no offence,' said Splendoursun. 'I sometimes forget the value you attach to your rustic ways.'

The green dragon glanced up. 'Perhaps one of the other riders murdered Maddie and threw her corpse into the river? My own rider, for instance, did not hold her in high esteem. She would not have murdered Maddie, but others may have done so. Many of them disliked the idea of the Queen having a foreign rider.'

Greysteel lowered his gaze. 'Then, we shall dredge the river; though I hope with all my heart that she has not been killed by another rider. Such a thing would be unforgivable. Nevertheless, I want each dragon here to question their own rider on this; we must investigate all possibilities while we await the Queen's return. Let us adjourn this meeting for an hour, to allow time for the riders to be interrogated.'

The assembled dragons bowed their heads, and began to disperse. Ashfall turned, and strode for one of the entrances, and Austin ran to keep up, his guards chasing after him. Ashfall continued until she emerged onto a high platform that sat atop a tower. She gazed out over the town of Udall in silence, as Austin and the guards caught their breath.

'I'm sorry for being angry with you before,' said Austin.

Ashfall ignored him.

'I didn't know why I'd been left alone, and I thought...'

'Be quiet, demigod,' said the grey dragon. 'I am thinking.'

Austin nodded, then sat on the low wall that ringed the platform. He looked down at the town, his eyes on the wide, brown waterway that flowed under the palace. He shuddered at the thought that Maddie's body might be lying at the bottom of the river. His eyes followed the water down to the harbour, where a collection of masts were poking up into the blue sky.

'Can I ask something?' he said.

Ashfall sighed. 'Very well.'

'Can dragons lie?'

'Why do you ask that?'

'It's just that I heard, back on Implacatus, that one of the great weaknesses of dragons was their inability to lie. Yet, Splendoursun accused you of lying.'

'I do not lie, demigod.'

'Alright, but that's not what I asked. Is it possible for dragons to lie? I mean, is it a matter of honour, or is it a biological impossibility?'

Ashfall turned to him. 'The very notion of lying fills me with such disgust, that I would never be able to utter an untruth. I have also never experienced another dragon lying. Whether it is a complete impossibility, however, I cannot say. Do you believe that one of the other dragons was lying in the chamber?'

'I don't know.'

'I cannot believe it,' she said. 'Obfuscation and word-twisting can happen, but not a direct lie. If a dragon answers a question with another question, that always raises my suspicions.'

Austin smiled. 'I know gods who do that.'

'You are a human, clearly,' she said. 'What do you think happened to Maddie?'

'I have no idea. When was the last time she was seen?'

'On the evening of the eighteenth, after she left a meeting of the inner council. She went back to her apartment, but when she didn't appear the following morning, humans were sent to summon her. That was when the body of her servant was found. She had been dead for several hours, therefore it is assumed that whatever happened, must have taken place during the previous evening. She could have walked out of the bridge palace without any dragon noticing. The palace is designed like that. The dragons occupy the upper floors, leaving the small and narrow halls and chambers on the lower levels for the humans. It could never have happened in Seabound.'

'Someone waited until Queen Blackrose was away; that seems obvious to me.'

'Do you have a suspicion?'

'Yes. The Unk Tannic. Maddie didn't like them, and I heard a dragon say that they didn't like her.'

'I, too, dislike the Unk Tannic,' said Ashfall, 'but their loyalty to

Queen Blackrose is not in question. I think they would rather die than displease their Queen. Besides, Ata'nix has an alibi.'

'Yes, if Splendoursun wasn't lying.'

'I refuse to believe that any dragon would lie about this. My thoughts point to the possibility that a jealous rider has killed poor Maddie. Many of them hated her, I am sad to report. Ahi'edo might be on Geist, but his influence has turned many of the riders against Maddie since our arrival. Someone might have killed her, then panicked, and disposed of the body.'

'If that's the case, then we should find out soon, if all of the riders in the palace are being interrogated by their dragons.'

Ashfall lowered her gaze. 'It is wrong of me to feel self-pity, but my heart has not only broken for Maddie, it has also broken for myself. With her disappearance, I remain the only outsider on Ulna; the only foreigner among a mass of native dragons. I almost wish I had a rider – someone with whom I could share my solitude.'

'I'm a foreigner,' he said.

'You are a prisoner, demigod. Try not to forget it.'

He held up his heavy gauntlets. 'I'm hardly likely to do that. Why don't you have a rider?'

'I don't care much for humans,' she said. 'They lie, they cheat, and they're too fragile. A dragon's relationship with a human is, to me, equivalent to a human's relationship with a rat. Tell me, would you adopt a rat, and carry it about on your shoulders all day?'

'But, rats can't talk. We can.'

'A fair point. Although, considering that most of what comes out of your mouths is trivial nonsense, I think my comparison stands. The only human I have ever carried on my back is Sable Holdfast, when I rescued her from the Fordian Wastes on Lostwell. I did not care for the experience. My younger sister Frostback, on the other hand, became besotted with her rider in a very short time, after many years of claiming that she would never allow a mere insect to clamber about on her shoulders. That surprised me.'

'Where is she now, your sister?'

'I am uncertain. Belinda was going to send her and her rider to safety, but I wasn't there to see it with my own eyes.'

'Hang on a moment, which Belinda?'

'The Ascendant.'

Austin gasped. 'What? You're joking, right?'

She eyed him. 'Do I need to remind you about what I said about lying?'

'You knew Lady Belinda, the Third Ascendant?'

'No. I did not know her. It is Maddie who knows her, not I. All I know is that Belinda had a device called a Sextant, and that she was using it to save as many people on Lostwell as she was able. After that, I am not aware of what happened.'

'Lady Belinda is back on Implacatus.'

'Is that so? Maddie will be most upset by this news, if she still lives.'

'Lady Belinda had a Sextant? I heard some rumours that a Sextant might be on Lostwell. It must have once belonged to Lord Nathaniel.'

Ashfall turned her gaze skyward. 'The Queen approaches.'

Austin noticed a couple of black specks against the blue sky. 'Should we go back downstairs?'

'Your hour is almost up, demigod,' she said. 'However, I do not wish to waste time by escorting you back to your cell. You may accompany me to the meeting chamber, in payment for the two hours you missed over the previous days.'

Austin got to his feet. 'Alright.'

The guards stubbed out their cigarettes, and joined them again, as Ashfall and Austin left the platform. The grey dragon strode quickly, and Austin had to run to keep up with her. They reached the grand cavern, and saw that Blackrose had returned. She looked exhausted, while Shadowblaze stood by her side, his eyes burning.

'We are doing everything we can, my Queen,' said Greysteel. 'We have searched Ulna, and sent scouts out in every direction. We have discovered no sign of your rider.'

Blackrose bared her teeth, and sparks leapt across her jaws. 'When I find out who is responsible, I will tear them to pieces,' she roared. She glanced around. 'Where is Ata'nix?'

'The leader of the Unk Tannic is currently carrying out investigations in the harbour, Queen of Ulna,' said the gold and white dragon. 'He has been working hard to get to the bottom of this most difficult matter.'

Blackrose stared at him. 'Who are you?'

The white and gold dragon raised his head. 'I am the noble Lord Splendoursun of Gyle, my wondrous Queen; your most recent, and soon to be only, suitor.'

Blackrose hesitated, her eyes tightening.

At that moment, Ata'nix entered the hall through the tall doors, leading two nervous-looking humans. He got to his knees in front of Blackrose.

'My noble Queen,' he said, raising his arms. 'I bear tidings.'

Blackrose glared down at him. 'Get on with it.'

Ata'nix stood, and gestured to a woman on his left. 'This woman works in a tavern by the quayside, my blessed Queen. She overheard something a few nights ago that might be of interest.' He nodded to the woman. 'Speak. Tell Queen Blackrose what you told me.'

The woman shuffled forward, and lowered her gaze. 'Your Majesty,' she said; 'two men were drinking in the tavern where I work, a few nights ago. They were drunk, and boasting about having bundled a woman onto their ship. When I looked for them a little while later, they had gone. I asked around, and I was told that they were crewmates of the *Little Sneak*, a ship owned by Captain Tilly of the Five Sisters.'

Several dragons cried out in anger.

'What were those filthy pirates doing in Ulna?' Blackrose said, her voice barely containing her rage. 'I explicitly forbade any contact with them.'

'Please forgive me, your Majesty,' said Ata'nix, 'but I fear my next witness may be able to provide an answer to that question. However, it is not an answer that will please you.'

'I am already well displeased, Ata'nix. Command your witness to speak.'

Ata'nix nudged the young man. 'Tell her Majesty the truth about what you saw.'

'Yes, sir,' he said. He swallowed, then looked up at the formidable array of dragons staring down at him. 'I also saw two pirates, here, inside the palace, on the afternoon of the eighteenth, not too long before Miss Jackdaw went missing.'

Blackrose's eyes smouldered. 'How did you know they were pirates?'

'One of them introduced herself, my Queen. She said her name was Captain Tilly.'

'The captain was inside the walls of the palace?' cried Blackrose. 'Why?'

The man raised a finger, and pointed it at Greysteel. 'She was talking to him, my Queen; she was speaking to Lord Greysteel.'

'No,' said Blackrose. 'I cannot believe it.'

'Compel this man to speak only the truth, your Majesty,' said Ata'nix, 'and then we shall know if this is a lie.'

Blackrose stared into the terrified man's eyes. 'I command you – speak no lie to me. Is what you said the truth? Was the pirate captain speaking to my uncle, Lord Greysteel?'

The man fell to his knees, trembling. 'It's the truth! I saw her talking to Lord Greysteel, just hours before Maddie disappeared.'

Every eye turned to the steel-grey dragon.

'Have you betrayed me, uncle?' said Blackrose, her voice edged with menace.

'No, your Majesty; I swear it.'

'Do you deny speaking to this pirate?'

Greysteel lowered his head. 'No, but I didn't conspire to have Maddie abducted, and that's the truth. I was interested in seeing if the pirates wished to restart the trading agreement that we once held with them. That's all.'

'It's too much of a coincidence!' cried a blue dragon.

'So it seems, uncle,' said Blackrose. 'You disobeyed my orders.'

'I did, your Majesty. I am sorry. My eye was on making a profit, I admit it to you all, and now I am shamed. We were discussing the Lostwell Hoard that day, and I contacted Captain Tilly, to see if she wished to barter raw iron for finished goods. The following day, she did not turn up for a further meeting that I had planned, and I assumed that she had reneged on our agreement, as is the way with pirates.' He gazed at Blackrose. 'I promise you, upon my life, that I had nothing to do with Maddie's disappearance.'

'I hereby strip you of your authority, uncle,' said Blackrose. 'Innocent or not, you invited the pirates into Ulna, only for them to make off with my beloved rider. You have proved that you can no longer be trusted. Lord Shadowblaze, you will now take command of Ulna in my absence.'

'Are you leaving again, your Majesty?' said Shadowblaze.

'I must. The Five Sisters have taken my rider, in revenge for their expulsion from Ulnan waters; it's the only explanation that makes any sense to me. If they have hurt her, then I will destroy them all; I will wipe out the entire family of the Five Sisters.' She shuddered. 'If they have killed her...'

Austin broke away from Ashfall, and approached Blackrose.

'Queen of Ulna,' he said. 'I have healing powers. I offer them to you, along with my services. If Maddie is wounded, I will be able to heal her.'

Blackrose stared at him. 'Why is this prisoner out of his cell? Wait; it matters not. I have more important considerations to occupy my thoughts. Ashfall, you shall accompany me on my journey to search for Maddie. You will carry the demigod, and prevent him from escaping.'

Ashfall looked disgusted, but tilted her head. 'As you command, my Queen.'

'We three shall leave within the hour,' Blackrose went on. 'I need to eat and rest before setting off again. Lord Greysteel, I advise you not to be here upon my return.'

The hall fell into silence as Blackrose strode away.

The moment she had gone, Ashfall turned to Austin. 'Why did you speak? This matter does not concern you.'

'I want to be released,' he said. 'Maybe, by helping Blackrose, I can achieve that. Besides, anything's better than sitting in my cell every day.'

She glared at him.

Greysteel stepped down from the platform, and the hall hushed again, as every dragon turned to stare at the disgraced uncle of the Queen. Greysteel glanced at the man who had seen him speaking to the pirate, then he turned, and left the hall. At once, a loud murmur of voices broke out among the others.

'Those vile pirates,' said the orange dragon. 'This is an outrage.'

Austin glanced at Ata'nix. The leader of the Unk Tannic was standing close to Splendoursun, the slightest traces of a smirk upon his lips.

'Silence,' cried Shadowblaze. 'You all heard the words of the Queen. I am now in command of Ulna. I shall constitute a new inner council, made up of the most worthy subjects of the realm. Ahi'edo and Ata'nix shall be the human members, while I consider which dragons should also be in attendance.'

'Might I recommend Lord Splendoursun, my lord?' said Ata'nix, bowing. 'He has vast experience of governing, and is descended from the most noble lineage in all of Dragon Eyre – none other than that of the sacred Gylean himself.'

'It is true, Lord Shadowblaze,' said the gold and white dragon. 'I am the sole remaining survivor of the line of the Gyleans, and I would be honoured to assist you in the inner council, now that the unfortunate Lord Greysteel's life has collapsed in shame.'

'Clear the hall,' said Shadowblaze. 'Ashfall, please remain for now, along with Lord Splendoursun.'

The other dragons bowed and departed, along with the two human witnesses that Ata'nix had brought along. Shadowblaze waited until the hall was cleared, then ordered the doors to be closed.

'This is a dreadful way to assume command,' said Shadowblaze, 'and I take no pleasure in the fall of Lord Greysteel. I wish you to know that I believe his claims of innocence in this matter. I refuse to believe that the Queen's uncle would allow Maddie to be abducted. However, having said that, it is clear that he disobeyed orders by beginning negotiations with the pirates, and for that reason alone, his expulsion from Ulna is deserved.'

Ahi'edo opened his mouth to speak, but seemed to think better of it.

'I agree with your every word, my Lord Shadowblaze,' said Splendoursun. 'It is clear to me that Queen Blackrose has chosen wisely, with her decision to place you in command of the realm in her absence. Now, shall we get on with business, my lord? I fear that Lord Greysteel's governance of Ulna left much to be desired.'

'I have an agenda ready to go over, my lord,' said Ata'nix.

'I shall leave you to it,' said Ashfall. 'Come, Austin; let us prepare for our departure.'

She strode from the chamber, with Austin alongside her. They went up a large ramp, and came out into the bright sunshine.

Austin exhaled. 'That was intense. So, it was pirates that did it? Poor Greysteel; I feel a little sorry for him, and Ata'nix seemed just a little too happy with the way everything went. Do you think...?' He paused, glancing at the slender grey dragon, who was gazing out over the town. 'Are you alright, Ashfall?'

She kept her eyes on the town. 'No, Austin. I am far from alright.'

'Look, I'm sorry about volunteering. I'll try not to be a nuisance.'

'You are the least of my concerns, demigod,' she said, turning to him. 'Something is rotten at the heart of Udall; something evil and manipulative is at work here. I shall be glad to leave for a while.' She lowered her head, then turned back to the ramp.

'Where are we going now?' said Austin.

She narrowed her eyes. 'To have a damned harness fitted.'

CHAPTER 8

TEN PER CENT

West of Tanroe, Olkian Archipelago, Western Rim – 3rd Essinch 5254 (18th Gylean Year 5)

Topaz kept his hands on the wheel as he glanced onto the deck of the merchant ship. It had been secured bow and aft to the *Giddy Gull*, another victim of Captain Lara's latest expedition. Twenty pirates armed with crossbows and swords had lined up the crew of the merchant ship, and were guarding them, as the goods it had been carrying were transported over to the *Gull*. Lara was standing next to Topaz on the quarter deck, along with the two officers from the captured vessel, who were both holding their hands above their heads.

Lara frowned, as she scanned a hastily drawn-up list. 'What am I supposed to do with eight hundred pairs of army boots?' she muttered.

'I could do with a new pair of boots, Captain,' said Topaz.

She eyed him. 'I already pay you enough, Master. You can afford better boots than the ones given out to the damn Banner forces. Well, you would, if you didn't spend all your money on booze, weed and whores.'

'I think you might be mistaking me for someone else, ma'am.'

She raised an eyebrow. 'I know the types of places you visit when you're ashore, Master. I have my spies.'

Topaz shrugged. There was little point in arguing with Captain Lara, especially in front of the two captured merchant officers.

'Bollocks,' she mumbled, as she read down the list. 'We'll be lucky to clear two hundred for this garbage.' She glanced at the officers. 'Where were you headed?'

The two men looked at each other.

'Yafra,' said one. 'We were on a simple re-supply trip, taking Banner supplies from Ectus to the main garrison in the capital of Olkis. Might I take this opportunity to state that the Sea Banner will hunt you down for this outrage?'

Lara smiled. 'Really? I certainly hope so. A hunt would be more fun than robbing you idiots.'

Topaz took a moment to glance around. In the distance, the cliffs of Tanroe were visible off their starboard side, but there was no sign of any other vessels.

'Calm yourself, Master,' said Lara. 'There's nothing out there.'

'Are you going to kill us?' said one of the officers.

'Are you the captain of that piece of crap?' said Lara.

The officer puffed out his chest. 'I am.'

She narrowed her eyes. 'Do you know who I am?'

'I am aware that your ship carries the standard of the Five Sisters,' he said. 'However, I am unaware of which particular sister you happen to be.'

'Good,' she said; 'because if you knew that, then I'd have to kill you, and your crew. Oh, by the way, I'm taking a few of your people. I need a new cook, and a sailmaker, and, um… what else do we need, Master?'

'A couple of young lads for the rigging would be handy, ma'am, and I'm always on the lookout for a decent master's mate.'

'You've already got a master's mate.'

'He's alright if we're going in a straight line, but I can't rely on him at night, or in fog, or too close to the shore, or if we need to out-run the Sea Banner, or…'

'Alright,' Lara snapped. 'I get your point, Master.' She glared at the two officers. 'I want your cook, your sailmaker, three young lads with a head for heights, and a damned master's mate. That makes six. Fetch them, and we'll let the rest of you go.'

The merchant captain nodded to the other officer, who frowned, then made his way off the quarter deck, escorted by two armed pirates.

'What a ball-ache,' muttered Lara. 'This was hardly worth getting out of bed for.'

A scream came from the deck of the merchant ship. Topaz turned, and saw Udaxa'osso, Lara's cousin, and the first lieutenant of the *Giddy Gull*, plunging his sword into the chest of one of the merchant crew.

'Hey, Dax!' Lara yelled. 'I said no killing!'

The lieutenant glanced over to the quarter deck of the *Gull*, and shrugged.

'Asshole,' muttered Lara.

'I must protest!' cried the captain of the merchant vessel. 'You have just added murder to your list of crimes. The authorities in Yafra will hear of this, have no doubt.'

'Shut up,' said Lara. She nodded to Topaz. 'Stay here.'

He watched as Lara strode from the quarter deck, her shoulders tensed. She hurried across the main deck, then clambered over the gap onto the other ship. She walked up to her cousin and slapped him across the face, in front of both crews.

'Your captain clearly doesn't have control of her people,' said the captain of the merchant vessel.

'Who asked you to speak?' said Topaz.

'You will all hang for this. Sub-created beasts.'

'Yeah? Tell me, who was it that slaughtered every inhabitant of Tankbar a few years back? Was it "sub-created beasts"? Or was it settler scum? Go on, answer me.'

The captain glared at him.

'And who annihilated half a million men, woman and children in six months on Gyle?' Topaz went on, his temper starting to get the better of him. 'You got an answer to that question, you piece of shit? No? Didn't think so. You can spare me the damned hypocrisy.'

Lara re-appeared back on the main deck of the *Giddy Gull*, along with six sailors from the merchant ship. Two of them looked barely old enough to be in their teens, and one of the lads was weeping, and calling out for his mother. Topaz felt a sickening twist in his guts, as he remembered how he had been impressed into the Sea Banner when he had been fourteen. The fear he had felt at that moment was seared into his mind, and a wave of guilt surged through him. Lara gestured to a few of the pirates, and they escorted the *Gull's* unwilling new recruits below deck. She turned to the quarter deck, and beckoned towards the captain of the merchant vessel.

'The next time I see you,' he said to Topaz, as he turned to leave the quarter deck, 'you'll be hanging from the gallows in Yafra harbour.'

The captain was shoved down the steps of the quarter deck by two pirates. Topaz watched him exchange a few words with Lara, then he jumped the gap between the two ships. Lara nodded to Topaz.

'Disengage!' he yelled, and the crew of the *Gull* began unfastening the ropes that held the two ships together. A midshipman ran onto the quarter deck, and Topaz gave him a stream of instructions to relay to the crew. Within moments, the square sails of the forward mast were billowing in the wind, and the *Giddy Gull* began to move away from the merchant vessel, heading north.

The lieutenant stormed onto the quarter deck, his cheek pink from where Lara had slapped him. He ignored Topaz and went straight into his cabin, slamming the door behind him.

'Dickhead,' muttered Lara, as she joined Topaz by the wheel.

'What was his excuse this time, ma'am?' said Topaz.

'He claims the guy was threatening him; said he had no choice. Bullshit. The lad was sixteen, if that. Completely out of order.' She frowned at Topaz. 'Don't give me that look. I know fine well that I've slaughtered the crews of many a damn ship, but they were all Sea Banner, not civilians. I have standards, Master.'

'Yes, ma'am. Shall we set a course for Pangba?'

'Nope. We'll be steering clear of that town for a while. Our appearances there are starting to raise suspicions, and after today's little incident, things are only going to get rougher. Take us round the north coast of Olkis, and we'll swing down by Cape Atar. I want to speak to my father about Dax; I've had enough of that asshole on my ship.'

Topaz frowned. 'Are we going to Langbeg?'

'Is that a problem, Master?'

'No, ma'am.'

'Then, why do you look so damn nervous? You do know how to navigate through Luckenbay, don't you? You're supposed to be the best pilot in Olkis.'

'I know how to do it, ma'am. It's just... well, I haven't been in Langbeg for a long time, and I know how some folk there will react to me having served in the Sea Banner for seven years.'

'You're my master, Topaz; you'll be fine. Anyone who messes with you, messes with the Five Sisters, and, believe me, no one in Langbeg messes with the Five Sisters. Right; I'd better go and administer the oaths of loyalty to our new crew members. Once that's done, I'll send your new apprentice master's mate up to the quarter deck, and you can check him out.'

'Thanks, ma'am.'

She flashed him a smile, then strode from the quarter deck. Topaz summoned the midshipman, and went over their new heading with him, providing him with a long list of instructions. He saluted, then scurried away, leaving Topaz alone on the quarter deck. He checked the position of the mid-morning sun, and the wind direction, then settled down into his job.

'I don't give a shit what the master of the merchant vessel told you,' Topaz yelled at his new apprentice; 'you'll do exactly what I tell you. Got it?'

'Yes, sir,' mumbled the miserable-looking teenager, his eyes lowered.

Topaz glanced to their port side, and saw Cape Endu in the distance, its volcano issuing a thin plume of light grey smoke. He felt bad for shouting at the newly-impressed lad, but the *Giddy Gull* was sailing through the most heavily-patrolled part of Olkian waters, and his nerves were strung tighter than the strings on Ryan's guitar. The main shipping lanes from Alef to Yafra, the capital of Olkis, ran through the gap between Cape Endu and the island of Qana, and to brave it in broad daylight was fraught with risk for any pirate vessel. Still, he thought, they had the advantage of speed on their side, and should be able to outrun anything the Sea Banner could throw against them.

'Did you see what that bitch did to me, Master?'

Topaz glanced to his right, and saw Lieutenant Udaxa'osso standing by his side.

'I don't know who you're referring to, Lieutenant,' he said.

'Yeah, right. Look, I get it; you swore an oath to her, but things change. One day, I'll have my own ship, and I want you to be my master.'

'I'm flattered, Lieutenant.'

'Cut the crap, Topaz. My little cousin has bitten off more than she can chew, and you know it. She's up to her eyeballs in debt for this damn vanity ship, and when we get to Langbeg, her creditors will demand the balance of what she still owes them. She ain't got it, and that's a fact. What do you think will happen then? What I'm saying is – don't tie yourself too closely to her. If she goes down, then it would be a terrible shame if you went down with her.'

He strode away before Topaz could respond, and went down the steps of the quarter deck. Topaz watched him whisper a few words to some of the crew as he passed along the main deck, then he disappeared out of sight.

'Pretend you never heard any of that,' Topaz said to his apprentice.

'Heard what, sir?'

'That's the spirit, lad. Tell me, where are you from?'

'Nankiss, sir.'

'That shithole? I'm only joking, lad; that's where I'm from too, though I ain't been there since I was seven years old. How long have you been sailing?'

'Four years, sir.'

Topaz nodded. 'Did you ever think you'd end up on a Five Sisters ship?'

The boy shook his head.

'What experience do you have as a master's mate?'

'I was the mate's assistant, sir. I did it for a few months.'

'Shit on a stick. Those bastards on that merchant's vessel have stitched me up, good and proper. I was supposed to get a master's mate, not a bleeding master's mate's assistant. Can you read charts, at least?'

'No, sir. I can't read.'

'What? You're illiterate? Dear gods. Right, off you go – tell the midshipman that I'm assigning you to the rigging.'

'But...'

'No buts, lad. I ain't got the time nor inclination to train someone up from scratch. I've already got one master's mate who can't tell north from south, and I certainly ain't taking on another. Maybe, after six months in the rigging, if you promise to learn how to read, I'll take another look at you. Off you pop.'

The lad looked like he was about to start crying, but did as Topaz ordered, and left the quarter deck. Topaz felt another twinge of guilt, but he couldn't afford to endanger the ship, just to please a young recruit. He frowned. His own master's mate, who they had picked up in Pangba, was lazy and useless, and Topaz was getting tired of the burden. He tried to remember the last time he had enjoyed a decent night's rest.

He summoned the midshipman.

'Yes, sir?' said the junior officer.

'Fetch me Vitz. Tell him to bring coffee and cigarettes.'

The lad saluted, and ran off.

Topaz closed his eyes for a second, feeling the wind on his cheeks. The ship had turned to the west as it had rounded Cape Endu, and it was baking hot on the deck. He opened his eyes, blinked, and focussed his concentration. Not a cloud was in the sky, and he could feel the perspiration running down his back.

'Afternoon, boss,' said Vitz, handing him a mug of coffee. 'I don't know how you can drink that in this heat.'

'I'd rather sweat than fall asleep, mate,' he said. 'Here; take a wheel for a second.'

Vitz stared at him. 'Is this a joke, boss?'

'No. Take the damn wheel.'

'But... the captain will have a hairy fit if she sees me pilot the ship. Where's your mate?'

'Sleeping off a hangover, the little dipshit. Don't worry, I ain't going anywhere. I just need to stretch my arms and legs for a moment, and have a quick smoke. I've been standing here for fourteen hours.'

Vitz glanced around, his eyes wary.

'Do I have to give you an order, sailor?'

The younger man sighed, and took hold of the wheel, as Topaz stepped aside. He stretched out his arms, groaning, then slurped down some hot coffee.

'Give me a cigarette, lad.'

Vitz reached into a pocket and threw Topaz his silver cigarette case. Topaz withdrew one, lit it, then sat down on the deck.

'Where are we going, boss?' said Vitz.

'Just point the ship in a straight line. Dear gods, my back is killing me. Hey, mate; how much do you remember of what I taught you on the *Tranquillity* and the *Winsome*?'

'A fair bit, I guess; not that any of it's come in handy recently.'

'Do you like being up the rigging?'

Vitz gave him a hard stare.

'Thought not,' said Topaz. 'That's it; I'm going to speak to the captain; see if we can get you made into a proper master's mate. She owes me a few favours. How does that sound?'

'It sounds great, boss, but I doubt she'll go for it.' He scanned the horizon. 'This isn't the way to Pangba.'

Topaz laughed. 'Well done. That's it – you've passed the test. Wait; one more question. In which direction are we heading? Think carefully, now, lad – your future career depends on it.'

'Don't take the piss, boss.'

'I noticed you didn't answer the question.'

Vitz sighed. 'West.'

Topaz laughed again.

'I assume you have a good explanation for this, Master?' came an angry voice.

Topaz shot to his feet. 'Captain; I didn't see you there.'

Lara glared at him. Topaz pushed Vitz out of the way, and took over the wheel again.

'Sorry, Captain,' he said.

'After all the trouble I went to, to find you a new master's mate,' she went on, her eyes tight, 'and you have this settler asshole on the wheel. Where's the guy I gave you?'

'He was no good, ma'am. The merchant ship pulled a fast one on us; the lad couldn't even read.'

'And so you called on this... this... thing, instead?'

'Vitz is a good sailor, ma'am. I just needed a break for five minutes. Vitz knows what he's doing. Can he please be my master's mate?'

'What, and make me the laughing stock of Langbeg? Talk about scraping the bottom of the barrel. Do you expect me to believe that a settler could be a better master's mate than a proper Olkian? Have you lost your mind?'

The lieutenant appeared on the quarter deck. 'What's all the shouting about?'

Lara glared at her cousin. 'Nothing. Go back to playing with yourself in your cabin.'

Dax gave her a look of contempt, then noticed the presence of Vitz by the wheel. 'Why is this fool up here? Boy; get off the quarter deck. You don't belong here.'

Vitz hesitated, glancing from Topaz to the captain.

Dax raised his fist, and swung a punch at Vitz. The young man stepped back, and the lieutenant's hand missed him by several inches.

'What do you think you're playing at?' cried Lara. 'Don't you ever lift your hands to one of my people. I'll kick your teeth in, you lazy-assed drunk.'

Dax smirked. 'I'd like to see you try.' He turned back to Vitz. 'Move. Get off my quarter deck.'

'Stay where you are,' ordered Lara, her eyes full of fury. 'This man is the new master's mate, Dax, so, suck it up.'

'What? He's a damn settler; a rich boy from the estates of Gyle.'

'So? He's a better damn sailor than you'll ever be.'

Dax shook his head, a look of bemusement on his features. 'Just wait until your father finds out about this. Dear gods, I'm looking forward to getting back to Langbeg. You're finished, Lara.'

The lieutenant turned, and strode back into his cabin.

Topaz kept his eyes averted from Lara's simmering anger.

'Shit,' she muttered. 'Look what you made me do, Topaz! I'll never live this down. A settler on the quarter deck; oh gods.'

'Captain,' said Vitz, saluting; 'thank you for the promotion. I won't let you down; I promise.'

Lara rubbed her face with a hand. 'Take the wheel, asshole. Topaz, come with me.'

He followed her into her cabin, and closed the door. Lara paced up and down for a while, as Topaz glanced around at the captain's meeting room. She walked to a table and took a large swig of gin from an open bottle, muttering curses under her breath.

'Right,' she said, 'before I rip your head off, Master, I need to know – is that boy actually any good?'

'He was my apprentice on the *Tranquillity* and on the *Winsome*, ma'am.'

'That's not what I asked, and you know it.'

'He's better than my existing master's mate, ma'am, and much better than the lad you sent me. He's a quick learner, and I'll stay by his side for his first few watches.'

'So, he's shit? That's what you're saying, yeah? Bollocks. Dax is going to have a fine time with this. He'll be telling the rest of the crew that I've picked a damn settler for the quarter deck. It'll be another thing to add to his little list of complaints about me, which he'll present to my father as soon as we get to Langbeg. He hates me.'

'Yes, ma'am; he does.'

'Maybe I should kill him.'

'That might look worse, ma'am. What would your father say?'

She smiled. 'I see that you're not opposed to it in principle.'

'He told me that he wants me as his master, ma'am. He thinks you're going to lose the *Gull* when we land.'

'And how does that make you feel?'

'I'd rather throw myself overboard than serve as Udaxa'osso's master, ma'am.'

'We have to stick together, Topaz; you and me. You're right, though; if I kill him on the voyage, then I'm finished. Do you have any money set aside?'

'A bit, ma'am; for my retirement.'

'If I don't come up with at least a thousand in gold by the time we reach Langbeg, then the creditors will try to repossess the *Gull*, and there's no way I'm allowing that to happen.'

'How much are you short, ma'am?'

She glanced down. 'About five hundred.'

He blinked. 'But, what about all of the ships we've robbed, ma'am? Surely you must have more than that saved up?'

'Do you have any idea how expensive the *Gull* is to run? Not to mention the fact that I'm always generous to the crew with our takings. Loyalty costs in this business, and it's cost me dear. Do you have five hundred or not?'

Topaz bowed his head. 'Yes, ma'am.'

'Where is it?'

'Locked up in my cabin, ma'am.'

She laughed, and slapped him on the back. 'You might just have saved my ass, Topaz. Give me the five hundred, and I'll forgive what happened out on the quarter deck.'

Topaz pursed his lips, and waited.

She stared at him, and he returned her gaze.

'Shit. Alright; what else do you want?'

'A share of the ship, ma'am. It cost five thousand, so let's say ten per cent.'

'You utter bastard.'

'I ain't been living frugally for the last two years for nothing, ma'am. I've saved every coin I could. Ten per cent is fair.'

'But, it's my beautiful *Gull*,' she said, her voice high. 'I demand the right to pay you back. The ten per cent is temporary, until I get the funds together to give you the five hundred. That's it. That's the deal. Take it or leave it.'

He held his hand out. She scowled at him, then took it, and they shook hands.

'Your cousin told me not to tie myself too closely to you,' he said.

She smiled. 'Too late for that, eh? We're in this together, and no mistake. Now, bugger off and get back to work.'

He saluted. 'Yes, ma'am. I'll deliver the gold to you this evening, once the watch bell sounds.'

She waved him away. He turned, and walked back out into the bright sunshine. Vitz cast him a nervous look from where he was standing behind the wheel, then noticed the smile on his face.

'What are you grinning about?'

'That's no way to address your immediate superior.'

Vitz snorted. 'What?'

'Check the look on your face,' Topaz said. 'It's done; you're the new master's mate. Congratulations, lad. Now, all I have to do is work out how to tell the other one.'

Vitz turned his gaze back to the bow of the ship. 'Do you trust me, sir?'

'What do you mean?'

'This is just me and you talking – Topaz and Vitz. You know what I really think about being a pirate. I'm asking you – do you trust me as master's mate; I mean, really trust me?'

'Yes.'

Vitz shook his head. 'Why?'

'Are you saying that I shouldn't trust you?'

'No. I'm asking you why you do trust me. I've done nothing but grumble and moan about the Five Sisters, and the captain; and I've thought about deserting many times.'

'I used to ask myself the same questions in the Sea Banner, and yet I never once disobeyed an order, and I always worked to the best of my ability. I did it because the crew felt like my family, and I did it out of pride, I guess. I trust you for the same reason that the captain of the *Tranquillity* could trust me.'

A tear slid down Vitz's cheek.

'Don't start all that,' said Topaz; 'please.'

'Sorry, sir.'

'Right; I'd better go and wake up the idler who's been masquerading as my master's mate for the last couple of months. It's time to give him some bad news. Keep the *Gull* on its present course; I'll be back in fifteen minutes.'

'Yes, sir, and...'

'And what, lad?'

Vitz smiled. 'Thank you, sir.'

CHAPTER 9

THE CENTRE OF THE OCEAN

East of Rigga – 4th Essinch 5254 (18th Gylean Year 5)

Maddie stared into the thick fog, her hands resting on the ship's railings. A light breeze was blowing; just enough to keep the *Little Sneak* sailing westwards, but Maddie could see nothing through the mist surrounding the vessel. For fifteen days, she had been on board the sloop, but in that time she hadn't seen a single other boat. On the afternoon of her first full day, she was sure that she had seen a few black specks in the sky overhead, as they had pulled away from the Ulnan mainland. Her spirits had soared at the sight, but nothing had come of it. Perhaps they had been birds, she had thought at the time. The crew had been anxious until the fourth day, then after that their mood had lifted a little, but it was subdued again. The drop in the wind, and the banks of fog had seen to that. The sailors were working in near silence, as if afraid to break a spell, as the hull of the small ship slowly ploughed through the ocean.

She wondered what Blackrose was doing. The ship was well out of her flying range, but Maddie was certain that her black dragon would be searching the seas and islands for her. If only there was some way to send her a message, to let her know that she was alright.

She looked up, and saw a patch of blue sky above. It was probably sunny and warm on Ulna, but out on the ocean, the fog had a chill that seemed to get through her clothing. The sails were glistening with condensation, and every surface of the ship seemed wet and slippery. She shivered.

'You still checking the skies, Miss Jackdaw?' said a familiar voice.

She turned, and saw Captain Tilly striding towards her.

'What are you expecting to see up there?' Tilly went on. 'We passed out of dragon range days ago.'

'I just wanted to see the blue sky again,' said Maddie.

Tilly nodded, and leaned on the railings next to her. 'We're not far from Rigga now.'

'How do you know? I mean, I can't see a thing through all the murk.'

The captain shrugged. 'We know our speed and direction; that'll suffice for now. My biggest worry is hitting the rocks on the east coast of the island.' She glanced at Maddie. 'Thanks for behaving. I admit that I had a few concerns about letting you roam free on my little sloop, but I needn't have worried. You've been a perfect passenger.'

Maddie glared at the young woman. 'Passenger, eh? In that case, perhaps you can kindly let me off at the next stop.'

Tilly laughed. 'A little late for that. I don't think I'll ever be able to show my face around Ulna again. That Unk Tannic asshole set me up as much as he set you up. If he'd mentioned that you were the Queen's rider, I would have told him where to go. I should have stuck with the deal that Lord Greysteel was offering me; but, on the other hand, if we can make it back to Olkis in one piece, I'll have enough money to live how I please.'

'What are you going to do with me when we get to Olkis?'

'I have no choice – I'll have to ask my father and sisters for their advice, as much as it pains me to say it. I'm going to blame the Unk Tannic, naturally. Everyone on Olkis hates them, so it shouldn't be a hard sell. After that, it'll be out of my hands.'

'Tell me about your sisters. I've met Ann and Lara, but only for a few minutes.'

'Ann's the oldest. She used to be wild, but she's old and boring now.'

'How old is she?'

'Ancient. Thirty-one. Then there's Ellie. Ellie and Ann had the same mother, but she died ages ago, and my father re-married, for a second time. Me, Lara and Dina are the children from that marriage. Our mother is also dead, and father is now on wife number four.'

Maddie frowned. 'His three previous wives have all died?'

'I think his first wife's still alive, somewhere on Olkis; I'm not sure. Ellie and Dina's mother was a pirate captain, like us, and she was captured and executed by the Sea Banner. My mother died of a disease she caught when we were hiding in the marshlands. The Banner were sweeping through Olkis, and everyone had to hide for a while. Dina was also very sick, but she pulled through; it was a rough time. I was only six. What about you?'

'My parents were killed by greenhides,' said Maddie.

Tilly nodded. 'Sorry to hear it.'

'My sister and brother are still alive, or, at least I think they are. Being on a different world sort of makes it hard to keep in touch. I wish I could see them again.'

'I feel shit for what's happened to you; you should know that.'

'But not so shit that you're willing to take me back?'

Tilly nodded. 'That's about right. It's bad luck, that's all. You're fortunate that it wasn't Lara who carried you off – that girl can be a little cracked at times. You should have seen the piece of crap that she sailed back from the Eastern Rim; the *Winsome* it was called. It's amazing that she made it all the way to Olkis. Now, she's bought herself some fancy boat, and she thinks she's the queen of the bleeding Western Rim. Ann, Ellie and Dina have their own ships too, but nothing like as swanky as Lara's shiny new brigantine. Bitch.' She spat into the dark ocean. 'Gods, I hate this fog.'

'How in Malik's name did five sisters from the same family all end up being the captains of pirate ships? That doesn't sound normal.'

Tilly laughed. 'It ain't normal, but our family ain't normal neither. You must have heard of my father?'

Maddie shrugged.

'The great Olo'osso?'

'No,' said Maddie. 'Is he famous?'

'He was the greatest pirate in Olkian history. Alright, he's past it now, but in his day, he ruled the seas of the Western Rim, from Alef to Ectus. He even raided a dragon palace in Gyle once, and got away with it. That was before the invasion; before I was born, but that's how he made his fortune. Then, after my mother died, he retired. He was ill at the same time, the same as Dina was, and it took him a long time to get over that and my mother's death. A lot of folk think he's dead, but that's just part of the legend he's tried to gather about himself – it gives him an air of mystery, or so he thinks. He set me and my sisters up with our own ships, and each of us pays him part of our annual takings. In return, he makes sure no one hassles us. He practically rules Langbeg now.'

'But, if women are accepted as captains, why are there none in the crew? Back where I come from, women served in the Blades, I mean, the army, alongside the men.'

Tilly raised an eyebrow. 'Really? Women serve in the army?'

'Yes, and it's completely normal. But here, and on Lostwell, the Banner soldiers are all men, and the crews of all the ships are men, too. Why?'

'There are women in the Banners,' said Tilly; 'on Gyle, Ectus and Na Sun Ka – the so-called Home Islands. But, as far as I know, they do the clerical work, or act as nurses and stuff like that. Me and my sisters are only captains because of father. We have to work twice as hard to prove ourselves to the crews we lead. Your world sounds a lot fairer.'

'I'm a Blade,' said Maddie. 'I was raised to be a soldier.'

Tilly laughed. 'You're a soldier?'

'Well, alright; I wasn't a particularly good soldier. I was terrible at obeying orders. But, my point stands – half of the Blades are women.'

'The men on Dragon Eyre wouldn't accept that. It's like, the dragons kept the humans down, and the men do the same to the women. Except for riders, of course. There are, or were, plenty of female dragon riders. That was the one way to break out of the bullshit. But, with the invasion, that's nearly all gone now. I don't think Implacatus has any plans to help women out, especially native women.'

'If I was back on Ulna, I would be in a position to persuade Black-rose to change things. I was already making progress. At first, the dragons excluded me from every meeting, saying no humans were allowed, but I managed to get that changed. But no, here I am, in the middle of the damn ocean.'

Tilly pulled a face. 'Oops.'

'I wonder if that's another reason why the Unk Tannic didn't like me,' said Maddie. 'I wasn't just uppity, I was an uppity woman.'

'It might have had something to do with it.'

'Land!' cried a voice from the top of the mast. 'Land ahead!'

'Holy shit,' yelled Tilly. She grabbed a passing sailor. 'Tell the master to slow down. I'll be on the quarter deck in a minute.'

'Yes, ma'am,' said the sailor, then he raced off towards the rear of the ship.

'Come on,' said Tilly to Maddie. 'Let's go take a look at Rigga.'

They walked along the deck, amid a growing level of activity among the crew. Sailors were scrambling up the rigging to adjust the sails, and doing a hundred other things that Maddie didn't understand. The two women reached the steps of the low quarter deck, and ascended. Her lieutenant was standing there, along with the master, who was barking out instructions to a young sailor.

Maddie turned when she reached the centre of the quarter deck, but could see nothing ahead of them through the thick fog. She was left alone for a while, as Tilly spoke to the senior members of her crew. The ship started to bank to the right, and they slowed down. On the left, a dark mass of rocks appeared through the murk, and the master began yelling his orders, his voice cutting through the frantic tempo of the working sailors.

The ship ploughed on, keeping the rocks to their left, then they emerged from the fog into a pocket of clear air, and Maddie caught a glimpse of a ragged, barren shoreline of cliffs and bare hillsides. The sudden glare of the sun made her narrow her eyes, and then it went dim again, and they entered more fog. It didn't last long, and soon they had left the fog behind, and were sailing in the clear light of a sunny morning. The atmosphere among the crew had improved with the sighting of land, and many were grinning as they worked, or slapping each other on the back.

'That was a little too close for my liking,' said Tilly, 'but we managed to get here without ramming into the rocks and breaking the hull, so I call it a success.'

'Is that Rigga?' said Maddie.

'I bloody hope so,' said Tilly. 'There's nothing else out here.'

'It looks bleak. Does anything grow here?'

'This is my first time in the centre of the ocean,' said the pirate captain, 'but there must be fresh water supplies; otherwise how would the Riggans survive, not to mention the thousands of Banner soldiers garrisoned here? That's our main job now – to find a river, so that we can replenish our water barrels before carrying on towards Olkis.'

'There's a Banner garrison?'

'There sure is. This place might be remote, but the Banner are here, presumably so that rebels can't use the island as a refuge. Their base is somewhere on the southern coast, which is why we're heading north. The last thing we need is to be spotted by a Sea Banner frigate.'

Tilly and Maddie kept their eyes on the uninviting coastline, looking for any signs of life. They sailed on for two more hours, but saw nothing except barren wastelands of bare rock. The wind fell again, until the sails were barely pushing them along, and Maddie noticed Tilly grow more anxious as time passed.

She was talking to the master about the possibility of breaking out their long oars, and refitting the sides of the ship to allow the crew to row the sloop onwards, when a loud cry came from the top of the mast.

'Village ahead!'

Tilly grinned, and clapped her hands together. She gestured to a crew member, and he ran off to assemble a landing party. Maddie walked to the railings on the left side of the quarter deck, and saw a ramshackle collection of mud-brick hovels clustered by the coast. A small stream was flowing down a valley, where a few crops were growing amid sheets of thick mud. Where the river met the ocean, a small pier jutted out into the water, and a few tiny fishing vessels were tied up. Natives began to emerge from the squat, brown buildings. They stared at the *Little Sneak* as it approached the pier.

'What are they holding?' she said to Tilly.

'Stone-tipped spears,' said the captain. 'There ain't much metal or wood here, or so I've been led to believe, and the people are somewhat, shall we say, primitive?'

The master guided the sloop over to the shore, and they drew to a stop a few yards from the end of the pier. The anchor was dropped, its chain making a loud grating noise that rattled through Maddie's ears. For a moment there was silence, as the crew of the sloop stared at the natives of Rigga, and the natives stared back.

Tilly nudged her lieutenant with an elbow, and the man stepped forward.

'Greetings' he cried to the natives. 'We wish to barter with you for access to the river, and for any spare supplies of food. We have gold, and weapons, and alcohol. May we come ashore?'

The natives didn't respond for a long few minutes, and Maddie started to wonder if they had understood the words spoken by the officer. At length, an old woman stepped forward onto the pier. She was using a spear as a walking stick, and was dressed in what Maddie would call rags.

'You are not welcome in our village,' the old woman shouted across to the ship. 'The Banner will enslave our children and take our food if we help pirates. You must leave.'

'Is there anywhere else on this coast to obtain fresh water?' the lieutenant called back.

'Yes,' said the old woman, 'but the villages there will give you the same answer, Olkian. Sail to the Banner base, and ask there.'

The lieutenant glanced at Tilly, who shook her head.

'Try again,' she said. 'This time, warn them of the consequences if they continue to refuse.'

The lieutenant nodded, then turned back to the pier. 'We cannot surrender ourselves to the Banner,' he cried. 'We have no alternative but to seek water here. If you cooperate with us, we shall reward you. We have crates of crossbows in the hold – we shall give them to you, in return for access to your river, and then you will be able to defend yourselves from the Banner.'

'Crossbows?' said the old woman. 'The Banner use bombs against our people. They destroy entire villages. What use is a crossbow to us?'

'I say again; we have no alternative. Our water supplies are too low to carry on. We shall be landing. Be warned. If you try to oppose us, we shall defend ourselves with vigour.'

Tilly signalled to a junior officer, who saluted, and ran to the bow. A large ballista was uncovered, its waterproof sheeting pulled away. Two crew members loaded it with a long, steel bolt, while the other members of the crew armed themselves with crossbows.

'I don't like this,' said Maddie.

Tilly shrugged. 'Neither do I, but what else can we do? If we don't pick up fresh water, we'll not survive the voyage to Alef.'

'Alef? I thought we were going to Olkis.'

'We are, via Alef. The ocean crossing is far shorter if we go north from here, then sail down to Olkis.'

Maddie wanted to ask more, but Tilly's eyes were tight, and focussed on the shoreline. She nodded to the lieutenant.

'This is your last chance,' he yelled to the natives. 'Stand back from the pier, and allow us to land.'

At these words, the Riggans raised their spears in the air, and began shouting at the ship. A few also had strange-looking bows, of a type Maddie had never seen before, and they waved them at the crew on the ship.

'Shit,' muttered Tilly. She glanced at a junior officer. 'Lower the rowing boat. I want a dozen armed men inside. The moment the Riggans begin hostilities, the crew are to loose a single barrage – crossbows, and the ballista. Target the old woman first, then aim for anyone with a weapon.'

'Yes, ma'am,' the officer said.

The shouting and chanting from the Riggans increased as the small rowing boat was swung over the gap between the ship and the pier. Empty barrels were lowered into it, along with twelve burly pirates, all wearing leather armour over their chests. The oars were fixed to the sides of the rowing boat, and its crew pushed off from the *Little Sneak*. At this, pandemonium erupted on the shore. A volley of stone-tipped arrows whistled through the air, along with hurled spears. Two in the rowing boat were struck immediately, along with a sailor up on the rigging, who fell with a scream. He landed into the water by the pier, an arrow in his back.

Tilly snapped her fingers, and a withering hail of crossbow bolts was loosed from the side of the sloop. The crowd on the shore screamed in panic as the first Riggans fell. A yard-long ballista bolt shot through the air. It struck the old woman on the pier, then passed through her body and hit a man standing behind her.

'Keep loosing!' cried Tilly. 'Those bastards started this, but we'll finish it.'

The pirates needed no encouragement. Over three dozen of them were standing or kneeling by the railings on the left side of the sloop, and they loosed volley after volley of bolts into the fleeing Riggans, until the bodies were piled up along the shore. The corpse of the old woman was lying sprawled on the flimsy pier, her lifeless eyes staring up at the blue sky.

Maddie looked away.

'Occupy the harbour!' Tilly yelled. 'Drive them back!'

The rowing boat docked at the pier, and the pirates tumbled out. One of them kicked the body of the old woman into the clear waters by the shore, while the others raced towards the village. The rowing boat pushed away again, heading back to the sloop, where another dozen armed pirates were waiting to make the short trip to the shore. By this time, the last of the Riggans had fled from the vicinity of the pier, and the shooting from the *Little Sneak* ceased. Bodies lay all along the shore, and the rocks were smeared with their blood.

'Idiots,' muttered Tilly, shaking her head at the sight. 'This could all have been avoided.'

'I feel sick,' said Maddie.

'It can be a nasty business, at times, Miss Jackdaw.' She gestured to her lieutenant. 'Set up a perimeter around the harbour, and start filling the water barrels. I want to be away from here within two hours. If you encounter any further resistance, crush it.'

'Seventeen dead Riggans, and two dead crewmen,' said the lieutenant. 'Plus another three members of the crew with injuries, ma'am.'

Tilly nodded from her comfortable chair. She glanced across her cabin towards Maddie, but said nothing.

'All water barrels have been replenished, ma'am,' the lieutenant went on. 'Shall we raid the village for food supplies?'

Tilly frowned. 'Do we have enough to reach Alef?'

'Barely, ma'am. If we have more trouble with the wind, then things could get rather tight.'

'Fine. Raid the village. Take whatever can be carried. Bring me one of those stone-tipped spears as well – I want a little souvenir.'

The lieutenant saluted. 'Yes, ma'am.'

Maddie waited until the officer had left the cabin, then she glared at Tilly.

'I don't know why you're giving me that foul look, Miss Jackdaw,' the captain said. 'What choice did I have? I can't let the crew die of damn thirst, can I?'

'You killed seventeen people.'

'They initiated the violence. We gave them plenty of warning.'

'A couple of children were among those killed,' Maddie cried. 'I saw them fall.'

Tilly shrugged. 'Unfortunate.'

'And the old woman's body was nearly ripped in two by that ballista bolt.'

'We only loosed one of those. We were restrained.'

Maddie shook her head, feeling a sense of nausea grow in her stomach.

'It was them or us,' Tilly went on. 'And, let's face it, the Riggans are little better than savages. My two dead crew were worth more than seventeen of them. If we'd been the Sea Banner, we would have blown their entire village up. They should be grateful that I'm not vindictive.'

'You can justify it any way you like,' said Maddie, 'but I can tell from the look on your face that you feel ashamed.'

'Shut up,' muttered Tilly. 'I did what had to be done for the good of my crew.'

'Maybe, but you know it was wrong.'

'Do you want to go back in the brig? Seriously, if you're that disgusted with me, then maybe you don't wish to be in my company any longer.'

Maddie hesitated.

'I thought not,' said Tilly. 'When we sail from here, I want you to remember this conversation, every time you take a sip of water – water you wouldn't have, were it not for my disgusting behaviour. Now, get out of my cabin; I'm sick of you judging me.'

Maddie got to her feet, and walked back out onto the quarter deck. The rowing boat was crossing the gap again, bringing crates filled with whatever had been looted from the homes of the Riggans. A few armed pirates remained on the pier, but it was clear that the operation was coming to an end. Maddie leaned on the railings. The bodies of the Riggans had been left where they had fallen, and a crow was pecking at the eyes of a dead man lying by the water's edge. In the distance, the surviving villagers were watching, keeping out of range of the pirates' crossbows. The rowing boat pushed off again, after unloading the crates, and the last pirates embarked for the sloop. When they had re-boarded the *Little Sneak*, the crane was pushed out, and the small boat was winched back up onto the main deck.

'Get us out of here,' said the lieutenant, and the master saluted. The wind was barely more than a breeze, and the sloop seemed to take forever to move away from the scene of carnage on the shore. The native Riggans re-occupied their village, and the cries of mourning and lamentation began; a terrible howling of pain and rage. Maddie glanced at the sailors. A few seemed troubled, but most had grins on their faces, their relief at leaving the village obvious. The full water barrels and looted food had been taken below deck.

The sloop edged along the shore, until, at last, the village disappeared into the distance.

'Sea Banner!' yelled a voice from the top of the mast.

At once, the atmosphere on board changed. Sailors ran around, climbing the rigging, or relaying new orders from the lieutenant. Tilly appeared on the quarter deck.

The lieutenant pointed behind them. 'A sixty-oared galley, ma'am,' he said. 'They're gaining on us.'

'The damn Riggans have betrayed us,' said Tilly. 'They must have sent someone to run to the nearest Banner base.'

Maddie hurried to the rear of the sloop, and stared out. A sleek, low galley was chasing them, its dozens of oars moving in rhythm as they smacked through the water.

'Full speed ahead,' cried Tilly.

'We're going as fast as we can, ma'am,' said the master. 'The wind is too weak to gain any more speed.'

'Shit, shit, shit!' yelled Tilly, her eyes wild. 'Battle stations! Get the ballista ready. Move!'

Maddie stared at the Sea Banner vessel. Without a strong wind, the oars of the galley were driving it on, and the gap between the two ships was decreasing with every second. On its deck, she could see sailors gathered around a large catapult by the bow.

'They're loading up a pisspot!' shouted a pirate.

Tilly put her hands to her face. 'We ain't going down without a fight,' she said, but her voice was low, and edged with despair.

Without warning, the wind began to pick up. Maddie's hair billowed as a renewed breeze caught the sails at last. The master barked out fresh orders, his eyes wild with hope, and the sloop raced off to the north. A thick bank of fog was to their right, and he piloted the ship into its path.

'Come on,' muttered Tilly, her fists clenched as she glanced between the galley and the approaching fog. 'We can make it; come on, my *Little Sneak.*'

A large projectile soared from the bow of the galley towards them, but the distance had grown too great, and it splashed down into the water, missing the stern of the sloop by two yards. At almost the same moment, the fog enveloped them, and the galley disappeared from sight. The crew remained quiet as they worked, except for the master, who was relaying instructions in a manic voice, his features strained as he coaxed as much speed as he could out of the vessel.

They broke through the fog, and the sun beat down on them again, along with a strong wind. The sails filled, and they shot off, the bow cutting through the ocean swell.

A great cheer rose up from the crew, and Tilly hugged her master, and then the lieutenant, a huge grin of relief etched on her face. She turned towards the probable position of the invisible galley, and made an obscene gesture in their direction, as the crew cheered and laughed.

Maddie panted in relief. As much as she had hated what the pirates had done, she had no desire to die at the hands of the Sea Banner. Tilly slapped her on the back.

'Luck is on our side today, boys!' she cried. 'Master, set a course for Alef.'

CHAPTER 10

PINNED DOWN

Nan Po Tana, Haurn, Eastern Rim – 5th Essinch 5254 (18th Gylean Year 5)

Sable took a long draw of the weedstick. 'I can't believe I'm doing this again.'

Meader paced up and down by the bench overlooking the little bay. 'You have to,' he said. 'If you can learn how to control them properly, it could mean...'

'What?' said Sable.

'I'm not sure, exactly.' He frowned. 'Why do you need to smoke so much first?'

'It helps,' she said. 'I need to prepare myself mentally. The inside of a greenhide's head is an unpleasant place to be.'

Millen walked through the archway, and stood under the shade of the olive tree.

'Am I too late?' he said.

'No,' said Meader. 'She hasn't tried yet; she's been too busy smoking her way through my stash of weed.'

Millen nodded, then stared across the bay at the abandoned village of Pot An. A solitary greenhide was roaming through the overgrown streets, sniffing around for the goat meat that Deepblue had dropped onto the village to attract it. The dragons had been told to allow a few greenhides to approach the temple. They had been reluctant, but Meader had managed to persuade them that it was essential to discover if Sable's previous trick had been a one-off. After that, they had waited for days before a greenhide had finally turned up.

Sable dropped the weedstick, and ground the butt under her sandal. The pain in her legs and back had been dulled by the narcotics, and she felt ready.

'Alright,' she said. 'What do you want me to make it do? Dance?'

Millen laughed. 'I'd like to see that.'

'Let's start off with some simple instructions,' said Meader; 'like, walk forward; halt; move one pace to the left – that sort of thing.'

'Nah,' said Sable; 'that's far too boring.'

She gritted her teeth and aimed her powers at the greenhide's insect eyes. She gagged. Just as before, the feeling was one of instant revulsion, like wading thigh-deep through a sewer. She sensed its thoughts. She felt a raw fear, from the beast's knowledge that dragons were close by, but, over-riding that, she could sense its ravishing hunger. It hadn't eaten properly in days, and could smell the goat carcass. It could also see the three humans by the bench on the opposite side of the bay, and greatly desired to devour them.

Stop moving.

The greenhide froze, half-stooped over the cracked road surface.

Climb up onto the nearest building.

It glanced up at the empty, white-washed houses, then leapt up in a single motion, landing onto a flat roof.

Dance.

The greenhide did nothing. It looked around, but otherwise remained motionless.

Wave your arms in the air, and shriek.

An awful sound came from the greenhide's mouth; a terrible wailing, as it lifted his long, taloned limbs above its head and swung them around.

Sable felt sweat roll down her forehead, and an ache was throbbing behind her temples. One more try, she thought.

Jump up and down.

The greenhide responded. It continued to wail with its arms in the air, but started to leap up and down at the same time. It lost its balance, and toppled from the roof, landing onto the road below with a crash; and the connection broke.

Sable gasped, then, before she could stop herself, she vomited down the front of her top.

'Shit,' she groaned, as sick dripped from her lips.

'That was amazing!' yelled Meader, a massive grin on his face.

Millen frowned at Sable. 'Urgh.'

'Well, that's this top ruined,' Sable said, wiping her chin.

'That was unbelievable, Sable,' Meader went on, oblivious to her discomfort. 'You made it dance; you made a damn greenhide dance.'

'Can someone get me a towel, and some water?' she croaked. 'And a clean top.'

'I'll be back in a minute,' said Millen, disappearing back through the archway.

'You were great,' said Meader. 'Oh. Are you alright?'

'No. I'm covered in sick, and my head feels like it's been in a vice.'

Millen hurried back, and passed Sable a mug of water. She swilled some round her mouth, then spat it out onto the path. He passed her a towel and a fresh tunic.

'Turn around,' she said to the two men.

They did so, and she pulled the vomit-stained top over her shoulders, trying not to let any drip on her. She folded the old tunic up, with the sick in the middle, and wiped herself down with the towel. Her back spasmed with pain for a moment, as she pushed her arms into the sleeves of the clean top, then she pulled it down over her head.

'What's it doing now?' said Millen, his eyes on the village.

'I think it's gone back to searching for the goat,' said Meader. 'Next time, we'll try giving it a more persistent command, like "don't move", and we'll see how long it works for.'

'What's all this "we" nonsense?' said Sable. 'It's me who's doing all the work.'

'Sorry,' said Meader, turning back to face her.

She handed him the folded-up tunic. 'You can deal with that.'

Meader pulled a face, then nodded. 'You did great, Sable. I know it's unpleasant, but think of the possibilities. I wonder if we could entice more greenhides into the village? I want to see how many you could control at the same time.'

'Why?' said Millen. 'I mean, it was hilarious, watching a greenhide dance, but what's the point?'

'He needs a project,' said Sable. 'I think he's bored.'

Meader frowned. 'I don't understand why you two are so lacking in enthusiasm for this. Do neither of you understand the ramifications? Greenhides were designed to allow only Ascendants the ability to control them; it was part of their strategy to enforce their control of everyone else. Along with the Banners, the greenhides are the main weapon the Ascendants can deploy. Imagine that one came here – they could order every greenhide on Haurn to storm the temple; sacrificing hundreds of them to break through. With Sable here, that would be impossible.'

'But there are no Ascendants on Dragon Eyre,' said Millen.

Meader ignored him. 'It's going to take a lot more practice. It'll get easier every time, Sable, just like any power.'

'Give me another smoke,' she said; 'my head is still throbbing.'

He reached into a pocket, took out a weedstick, and lit it for her. 'I'm almost out of matches,' he said, handing it to her.

'Get more when the next boat arrives,' she said, 'or, better still, buy one of those metal lighters that some of the Banner officers carry, and then you'll never have to worry about running out of matches again.' She took a draw, and sighed as her headache lessened a little. She passed the weedstick back to Meader, gripped the head of her walking stick, and pulled herself to her feet. 'I might need to go for a lie-down,' she said. 'I feel terrible.'

'I'll help you walk to the tower,' said Millen, taking Sable's arm.

They went through the archway, with Meader following them, the weedstick in one hand, and the soiled tunic in the other.

A shadow flitted overhead before they could enter the tower, and Deepblue landed in the large courtyard.

'Did you see what Sable did?' said Millen.

'I did, rider. However, that is not why I have landed. I am here to tell you that Blackrose is on her way; I have just seen her in the distance, to the north. She is approaching, with Ashfall.'

Sable's eyes widened. 'She's found me. Shit.'

At that moment, Evensward swooped over, and she landed close by.

'Two strange dragons are coming,' said the leader of the Haurn colony.

'It's Blackrose,' said Deepblue.

Badblood's head appeared between two buildings. 'Blackrose is here? Rider, come; should we flee?'

'There is no need to flee,' said Evensward. 'I will not allow any hostile enemy to harm you. I have forty dragons in my colony who are ready and willing to defend this temple from anyone. If Queen Blackrose tries anything, we shall kill her. You are all under my protection – do not forget.'

Evensward extended her wings and sprang into the air. She circled once, then sped off to the north.

Sable staggered over to a bench that sat outside the front door of her tower. She lowered herself onto it, and waited. Badblood strode into the courtyard, his good eye scanning the skies.

'I'm scared,' said Deepblue. 'Why has Blackrose come here? All we want to do is live in peace.'

'Don't worry,' said Badblood. 'As we are under Evensward's protection, you are under mine.'

'What should we do?' said Millen.

Sable shrugged. 'Nothing. We all wondered if this day would come. If Blackrose wants a fight, then I'm sure Evensward and her colony will give her one. Let me take a quick look, so I can see what's happening.'

She sent her vision out, and hurled it up into the sky. She looked around, and saw several specks. Four were moving at speed towards two that were coming from the north. Sable's vision crossed the distance in seconds. Evensward was leading three of her strongest dragons in the direction of Blackrose and Ashfall. Something seemed wrong, and then she noticed what it was. Blackrose was wearing a harness, but Maddie was not on it, while, upon Ashfall's shoulders, a man was sitting. Sable blinked.

'Austin?' she mumbled.

'What did you say?' said Meader.

Sable glanced at him. 'Your brother is on Ashfall's back.'

'Dear gods; is he alright? What's he doing on the back of a dragon?'

Sable turned to Millen. 'Now the bad news; there's no sign of Maddie on Blackrose's shoulders.'

'You have to communicate with Evensward,' said Meader. 'Tell her not to attack; please.'

Sable nodded. 'Sure.'

She shot her vision back over the miles of sky, and entered the mind of the dark green dragon.

Evensward; it's Sable. Apologies for entering your mind without asking first. You need to know that the man on the shoulders of the grey dragon is Austin – Meader's young brother.

Understood, Sable.

She severed the link. 'Done.'

'What are they doing up there?' Meader said.

'Let's wait and see,' said Sable. 'I'm still tired and achy from the dancing greenhide.'

Meader began pacing up and down again, his fists clenching and unclenching as he peered up at the blue sky. The sun was beating down with its usual ferocity, and Sable relaxed in the shade cast by the tower as they waited. Millen sat down by Deepblue, whose eyes were lined with anxiety. Badblood puffed his chest out, and stretched his forelimbs in readiness for battle. A few minutes passed, and then several black specks appeared overhead. They descended slowly, in wide, lazy circles, until their colours became visible. Evensward was talking to Blackrose as they lowered, and neither looked as though they were about to commence hostilities.

The dragons landed in the field close to the courtyard, and Meader broke into a sprint, running towards the grey dragon. Austin clambered down from the harness, then stared, his mouth hanging open, as his brother raced across the field and threw his arms around him.

Sable smiled.

Evensward and Blackrose were still talking to each other as they strode towards the courtyard, and Sable took a deep breath.

'It can't be all bad,' said Millen. 'Evensward wouldn't be allowing Blackrose to get close if she thought she was a threat.'

'Let us hope you are right,' said Badblood.

Evensward entered the courtyard.

'The Queen of Ulna wishes to speak to you in private, Sable Hold-fast,' the dark green dragon said. 'She has given her word that she will cause no harm during her visit here. However, I want to respect your wishes. If you do not desire to speak with the queen, then I will send her away.'

'Let her approach,' said Sable.

Evensward tilted her head. 'As you wish. I will keep the grey dragon close to me, in case there is a hint of betrayal.'

'I have given my word,' said Blackrose, her voice strained. 'I shall not break it.'

'I have not forgotten what your subjects did to Sable and Badblood in Seabound, Queen of Ulna,' said Evensward.

'That was done while I was unconscious, noble Evensward of Haurn,' said the black dragon. 'I did not order the attack.'

'Very well,' said the dark green dragon. 'We shall withdraw from the courtyard, to allow you to speak to Sable. Please remember, she is dear to the dragons of Haurn.'

'I understand.'

Sable glanced at Badblood. 'Leave us, my beloved. It'll be fine.'

Badblood glared at Blackrose, then he, Deepblue and Millen left the courtyard, and Evensward also retreated. Blackrose stepped forward, until her head was a few yards from the bench where Sable was sitting.

'Holdfast witch,' she said. 'How goes it?'

Sable narrowed her eyes. 'Where's Maddie?'

'I see that you have retained your usual contempt for pleasantries, witch. You have gone straight to the heart of my visit here.' She bowed her head, her eyes filled with sorrow. 'Maddie Jackdaw has been abducted by pirates.'

Sable swallowed her initial reaction, and merely nodded. 'When?'

'Seventeen days ago. I was in Geist, meeting with some dragons from Wyst, when she was taken. Ashfall and I have searched everywhere along the Eastern Rim. We did not originally plan to come here, but I heard a rumour from a dragon who dwells on the islands between Haurn and Throscala that a wounded witch was living here, and I knew it had to be you.' She looked Sable in the eye. 'Please help me.'

'How am I supposed to help you, exactly?'

'Have you seen any sign of a Five Sisters vessel?'

Sable raised an eyebrow. 'The Five Sisters took her? Please don't tell me it was Lara.'

'The sister in question is named Tilly, I believe.'

'I haven't seen any Five Sisters ship pass southern Haurn. Sorry.'

'I already know that, witch. I need you to use your powers to search for her. My heart is unravelling, and I can barely find the strength of will to do anything other than continue my search. My realm is being governed by others in my absence, and yet I hardly care. I would do anything to get Maddie back; even declare a truce with you.'

'How far have you searched?'

'All the way from Wyst in the north, right down to here. I do not understand it; we should have seen some sign of them.'

'Several possibilities present themselves. The ship could have sunk.'

Blackrose emitted a low groan.

'Or,' Sable went on, 'they might have sailed via Rigga. That's out of your flying range, isn't it?'

'It is.'

'If they went in that direction, then they would already be halfway to Olkis.'

'If they are going to Olkis.'

'Where else could they go? They must know that they've taken a dragon rider. The Five Sisters aren't stupid, regardless of your personal feelings about them. They'll know that you'll be looking for them.' She frowned. 'I'm a little confused about their motives, however. Do you know why they took Maddie?'

'It must be for revenge. I forbade them from entering Ulnan waters, and this is their response. They want to punish me.'

'I don't want to contradict you, Blackrose, but that sounds unlikely. I mean, where's the profit? Have they asked for a ransom?'

'No, nor would I pay one. I do not submit to blackmail.'

'Not even for Maddie?'

Blackrose paused, and Sable shifted on the bench, the pain in her legs flaring.

'Are you injured?' said the dragon.

'I'm fine.'

'You do not appear fine, witch. I can tell by your posture that you are experiencing discomfort.'

'Now, about a possible ransom,' said Sable, ignoring her. 'If I could somehow find out where they have taken your rider, would you be prepared to pay for her release? I assume that you still have plenty of gold left from the Lostwell Hoard?'

'Not as much as you might think. The last time I checked, there was little left of the gold.'

Sable frowned. 'What have you been spending it on?'

'I am not sure. I delegated control of the finances of the realm to others. The resettlement of the town of Udall has presumably cost much in gold.'

'Who has access to the hoard?'

'Why? This is irrelevant. How does this help me in my search?'

'I'm just trying to piece it all together. Don't get angry, but is it at all possible that someone paid the pirates to take Maddie? I can't see why else the Five Sisters would have done it. Profit is their sole motive. Could someone have bribed them to take such a risk?'

Blackrose glanced away. 'My uncle was caught in the act of speaking to the pirates, just hours before they took my rider. He disobeyed my orders, but I cannot believe that he would have betrayed me to such an extent that he would bribe pirates to take my rider.'

'Greysteel was talking to Captain Tilly? Why?'

'He claims he was trying to renegotiate the same deal that you struck with Captain Ann.'

'That sounds plausible.'

'I believe that the abduction was opportunistic. The vile pirates were in the palace, and they saw a chance to spite me.'

'For no gold?'

'That is quite enough about the gold, witch,' said the dragon, her temper rising. 'This is getting us nowhere. If, as you believe, they have taken her to Olkis, then I have no choice. I too, must go to Olkis.'

Sable stared at her. 'That would be suicide, and you know it. To fly to Olkis, you would have to go via the Home Islands. If the Banner and gods don't find and kill you on Na Sun Ka, then they would certainly do so on Gyle. You'd never make it as far as Ectus, never mind Olkis.'

'I might, if you came with me, witch.'

Sable laughed. 'Come on. Are you saying that you trust me now, after everything that's happened?'

'Tell me, witch; are you fond of Maddie?'

'Of course I am.'

'Then I would trust you to the extent that you would help me find her.'

'Did you bring the Quadrant with you?'

'No. It remains on Ulna.'

Sable exhaled in frustration. 'Alright. Go back to Ulna, and bring the Quadrant here. Then, give it to me. I can go to Olkis, and bring Maddie back, if she's there.'

Blackrose's eyes flared with rage. 'Absolutely not! For one thing, I cannot allow myself to trust you with it, not alone. And for another, you are clearly in no fit state to rescue anyone. You may claim to be "fine", but I can sense that you are in great pain, witch.' She turned her head to face the other dragons. 'Bring me Austin; at once.'

'Why are you summoning him?' said Sable.

'Austin can heal your wounds, witch. You know this. Why have you not asked to be healed?'

'Maybe I don't want to be. Maybe, I'm happy living my quiet life here, in the temple. I said I would help rescue Maddie, but that's only because she is a friend. I have no desire to involve myself in the affairs of this miserable world any longer. And, even if you force Austin to heal me, you've already said that you won't give me the Quadrant, so what would be the point?'

'I said "not alone", witch; do not twist my words. Austin is from Implacatus; he will know how to use a Quadrant.'

They turned as Ashfall approached, with Meader and Austin walking alongside her.

'I asked for Austin only,' said Blackrose.

'I am responsible for him, my Queen,' said Ashfall. 'You ordered me never to allow him to leave my sight.'

'And I'm his brother,' said Meader.

Blackrose tilted her head. 'You are his brother? You are Meader, the rebel demigod? Do you know that the gods of Gyle are claiming it was you who destroyed the fleet outside Seabound?'

Meader narrowed his eyes. 'I am aware of that, yes.'

'It's true,' said Austin, his cheeks flushed with anger. He pointed at Sable. 'That bitch forced him to do it. She manipulated him, and made him slaughter tens of thousands of sailors and soldiers. Meader's told me all about it.'

Blackrose looked stunned for a moment. She turned her fiery gaze to Sable. 'Is this true, witch?'

Sable shrugged.

'You... you saved me from Seraph,' said the black dragon, 'and then you saved Seabound? I owe my life and my realm to you? Sable, why didn't you tell me this?'

'It was irrelevant to our discussion.'

'Austin,' said Blackrose; 'heal her, immediately.'

'No,' he said. 'Why should I? She turned my brother into a mass murderer; she doesn't deserve to be healed.'

Blackrose roared in rage, sparks flying out from her jaws.

'Do it,' said Meader. 'Heal her.'

'But, brother,' said Austin, 'she destroyed your life. The Banner are hunting you, because of her; because of what she forced you to do.'

'I know. I forgive her.'

Austin stared at Meader in disbelief.

'The time has come, brother,' said Meader. 'I'm so sick of doing the dirty work of Implacatus. The slavery, the destruction, the slaughter – it's wrong; it's all wrong. I've made my mind up. I will never help the cause of Implacatus again.'

'Well said, demigod,' said Blackrose, calming a little. 'Austin, I ask you once again. I require Sable to be at her full strength, so that she can rescue my rider.'

'Do as the Queen commands,' said Ashfall.

Austin folded his arms across his chest and shook his head.

'What if,' Ashfall went on, 'the Queen ordered your release in return for this favour?'

'I would be willing to do so,' said Blackrose; 'after you have completed one final task for me.'

'What task?' said Austin.

'Heal Sable first, and I shall tell you.'

Austin sighed. He glanced at Meader, who nodded, then he raised his right hand. 'Fine.' His expression dropped. 'Wait; I can't sense her. It's as if she's protected from my powers.'

Sable smirked. 'What a pity. Oh, well.'

'You'll have to touch her,' said Meader. 'Her blocking skills are only effective through the air.'

'Damn you, Meader!' yelled Sable. 'I told you that in confidence.' She gripped the walking stick, and pushed herself to her feet. 'No one's healing me; not today, not ever. Leave me alone.'

'Ashfall,' said Blackrose, 'hold the witch down.'

The slender grey dragon raised a forelimb, and pushed Sable down to the dusty ground of the courtyard, her claws splayed out on either side of her. Sable groaned in agony, her back howling in pain.

'I am sorry for this, witch,' said Ashfall.

'Austin,' said Blackrose. 'Place your hand on her head; she is at your mercy.'

Sable tried to use her vision powers to stop the young demigod, but the pain was too much. Her legs and her back were dominating every thought, and tears came from her eyes. Austin knelt down beside her.

'I could kill you, Sable,' he said, lifting a hand. 'I also have flow powers.'

'You would be the next to die,' said Blackrose. 'Heal her, and you shall be freed; kill her, and I will rip your head from your body.'

Austin placed a hand onto Sable's brow, and she felt a torrent of power surge through her. It started in her toes, and worked its way up, through her legs, then her back and torso, until it reached her head. She convulsed, then fell still, panting. The pain had gone. For the first time since she had been standing on the cliffs of Alg Bay, there was no agony accompanying her every waking moment. She gasped, and opened her eyes.

'Is it done?' said Blackrose.

'Partly,' said Austin.

'What do you mean?' said the black dragon.

'I've fixed her right leg, and her back, and driven out the infection in her blood, but her left leg cannot be healed.'

'Why not?' said Meader, his eyes full of concern.

'Her left leg has been broken in several places,' said his brother, 'and the bones have already set. In other words, her body believes that it has already healed, and I can't change that.'

'Not good enough,' said Blackrose. 'I need her whole. What can be done? There must be a way.'

Austin frowned. 'There is a way, but it's too cruel, even for Sable.'

'Explain yourself.'

'Well,' said Austin, 'if we were to re-break her leg in the same places, then I might be able to heal it properly.'

'No,' gasped Sable. 'Please; leave me alone. I don't want this. All I want is to live in peace.'

Blackrose ignored her. 'Point out where her leg was broken, and I will break the bones.'

Austin grimaced. Millen had also appeared in the courtyard, his eyes wide at the sight of Ashfall's huge limb pinning Sable to the ground. He crouched down next to Sable, and took her hand.

'Be brave,' he said, his eyes welling.

Austin picked up a chalky piece of stone from the ground, and marked the fabric running down Sable's left leg. 'Here, here, and here.'

'Brace yourself, witch,' said the black dragon, then she lifted a thick claw, and rammed it down onto the first mark, snapping the bones above her left ankle.

Sable screamed, then again, and again, as the dragon broke her leg two more times, until her cries filled the air. She began to lose consciousness, her eyes clenched shut, then she felt Austin's powers fill her again, and the pain ceased.

'I've done it,' said Austin. 'Her left leg has now set properly.'

'Release her,' said Blackrose, and Ashfall lifted her forelimb.

Sable opened her eyes. Millen and Meader were crouching alongside Austin, and the three men were gazing down at her. Meader and Millen looked distraught, but Austin kept his features guarded.

'Are you alright?' said Millen. 'That was horrible.'

'What is happening?' roared Badblood, as he stormed into the crowded courtyard. His bulk pushed Ashfall aside as he approached. 'If you have hurt my rider...'

'We have healed her, son,' said Blackrose. 'She is whole again.'

Badblood used his head to shove the three men away, then stood over Sable, his eye flashing a warning.

'My beautiful rider,' he cried. 'I am sorry; I was not here to protect you. Say the word, and I will kill them all. You are all that matters to me; you are everything. The dragons of Haurn will help me; say the word. I love you.'

'I love you too, Badblood,' she said. 'But it's true; they healed me, whether I wanted it or not.'

'Can you stand?' said Meader.

Sable got to her feet, then wiped the tears from her cheeks, and the dust from her clothes. She shot Austin a look of hatred, then placed her hand by Badblood's good eye. Her body felt wonderful – healed, whole, and without any hint of pain. She noticed that she still had the scar on her left hand where the bolt had ripped through her palm, but all sensation had returned to her remaining fingers.

'Are you fit and ready, witch?' said Blackrose. 'Will you help me rescue Maddie?'

She lowered her gaze, and nodded. 'Fine; I'll help you, but I need to train first. I haven't exercised in months. I'm out of shape.'

'You have eight days, witch,' said the black dragon.

'Why?' she said. 'What will happen in eight days?'

'That is how long it will take for Ashfall and Austin to return to Ulna and retrieve the Quadrant,' she said. She gazed at the demigod. 'This is the last task I mentioned. Do this, and I will release you; you will be free.'

'Aren't you coming with us?' said Ashfall.

'No. I am near the limits of exhaustion, both mental and physical,' said Blackrose. 'Without rest, I will be unable to continue with the search for Maddie. I will stay here, with Sable, Badblood and Deepblue, if the dragons of Haurn allow it. Go to Udall, collect the Quadrant, and ensure that Austin does not attempt to flee with it.'

Ashfall bowed her head. 'Yes, your Majesty.'

'Will you do this for me, Austin?' said Blackrose.

'When we get back,' he said, 'I will be completely free? No more tasks or conditions?'

'You have my word, demigod.'

'It's the right thing to do, brother,' said Meader. 'You know in your heart that the invasion and occupation are wrong. This is our chance to be on the right side, for once.'

Austin frowned, then nodded. 'Alright, dragon; you have a deal.'

CHAPTER 11

PALACE COUP

South of Serpens, Ulnan Archipelago, Eastern Rim – 8th Essinch 5254 (18th Gylean Year 5)

Austin reclined in the shade of a large tree as Ashfall drank from the stream. It was another hot morning – the sky a deep blue, and the glare from the sea around the small island was almost too bright for Austin's eyes. The branches of the tree swished over his head in the warm breeze, and he could hear the calling of some birds, but they were keeping their distance from the dragon.

Ashfall lifted her head from the stream, and glanced at him.

'Have you eaten?' she said.

'Yes,' said Austin. 'That's the last of the supplies we got from Haurn finished.'

'We shall be in Udall in a few hours,' said the dragon. 'I estimate that we still have two hundred miles to go. Once there, we shall rest for a day before starting the return journey.'

'Will you go with Blackrose to Olkis?'

'I will do whatever the Queen commands,' she said. 'Now, it is time for us to have a little talk. Queen Blackrose told us that the Quadrant is locked away in Maddie's apartment.'

'Yes?'

'As you know, Austin, only a human can enter the small rooms where she lived. I cannot. I need you to promise that you will not take advantage of the trust we have placed in you. If you use the Quadrant to flee, you will have committed a gross betrayal, and I would fear for your brother's safety when Blackrose discovers your crime.'

'Is that a veiled threat?' he said, smiling. 'Look; you don't need to worry. I was only ever taught the bare minimum about how to use a Quadrant, and I've never actually even touched one before. I wouldn't know how to use it to take me to Gyle, or anywhere else on Dragon Eyre.'

The grey dragon tilted her head. 'Why did you not mention this to Blackrose? She is under the impression that you are knowledgeable about these things.'

'She never asked, and that wasn't part of the deal. We bring her the Quadrant, and I'm free. I'm not going to jeopardise that.'

'Very well. What will you do with your freedom?'

'I don't know. I'm going to try to talk my brother out of joining the rebellion, but after that?' He shrugged.

'I do not believe that you will succeed in convincing Meader to change his mind. He seemed determined.'

'He's confused. Sable did things to his mind. He has the deaths of thousands of people on his conscience, because of her, and he's not thinking straight.'

'What do you think he should do?'

'He needs to hand himself over to the authorities, and explain what happened; that it wasn't his fault.'

'You want him to betray Sable, Badblood and the others? Be very careful with your next words, human, for I will not carry someone who is planning to run off to the occupiers the moment he is freed. Remember, I am not your friend. I would happily leave you here, upon this barren rock.'

Austin blinked. 'That's not what I meant.'

'No? What did you mean? If Meader were to inform upon Sable, he would lead the gods directly to the temple on Haurn. How is that not a betrayal?'

'I cannot betray a cause that I am not a part of. But, I promised to deliver the Quadrant to Blackrose, and that's what I'm going to do.'

'You wish the rebellion to fail, don't you? You want the dragons to be annihilated? For, make no mistake, that would be the outcome, were the forces of Implacatus to prevail.'

Austin kept his mouth shut. Three times, he had made a bargain with the dragons – for his life, for the chance to get out of his cell, and for his freedom. Did that make him complicit in the rebellion? If he returned to Gyle, Governor Horace would read his every thought, and use that intelligence to attack Sable and the others. Did he care? What if his brother decided to become an active member of the rebellion? If Horace read his mind, then Meader would also be condemned as a traitor.

'Answer me,' said Ashfall.

'I don't know,' he said. 'If my father was still the governor, things would be different, and my choices would be clearer. My father was content to allow the dragons to live in peace, as long as they didn't rebel, but Lord Horace is less restrained. All the same, you can hardly expect to me to turn my back on everything that I believe in.'

'What do you believe in, Austin?'

'The essential righteousness of Implacatus,' he said. 'The rule of the Ascendants. Only they can guarantee stability and peace upon the worlds; without them, everything would fall into anarchy. I'm not saying the Ascendants are perfect; I know they've made mistakes here on Dragon Eyre, but I'm still loyal to them.'

Ashfall's eyes blazed. 'Edmond destroyed my entire world, human. My home. How many people were on Lostwell when he decided to obliterate it? How many families; how many children? You disgust me.'

'I don't know why he did that, but he must have had his reasons.'

Ashfall turned her back to him, and he could sense the growing rage simmering inside her. He glanced at his hands. He could kill Ashfall, if he wanted to. He could send a rolling wave of flow powers through her body, stopping her heart, or filling her head with so much blood that it exploded, just as he had done to the group of Unk Tannic terrorists who had attacked him outside Port Edmond. His metal gauntlets were somewhere within the baggage compartments attached to the dragon's harness. Blackrose and Ashfall trusted him, despite his allegiances; did that make them stupid, or noble? He pushed the thought from his mind.

'I'm sorry,' he said. 'I can't explain what happened on Lostwell. At school, I was taught that the Ascendants were wise and all-powerful, the guardians of civilisation; our protectors. I'm descended from them – every god and demigod is; they are the original source of immortality, and all of our powers. And yet, I know that Lostwell isn't the first world that they have destroyed.'

'They throw away the lives of mortals as if we were worthless,' said Ashfall. 'To you, I am a sub-created beast; a being of no value. At least your brother is attempting to make some amends; you, I fear, are a lost cause.'

Austin tried to smile. 'That's a little harsh.'

She turned back to face him, her head just inches from his. 'Is it? Tell me, demigod, what further atrocities would the Ascendants have to carry out, before you saw them as they really are? The extinction of the dragon race? The slaughter of every native on this world? How many children would they have to kill before you condemned them?'

'What about the Unk Tannic?' he cried. 'They kill children too.'

'I despise them also,' said the dragon, 'but, we are talking about the Ascendants.'

'Sometimes... sacrifices have to be made, for the sake of stability.'

'Do you see much stability on Dragon Eyre? Climb onto my back. I want to get this over with as quickly as possible. I no longer care for your company, demigod.'

Austin got to his feet, his eyes lowered as Ashfall stared at him. A rising sense of shame crept over him, and he tried to brush it away. He had done nothing to be ashamed of, yet the words of the grey dragon had bitten deep. He clambered up onto the harness and strapped himself in. The dragon took off without another word, and soared away to the north.

It took four hours of flying to reach the town of Udall. Ashfall had skirted the islands of Serpens and Tunkatta, and then passed to the east of the volcano that stood on the southern tip of Ulna. A few boats were in the harbour of Udall, and they sped over them, heading for the palace on the bridge. Austin's heart sank at the sight of the place of his imprisonment, and he tried to console himself that they wouldn't be staying long.

Ashfall hadn't uttered a single word to him during the flight, and she remained silent as they alighted onto a large, square platform atop one of the palace towers.

'Place the gauntlets back onto your hands,' Ashfall said, without looking at him.

'I can't do the buckles up,' he said.

'It matters not; even loose, they will give the impression that you are powerless. Do it.'

He reached over, and looked through the baggage pouches hanging from the harness. He found the large, metal gauntlets, and picked them up, then slid down to the ground. He pushed his hands into the gauntlets, then held them up at an angle so that they wouldn't fall off.

'You still trust me, then?'

'I trust you not to do anything stupid,' she said. 'If you attempt to use your powers on anyone, I will kill you.'

She strode down the ramp into the interior of the palace, and Austin followed. It seemed quiet at first, with most hallways empty, but a huge green dragon was standing outside the entrance to the great reception hall, blocking the tall doors.

'Halt,' he said to Ashfall.

'I need to speak to Shadowblaze,' said the grey dragon, as Austin stood close by. 'I have orders from the Queen.'

The green dragon narrowed his eyes. 'Who are you?'

'My name is Ashfall; I am a member of the inner council. Who are you?'

'I wasn't informed that you were arriving,' he said. 'Entry is forbidden to those without a proper appointment.'

Sparks flew from Ashfall's jaws, and the green dragon tensed. He was far larger than the slender grey dragon, and Austin began to edge away.

'Tell Lord Shadowblaze that I am here,' Ashfall growled.

'I can't,' he said. 'My job is to guard this entrance. I cannot leave my post.'

'I don't have time for this nonsense,' she said. She glanced at Austin. 'Go. Find what we came to collect, while I deal with this imbecile.'

Austin frowned, then turned, and ran off down the hallway. The sound of raised dragon voices echoed behind him, but he didn't look back. He remembered where Maddie's apartment was, though he had never been inside, and saw no one on the way there. Standing outside her front door, however, were two men in black robes, armed with crossbows. Austin slowed to a stroll as he approached, trying to appear calm and nonchalant.

'Hello,' he said. 'I need to get into Maddie's room; I have direct orders from Queen Blackrose herself.'

The two Unk Tannic men glared at him.

'Lord Ata'nix told us not to let anyone in,' said one. 'The former rider's quarters are sealed off.'

'Yes, but I need to look for something,' said Austin. 'It's very important. Queen Blackrose insisted.'

'Can you prove that? Who are you?'

'He's the captive demigod,' said the other guard. 'I recognise him; and look – he's wearing gauntlets to stop him using his powers on us.'

'If you're a captive,' said the first, 'then why are you out of your cell?'

'I'm helping Queen Blackrose look for Maddie Jackdaw,' Austin said. 'Princess Ashfall brought me back to Udall. I just need a minute inside, to look for something.'

'What are you looking for?'

Austin felt his temper start to fray. 'That's none of your business.'

'It is very much our business, demigod. Do you think we're scared of you?' He glanced at his colleague. 'Place him under arrest.'

The guard raised his crossbow and aimed it at Austin's chest.

'You're making a mistake,' said Austin.

The guard lifted a hand to grab him.

'Don't touch me, you Unk Tannic scum,' Austin snarled.

'Shoot him,' said the first guard. 'He's a demigod; he'll be fine.'

Austin turned, but not quickly enough. The second guard loosed a bolt in his direction, and it struck him in his left side, sending him flying to the ground. His gauntlets fell off, and clattered onto the stone floor a few yards away.

'Kill him!' cried the first guard. 'He has powers!'

Austin suppressed the pain in his side, and raised a hand. His powers leapt out, striking the two men. Blood burst from their eye sockets, and they slumped to the ground in a heap by the doorway. Austin groaned, and reached for the bolt in his side. He clutched it in his right hand, and pulled, ripping it out of his flesh. He dropped it onto the ground and lay still, panting, as his self-healing took over.

'Shit,' he muttered. He glanced down the hallway, but there was no one else there, so he pulled himself back onto his feet. He stared at the bodies of the Unk Tannic guards lying in front of Maddie's front door. Two more deaths to add to his name. They had wanted to kill him, he told himself, and besides, they were Unk Tannic terrorists, just like those he had slain on the road outside Port Edmond. Despite that, he felt sickened. He wished there was a way he could use his powers in a more subtle way – to render victims unconscious, rather than dead. Experienced gods with death powers could take someone to the brink without snuffing out their life, but Austin's flow abilities seemed clumsy and brutal, a blunt weapon.

His thoughts turned to escape. He should flee the palace, and try to make his way to the harbour. Perhaps a boat would be willing to carry him from Ulna, before the bodies were discovered. Once that happened, the Unk Tannic would be hunting him. A braver god might decide to confront the rest of the rebels in the palace. He would stride into the hall where the inner council were meeting and destroy them all – humans and dragons alike. He could end the rebellion. But Austin was not that god. Besides, hadn't he made a deal with Blackrose?

He cursed. The Quadrant. Of course. If he could get his hands on it, then that would change everything.

He stepped over the bodies and tried the handle of the door. Locked. He crouched down, trying to ignore the bloody holes where the men's eyes had been, and rifled through the inside pockets of their black robes. He found a set of keys, and took it out. He tried each of them in the lock, but none fitted. He shoved the keys into a pocket, and picked up a crossbow. The butt-end was covered in a strip of metal, and he rammed it down onto the lock. He tried it again, using both hands to grip the shaft of the bow. On the third attempt, the lock gave way with a loud crack, and the door swung open. He tossed the crossbow to the ground, and entered Maddie's apartment. The shutters had been drawn, and the main room was in darkness, so he felt his way to the window, his shin hitting a low table on the way. He pulled open one of the shutters, and sunlight spilled into the room. He glanced around. A bloodstain marked the floorboards by the table, and he remembered that Maddie's servant had been murdered in the apartment.

He opened the side doors until he found the bedroom. Whatever else Maddie was, he thought, she wasn't the tidiest of people. Clothes littered the floor, and the bed was a tangled mass of sheets and blankets. He crouched down, and looked under the bed. Blackrose had told him that Maddie kept the Quadrant in a leather satchel, and his heart leapt as he saw it. He pulled it out by the straps, and sat down. The bag had no lock, but when he opened it, he realised it was empty.

'Shit.'

For a few minutes, he sat in dejected silence, his eyes staring into the empty satchel. He tried to pull himself together, but despair was weighing upon his shoulders. He stood, and began searching the rest of the room, poking through the piles of clothes, and lifting the mattress to check beneath it. His movements became more frantic with every passing second, and he only realised that others had entered the apartment when the first two crossbow bolts struck his back. He toppled to the floor, and another pair of bolts hit his chest. Before he could raise his hands, a black-robed man stood over him, aimed a crossbow into his face, and loosed.

———

For the next hour, all Austin knew was pain. His self-healing was keeping him alive, but with his hands again enclosed inside the thick gauntlets, he had no way to pull the bolt from his left eye. It had lodged itself deep within his head, almost as if he were wearing a god-restrainer mask, and the torment was unlike anything he had ever experienced. He was aware that he was howling and screaming, but strong hands were gripping onto him. He had been carried somewhere, but his mind couldn't focus on his location; all he cared about was the pain.

He heard angry shouting, and then the bolt was ripped out of his eye socket. Immediately, the agony started to fade, as his self-healing took over. His left eye had been severely damaged, and would take time to heal, but he didn't care. He lay on the cold ground, panting with relief, his body shaking.

'He should be executed!' cried a voice. 'He murdered two of my men.'

'We don't know what happened,' said Ashfall. 'Let him speak, before you condemn him to death.'

There was a pause, and Austin sensed a presence close to his face. He opened his right eye, and saw Ashfall staring down at him.

'Tell us what happened,' she said.

'The two men were going to kill me,' he gasped. 'It was self defence.'

'See?' said Ashfall. 'Once again, Ata'nix, you have jumped to the wrong conclusion.'

'He's lying,' said the Unk Tannic leader. 'Why would my men attempt to kill him, as he claims? They were under orders to restrict access to Miss Jackdaw's apartment; this demigod had no right to be there. He murdered them for doing their jobs.'

'I agree with Ata'nix's analysis,' said Splendoursun.

Austin turned his head, and saw that he was inside the large, domed reception hall. Shadowblaze and Ahi'edo were there, along with Splendoursun and Ata'nix, and several other dragons he didn't recognise. Close by his head, he saw more Unk Tannic men in black robes, each pointing a crossbow at him.

Ashfall moved her head closer. 'Did you find it?'

'No. It wasn't there.'

'Find what?' said Ata'nix. 'What was he doing in Miss Jackdaw's apartment?'

'He was carrying out the Queen's orders,' said Ashfall, 'as was I. Who are you to question me like this?'

'I have been appointed as leader of the humans of Ulna,' said Ata'nix, 'and I am a member of the inner council. I have nothing to hide. You, on the other hand, my dear princess, have aroused our suspicions. You arrive here, unannounced, and send this vile, murderous, demigod off to do your secret bidding, while you attempt to distract us with tales of Haurn. How do we know that you are telling the truth? Lord Shadowblaze, I call upon your leadership. This dragon should be exiled, while her rider must be executed for his crimes.'

'Austin is not my rider,' Ashfall said.

'So, you are trying to distance yourself from his actions?' Ata'nix went on. 'Yet, you were the one who brought him here, and you are wearing a harness. The evidence seems stacked against you, does it not?'

Ashfall exploded in rage. Sparks flew from her jaws, and she lifted a forelimb, her claws extended. Three other dragons moved forwards, and took up a defensive stance around Ata'nix, their claws also raised.

'I have heard and seen enough,' said Splendoursun. 'Lord Shadowblaze, you must act, or I shall. Princess Ashfall has clearly lost her mind. She does not belong here – she is a foreigner, who understands nothing about Dragon Eyre.'

Shadowblaze cast his amber eyes over Ashfall. 'I order you; tell us what you were looking for.'

'I will tell you in private, my lord, but not with these Gyle dragons present, and certainly not with Ata'nix here.'

'Do not be taken in by her tricks, my lord,' said Splendoursun. 'Without my kinfolk from Gyle here to protect you, who knows what she would attempt?'

'I ask you again, Ashfall,' said Shadowblaze; 'what did you send the demigod to find? If you do not answer, we will have no choice but to punish you.'

'What has happened to Udall in our absence?' cried Ashfall. 'Do Splendoursun and Ata'nix now rule Ulna? Lord Shadowblaze, I appeal to you; you know I am not a traitor. Dismiss the others from the hall, and then we can talk.'

A flicker of doubt passed over the grey and red dragon's face, then his amber eyes hardened. 'This is your last chance, Ashfall.'

'Very well,' she cried. 'We were sent here to collect the Queen's Quadrant. She has need of it.'

The hall fell into silence.

'We assumed that the Queen had the Quadrant,' said Shadowblaze after a while. 'It is not in the palace.'

'Are you sure?' said Ashfall.

'I personally searched the Queen's lair,' said the grey and red dragon. 'Maddie's quarters have also been thoroughly checked. This is grim news; we must presume that the pirates are now in possession of it.'

'Who searched Maddie's rooms?' said Austin.

'Silence, insect,' cried Splendoursun. 'You do not have permission to speak.'

'If he talks again, shoot him,' said Ata'nix.

The guards by Austin's head tensed, each staring down the shafts of their crossbows at him.

'I would like to know the answer to his question,' said Ashfall.

'My men conducted the search,' said Ata'nix. 'There was no Quadrant to be found. I am willing to undergo a truth spell on this matter. I swear that the Quadrant was not in the apartment when my men searched there. Would any noble dragon like to test my honesty?'

'That will not be necessary,' said Splendoursun. 'Ata'nix can be trusted.'

'I do not trust him,' said Ashfall, 'but I lack the ability to force the truth from a human. Lord Shadowblaze should test him.'

'Lord Shadowblaze is not yours to command, foreigner,' said Splendoursun. 'Your arrogance astounds me. Princess or not, you are no longer welcome in the inner council.'

Ashfall met the gold and white's dragon's gaze. 'You don't have the authority to expel me.'

Splendoursun laughed. 'You are wrong. I am the Queen's sole remaining suitor, and in Lord Greysteel's unfortunate absence, I have also been appointed as the Queen's agent regarding all matters relating to the courtship. While the Queen is engaged on personal business, I have stepped in, as Regent-in-Waiting. Little over a month remains before the courtship period expires. Upon that date, if the Queen has not returned, then I shall be Lord of Ulna by default. I most certainly do have the authority to expel you, or imprison you, or, indeed, to have you executed as a renegade.' He turned to Shadowblaze. 'Is this not so, my lord?'

Shadowblaze said nothing for a moment, his eyes revealing the conflict going on in his mind. 'Legally speaking,' he said, 'Lord Splendoursun is correct. If no other suitor comes forward, he shall be anointed as Blackrose's mate, unless she returns to refuse him.'

'You see, my dear Princess?' said Splendoursun.

'Then I shall take my leave,' said Ashfall, 'and fly to Blackrose, to warn her of this. Once she hears what has been happening in her absence, her rage will destroy you.'

'I think not,' said Splendoursun. He gestured to several other dragons, none of whom were wearing rider's harnesses. They surrounded Ashfall and Austin.

'Princess Ashfall,' Splendoursun went on, 'you are under arrest. You shall be taken to the dragon dungeon that lies beneath this hall, where you shall be incarcerated until my anointing as Lord of Ulna. If you resist, my kinfolk will kill you, here and now.'

'Shadowblaze!' cried Ashfall. 'You have to stop them. Blackrose appointed you as leader, not this repugnant lizard.'

'I cannot interfere,' said Shadowblaze. 'The law is clear.'

Ashfall roared in frustration.

'Take her away,' said Splendoursun. 'If she gives you even the slightest trouble, rip her wings to shreds. Oh, and place her little rider back into his cell; he may still have some value as a hostage.'

'I made an oath to the Queen!' cried Ashfall. 'You are making me break it. Blackrose will kill you all for this treachery; this is nothing less than a coup.'

'I am sorry,' said Shadowblaze; 'truly.'

'Traitors!' roared the grey dragon.

A huge red dragon raised his claws, and Austin flinched back, convinced that Ashfall was going to make a last stand, but the slender grey dragon bowed her head, her eyes red with rage and despair. The other dragons shoved her along, and she strode away, surrounded. Two men grabbed Austin by his shoulders and hauled him to his feet.

'You won't be getting back out again, not this time,' said one, a smirk on his lips.

They placed a hood over his head, and he was led away, to the sound of laughter coming from Splendoursun.

CHAPTER 12

LANGBEG

Luckenbay, Olkis, Western Rim – 8th Essinch 5254 (18th Gylean Year 5)

Topaz kept his eyes on the sky. The earlier rain had cleared up, and the moon was shining down through a break in the clouds, illuminating the way ahead. To the right of the moon, some of the brighter stars were visible, and he marked the ship's direction. He recited some orders to the midshipman, who scampered off into the darkness.

Vitz handed Topaz a mug of coffee.

'Cheers, mate.'

Vitz nodded. 'How's it going, sir? Are we nearly there?'

'We should be arriving at Langbeg for dawn.'

Vitz shook his head. 'I have no idea how you're doing this, sir; I can't see a thing. Sea Banner vessels can't navigate through this bay in daylight, never mind in the middle of the night.'

'That's because they weren't brought up here. I spent four years as a boy on these waters, crossing the bay back and forth, and learning how to avoid the sandbars and Skerries. It's not something you ever forget.' He pointed. 'Do you see the way the water looks different over there? That means there's a sandbar close to the surface. Anyone can memorise the positions of the rocks in Luckenbay, but they don't bleeding well move. The sandbars are always shifting.'

He took a slurp of coffee and sighed. 'Good stuff, mate. Gods, I'll sleep after this, and then, tomorrow night, I'll take you out on the town.'

'Is that wise, sir? Isn't Langbeg a nest of pirates and rebels? Sounds like it could be dangerous for someone like me.'

'The town militia keeps order, most of the time. They're the ones you want to watch out for, lad. Give those boys any cheek, and you'll end up with a broken nose, as well as a night in the cells. You been practising your Olkian accent?'

'Ryan laughs at me whenever I try, sir.'

Topaz broke off from the conversation to make an adjustment to the wheel. The *Giddy Gull* was advancing at a slow speed, inching its way between the multitude of natural barriers that littered Luckenbay. One wrong move, and the hull would beach on a sandbar, or worse, strike one of the hundreds of rocky Skerries. Dozens of wrecked ships adorned the large bay, from small fishing vessels, to the pride of the Sea Banner fleet, and everything in between. In Olkian waters, if a master couldn't navigate through Luckenbay, then many would doubt if he was a true master after all; it was the place where masters proved themselves, and many had failed the test. To accomplish the feat in darkness was deemed almost supernatural, and it was a sign of Lara's supreme confidence in him that she had gone to bed the night before, leaving Topaz to get on with it.

He drew on his mental map of the bay. He had been forced to commit it to memory as a boy-sailor; every rock, every cliff, every cove, and every damn Skerrie.

The clouds drifted over the moon again, and the faint light dimmed. Topaz muttered a curse, but kept calm. He had taken a decent bearing, and knew what lay ahead. To starboard, a lighter plume of water marked a reef that hid beneath the surface, a reef that could rip out the bottom of the brigantine's hull. The lives of the entire crew were in his hands that night, and he knew it.

'My nerves are shredded, sir,' said Vitz. 'Just watching you is giving my heart palpitations.'

'Don't use big words like that when we're out drinking in Langbeg, lad; that's my first piece of advice.'

'We'll have to do all this again on the way back out, sir, won't we?'

'More than likely, lad. The only reason that Sea Banner frigate didn't follow us yesterday evening, is because we steered right into the bay. Now they know that we're in here, there's a good chance they'll be waiting for us when we try to leave. Don't worry about it, though; we'll slip back out at night when no one's looking.'

A cabin door opened and closed behind them, and he heard a loud yawn.

'Morning, boys,' said Lara, wrapped up warm in a battered old overcoat. She glanced to the east, where the sky was starting to brighten.

'Good morning, Captain,' said Topaz, as Vitz saluted.

Lara eyed the young settler. 'Get me some coffee, asshole; make yourself useful.'

'Yes, ma'am,' said Vitz.

'How's he doing?' said Lara, as she watched Vitz hurry away.

'He's not up to Luckenbay standards quite yet, ma'am, but he's getting there.'

Lara frowned. 'Just make sure you don't get yourself killed in a bar fight, or we'll never be leaving Langbeg.'

'Nice to know you care, ma'am.' He glanced down the deck. 'Hey, Middie!'

The midshipman ran up onto the quarter deck. 'Yes, Master?'

'Tell the lads to open up the forward sails; we're clear of the last reefs. We'll bring the *Gull* up to seven knots and hold her there.'

'Yes, sir,' said the young officer. He saluted the captain, then ran off.

A few moments later, the ship began to pick up speed, and then the sun appeared over the horizon with a dazzling burst of light. At once, the bay opened out in front of them. Ahead, a long line of cliffs marked the southern shore. It was pocked with creeks and tiny bays, while, to their right, the tall, isolated mountain peak of Skythorn dominated the view. Dragons were wheeling and circling round its bare summit, their wings glistening in the dawn light.

Topaz grinned.

'When's the last time you were here?' said Lara.

'Gods, a while back. Nine years, maybe?'

She frowned. 'What?'

'We'd just left Luckenbay when the ship I was on was stopped by the Sea Banner, and I was taken into their crew. I was fourteen.'

Lara's face paled. 'You mean, you haven't navigated the bay since you were fourteen? Holy shit.' She spat overboard. 'I'm glad you didn't tell me that last night; I wouldn't have slept a wink.'

'The route's imprinted on my memory, ma'am.'

'If you'd wrecked my ship, I would have killed you; slowly and painfully.'

'That was an added incentive to me getting it right, ma'am.'

He stretched his arms and neck, and felt some of the tension go, as the daylight grew stronger. The area to the north of Langbeg was clear of rocks, and a couple of fishing boats were out. Topaz turned the wheel, and the *Gull* banked to the south-west. In the distance, he saw a large, brooding fortress on top of a cliff. It was Befallen Castle – the home of the Five Sisters.

'Which sisters are you expecting to be in Langbeg, ma'am?' he said.

She shrugged. 'Ann's there, but I don't know about the rest. I think Tilly's over in the Eastern Rim; she's always trying to copy me.'

They glanced up as they passed the castle, and Topaz felt some nerves grow in his stomach. For years, Olo'osso had been a myth to him; a famous name, evocative of a legendary past before Implacatus had invaded. In his youth, he had often looked up at the towering fortress perched on the cliff, without knowing that Olo'osso had chosen it as his hiding place. Part of the castle was in ruins, which was probably deliberate, he realised – another part of the deception, to make it look as though the fortress was abandoned.

'Does your father ever go into Langbeg?' he said.

'Sometimes. His days of pretending to be dead are over, even if most folk outside Langbeg don't realise it. He attends weddings and funerals of the other big pirate families these days, and occasionally appears at meetings of the town council. He doesn't seem to care that there's a reward of twenty thousand on his head. No one will touch him in Langbeg.'

Topaz whistled. 'Twenty thousand? Damn. And I thought I was a big shot, having a bounty of a thousand on my own head.'

'It's not bad for a master. Promise me, though, that you won't mention bounties in front of my sisters. It always starts a row about who's got the biggest. Dina's never forgiven me for having a larger bounty than her.'

'I doubt I'll be meeting any of your sisters, ma'am, but I'll bear it in mind.'

'What are you talking about, Topaz? I'm taking you to Befallen to meet father – did I not mention this?'

Topaz stared at her. 'No, ma'am; you didn't.'

'You're one of the best masters on Dragon Eyre, you dipshit. Of course I'll be showing you off to father. I want Dina to see you, especially. Her master's shit in comparison. He rammed their hull into a sandbar six months ago, the twat. Besides, Ann's already met you.'

'It's not Ann I'm worried about, ma'am. Your father... he, eh... well, he's a folk hero.'

'He's just an old guy, Topaz. Don't be intimidated by the myth he's tried to wrap himself up in. Most of it's bullshit.'

The *Giddy Gull* rounded the headland where Befallen Castle sat, and a narrow bay opened up before them. At its centre, three miles from the castle, lay the town of Langbeg, its houses and streets piled up on steep terraces overlooking the waters of the bay. The harbour was almost as large as the town, with two enormous breakwaters that each stretched out for over a hundred yards. Within the wide basin, dozens of masts were visible, and Lara squinted as she looked for the flag of the Five Sisters among them.

'One, two... three,' she counted. 'Tilly's missing; the others are all here. Bring us in, Master.'

Vitz appeared with a steaming cup of coffee.

Lara eyed him. 'You took your time, asshole. Where's my cigarette?'

'Sorry, Captain,' he said. He handed her the mug, then lit a cigarette and passed it to her.

'One for the master, too,' said Lara.

'Yes, ma'am.'

Topaz grinned as Vitz handed him a cigarette. 'Take the wheel for a minute, lad.'

Topaz stepped aside, and did some stretches. The watch was changing on board the ship, and the fresh sailors were staring at the sight of Langbeg. A few of them cheered, and Topaz wondered how many had spent an anxious night as they had snaked their way through Luckenbay.

'They think you're a damned god, Topaz,' Lara muttered. 'Look at their cheery wee faces. Luckenbay at night, eh? That'll impress father.'

Lara and Topaz smoked by the railings of the quarter deck, as Vitz steered the ship closer to the harbour entrance.

'Half the speed, lad,' Topaz called over to his mate.

Vitz nodded, then called for the midshipman.

'Do I really have to meet your father, ma'am?' Topaz said, turning back to Lara.

'Yes, so there's no point arguing about it. He'll probably rip the piss out of you for being in the Sea Banner, but he's a cuddly bear at heart.'

They passed the first breakwater, and Topaz flung his cigarette over the side. He retook the wheel, and guided the *Gull* to a berth that Lara pointed out. The crew were grinning from ear to ear. The *Giddy Gull* was by far the most beautiful ship in the harbour, and several sailors were staring at it from the other boats. They pulled alongside the pier, and the *Gull* was secured fore and aft.

Lara summoned her crew.

'Well, lads,' she cried; 'thanks to our magnificent master, we not only evaded a Sea Banner frigate, but we made it unscathed through the Skerries on a cloudy night. As a little reward for your services, I have something extra for you to take ashore, over and above your usual pay. See the purser on your way off the *Gull*, and he'll give you each an extra twenty gold to spend in the taverns of Langbeg.'

'A cheer for the captain!' cried Topaz.

The crew cheered, slapped each other on the back, and a few hugged their comrades. They began to disperse, laughing and joking.

Topaz frowned. 'Can we afford that, ma'am?'

'Shut up,' said Lara. 'I want the lads singing my praises in the taverns tonight, and I want everyone in Langbeg to be jealous of the *Giddy Gull*. That's worth a few hundred in gold.'

'Is the thousand still intact? If we don't pay the latest instalment, we're screwed.'

'Of course the thousand is intact; stop worrying.' She turned to the midshipman. 'Go and wake up my asshole of a cousin. Wait; on second thoughts, leave him. If he's too hungover to get out of bed, he can look after the *Gull* while we're ashore. That'll teach the prick. Come on, Topaz; grab your shit, and we'll go.'

'Stick with Ryan for the day,' Topaz said to Vitz. 'I'll find you when I get back from the castle.'

'Yes, sir,' said the master's mate.

Lara disappeared into her cabin, and Topaz slipped down a deck to his own, tiny room. He quickly washed, then pulled on a fresh set of clothes. By the time he was back on the main deck, Lara was waiting for him. He blinked. She was wearing a dress, for the first time since he had known her.

'Don't say a bleeding thing,' she muttered.

'Eh... alright, ma'am.'

She gestured to the two sailors standing behind her. 'Take my stuff straight up to the castle. Hire a cart. Tell my father I'll be a couple of hours.'

The sailors saluted, then began ferrying the chests up the gangplank.

'Let's get a drink down our necks before we head up, Topaz,' Lara said. 'My nerves are a little strained.'

They strode up the gangplank and walked down the pier, passing members of their crew, who each saluted with broad smiles on their faces.

'They bleeding love us,' Lara smirked. 'We make a shit-hot team, Topaz.'

He glanced up at the town as they strode towards the busy quayside. Many of the houses were brightly painted, in yellows, pinks and shades of blue, and flowers in baskets were hanging from a hundred windows.

'It looks smaller than I remember,' he said.

'That's because you ain't fourteen any more, you pillock. Langbeg ain't changed in years.'

They passed a group of fishermen, who were staring down at the *Giddy Gull* as they sat repairing their nets, and Lara smiled. Along the quayside was a long row of nothing but taverns, several of which were open, despite the early hour. They walked into one called *Bo'sun's Droop*, and went to the bar. An old man approached, wearing an apron, and his eyes widened as he saw who had entered his tavern.

'Captain Lara!' he beamed. 'Welcome home. Is that you just in?'

'Not ten minutes ago. The *Gull* is sitting in the harbour.'

'Ahh, so it's true, eh? You bought the new brigantine? Business must be good.'

'Line up the ales, and get some breakfast warmed up for us. This here's Topaz, my master. He's just brought us through Luckenbay, so he'll be needing a drink.' She handed over a bag of gold. 'If any of my boys come in, that should pay for a few of their rounds.'

They took a table and had breakfast together. Lara told him a few stories about her father, but Topaz was exhausted, and his nerves were starting to build.

They were on their third ale, their plates empty, when the owner hurried over to their table.

'I don't wish to alarm you,' he said, 'but there are a couple of debt collectors outside, and I heard one of them mention your name, Captain.'

Lara scowled, then stood up and peered out of the window.

'Shit,' she muttered. 'Topaz, we need to get out of here, now.'

'I suggest leaving by the back door,' said the tavern owner. 'I'll hold them off for you.'

'Thanks; you're a gent,' said Lara. She picked up her bag, then she and Topaz ran through the tavern. They raced across the kitchen, avoiding the cook, and headed out the back door, emerging into a narrow lane. Lara kept running, and Topaz chased after her. When she finally stopped, she placed her hands on her knees and started laughing.

'That was a close one,' she cackled.

'I don't understand,' Topaz panted. 'Why did we run? We have the money.'

'Eh, not exactly.'

'What? You said we needed a thousand to pay off the next instalment.'

'Did I? Well, the truth is that I'm hoping a thousand will satisfy them for now, but technically, I'm supposed to come up with the entire three thousand.'

'When's the deadline?'

'Oh, we passed that a few months back.'

He narrowed his eyes. 'You're in deep shit.'

'Hey, you own ten per cent; you're in the shit too, Topaz. Don't worry, though, my father will sort it all out.' She straightened herself. 'It's probably time to head up to the castle. I'm not quite as drunk as I wanted to be, but father's bound to ply us with gin. Come on; we'll hail a cart.'

They walked along the rest of the alleyway, then appeared on one of the main roads. Lara glanced up and down the pavement, then approached one of the pony-carts that were lined up in front of a bakery.

A young man smiled down from the driver's bench. 'Where to?'

'The castle,' Lara said, as she and Topaz climbed up onto the back of the cart.

The driver raised an eyebrow. 'Sure thing.'

He urged the two ponies on, and they moved off. Topaz lit two cigarettes and passed one to Lara.

'Cheers, Master,' she said.

'Are you the master of a ship?' said the driver.

Topaz nodded.

'Which one?'

The road wound up the side of the cliff, and they could see the harbour basin below them. Topaz pointed at the *Giddy Gull*.

'That one,' he said.

The driver's mouth fell open. His gaze darted to Lara. 'Are you...?'

'Keep your damn eyes on the road,' she said. 'Never you mind who we are.'

The driver turned, and Topaz and Lara settled down in the back. The way was steep, but the ponies made light work of it, as they pulled the cart along the switchback road, climbing ever higher as they went. They reached the top of the cliff, and followed the road as it wound by the rugged coast. Topaz gazed down at Langbeg. Bathed in sunshine, it looked stunning, but he remembered how rough it could be, especially at night, when the taverns were packed full with drunken sailors. Ahead of them, Befallen Castle loomed ever closer. The ruined sections all faced the coast, so that it would appear derelict to any passing ship, but the other sides were still standing. Topaz counted three square towers, linked by a pair of two-storey galleries. The buildings enclosed a courtyard on three sides, protected by an imposing gatehouse, which had been fortified. A few sentries were standing up on the battlements, some with their eyes on the bay, while the others were watching the road.

The driver halted the cart when they were still twenty yards from the gatehouse.

'This is as far as I'm allowed to go,' he said. 'The guards sometimes shoot if you get any closer.'

Lara smiled as she handed over some coins. 'I'm sure we'll be fine.'

They clambered down from the cart and strode towards the gatehouse.

'Stop there!' cried one of the sentries.

'It's me,' Lara cried back. 'The youngest and prettiest of the Five Sisters. Let us in, you dipshits.'

Moments later, the gates were pulled open, revealing the courtyard beyond. Lara and Topaz walked through, and entered the castle.

'Your men were here earlier, ma'am,' said a sentry. 'They brought your chests up from the harbour.'

Lara nodded. 'Is my father up and about?'

'Yes, ma'am. He's waiting for you on his private loggia.'

'Cheers; I'll head up now. Are any of my sisters there?'

'I don't know, ma'am. Ani, Elli, and Adina are currently staying in the castle, but I don't know if they're up yet.'

'Let's hope they're still asleep,' said Lara, then she set off for the central tower.

'Why did the guard call them that?' Topaz said, as they entered the tower.

'It's my father's habit,' she said. 'He calls us by the first parts of our Olkian names. I'm Alara, to him, so don't be surprised if he decides to call you Oto.'

'What do I call him?'

'Sir.'

They climbed up several flights of stairs, passing a few more armed sentries on duty, then emerged onto the wide loggia. The side facing the bay was open to the elements, and sunlight was streaking through the gaps between the thick pillars holding up the roof. A large, round table was in the middle of the loggia, and seven people were already sitting there, sharing breakfast. Lara narrowed her eyes as she and Topaz approached.

Sitting in the largest, almost throne-like chair was a middle-aged man with grey flecking his shoulder-length hair and beard. His blue eyes caught sight of Lara, and he smiled.

'There you are, my girl,' he said, rising. 'Come and give your old dad a hug.'

He opened his thick arms, and Lara ran up to him. They embraced, as Topaz stood awkwardly to the side. Around the table, the only person he recognised was Captain Ann, and he assumed that the two other young women must be Ellie and Dina. There was a slightly older woman, whom he guessed was Olo'osso's new wife, but he had no idea who the other two men were.

'Take a seat, Alara,' said her father. 'Have some breakfast.'

'Topaz and I have already eaten,' she said, sitting.

Olo'osso turned to him. 'Topaz, eh? Or, Oto'pazzi. Yes, I've heard a fair bit about you, lad, and not all of it good. I watched you pilot the *Gull* into harbour this morning. Come through Luckenbay at night, eh? Do you think that sort of thing impresses me?'

'I... uh...'

'He's joking,' said Lara. 'Sit your ass down, Topaz.'

'Did I say he could sit, my sweet little Alara?' said Olo'osso. He turned back to Topaz. 'Seven years in the Sea Banner; that's what I heard. Am I wrong, boy?'

'No, sir,' said Topaz. 'I was pressed into the Sea Banner when I was fourteen.'

The old pirate glanced back at Lara. 'And what's this I hear about you taking on a settler lad as master's mate? Are you deliberately trying to goad me, daughter?'

Lara's face went scarlet. 'No, father. It was, eh... Topaz's decision. He insisted, and, well, you know, I needed to keep my master happy. He's the best master in Olkian waters.'

Olo'osso raised an eyebrow. 'I very much doubt that. Seven years of kissing Sea Banner ass is hardly likely to have turned him into an expert. Anyway, I'm being rude; let me introduce you to everyone, Oto of the Sea Banner.' He gestured to Ann. 'This is Ani, my eldest.'

'I've already met Topaz, father,' said Ann. 'I was there when Lara captured his sloop.'

'Ah, yes,' said Olo'osso, looking a little aggrieved at having been interrupted. 'Next is Elli, then Adina, two of my other daughters, and this is my soon to be ex-wife, Opina.'

Lara stared at him. 'What did you say? Are you getting divorced?'

'Indeed, my little princess.'

Opina looked away, scowling.

'Then,' Lara went on, 'why is she here, at breakfast?'

'Opina still handles much of my finances,' he said; 'and finances have been the subject of our discussions this morning, brought about, I might add, by your unexpected arrival.' He turned to the two men also sitting at the table. 'These gentlemen are from your creditors, my dear Alara. They seem to think that you are late in paying them over three thousand in gold, for the *Giddy Gull*. Tell me it isn't true.'

'Of course it's true,' snapped Dina. 'Everyone in Langbeg knows that Lara is up to her eyeballs in debt, for a ship she should never have bought.'

'Hush, dear,' said Olo'osso; 'I want to hear Alara's side of the story.'

'I have a thousand,' Lara said, her voice high. 'I can pay them one thousand, right now.'

Olo'osso glanced at the two men. 'Would one thousand satisfy you for now, gentlemen?'

'I'm afraid not, my lord,' said one. 'The terms of the loan were clear, and your daughter is late, by three months. She pledged to pay us in full, and we are under orders not to leave Langbeg until we have one of two things – the balance, or the boat.'

'And how much does the balance come to?'

The man consulted a notebook. 'Three thousand, two hundred and eighty-one gold sovereigns, my lord.'

'I see. Opina, would you please be a dear, and pay these two gentlemen what Alara owes them, minus the one thousand that she has?'

'This is ridiculous,' cried Opina. 'Yet again, you are coming to the rescue of one of your idiot daughters. They'll never learn, if you keep doing this. Alara should never have bought such an expensive ship; she must have known that she wouldn't be able to pay off the loan.'

Olo'osso glanced around the table, and gave a weak smile. 'This is why we're getting divorced; well, one of the many reasons. Opina thinks

I spoil my girls too much. What do you think, Oto of the Sea Banner? Do I spoil them?'

Topaz, who was still standing, glanced up. 'Any father lucky enough to have five such beautiful daughters would be a fool not to spoil them, sir.'

Olo'osso slapped his thigh and laughed. 'That was the correct answer, my lad. You may sit.' He glanced at his wife. 'I still appear to be waiting for you to pay the two gentlemen, dear.'

Opina got to her feet, threw down a napkin, then gestured to the two men.

'My thousand is in the smallest of my three chests, Opina,' said Lara.

The older woman glared at her, then led the two men away.

'Thank you so much, father,' Lara said, grinning.

'This is so typical,' said Dina. 'Lara screws up, again, and gets away with it, again.'

'Not so fast,' said Olo'osso. 'I do believe that a controlling share of the *Giddy Gull* now belongs to me, and I haven't yet decided what I shall do with my new acquisition.'

The colour drained from Lara's face.

'I'd like to point out that I own ten per cent of the vessel,' said Topaz.

'Is this true, little petal?'

Lara nodded. 'Yes, father.'

'Then Oto of the Sea Banner shall remain its master; that, at least, is clear. Now, I just have to find a suitable captain. My first thoughts were of my sister's son, Udaxa. His mother has been pestering me for a while about finding the lad a ship of his own. Of course, the *Giddy Gull* would remain mine, but Udaxa could captain it for me, for a good slice of the takings.'

'No,' said Lara, her eyes starting to well. 'Please, not Dax. Anyone but Dax. He's a complete asshole, father. I'd rather Dina captained the *Gull* compared to him.'

Olo'osso raised an eyebrow. 'You'd rather Adina did it? My; you must really hate Udaxa. Oto of the Sea Banner, what is your considered opinion of my nephew?'

'I feel that it would be wrong of me to insult one of your relatives, sir. No uncle wants to hear about how incompetent, unpopular, and lazy his nephew is.'

Olo'osso drummed his fingers on the table top.

'Please, father,' said Lara; 'give me one more chance. You can have the entire take from my next trip.'

He sighed. 'Very well; seeing as how you went to the trouble of putting on a dress. I know how much that must have pained you. I calculate the shares of the *Gull* as the following: six parts are mine, one part belongs to Oto, and the remaining three parts are yours, little Alara. Do you both accept this state of affairs?'

Lara nodded.

'Yes, sir,' said Topaz.

'Then, it's settled,' said Olo'osso. 'You shall remain the captain of the *Giddy Gull*, Alara, for now. You shall deliver the entire takings to me from your next voyage, as you agreed, and then we shall see.'

Lara threw her arms round her father's neck. 'Thank you.'

'If you let me down again, sweet girl,' he said, 'then you will be working for Captain Udaxa. Am I understood?'

'Yes, father.'

Around the table, the other sisters sighed and glanced at each other, while Dina shook her head in anger.

'Right,' said Olo'osso; 'back to breakfast. Oto's going to tell us all a story about his time in the Sea Banner.'

'Am I?' said Topaz.

'Yes, lad, you are,' grinned the old pirate; 'and it had better be a good one.'

CHAPTER 13

THE LAST RESORT

South-East of Alef, Western Rim – 18th Essinch 5254 (18th Gylean Year 5)

Maddie sat in the tiny, cramped cabin, staring at the door as a key turned in the lock. The door opened, and Captain Tilly glanced inside.

'You can come out,' the captain said.

'Oh, I can, can I?' Maddie snapped. 'That's very generous of you; I mean, you've only had me locked up for hours.'

'I couldn't concentrate on my job. Your never-ending questions and chatter were driving me insane.'

'That's it? No apology?'

Tilly shrugged. 'I can lock the door again if you aren't satisfied.'

'Is it sunny outside?'

'Yes.'

'Then, I want to go back up on deck.'

'I have a couple of conditions. First, you have to stop distracting my crew. They're busy enough, without you peppering them with a hundred questions. Second, if I raise my finger then that means you have to stop speaking immediately. Third, no more questions about my damn sisters; I'm sick of talking about them. Do you agree to all this?'

'What if I say no?'

Tilly dangled the keys in front of her. 'If you refuse, then I'll lock the door and come back in another few hours. It's your decision.'

Maddie frowned. 'You're not very nice.'

'I have a damn ship to run,' Tilly cried. 'I need to concentrate, and I can't do that if all I can hear is your voice in my ear. Look, Miss Jackdaw, I think I've been more than fair – you're a prisoner, not a damn guest, and I've tried to make your journey as pleasant as possible. Lara would probably have had you locked up in chains for the entire voyage.'

'I thought you said you didn't want to talk about your sisters?'

'Right; that's it. I'm locking the door again.'

'No, wait! Fine. I agree to these stupid conditions. I feel sick sitting in this tiny cupboard. The boat is rolling up and down, and it's making my stomach feel funny. It's not as bad up on deck. Why is that? It's weird, if you think about it. Why would...'

Tilly raised a finger.

Maddie frowned, and stopped talking.

'It's something to do with the horizon,' the captain said. 'If you can see the horizon, then the sea-sickness doesn't feel as bad. I don't know why, so don't ask.'

She stepped to the side, and Maddie got to her feet and squeezed by her. They walked along the narrow corridor, and up a flight of steep wooden steps. Maddie smiled as the sunlight hit her face. A fresh breeze was blowing, and the sea was shimmering in shades of turquoise.

'Are we back on course?' she asked Tilly. 'I mean, after those storms? Are we heading in the right direction again? Am I allowed to ask that?'

'We lost about four or five days altogether,' Tilly said. 'The winds blew us too far to the north, and now we have to navigate our way past Alef.' She pointed to a small island in the distance. 'That's a small part of the Alef archipelago right there.'

Maddie peered at the tiny island. It looked rugged and uninhabited, but had a beautiful long stretch of golden sand along its coast. Maddie remembered the small beach near Pella on her own world, and how much it was prized by the Reapers who lived there. It was barely a mile long, whereas, on Dragon Eyre, she had seen hundreds of beaches, including some that stretched for over a dozen miles. She turned to ask Tilly something, but the captain had walked away, and was speaking to her lieutenant about something.

A sailor winked at her as he passed by on the deck, and Maddie raised an eyebrow. Most of the crew seemed friendly, but they were the same men who had killed so many of the natives on Rigga, and she had made it a point of principle not to become over-familiar with any of them. A cry came from the rigging, and Maddie looked up. Two sailors were bickering as they climbed the ropes attached to the mast. One of them swung a punch and missed, and Tilly's lieutenant began shouting at them.

The two sailors came down from the rigging, looking shame-faced, and the lieutenant gave them both an earful of abuse, then sent them back up the mast again.

'What was that about?' said Maddie.

Tilly glanced at her. 'The nerves of some are getting a little strained.'

'Why? The storms are over.'

'My lads don't mind a few storms. This is more serious than that – we're out of tobacco, coffee, weed, and we're running perilously low on gin. We should have stocked up on more supplies in Ulna, but we had no idea who you were when we left harbour, so we didn't think it would be necessary. This voyage has stretched our supplies to breaking point.'

'But we have enough food and water, yeah?'

Tilly nodded. 'We ain't going to starve, but it's the little luxuries and comforts that keep the crew going. We'd better hope we run into an unarmed supply vessel soon, or things are only going to get worse.'

The sloop shifted to a more southerly direction, away from the little island.

'Why are we turning?' said Maddie.

Tilly sighed. 'We're tacking into the wind. We can't sail directly into it, so we have to zigzag.'

'Why?'

'When we get to Olkis, I'll find you a book on sailing.'

'Do you have books in Olkis? I thought most people were illiterate.'

'A lot of the skilled jobs on board require the ability to read. We're not all savages.'

'So, pirates are more literate than the general population? I wouldn't have guessed that.'

'Yeah? Well, now you know.'

'And how...'

Tilly raised her finger, then strode away.

Maddie almost chased after her, but decided not to chance her luck. Her nausea had faded since coming out on to the deck, and she didn't want to be placed back inside the tiny cabin again. She glanced out at the view of sea and sky. If it weren't for the fact that she had been taken from Blackrose, she reckoned she might enjoy travelling by ship. The little sloop had seemed flimsy and fragile when they had sailed through the storms, but she had never thought they were going to sink, no matter how hard the wind had blown. Now that the sea was calmer again, and the sky was a deep blue, everything seemed almost idyllic.

The ship turned again, banking back towards the north, and Maddie saw two more islands appear on the horizon. To the left of them, a faint line of smoke was drifting up into the sky. Was a ship on fire? She squinted into the distance, but couldn't see the source of the smoke. She glanced at Tilly. The captain was in a deep conversation with the bosun and master up on the quarter deck, and looked as though she didn't wish to be distracted. The lieutenant walked by at that moment, his eyes on the two sailors up in the rigging.

'Excuse me,' said Maddie.

The lieutenant glanced at her.

'Do you see the smoke?' she said. 'Just thought I'd point it out, in case, you know, you'd missed it.'

'I see it,' he said, then turned away again.

'What's causing it?' she said, before he could walk away.

'A giant oil refinery,' he said. 'It's about a dozen miles away; so far that you can't yet see the island where it's based. Every drop of oil on

Dragon Eyre goes through its doors, then gets shipped off to the rest of the islands.'

'Thank you. That was a good answer.'

He gave her a half-smile, then strode away.

She gazed back at the view, feeling pleased with herself that she knew what an oil refinery was, having seen the one in Tarstation. She smiled as she recalled how she and her little sister had robbed the governor of the freezing cold settlement, just like pirates would have done. Dragon pirates. Her smile vanished as she thought about Blackrose, and a familiar ache appeared in her chest. What Tilly didn't realise was that she needed to keep talking, to distract herself from thinking about Blackrose.

'Hey,' she called out to a sailor. 'What date is it?'

'The eighteenth, love,' said the young man.

The eighteenth. Maddie sighed. She had been missing for exactly one month. More than that, she had been on board the *Little Sneak* for a whole month, and yet they seemed no closer to Olkis. Their route must have confused whoever was searching for her. She remembered someone telling her that no dragon could fly between Wyst and Alef – the distance was too great for a single flight, which meant that the only way Blackrose could reach Alef would be to fly right round the other side of the two rims, via Gyle. But, of course, Blackrose would have no idea that she was in Alef, so it was pointless trying to speculate. She had a vague hope that her black dragon might be waiting for them in Olkis, but she had learned not to raise her expectations.

'Right,' said Tilly, appearing by her side. 'I'm free again. Ask me anything.'

'Can a dragon fly all the way from Ulna to Olkis?'

'It's difficult, but possible. The hardest stretch is between Na Sun Ka and Gyle. The distance is just within the range of most strong dragons, but they would arrive on Gyle utterly exhausted. That wouldn't have mattered in the old days, but now the Banner forces would be able to pick them off easily. Even if they survived that, there's another long flight to Ectus, which is armed to the teeth. In other words, Miss Jackdaw, it's highly unlikely that even Blackrose would be able to make it all the way to Olkis in one piece.'

They sailed on for another few hours, and Maddie kept to herself, staying out of the way of the busy sailors as they worked. Every twenty minutes or so, they would alter course, and Maddie gazed out at the islands in the distance. The smoke from the refinery grew closer, but there was still no sign of the island where it was located. She found a place to sit to get out of the midday sun, on the steps leading to the quarter deck, which was in the shade of the main sail.

Tilly's last words to her had brought her spirits down. Blackrose would not be waiting for her in Olkis, that seemed certain, and now Maddie was worried that the dragon would attempt the trip regardless of the risks involved. If so, then the Banner, or the gods of Gyle or Ectus would strike her down.

She glanced up, and noticed they were steering close to one of the larger islands in the archipelago. Its mountainous flanks were covered with a thick forest that ran right down to the long beach by the shore. Maddie got to her feet and stepped up onto the quarter deck.

'What are we doing?' she said to Tilly. 'Why are so close to that island?'

'We're looking for an opportunity to take on more fresh water, Miss Jackdaw,' said the captain. 'Is that alright with you?'

Maddie shrugged. 'Are you going to kill more natives?'

'We're unlikely to see any native Alefians out here,' said Tilly. 'Settlers, maybe; Banner soldiers, possibly; but the majority of the natives are corralled on the main island of Alef itself, where they slave away for their masters in the oil fields and refinery. Do you have any objections to us shooting settlers?'

'Yes, if by settlers you mean families. Who knows what Implacatus told them before they packed up their belongings and made the trip to Dragon Eyre? Just because they're here, doesn't mean...'

Tilly raised a finger.

Maddie glared at her, but the captain's attention was already elsewhere.

'Take us in a little closer, Master,' Tilly said. 'I think I see the sparkle of a waterfall through the forest cover.'

'Yes, Captain,' said the master, who turned the wheel.

'Everyone,' said Tilly; 'eyes on the coast. There must be fresh water here somewhere; those storms brought a lot of rain.'

'That could be a small stream,' said the lieutenant, pointing at the shore. 'There, where the water looks disturbed.'

'Looks a bit marshy, but it'll do,' said Tilly.

Maddie glanced away from the coast, as the others debated the best course of action. She savoured the feel of the warm breeze of her face, and wondered if she was getting a tan. Back in Ulna, she had spent too much time indoors, either in Seabound, or in the bridge palace of Udall, when she should have been outside sunbathing.

She blinked. In the distance, a few miles away, seven ships were rounding a headland, and turning towards the *Little Sneak*.

'Uh, Captain?' she said.

'Not now, Miss Jackdaw; can't you see we're busy?'

'You might want to look in the other direction for a moment.'

'What is it?' Tilly sighed, turning. Her eyes widened. 'Holy crap; Sea Banner! What were those useless assholes up on the mast doing?'

'They were staring at the coast, as you ordered, ma'am,' said the lieutenant.

'Shit! Battle stations!' she cried. 'Master, get the sloop moving; full speed.'

'Yes, ma'am.'

Tilly and her lieutenant strode to the starboard side of the quarter deck, and Maddie tagged along.

'Three oil-carrying transports and four frigates,' muttered the lieutenant. 'We have fifteen minutes, I'd guess, ma'am, before they catch up with us.'

Maddie glanced up at the mast, but the flag of the Five Sisters had been taken down several days before.

'Could we not just pretend to be a merchant ship?' she said.

'All sea traffic in Alefian waters is restricted, because of the oil,' said Tilly. 'It's effectively a militarised zone, unless you've got the proper paperwork, which, as you can probably guess, we don't. They'll realise who we are as soon as they board us.' She glanced at the lieutenant. 'Get the pisspot catapult ready; we ain't going down without a fight.'

'Yes, ma'am,' said the officer, then he turned and hurried away.

'We have a pisspot on board?' said Maddie.

'Just the one,' said Tilly. 'The last resort, as I call it.'

'But there are seven ships heading towards us.'

'I am perfectly aware of that!' she cried.

'Shouldn't we surrender?'

'They'll slaughter us all; the Sea Banner don't take prisoners from pirate vessels, Miss Jackdaw; they kill them. They might spare me, so that they can take me to Ectus for execution, but I'll kill myself before I allow that to happen. Shit.'

The change in atmosphere among the crew felt tangible to Maddie. A few minutes before, they had been happily going about their duties, but now each one was staring at the approaching vessels with a look of despair on their faces. By the bow of the ship, next to the ballista, a catapult was being hastily assembled by four men. Wooden pegs were being driven home by mallets, and the device was put together in under a minute, then its long arm was winched back into position. Two sailors appeared from below decks, one cradling a large ceramic object in his arms, while the other cleared a path through the deck for him.

'Upon my signal, Master,' said Tilly, 'I want you to swing the *Little Sneak* about, so that we're facing the nearest frigate. We'll loose the pisspot, then bolt into the Outer Ocean.'

The master frowned. 'Yes, ma'am.'

'Is this it?' said Maddie. 'Are we going to die?'

Tilly shrugged. 'It's a fine day for it.'

The lieutenant returned to the quarter deck. 'The catapult is

loaded and ready, ma'am. The frigates are also arming their own catapults and ballista stations, and marines are starting to line up along
their decks.'

'Bastards,' muttered Tilly. 'We'll make sure some of them suffer
before they get us.'

A series of flags were raised by a sailor standing on the bow of the
closest frigate – red, then green, then black.

'What does that mean?' said Maddie.

'No idea,' said Tilly. 'It's probably a coded message. Ships allowed to
be in these waters will know the correct response.' She nodded to the
midshipman. 'Wave a green flag back at them. It might confuse them
for a minute or two.'

The young officer ran to the rear of the sloop. He crouched down,
opened a box, and lifted a green flag high above his head in the direction of the pursuing frigates, which were closing fast.

'Try a white one now!' Tilly shouted up to him. 'And then any colour
you damn well feel like.'

'Yes, ma'am,' the midshipman called back.

'The second frigate is moving to intercept us off the port side,' said
the lieutenant. 'They have just entered ballista range, ma'am.'

Maddie shrank back against the railings that surrounded the
quarter deck. Of the four frigates, two were speeding towards them. The
Sea Banner sailor who had been waving the flags from the bow had
gone, replaced by a ballista, while, next to it, a large catapult was being
loaded with a ceramic object.

'Halt!' cried a voice over the water. 'Halt, or we will attack.'

Maddie saw an officer standing by the bow of the second frigate, a
large cone-shaped horn held to his mouth.

'I repeat,' the officer shouted through the horn; 'bring your vessel to
a halt!'

'Someone shoot that bastard,' said Tilly.

'The ballista isn't ready, ma'am,' said the lieutenant, 'and we're still
out of crossbow range.'

Tilly clenched her fists in rage. 'Swing us about, Master! Lieutenant, get up to the bow and await my order to loose the pisspot. Middie, get down here.'

Maddie glanced over. 'What?'

'Not you!' cried Tilly. 'The middie – the damn midshipman.'

The young officer threw the flags back into the box by his feet then turned. As he was about to jump down to the quarter deck, a yard-long steel bolt was loosed from the closest frigate. It struck the midshipman between his shoulders and carried on through him in an explosion of blood. Everyone on the quarter deck dived as the bolt sped past. It ripped through the canvas of the main sail, leaving a large, ragged hole, then splashed down into the sea next to the sloop. Maddie grasped onto the railings as the Master turned the wheel. The sloop banked, its decks sloping to the left as the craft turned in a tight circle. Another ballista bolt flew overhead. No one was struck, but a chunk was ripped out of the mast, and several ropes snapped, leaving one of the topsails fluttering uselessly in the wind. More bolts were loosed at the *Little Sneak*, but its sudden turn had surprised the crews of the two chasing frigates, and most flew past them. One hit a sailor halfway down the main deck, knocking him off his feet and into the sea with a scream.

'Loose the pisspot!' Tilly yelled.

The sloop collided with its own wake at that point, and the bow rose up over the heavy swell as the catapult shot the ceramic device at the closest frigate. The angle was all wrong, and the device soared into the sky. It passed clean over the first frigate, and Tilly cursed loudly. Then, the device fell, having travelled further than intended. It crashed down, striking the bow of one of the oil transporters, where it exploded with a tremendous roar. A larger, secondary explosion went off moments later, and the front of the oil transporter blew apart. Heavy, thick black smoke billowed up into the sky, as the oil on board caught fire. There were more explosions from the transporter, and it began to slow, dead in the water. Its masts and sails were aflame, and smoke was pouring out from the battered vessel.

'Into the smoke!' cried Tilly.

The master nodded. 'Yes, ma'am.'

The wind was blowing the dense, black smoke over the ships, and the remaining oil transporters slipped out of sight, hidden behind the thick curtain. The two frigates were still closing on the sloop, but were now heading in the opposite direction, and Maddie realised that the *Little Sneak* was about to pass between them.

'Everyone down!' screamed Captain Tilly, as the frigates got within crossbow range, one on either side of the sloop. A withering hail of bolts shot out from both frigates at once, and the main deck of the *Little Sneak* started to resemble a slaughterhouse, as pirate sailors fell, their bodies studded with bolts. Screaming sailors plummeted from the rigging, and Maddie closed her eyes, as she lay on the quarter deck. After a few seconds, it was over, and the two frigates passed by the stern of the sloop, and began to turn.

Maddie raised her head a little. Two yards from her, the lieutenant was lying dead, his eyes staring upwards at the smoke-filled sky. Next to him, Tilly pulled herself to her feet. She glanced around, then saw the body of her lieutenant. She stared at him, her mouth open, then the sloop was enveloped by the impenetrable clouds of black smoke, and Maddie could see nothing. She coughed, her eyes stinging from the acrid smoke, and gripped the railing.

'Master!' cried Tilly through the darkness. 'Are you alive?'

'Yes, ma'am,' came a voice from the rear of the quarter deck.

'Praise the gods for that,' said Tilly.

The sloop was still cutting through the water, though Maddie had no idea of the direction in which they were heading. They could hit one of the other ships, perhaps the burning one, or maybe even the coast. The smoke was getting worse, and she remained crouched by the railings, her breath ragged, and her throat scorched. A bright flicker of flame passed them on their right, and she could hear the cries and groans of injured sailors over the sound of the fires raging on the oil transporter.

They sailed onwards, the smoke seeming endless, with every moment filled with terror for Maddie. She closed her eyes and retreated into herself. If she was going to die, then she hoped it would happen soon.

The wind changed a little, and the *Little Sneak* shot out of the thick banks of smoke and back into the clean, fresh air. Even with her eyes closed, Maddie could feel the difference. She glanced up, and saw only blue skies ahead of them. She pulled herself to her feet and turned to gaze at the dense wall of smoke behind them. Flames were leaping upwards from within the inferno, but none of the other ships were visible.

'Full speed, Master,' said Tilly. 'Get us out of here.'

Maddie thought back to their previous escape, when they had raced through a bank of fog to flee from a Sea Banner vessel. That time, the crew had cheered, but there were no cheers this time. Bodies littered the main deck, which was covered in pools of blood. Three bodies lay on the quarter deck – the lieutenant, the midshipman, and the master's mate, while only Tilly, Maddie and the master had survived.

The sloop reached the headland from where the convoy had appeared.

'Where to, ma'am?' said the master.

Tilly pointed directly ahead. 'Straight into the Outer Ocean, Master. It's our only chance.'

'Yes, ma'am.'

Maddie noticed that the captain's hands were shaking, and she looked drained of all energy. Down on the main deck, the surviving sailors were getting to their feet, each staring at the bloody bodies of their fallen crewmates.

'Get back to work!' Tilly screamed. 'Work, or those bastards will catch us!'

She ran down the steps to the main deck, and began shoving the sailors back to their positions. She slapped one who was weeping, and pushed him towards the rigging.

'Are you alright, lass?'

Maddie turned, and saw that it was the master who had spoken. His hands were on the wheel, where they had remained throughout their ordeal. Blood was coming from a cut across his cheek, from where a crossbow bolt had grazed him.

She nodded.

'Good, lass. Now, start helping with the bodies.'

'What should I do with them?'

'Line them up by the side of the ship, so that the crew can do their jobs without worrying about stepping on any of their friends.'

'And then what?'

'Then, lass, we'll bury them at sea. They belong to the ocean now.'

CHAPTER 14

GETTING WET

Nan Po Tana, Haurn, Eastern Rim – 20th Essinch 5254 (18th Gylean Year 5)

Sable gripped the hilt of the sword, her hair still dripping with water from having swum across the small bay. The two greenhides in the narrow lane ahead of her had yet to notice her presence, engrossed as they were with devouring the goat carcass that Deepblue had dropped over the abandoned village.

Sable leaned over, picked up a small stone, and threw it at the nearest greenhide. It bounced off the toughened outer skin on its rounded back, and the beast paused, then glanced in her direction, its insect eyes scanning her.

She drove into its mind, suppressing the powerful wave of revulsion. *Do not move. Stay exactly where you are.*

It continued to stare at her, frozen to the ground, while the other greenhide ignored what it was doing, content to have the rest of the goat to itself. Sable approached, her wet boots squeaking on the dusty cobbles of the narrow village street. The greenhide closest to her remained unmoving. She had imprinted her command with more force than usual, testing how long it would persist in the greenhide's mind. Would it allow her to kill it without resisting? She approached to within a yard of the beast, its stench filling her nostrils, and raised her sword. It was an old weapon, discovered on one of the tiny islands where refugees still lived, and then sold to Sable by visiting merchants; and she hoped the blade was strong enough.

She inched closer, her vision ready to dive back into the beast's mind if necessary, but it didn't move. She drew her right hand back, then plunged the blade deep into the greenhide's face, killing it instantly. It fell, and the weight of the beast nearly ripped the sword from Sable's hand, but she managed to pull the blade out, its edge coated in green blood.

The other greenhide jumped back, at last noticing Sable's presence. It lifted its long talons and shrieked, then charged. Sable ducked a lunge from the sharp claws. She swept her arm out, and her blade connected with the tough hide around its upper arm. It left a long mark, but didn't break through its skin. The greenhide's head jabbed down at her, its teeth red from the goat carcass, and she rammed the end of the sword into its mouth. The greenhide shrieked in agony, then collapsed on top of her. It writhed for a moment, and she pushed the sword in deeper, until the beast stopped moving.

She grunted, then used her battle-vision strength to push the beast off her. Green blood was covering the front of her thin leathers, and was running down her right arm. She pushed herself to her feet, and glanced at the ground. Two dead greenhides – her first. True, she had tricked one using her powers, but she had killed the second in a fair fight, and, of the two deaths, that was the one she was most proud of.

A shadow flitted overhead, and she looked up to see Deepblue hovering above her.

'Well done, Sable,' the dragon said.

'I didn't know you were watching.'

'Badblood asked me to make sure you were alright, but I wanted to let you try on your own; and you did it. Would you like me to carry you back to the temple?'

'Thanks, but a swim will help wash off their blood. It stinks.'

'Very well. I will see you in a moment.'

The small dragon extended her wings and flew to the other side of the bay. Sable walked past the two greenhide bodies and onto the little quay that stood at the edge of the village. She crouched down, and washed the blood from the sword, then secured it in the sheath that was strapped over her shoulder. She glanced down into the crystal clear waters of the little bay, then dived in, disturbing the little silver fish that clustered by the old harbour. She swam the length of the bay, then clambered out by the rocks on the other side, her clothes and tied-back hair dripping.

She heard a ripple of applause when she reached the path that ran up the low cliff. She looked up, and saw Millen sitting on the bench under the olive tree.

'That was very impressive,' he said.

'I thought so, too.'

'Everything work all right?' he said. 'No pain or stiffness?'

'I'm still not at my peak,' she said, sitting down on the bench next to him, 'but I'm moving without any problems. To be honest, I don't know if I'll ever reach my peak again. It's been two years since I last fought, and I'm not in my twenties any more.' She felt the rays of the sun start to dry her out. 'Still, does it matter? Once we've rescued Maddie, I don't intend to do any more fighting.'

'Don't say that in front of Meader,' said Millen. 'You'll set him off on another rant.'

'He has all the zeal of a new convert,' said Sable, 'mixed with the dire warnings of a prophet of doom.'

'He's worried about his brother.'

'I know. However, I doubt that Austin shares Meader's desire to join the rebellion. When he and Ashfall get back here, I suspect that there might be a rather large argument in store.'

'If he gets back, not when,' said a voice from behind them.

Sable and Millen turned. Meader was standing in the shade of the archway.

'Stop lurking, Meader,' said Sable.

'It's been fifteen days since Austin and Ashfall left to get the Quadrant,' Meader went on. 'Something's gone wrong.'

'Maybe.'

'It only takes three days for a dragon to fly to Ulna; four if they take their time. With a two-day stop-over on Ulna, that still only comes to ten days.'

'There's no point in worrying about it,' said Sable. 'There's nothing we can do.'

Meader gave a grim laugh. 'That's easy to say, but he's my little brother, and asking me not to worry is an exercise in futility. Anything could have happened. They might have been attacked over Throscala – Lady Ydril is still on that island, and she could knock Ashfall out of the sky with ease.'

'Or,' Sable said, 'Austin might have taken the Quadrant and used it to go back to Implacatus.'

'He wouldn't do that; he wouldn't leave without saying goodbye. Besides, he made a deal with Blackrose.'

'You know him better than I do, I suppose.'

Meader frowned, then lit a cigarette with his new lighter, which he had bought from the visiting merchants at the same time as Sable had purchased her sword.

'I don't actually know Austin all that well,' he said. 'In Gyle, I tried to show him as much as possible, but he still had the lessons from school stuck in his head. You know – the Ascendants are always right, and that sort of thing. I need him to come back, so that I can try to persuade him that what he was taught is bullshit. I have to change his mind before Implacatus sends reinforcements to Dragon Eyre.'

Sable shrugged. 'It's been a while since their defeat in Alg Bay. Maybe they're not going to send anyone else. Maybe they've given up.'

Meader laughed, but it wasn't a happy sound. 'You're delusional if you believe that, Sable. Of course the Ascendants haven't given up; it just takes time to put together a new army. The Banners like to have a full year with new recruits, to train them properly, and Lord Edmond can be very patient. With every day that passes, more opportunities slip through our fingers. In two years, we should have re-conquered all of Dragon Eyre; instead, we've done nothing to consolidate the victory in Ulna. The Home Islands are still secure; the Western Rim remains under the heel of the Banners, and, worst of all, Throscala is still in their hands.'

Millen sighed.

'I'm sorry,' snapped Meader; 'am I boring you?'

'Don't be rude to my rider,' said Deepblue, her long neck arching down towards them.

'Why is everyone lurking around today?' said Sable.

'I wasn't being rude,' said Meader. 'I'm just frustrated that no one else seems to be taking this seriously.'

'There are plenty of rumours among the dragons of Haurn,' said Deepblue. 'Many of them believe that this is only a short respite, and that the Sea Banner will soon be back in force. They say that they've seen this happen before, especially during the last rebellion of the Eastern Rim.'

'I remember that,' said Meader; 'and I remember what happened next. We need to be prepared.'

Sable closed her eyes and reclined on the bench, savouring the warm sunshine on her skin. 'I am prepared.'

'What does Blackrose think?' said Millen.

'Blackrose only cares about her missing rider,' said Meader. 'She's not interested in any further offensive actions against the authorities in the Home Islands. I've tried speaking to her about it, but she told me to shut up.'

Sable felt a shadow cross her, and she opened her eyes. A dragon was approaching. She glanced through the archway as Evensward landed in the courtyard.

'Sable,' the dark green dragon said. 'A single ship is sailing towards Haurn from the west, on a course that will bring it here.'

Sable sat up. 'A merchant ship?'

'No. Sea Banner. What you would call a frigate.'

'How close is it?'

'About twenty miles away. One of my kin spotted it, and I flew out to take a look. I was tempted to attack, but decided to tell you first, in case a god is on board. I have also summoned Queen Blackrose; she is on her way.'

Sable yawned, and stretched her arms. 'Millen, could you make me a coffee? And, Meader – do you have any keenweed left? I'm a little frazzled from controlling that greenhide earlier.'

'I thought it was getting easier?' said Meader.

'It is. I managed not to be sick this time, but it's still an effort.'

'Tough. I'm out of keenweed. I have tobacco.'

'No, I don't want to start smoking that again. Coffee will have to do.'

'I'll get it for you,' said Millen, standing.

Meader frowned. 'She's not an invalid any more, Millen; she can get her own coffee.'

'I know,' he said, 'but I like to be helpful.'

Sable flashed him a smile. 'Thank you.' She waited until he had disappeared through the archway, then took a breath, concentrating. 'Here goes.'

She lifted her vision clear of her body, and gazed down at their tiny corner of southern Haurn. The temple complex was shining in the sunlight, and workers were out in the little fields and groves. She turned towards the west, and sped her vision across the sea, crossing the coast in seconds. She left Haurn behind, and scanned the ocean. Reaching what she guessed was about twenty miles, she slowed, and looked around for the frigate. She spotted its wake first, then chased it until she reached the stern of the ship. She homed in on the quarter deck, and saw the usual selection of officers, along with a young-looking man dressed in civilian clothes, who was standing close to the captain.

She went into his mind without hesitation, noticing how pleasant an experience it was, compared to entering the consciousness of a greenhide.

The man was a demigod. She searched for his powers, and found that he possessed the ability to deliver death, but in a weakened form – he was no match for an Ancient like Seraph, but he would still be able to kill a dragon that flew too close to the ship. She examined some of his memories. He had been sent from Na Sun Ka, on a mission to arrest Lord Meader. A rumour was circulating that the renegade demigod was hiding in a temple on a remote corner of Haurn. Fishermen had been interrogated; fishermen who had seen Meader with their own eyes. The frigate also had sixty armed Banner soldiers on board, along with a few dozen marines, to assist in the capture of Meader, and the demigod on board was looking forward to apprehending him – it would do his faltering career a world of good.

Sable severed the connection, and noticed that Millen was holding out a small cup of freshly-made coffee for her. She smiled and took it, then glanced at Meader.

'They're here for you.'

Meader stared at her. 'What?'

'You were seen in these waters by some fishermen, who are now in the custody of the colonial authorities in Na Sun Ka. You might not have been as discreet as you'd imagined.'

'Is there a god on board the ship?' said Evensward.

'Yes. Not a particularly good one, but he has death powers that are strong enough to kill a dragon.'

'I was correct to come to you first, witch.'

'You were. They also have sixty Banner soldiers and forty Marines on board.'

'What should we do?' said Deepblue.

Blackrose came striding into the courtyard. 'We should attack.'

'I agree,' said Meader.

'And I,' said Evensward.

'Woah,' said Sable; 'hang on a minute. Let's think this through first, before we do anything rash.'

'I didn't take you for a coward, witch,' said Blackrose.

Sable gave the black dragon a glance, and decided to ignore the comment. 'Did no one hear me say that the authorities on Na Sun Ka know that Meader is here? Or, at least, they strongly suspect it. If we destroy that ship, it will confirm it.'

Blackrose tilted her head. 'Are you saying that we should allow them to arrest Meader? That's a little callous, even for you, witch.'

'I was suggesting no such thing,' said Sable. 'We should evacuate – all of us. The humans and the entire dragon colony. We can hide on the other side of Haurn until they've gone.'

'They'll see the fields and farms within the temple walls,' said Meader. 'They'll know that someone lives here. They might even destroy the temple, out of spite.'

'We can rebuild,' said Sable. 'After we've rescued Maddie, I intend to live here. We can't do that if we sink the frigate and kill the god on board.'

'You're dreaming again,' said Meader. 'There's a powerful god with vision powers based on the island of Yearning, who is capable of sending messages to Lady Ydril in Throscala. He will have seen me here by now, and you, Sable; and you too, Blackrose. If I were him, then right now I'd be inside the mind of the demigod on board the frigate, telling him what to expect. In fact, I might even be advising him to turn around and fetch someone more powerful from Na Sun Ka to deal with us.'

'That settles it,' said Evensward. 'We must attack. If the gods are aware of our presence here, then my colony is no longer safe. Once the ship has been destroyed, we shall have to look for an alternative place to live.'

Sable shook her head. 'You led them to us, Meader.'

'I didn't intend to,' he said. 'Sorry, everyone.'

'It was a foolish mistake to make,' said Evensward, 'but I accept your apology, as you did not mean for this to happen. Now, how shall we go about the destruction of the ship? Sable, do you have any explosive devices left?'

'I still have the four we brought back from Ulna,' she said, 'but we have no way of getting them on board.'

'Could dragons dive from a high altitude, and drop them on the ship?' said Meader.

'That'll never work,' said Sable. 'It would be like dropping an olive stone onto an ant from six feet. A moving ant, I might add. And, any dragon that tried it would be hit by the god's powers.'

'Perhaps we should drop you, witch,' said Blackrose. 'You could slay the god, and then we could burn the vessel.'

Sable stared at the black dragon. 'Right. I see. You think I need my legs broken again? Not to mention the dozen crossbow bolts that'll hit me as I lie writhing in agony on the deck; that's if I even landed on the deck, and didn't just splash into the ocean.'

'I could jump with you,' said Meader, 'and cushion your fall. I can heal a few broken bones.'

'Are you all out of your minds? Badblood, where are you?'

The dark red dragon appeared in the courtyard. 'Yes, my rider?'

'You should hear what these clowns are suggesting.'

'I heard them,' he said. 'Do not fear, rider; I will not allow anyone to drop you onto a ship.'

'She'd be safe,' said Meader. 'I'd act as her shield. I can take the crossbow hits, and the demigod's powers don't sound strong enough to be able to kill me outright. She cuts his head off, then we dive overboard.'

'You used to approach these matters as if they would be fun, witch,' said Blackrose, 'and you have performed feats far riskier than this. Where has your courage gone?'

'Do not insult my rider, Blackrose,' said Badblood. 'She is not your weapon.'

'I was merely trying to encourage her, son.'

'Why do you persist in calling me that?'

'Because it remains true. I adopted you in the Catacombs, and I do not relinquish my responsibilities lightly.'

'I cursed your name in Seabound.'

'And I have forgiven you. You were unaware that I had no part in the attack upon Sable.'

'What about the time before that, when you tried to kill her?'

Blackrose's eyes flared. 'She set my oldest friend upon me! I still have a scar from Shadowblaze's attack.'

'Stop arguing,' cried Sable. 'Shit; alright, I'll do it. Badblood, you're staying here. I'm not risking your life. Blackrose can fly us to the ship, if she thinks it's such a good idea. She can take her chances with the demigod's death powers.'

'So be it,' said Blackrose. 'I shall enjoy dropping you from a great height.'

———

The black dragon was flying so high that Sable was shivering on the harness. Below them, the blue ocean stretched out relentlessly, the horizon merging with the sky. Meader was leaning over, staring down at the surface of the water. Sable glanced over her shoulder, but the coastline of Haurn had faded into the distance. She hoped Badblood was alright. He had been enraged by her acceptance of the plan, and even more angered by her insistence that he remain behind. She had hated having to tell him not to come along, but she didn't want him to get hurt, and had known that he would have had difficulties flying back to Haurn alone, without her there to help guide him.

It felt strange being on another dragon's shoulders, and stranger that she didn't have to keep her mind connected to the dragon. She wouldn't do it again, she said to herself. One time only.

'I think I see it,' said Meader. 'Gods, it's so tiny from up here.'

'And you wanted dragons to drop pisspots onto it,' said Sable.

'I am ready to commence diving,' said Blackrose. 'Once you have killed the god, and jumped into the sea, signal to me using your powers, and I shall incinerate the ship.'

'You make it sound so simple,' said Sable.

Sable and Meader unbuckled the straps holding them to the harness, then Meader wrapped his arms round her.

'This is cosy,' she said.

'Don't get any funny ideas,' he said. 'You hang onto the harness strap, then let go when we're over the ship.'

Blackrose started to dive. She pulled her wings in, and they plummeted from the sky, their speed increasing with every second. Sable gripped onto the leather handle, and half-closed her eyes as the ocean hurtled towards them. The ship came into sight, a long, narrow shape cutting through the water towards Haurn. The sails became visible, then the tiny figures moving about on the decks.

'They have seen us,' said Blackrose, and Sable felt the dragon tense in readiness.

The death powers arrived a few moments later. Meader grunted, while a tremor passed through Blackrose. Sable craned her neck, and saw the demigod standing on the quarter deck of the frigate, his right hand in the air.

'Get ready,' said Blackrose, her voice straining from the pain.

The black dragon twisted in the air, turning upside down, and Sable let go of the handle. She and Meader tumbled through the air, his arms wrapped tightly round her as Blackrose soared away to safety.

Meader smiled at her as they dropped through the sky. 'Fancy meeting you here.'

'It's very romantic, but you should know that this isn't the first time I've been dropped by a dragon.'

Blackrose's aim had been true, and the ship grew larger and larger as they fell. They passed the top of the mast, then Meader's foot struck one of the many ropes attached to it, and they spun through the air. Meader's back cracked off a horizontal boom, then they fell onto the main deck of the frigate.

Sable powered her battle-vision and sprang to her feet, leaving Meader groaning on the boards of the deck. She drew her sword, as the sailors turned to stare, their mouths falling open.

'Get the marines!' cried an officer. 'We're under attack.'

Sable pushed a sailor over the side of the ship and sprinted towards the quarter deck. Most of the marines and Banner soldiers were still below deck, and the sailors were unarmed. A small number of Banner soldiers were close to the quarter deck, and were loading their cross-bows as Sable charged towards them. A sailor tried to block her path, and she sliced his arm off at the elbow with a savage downwards blow, then ducked as the first crossbow bolt sped over her head.

She ran headlong up the steps onto the quarter deck, ignoring the soldiers and everyone else, and made straight for the demigod, who was pointing at her with a look of terror mixed with disbelief on his face.

Another bolt flew past her waist, then an officer ran in front of the demigod to shield him from her attack, but was hit by a surge of death powers, and collapsed, dead. The demigod screamed, then turned and started to run for a cabin door. A stray crossbow bolt struck him in the leg, and he tripped. Sable rolled as more bolts sped past, then she raised her right arm and brought the edge of her sword down onto the demigod's neck, severing his head from his shoulders.

'Bring her down!' shouted the captain.

Sable lifted the body of the dead officer, and held it up in front of her as a shield, her head lowered. The body jerked and shuddered as bolts struck it. She flung it towards the approaching soldiers, and raced for the side of the ship. She vaulted the railings with a leap and fell, dropping her sword as she struck the water. She kicked with her legs, and went deeper, then held her breath for as long as she could as the frigate sailed by. When she re-surfaced, the back of the frigate was only a few yards away, and she was bucked up and down in its wake. A sailor pointed down at her and shouted, and she took a deep breath and plunged down again, under the water. She swam away from the ship, feeling her battle-vision power her movements. She surfaced again, and smiled. The frigate was now forty yards away. She cast her vision around for Meader, and found him over to her left, treading water. She swam over to him, and together they watched as the frigate started to turn.

'They're coming back for us!' Meader cried.

'Of course they are,' she said. 'Did you see what I did to their little god?'

'I saw,' he said.

'How are your bones?'

'Healed. I jumped overboard as soon as I was able to stand. By that time, you'd already killed the demigod. You're insane.'

'If I was sane, I would never have agreed to this plan.'

She sent her vision skywards, found Blackrose, and entered her mind.

You can burn the ship now.

The black dragon didn't respond. Instead, she pulled her wings in again and dropped from the sky like a stone. When she was fifty yards above the ship, she opened her jaws, and poured out fire over the deck of the frigate. She aimed for the ballista stations first, then scoured the entire deck from bow to aft, incinerating everything. She swooped away, then turned for a second pass. As she was about to reach the ship again, a massive explosion ripped through the stern, lifting it clear of the ocean for a moment as it disintegrated into a million fragments.

'There go the pisspots,' said Meader.

The shattered hull of the frigate settled back into the water, and it began to sink, stern first. The bow rose into the air until the ship was almost vertical, then it slid down into the depths, all traces of it gone, bar the flotsam left over from the explosion.

Blackrose dived towards Sable and Meader and plucked them from the water with her giant forelimbs.

Sable laughed as the dragon bore them away. 'You were right,' she said. 'That was fun.'

'We have a decision to make,' said Blackrose, to the dragons and humans assembled in the courtyard. 'With the destruction of the frigate, the gods of Na Sun Ka, and of Gyle, will soon know that we are here. Ashfall and Austin have not returned, and with fifteen days having elapsed, I am forced to the conclusion that they have been in some way delayed or obstructed. I cannot afford to waste more time going back to Ulna to find out what happened; therefore, I have decided to press on, alone if necessary, to Olkis.'

'Olkis?' said Meader. 'You'll never get to Olkis, not by flying.'

'Without a Quadrant, flying is the only way.'

'The vision god on Yearning will see you,' said Meader, 'and alert Na Sun Ka. Then there's the huge distance between Na Sun Ka and Gyle to cross. It's suicide.'

Sable glanced up. She was leaning against the side of the dark red dragon, and caught his eye.

What do you think? she said inside Badblood's mind.

I think that we should help find Maddie, my rider, Badblood said.

It will be dangerous, my love.

I know.

Sable nodded, then turned to Blackrose. 'Badblood and I will come,' she said.

'Maddie is our friend,' said the dark red dragon; 'we are not going to desert her.'

'Thank you,' said Blackrose.

'Millen and I shall also come,' said Deepblue.

The black dragon gazed at her. 'I forbid it. Little Deepblue, your courage is not in question, but you do not possess the strength to complete the journey from Na Sun Ka to Gyle. I have done it myself, once in my youth. It is an exceptionally demanding flight of over five hundred miles without a break. You would fall from the sky before you ever reached Gyle.'

'But Maddie is our friend too,' said the small dragon.

'Someone has to remain here,' said Sable, 'to look after the place in our absence. I'm sorry, Deepblue, and Millen, but Blackrose is right. Only the very strongest dragons will be able to make the series of journeys that we're planning. Evensward, will you evacuate the colony?'

'Yes. I already have dragons out scouting for a suitable location. Deepblue and Millen will be very welcome to remain with us.'

'It's probably best if we stay by the temple, in case Ashfall and Austin do finally appear,' said Millen, a miserable look on his face. 'Deepblue and I can join you if we come under attack from more ships.'

'I feel so useless,' said Deepblue.

'You saved my life by Seabound,' said Sable, 'and I'll never forget it.'

Blackrose lowered her head to face the small blue dragon. 'As I said, dearest Deepblue, no one here is questioning your courage. You can remain here without any shame. Badblood, Sable and I will find Maddie.'

'I'd better come too, if you're sure about this,' said Meader. 'You'll need me in Gyle – I know the place like the back of my hand. I also know the locations of a few abandoned dragon palaces in the mountains where we'll be able to rest in safety.'

'Agreed,' said Blackrose.

'I shall also accompany you,' said Evensward, 'along with one of my strongest young dragons. The Banner were intending to attack my home today, just as they reduced Haurn to a greenhide-infested wasteland some years ago. I do not know Maddie, but I thirst for vengeance all the same. I want to burn the palaces of the gods to the ground.'

Meader shook his head. 'This is madness.'

Sable laughed. 'Weren't you complaining this morning about our lack of action? Well, here's a plan that will take us right through the heart of the Home Islands. Think of the damage we could do before we reach Olkis.'

'I did say that, didn't I?' He sighed. 'Fine. When are we leaving?'

'In a few days,' said Blackrose. 'Each dragon who is going will need to eat and rest before departure.'

Sable got to her feet.

'Where are you going, rider?' said Badblood.

'Back to work,' she said. 'Anything could be waiting for us out there, and if we have a few days, then I need to be training.' She smiled. 'Let's see if I can find a few more greenhides.'

CHAPTER 15
DIVIDED

U dall, Ulna, Eastern Rim – 22nd Essinch 5254 (18th Gylean Year 5)

Austin had decided that he hated Ulna. He also hated the dragons, but most of his contempt was aimed towards the Unk Tannic. Gyle seemed so civilised in comparison to Ulna, and it was clear to him that dragons were not meant to rule. They had no patience with organisation or institutions, but instead were bound to pointless traditions that were handed on from generation to generation. As far as Austin knew, in the long history of Dragon Eyre, not a single constitution or code of law had ever been written down, and that was no way to run a world.

He sat amid the gloom and stared at the bare walls. He had been placed into a different cell after his arrest, and no longer even had the sound of the river for company. In fact, there were no openings at all, and the cramped cell was in constant darkness. His meals had been reduced to one a day, but, as he had no idea when each meal was delivered, he had lost all track of time. The one feature that his new cell shared with the previous one was the hatch system that brought his tray of food. He knew it was designed to protect the guards from his powers, but he was again desperate for company, and even missed talking to

Ashfall. The slender grey dragon loathed him, but at least she had spoken to him. He thought a lot about his journey from Haurn to Ulna, regretting the missed opportunities to make his escape. Foolishly, Ashfall had trusted him. He could have easily killed her along any part of the route, and fled; but he hadn't, and now he was paying the price.

More and more, he found himself thinking about the fate of his mother. If he had escaped, then he would have been free to begin his search for her. He longed to see her again; to tell her that he hadn't forgotten about her. Slaves were cheap on Implacatus – he would have been able to buy her back from whichever lord or lady of Serene had bought her, and then he would have found her somewhere to live; somewhere she could be free. It was a dream, but it had turned to dust.

They were going to execute him – it was only a matter of time. Splendoursun may have mentioned something about him being a useful hostage, but that was nonsense. Governor Horace would never lift a finger to help him, and would certainly never negotiate with rebels and terrorists. As soon as the dragons realised this, then Austin's life would be over. His only hope was that reinforcements would soon arrive from Implacatus, and sweep up the Eastern rim in a storm of destruction. They would annihilate his captors, and he would be free. He smiled. It was a vain hope, but it was all he had to cling on to.

He tensed as footsteps passed outside his cell door, but they kept walking, and soon faded away again. Probably just a change of guard, he thought. The sound of footsteps appeared again, and paused in front of his door. Austin braced himself. If the door opened, then it was time to die. Why else would anyone come to his cell? If the door opened, he would be sprayed with crossbow bolts, and his head would be hacked off by a black-robed fanatic from the Unk Tannic. He would cease to be Austin, and become just another victim of Dragon Eyre, added to the grim statistics that detailed the never-ending conflict.

He stared at the door. The person was still there. No further footsteps had been heard, so they must be. What were they doing? He raised his right hand, and readied his powers. If they had come to kill him, then he had an obligation to take down as many as he could. His flow powers surged through him in preparation for a last stand.

The door opened a tiny crack.

'Hey; you in there – demigod, are you awake?'

Austin frowned.

The door opened a little more, and a face peered through the gap. His eyes caught sight of Austin sitting on the floor, and he jumped in fright.

'Don't kill me!' the man hissed, his voice edged with terror. 'I'm here to let you out.'

Austin said nothing. It was probably a trick. The man was trying to lull him into becoming complacent, and lowering his guard.

'Shadowblaze sent me,' the man went on; 'you have to hurry. The guards will be back in a few minutes.'

Austin squinted through the gloom at the man's face. It seemed familiar.

'I'm Shadowblaze's rider,' the man said. 'Come on; move.'

'Ahi'edo?'

'Yes. I'm here to take you to Shadowblaze.'

'Why?'

The young man's face twisted in exasperation. 'Hurry up. If the Unk Tannic come back, then I'll end up in the next cell along.'

Austin got to his feet and glanced out of the door. No one but Ahi'edo was in the corridor, and the rider was unarmed.

'That's it,' said Ahi'edo; 'quickly.'

Austin walked out of the cell, and Ahi'edo re-locked the door.

'With any luck, it'll take a while before anyone realises you're not in there,' said the rider. 'Now, follow me.'

'Why does Shadowblaze want to speak to me?'

'Hush. Keep your voice down.'

Ahi'edo raced off along the corridor, and Austin followed on behind him. Maybe it wasn't a trick. A tingle of hope appeared inside him, and he tried to quash it. He had to stay wary and alert, and trust no one.

There was another door at the end of the corridor, and Ahi'edo took a moment to check that the way was clear, before they passed through the doorway and headed up a flight of stairs. The stairwell was lit by oil lamps, and Austin realised that it was night-time. He glanced out of a narrow window slit, and saw a few lights coming from the town on either side of the great river. They stopped at the top of the stairs, and Ahi'edo removed a long black cloak from a bag strapped over his shoulder.

'Put this on,' he said.

'It'll make me look like I'm in the Unk Tannic.'

'That's the point. Only dragon riders and Unk Tannic are allowed outside their quarters at night in the palace.'

Austin took the cloak, and pulled it on.

Ahi'edo glanced at him, then nodded. 'Keep your mouth closed from now on. If we get stopped, let me do the talking.'

The dragon rider set off again, and Austin kept up with his brisk pace. They crossed a large, empty hall, then ascended more stairs. They heard voices at the top, and hid in the shadows for a few minutes until the sound of footsteps fell away. They emerged from the darkness of the stairwell, and carried on, until they reached a doorway. Ahi'edo unlocked it, and they walked into a huge, cavernous space, where a dragon was waiting for him.

'Thank you, rider,' said Shadowblaze, his amber eyes trained on Austin. 'Lock the door; I do not want this little meeting to be interrupted.'

'Yes, master,' said Ahi'edo.

'So, Austin the demigod,' said the grey and red dragon; 'answer me this – do you know how to use a Quadrant?'

'Yes.'

'Will you honour the bargain you made with Queen Blackrose, and take the Quadrant to her?'

'Yes.'

Ahi'edo muttered something under his breath.

'I am aware that you do not trust him, rider,' said the dragon, 'but our position here has become desperate.'

'May I speak freely, master?' said Ahi'edo.

'I would be insulted if you didn't, rider.'

'I don't understand why we're doing this, master. I obeyed your command, and released the enemy demigod, but I don't agree with this decision. Blackrose has deserted us; she's travelling the world to search for that stupid bitch, Maddie – someone who should never have been the Queen's rider. Blackrose cares more about her than she does about Ulna.'

A flicker of anger flashed across Shadowblaze's eyes. 'I have known Queen Blackrose for hundreds of years, rider, and I have warned you before about denigrating her rider. I do not want to hear such words come from you again.'

'You said I could speak freely, master.'

'And I am telling you to stop insulting Maddie Jackdaw. It is most disrespectful.'

'But you hate her too, master.'

'You are mistaken, rider. When I first met the Jackdaw girl, I admit to having had some serious reservations about her suitability for the role, but that is in the past. I have long since accepted that the Queen shares a strong bond with her. You should do so also.'

Ahi'edo closed his mouth and folded his arms across his chest, the look on his face making it clear what he thought of the dragon's suggestion.

'Now, demigod,' said Shadowblaze, turning back to Austin; 'are you aware of the current political situation that pertains in Udall?'

'Not really,' said Austin.

'I am alone,' said the dragon. 'Greysteel, Maddie and Ashfall have gone, and the Queen has been away for far too long. In their absence, the palace has been inundated with allies of Splendoursun, along with their filthy little Unk Tannic acolytes. The Queen may have left me in charge, but my authority here is withering away with each day that passes. Splendoursun barely listens to anything I say, and my orders are routinely ignored. More importantly, if the Queen does not return by this time next month, then Lord Splendoursun will legally be her mate, and will be able to wield unlimited power over Ulna.'

'What's this got to do with me?' said Austin.

'You say that you know how to operate the Quadrant.'

'So? It's not here.'

'What if I was to tell you that I have discovered its location? What if I was to say that I also know that it was stolen from Maddie Jackdaw's apartment by a certain member of the Unk Tannic?'

'Well, that would change things.'

'Indeed.'

'Where is it?'

'It is being kept in a location within the palace that is both guarded, and inaccessible to dragons. You must go there, find it, and use it to escape Ulna. But first, you must swear to me that you will deliver it to the Queen. Do you swear this?'

'But, master!' cried Ahi'edo. 'I must protest. We cannot trust this creature of Implacatus.'

'Why not? Ashfall trusted him, and I trust her. Ashfall stated that Queen Blackrose also trusted him, and that is enough for me.'

'I swear it,' said Austin. 'I swear I will take the Quadrant to Blackrose.'

'This is wrong, master,' said Ahi'edo. 'Please reconsider; I beg you.'

'Silence, rider,' said the dragon. 'My loyalty is to Queen Blackrose, not to the Unk Tannic, and certainly not to Splendoursun. The Gyle dragons think themselves superior to us – look at the way they have driven off so many Ulnan dragons from Udall. If Splendoursun succeeds, then we shall all become his slaves.'

Austin watched the dragon and his rider stare at each other. The dragons in Ulna were hopelessly divided, he realised, and so were the humans. Best of all, if the Quadrant was hidden somewhere within the palace, then he might be able to make his escape. He tried to keep his wild hopes under control.

'Tell me where the Quadrant is,' he said, 'and I will take care of the rest.'

'He will kill the Unk Tannic guards,' said Ahi'edo. 'Those deaths will be your responsibility, master.'

'I know that,' said Shadowblaze. 'With any luck, he will kill every Unk Tannic agent in the palace.'

'How can you say that, master? The Unk Tannic saved Seabound when the Banner attacked.'

'They helped us because it furthered their aims, rider. If you want to know the truth, I believe that the Unk Tannic were the ones who placed Maddie Jackdaw in the hands of the pirates, in order to ensure the Queen's absence from Ulna. They have been in league with Splendoursun from the very beginning; don't you see?'

'No, master; I don't see that. But, even if it were true, then I'm glad they got rid of Maddie. In fact, I hope the pirates have already killed her.'

Sparks flew round Shadowblaze's jaws. 'You go too far, rider. You test the limits of our bond.'

'You are the one contemplating treachery, master; not I. My conscience is clear.'

'Not another word from you, rider, lest my anger override my feelings for you.' He glanced down at Austin. 'The Quadrant is being kept inside a chest, within the rooms of Ata'nix. Do you know the location of his quarters?'

'Yes. Where is the chest, exactly?'

'I don't have that information. I only know that it lies somewhere in his rooms. I overheard Ata'nix tell one of his minions this – humans sometimes forget how sharp the ears of a dragon can be. Go, and do what you have sworn to do.'

Austin frowned. 'What will happen to you when the others discover that you let me out?'

'My loyalty to the Queen outweighs any considerations regarding my personal safety.'

'And Ashfall? Is she still locked up?'

'She is. Do not attempt to rescue her; nothing must imperil the delivery of the Quadrant to the Queen.'

Austin frowned. 'Is she suffering?'

'She is confined to a prison lair, but is otherwise healthy,' said Shadowblaze. 'Do not be distracted, demigod. Ashfall is loyal to the Queen, and will understand.'

'Alright. Is Ata'nix in his quarters; do we know that?'

'He is currently addressing a group of Unk Tannic. That is why it must be done now – this may be our only chance.'

'Understood. Thank you, dragon. I'll go now, and try my best.'

'You are a good man, demigod. I wish you well.'

Austin bowed his head, then strode towards the door. Ahi'edo followed him, the anger in his eyes unmistakeable. The rider unlocked the door, and Austin slipped out. He pulled the hood of the cloak up to shield his features, and set off down the hallway.

He had lied several times to the large grey and red dragon, but his conscience was clean. As he had told Ashfall, it was impossible to betray a cause that he wasn't part of. If Shadowblaze suffered because of his actions, then it was the dragon's own fault. They were all rebels, as far as Austin was concerned, and were idiots to trust him. He flexed the fingers in his right hand as he walked towards the quarters of the Unk Tannic leader, feeling his flow powers.

His first lie had been about the Quadrant. A half-lie, Austin thought, correcting himself. He had been taught the bare minimum about how to use the ancient devices – the two easiest actions, the same two that every demigod was taught. The first action would take the bearer of the Quadrant to the last place the device had been used. That would be no good, he thought. Sable had probably been the last person to activate the device, so the first action would most likely take him close to Seabound Palace, which would be useless. It was the second action that he was focussing on. That would take the bearer of the Quadrant to the first place it had ever been used – Implacatus. Where on Implacatus, he had no idea; he assumed that, out of the hundreds of Quadrants that had once existed, many would have been first used in different locations upon his home world. The devices were thousands of years old, relics from an era that had also seen the construction of the legendary sextants, back when Implacatus was the sole inhabited world. If he had known more about the history of the Quadrant lying in Ata'nix's quarters, then he might have been able to make a rough guess as to where the second basic action would take him. Only around a dozen of the precious devices still existed, or so he had been taught, and quite a lot was known about the individual Quadrants that had survived the long millennia since being created. The device held by the Governor of Dragon Eyre, for example, had once belonged to Albrada, the Blessed Eleventh Ascendant, who had first activated it within a palace close to Serene. With any luck, the Quadrant in Udall would have a similar past, and it would take him to Serene or Cumulus. He thought of his mother again, and his heart started to race.

He slowed as he reached a stairwell leading down into the human-sized levels of the bridge palace. A few lamps were lit, but the place was in silence. He crept down the stairs, his ears alert for any noise, and came out into a narrow corridor, lined with doorways. Austin had been there once before, while being escorted from his cell to meet Ashfall, back in the days when she had been responsible for guarding him during his daily outings. He searched his memory, trying to remember which door led to Ata'nix's quarters. He turned a corner in the corridor, and saw two Unk Tannic guards standing outside a doorway. He smiled.

The two guards were armed with crossbows, but had them slung over their shoulders. They glanced at Austin as he strode towards them, their eyes narrowed.

'Brother,' said one; 'you need permission to be down here; this area is restricted.'

Austin raised his hand, and the heads of the two men exploded, sending bloody fragments outwards that covered the walls and ceiling of the corridor. The two bodies tottered, then slumped to the floor. Austin frowned. It was getting easier to kill; should he be worried? Unlike the previous times, he didn't feel an immediate surge of horror, shame and disgust. The two men were enemies, who would have probably relished executing him – why should he feel bad for them? Hadn't

Shadowblaze encouraged him to kill as many of the Unk Tannic as possible?

He stepped over the corpses and tried the door. It opened, and Austin barely suppressed a laugh of relief. He stepped inside the apartment. It was in complete darkness, and he spent a few moments stumbling about before he found a lamp. He lit it, and gazed around the room. A long table sat by a set of shuttered windows, its surface littered with papers and maps. On the other side of the room were a few comfortable chairs, and a bookcase filled with battered old volumes, their spines cracked and repaired. Two other doors led off from the room, and he tried the first, only to see a small toilet chamber. He backed out, and went to the other door. He pushed it open, and entered a bedroom. A single bed sat in one corner, and at its end was a large chest.

Austin set the lamp down on the rug by the bed, and crouched next to the chest. He tried to open the hinged lid, but it was locked. Austin cursed. Of course it would be locked, especially if it contained a Quadrant. He glanced around the bedroom, looking for something he could use to prise it open. A sword would do, or a long knife, but he saw no weapons anywhere. He remembered the two guards, and hurried back out through the main room and into the corridor.

His eyes scanned the blood-spattered clothing of the two men. Each had a short sword attached to their belts, and Austin slid one out of its scabbard, then froze as the sound of footsteps and voices approached from the corner of the corridor. One of the voices belonged to Ata'nix; he recognised it from their previous meeting. Austin jumped to his feet and ran back into the apartment. He needed to remain calm, but his hands were shaking as he knelt down by the chest. He rammed the blade into the crack under the lid, but it slipped and sliced through the back of his left hand. Austin suppressed a cry of pain, then watched as the wound on his hand started to heal. Dripping blood onto the rug, he tried again. This time, the blade penetrated the outside of the chest. He leaned on the hilt, pushing down, and the lid sprang open, the lock broken.

Shouts arose from the corridor, and Austin began throwing out everything he could see within the chest – clothes, leather pouches and bags, a knife, some books, until, at the very bottom, he caught a glimpse of copper-coloured metal. He pulled the Quadrant out from the chest, and stared at it, his mind foggy with panic. He saw the two locations that he had been taught, but his memory of which was which went blank.

'He's in the bedroom!' cried a voice from outside the door. 'Bring crossbows!'

'This time,' said Ata'nix, 'I want the demigod's head.'

Austin glanced from the Quadrant to the door. Unk Tannic agents would be entering within seconds, to kill him. He was sure he would be able to deliver death to a few of them, but they had managed to subdue him twice before, and if they caught him again, he would surely die. But which location should he touch on the Quadrant?

He swiped his trembling fingers over the surface of the device just as the door to the bedroom was kicked open. The air shimmered, and everything went dark. He was falling through the night air, the stars above him. He looked down, and saw the waters of Alg Bay rushing up towards him.

'Damn it,' he cried, realising that he had been transported to where Sable had last used the device. A huge chunk of cliffside was missing, destroyed by his brother when he had created the massive wave that had sunk the fleet. With seconds to spare before he struck the surface of the dark water, he swiped the Quadrant again, and his surroundings shimmered and changed.

He fell onto rocks and sand, a howling wind gusting over him. He groaned. His back had struck a jagged rock, and pain rattled through him. The wind was whipping sand into his face, and he struggled to see anything as he lay on the ground, waiting for his self-healing to repair his injuries. A dim orange light suffused the air, though no sun was visible.

Was he on Implacatus? It was like being in a desert in the middle of a sandstorm. The only places he had been on Implacatus were Serene and Cumulus, both high up on a mountainside. It was hard to breathe, not just because of the hot sand that was hitting his face, but also because the air itself seemed wrong; tainted even. He coughed and spluttered. His powers had healed the damage done to his back in the fall, and he struggled up onto his feet. He glanced around, but every direction looked the same – a swirling mass of gusting sand, with barren rocks covering the ground. He could only see for a few yards in front of him, so chose a direction at random, and started walking, after tucking the Quadrant into his clothing.

He wondered what was happening within the palace in Udall. The Unk Tannic would know that he had disappeared with the Quadrant, but he was well out of their reach now. He felt a tiny twinge of guilt about abandoning Shadowblaze and Ashfall, but they had been fools to trust him, and it wasn't his fault that they had done so. He had also broken his word to Blackrose, but what else could he have done? He didn't know how to use the Quadrant to travel around the islands of Dragon Eyre, and the Unk Tannic guards would have killed him if he hadn't activated the device.

He trudged along, keeping his head down. A rash was appearing on the skin on the back of his hands. His self-healing was repairing it as soon as it appeared, but it kept coming back, and he coughed again. It was as if the air itself was poisonous. He pushed his guilt to the back of his mind and kept going, the roar of the wind drowning out everything else. He coughed, and noticed blood come from his mouth, so he stopped, and wrapped a strip of cloth over his face, leaving a narrow space for his eyes, then he pulled the cloak's hood down to protect his head. He had no water, food or money on him; all he had were his clothes and a Quadrant. He noticed that the ground was rising to his left, so he set off in that direction. Perhaps if he got to higher ground, he would be able to see the mountains where Serene lay. For half an hour, he staggered onwards, but the wind showed no signs of abating. His feet went over a loose rock, and he slipped, then tumbled all the way back down the slope, bringing rocks and sand falling around him as he fell.

He landed at the bottom, and held his hands over his head to shield himself. This couldn't be Implacatus, he thought; he must have made a mistake. The rash on his exposed skin was getting slowly worse, but he pulled himself back to his feet. What choice did he have? He couldn't use the Quadrant to return to Ata'nix's rooms; that would mean certain death. All he could do was press on, and hope that the storm would die down.

He pulled the cloak around him, and set off again.

CHAPTER 16

BEFALLEN

Langbeg, Olkis, Western Rim – 30th Essinch 5254 (18th Gylean Year 5)

The three sailors walked into *Bo'sun's Droop*, and went up to the bar.

'Master Topaz,' said the tavern owner; 'I assume the *Giddy Gull* has successfully returned from her latest voyage?'

Topaz nodded, his eyes bleary from lack of sleep. 'We're back,' he said, 'though whether "successfully" or not remains to be seen.'

The tavern owner resisted the urge to ask any further questions. 'Ale?'

'And food,' said Ryan.

'And gin,' said Vitz.

'Ale's fine for me,' said Topaz, handing over a purse of money. 'That should cover us for the day.'

The tavern owner peered inside the purse. 'Very generous, Master.'

'You haven't seen how much Ryan can eat and drink yet,' said Topaz.

'He can drink for free, if he plays that guitar hanging over his shoulder for a few hours later on,' said the tavern owner, as he poured out three pints of ale. 'The folk in here are always asking for a sing-along. Is he any good?'

'I'm excellent,' said Ryan, 'and I have a voice like a nightingale.'

'More like a gull caught in a net,' said Vitz.

'Get yourselves a table, lads,' said the tavern owner, 'and we'll see how he goes. Oh, will your captain be popping in later?'

'She's gone straight up to Befallen Castle,' said Topaz, taking his ale.

They passed through the quiet tavern, and selected a small table in a dark alcove. They sat, and Ryan downed his pint in one.

Topaz frowned at him. 'You should have done that at the bar before you sat down, you dozy pillock,' he said. 'Now, you'll just have to get back up and order another one.'

Ryan belched, then lifted his empty mug. 'More ale!' he cried at the tavern owner.

Vitz laughed.

'Don't encourage him, lad,' said Topaz, yawning. 'Dear gods, I can hardly keep my eyes open.'

'I had a wonderful night's sleep,' said Ryan. 'I dreamt I was with these two stunning redheads, and...'

'Spare us, mate,' said Topaz. 'While you were snoring, some of us were working all night.'

'That's the perils of being a master, eh, mate? It's what you always wanted.'

'I know, but I've taken the *Gull* through Luckenbay three times in the last twenty-odd days, and I'm knackered. Worse, judging by the measly haul we got from that Alefian merchant ship, we'll be back out again soon, while all of our takings are going straight up the road to Olo'osso.'

Ryan frowned. 'Is that why we didn't get a landing bonus? Why's he getting the takings?'

'Shit,' muttered Topaz. 'Forget I said that.'

'No chance, mate,' said Ryan.

'I can't tell you; Lara will kill me.'

'You'll have to tell us now,' said Vitz. 'The crew suspects that something's going on. The captain's usually generous when we land, but this morning she hardly said a word to us – she just loaded a cart with everything we took from the merchant ship, and set off up the cliffside.'

Ryan nodded. 'Her old man paid off her debt, didn't he? And now we're working for him.'

Topaz narrowed his eyes. 'Who told you that?'

'It's pretty obvious,' said Vitz.

'I see you ain't denying it, mate,' said Ryan. 'Shit, so Olo'osso now owns the *Gull*? You know, it's not all bad. No one will ever mess with us now, not if we're on his lordship's boat. Folk are scared of Lara, but they're shit-in-their-pants-scared of old Olo'osso. I hope he's as generous as his daughter.'

A young barmaid brought over another ale for Ryan, and he grinned at her.

'Alright, darling?' he said. 'I'll sing you a song if you give me a kiss.'

'Yeah?' she said, setting the ale down on the table. 'Do you know the one called "Piss off, I'm working?"'

Ryan laughed. 'No, but I could sing it to you later while you take your clothes off.'

The young woman muttered something under her breath and strode away.

Ryan turned back to the others. 'She reminds me of one of the girls from last night's dream. Are there any decent brothels in Langbeg?'

'Do you ever think of anything else?' said Vitz.

'Not if I can help it, lad,' said Ryan, taking a drink from his second ale. He glanced at Topaz. 'Shit on a stick, mate, you look like you're about to fall asleep; we can't be having that. I'm up for an all-nighter.'

'It's not even noon yet,' said Topaz.

'I know. And?'

'Maybe I should get some sleep now, so that I can join you two later in the evening.'

'No chance,' said Ryan. 'You'd be sober and fresh, while me and the lad would be rat-arsed. You promised us a night out.'

'I'm paying for it, ain't I?'

'And I'm grateful,' said Ryan. 'But, let's face it, your pay as a master is a little higher than ours, and you can afford it.' He picked up his guitar, and strummed a chord. He stopped, and re-tuned one of the strings.

'You ain't bailing on us, though, mate. If you fall asleep, I'm emptying your pint over your head.'

The barmaid returned to their table. 'Who's wanting fed?'

'I could eat you,' said Ryan.

'Apologies, miss,' said Topaz. 'Ryan always gets a little over-excited after a few days at sea.'

'She works in a sailors' tavern, mate,' said Ryan. 'I'm sure she's heard worse.' He winked at the barmaid. 'I'll have some breakfast, darling, if it's still on offer.'

'Sure. Three breakfasts?'

'Yeah, go on,' said Topaz.

She strode away, and Ryan began strumming his guitar.

Topaz eyed Vitz. 'You did some good work last night, lad.'

'All I did was bring you coffee and cigarettes,' said Vitz.

'You did a lot more than that. You're already much better than the *Gull's* last master's mate. Next time we're out, I'll let you take a full watch. You think you're up for it?'

'Yeah, definitely. Thanks.'

'It'll be once we're clear of Luckenbay. You ain't ready for that yet.'

'I know. I've been reading the charts, though; trying to memorise the location of all the Skerries.'

Ryan yawned loudly, and the two others glared at him.

'There's nothing more boring than having to listen to master-speak,' said Ryan. 'Do I prattle on about carpentry? No, I do not.'

'That's because you know bugger all about carpentry, mate,' said Topaz.

Ryan tapped his guitar. 'Oh yeah? And who built this little beauty, eh? Assembled from scraps, and now it's a bleeding work of art. This guitar is guaranteed to get me a girl tonight; the ladies love a handsome musician.'

Topaz tried to think of a retort, but his eyes were starting to close. Just a quick nap, he thought. He felt an elbow nudge his ribs, and his eyes snapped open to see Ryan about to pour an ale over his head.

Ryan narrowed his eyes at Vitz. 'I nearly had the bastard; why did you have to wake him up, lad?'

'Sorry, guys,' said Topaz. 'I think I might book a room for the day. I can't keep my eyes open.'

Ryan put down his guitar and got to his feet. 'Wait here, and don't eat my breakfast.'

Topaz frowned as he watched Ryan hurry out of the tavern.

'Where's he going?' said Vitz.

Topaz shrugged. 'Who knows?'

The barmaid walked over with a large tray, and deposited three huge plates onto the table. She glanced at the empty seat.

'Is your mate coming back?'

'He's left his guitar,' said Vitz, 'so he must be, I guess.'

'That's a funny accent,' she said. 'Where are you from?'

'Uh, Gyle.'

She frowned. 'Gyle? Shit; you're not that settler who got promoted to master's mate, are you?'

'How do you know about that?' said Topaz.

'The whole town knows about it,' she said.

'Does it bother you?' said Vitz.

She looked him in the eye. 'I hate settlers.'

'He swore an oath to Captain Lara, and to me,' said Topaz. 'He's one of us now.'

'He may have sworn an oath,' she said, 'but he'll never be one of us.'

She walked away, and Vitz glanced down at the floor.

'That could have been a lot worse,' said Topaz. 'She didn't throw the food in your face.'

'I need to work harder on getting rid of my accent,' Vitz said. 'I nearly got into several fights when we were last in Langbeg.'

Topaz picked up a fork. 'I wasn't out with you then, lad. If anyone wants a piece of you today, they'll have to come through me and Ryan first.'

They got stuck into their breakfasts, and all conversation ceased for a few minutes as the two hungry sailors wolfed down their plates of fried fish, fried eggs, beef sausages and blood pudding. When he had finished, Topaz pushed his plate away, and sat back in his seat. It felt good to have a full stomach, but the food had made him sleepier, and he could sense himself slipping into a stupor.

'Master Oto'pazzi?'

Topaz blinked, and looked up. Two men were standing next to their table.

'Who wants to know?' he said.

'Lord Olo'osso is hosting a party in Befallen Castle this afternoon, and all officers and petty officers from the *Giddy Gull* are invited. A few wagons have been organised to take everyone up to the castle, leaving at noon from the eastern pier.'

'Maybe another time,' said Topaz.

'Your attendance is mandatory, Master,' said one of the men. 'The "invitation" bit was just a courtesy. We'll see you at the pier in half an hour.'

Topaz scowled as the men turned and walked out of the tavern. 'So much for a nice day out.'

'I'm a petty officer,' said Vitz.

Topaz chuckled. 'Well done, lad.'

'That means I have to go too. Bugger and damnation. Why does Olo'osso want us all together up in the castle?'

'You know as much as I do, lad. Maybe he just wants to say hello to the senior crew of his new ship. My advice is, keep your mouth shut as much as possible.'

'I'll be the only settler there, Topaz.'

'Hence my advice.'

Ryan appeared back in the tavern at that moment. He grinned as he approached their table, then sat down and began eating his breakfast.

'Where did you go?' said Topaz.

Ryan mumbled something, but his mouth was so full of food that the words were unintelligible.

'We've been invited to a party,' said Vitz.

Ryan swallowed. 'Who else will be there?'

'Us,' said Topaz, 'and the captain.'

'Eh?' said Ryan.

'It's in Olo'osso's big castle,' said Vitz.

'What? In Befallen? And I'm invited? That doesn't make sense.'

Topaz yawned again. 'Just finish your breakfast, mate. I need some fresh air before I can handle a bleeding party.'

They waited for Ryan to shovel down the rest of his food, then they went up to the bar.

'That's us away,' said Topaz to the tavern owner.

'Already? You've hardly made a dent in the bag of gold you gave me.'

'Can you hold it over until another time? We've been summoned to Befallen.'

'Certainly, Master. Good luck.'

The three sailors walked out into the sunshine. The sun was burning overhead, and the water in the harbour was glistening brightly. Over by the eastern pier, a few wagons were sitting in a line, and several petty officers from the *Giddy Gull* were clambering up into the back of one.

'We should probably get onto a wagon,' said Topaz. 'The sun is too bright for me today.'

'Don't you worry, mate,' said Ryan; 'I have the cure.'

'What are you on about?'

Ryan delved into a pocket and produced a thick weedstick. 'I have a present for you, mate.'

'Dreamweed? One puff of that and I'll be asleep in seconds.'

Ryan grinned. 'It ain't dreamweed, you dozy beggar. It's keenweed. It'll wake you right up.'

'Yeah? Where did you find that?'

'The purser on the *Gull* can get his hands on just about anything, mate,' he said, handing it to Topaz.

'Cheers, I guess. It's been a long while since I touched any of this stuff.'

'Well, don't just stare at it, mate; spark it up.'

Topaz lit a match, and lifted the flame to the end of the weedstick, then he inhaled.

'No, no, sir,' Topaz said, 'that was the first time I'd met your daughter; the second time was when I was in jail in Throscala because I'd been abducted by the Unk Tannic, and then the Banner had freed me, but they were suspicious on account of me being from Olkis, and so they put me and Lara into the exercise yard, to see if we'd talk, and that's when Sable Holdfast appeared with a Quadrant, and she killed the four guards, then took me and Lara off to my old frigate, where she punched me in the face and told me I had ten seconds to get off the ship before she blew it into a million pieces.'

Olo'osso raised an eyebrow. 'Have you finished?'

Topaz nodded. 'Yes, sir.'

'I'm tempted to ask more about this Sable Holdfast,' said the old pirate, raising a glass of wine, 'but I'm slightly worried that you'll launch into another long, breathless, speech, Oto of the Sea Banner.' He turned to Lara, who was sitting a few spaces away down the side of the dining table. 'I didn't know your master was so talkative; he hardly said a word the last time he was here. Still, I'm glad you have a good relationship with him – the bond between a captain and their master is the most important one on any ship.'

Topaz grinned, the keenweed buzzing through his system. He swigged from his glass of wine, and grinned again. Several dinner tables had been arranged under the shade of the loggia, but he was sitting next to the great Olo'osso, while the rest of the officers and petty officers had been distributed at the smaller tables.

Lara gave him a funny look. 'I'm surprised he's still awake, father. He was up all night, and he's drunk about four gallons of wine since he sat down.' She nodded towards Topaz's untouched plate of food. 'You should probably eat something.'

'Don't nag the man,' said Dina, who was sitting between Lara and their father. 'It's supposed to be a party.'

'Shut your mouth,' said Lara. 'He's my master, not yours, so keep your sweaty hands off him.'

'Don't squabble, girls,' said Olo'osso. 'Technically speaking, Oto of the Sea Banner is *my* master. At the moment, I have decided to loan the *Giddy Gull* and its master to you, Alara. Who can say how long this arrangement will last?'

Lara scowled at her father, but said nothing, while Dina sniggered.

Ellie shifted in her chair, her glance on the waters of the bay below them.

'Getting bored, my sweet Elli?' said Olo'osso.

'No, father,' she said. 'I'm just looking forward to the wind changing, so I can get back out to sea.'

'Of course. It'll be any day now. Where are you planning on going?'

'Tankbar, father,' said Ellie. 'The first big convoys of the New Year will be leaving Alef in a few days, and I intend to catch a few merchants heading to Ectus.'

Olo'osso nodded. 'That sounds sensible.'

'It sounds boring,' said Lara. 'I want to go back to the Eastern Rim. If the settlers evacuate from Throscala, there will be plenty of easy pickings.'

'That's what I was thinking,' said Ann.

'Maybe we could team up,' said Topaz. 'I know the waters there as well as I know Olkis; maybe better. The rebellion on Ulna is bound to be crushed sooner or later, but the anarchy that exists there at the moment means that there will be opportunities to...'

'Let me stop you there, Oto of the Sea Banner,' said Olo'osso, his eyes glinting. 'I have already given permission for Ani to sail for the Eastern Rim next month, but I have other plans for the *Giddy Gull*.'

Lara narrowed her eyes. 'What plans, father?'

'I will speak to you and your crew after dinner, my little princess. Tell me more about this Sable woman. Did you know her well?'

Ann started to laugh, then she saw the glare coming from Lara, and stopped.

'What's so funny, dear?' said Olo'osso.

'Nothing, father,' said Ann.

The pirate glanced at his two daughters. 'Well, Alara? Did you know Sable well?'

'I guess so, father,' said Lara, her cheeks flushing. 'She and I... well, you know...'

'I see. Well, each to their own. Do you think she could be persuaded to become an ally of ours?'

'She's already helped me twice, father. Once when she freed me from jail, and a second time when she delivered the *Winsome* to me.'

'I thought Oto of the Sea Banner was responsible for bringing you that old sloop.'

'Sable forced me to do it, sir,' said Topaz. 'She did... something to my head, and made me pilot the sloop straight into a trap. Then Lara killed the rest of the crew.'

'The Sea Banner killed my entire crew when you first captured me,' cried Lara.

'I know,' said Topaz. 'I wasn't apportioning blame, ma'am. It's war, isn't it? Bad things happen.'

Olo'osso regarded Topaz with a stare. 'How is it possible that Sable could force you to do something? Gods can implant little suggestions into your mind, but they cannot force you to carry them out.'

'She's a Holdfast, father,' said Lara. 'She has a bunch of weird powers. Still, I think she might be dead. We've not heard anything about her for nearly two years.'

'She had no interest in helping us,' said Ann. 'It's true that I forged a deal with Sable, but it was purely business – she had her own agenda.'

'Did she keep her end of the bargain?' said Olo'osso.

'She did, father,' said Ann. 'The gold and iron I brought back from Ulna bears witness to that.'

'Then, it is immaterial if her heart is with us. If she ever re-surfaces, seek her out when you visit the Eastern Rim; there may be more deals to be had.'

'I shall, father.'

Lara cast her glance down.

'Don't be despondent, my little flower,' said Olo'osso. 'It's clear that you still have some personal feelings towards Sable. For that reason, it is wiser to send Ani to the Eastern Rim. Our line of business requires a cool head, and a ruthless detachment.' He glanced around the table. 'Has everyone finished eating? Good. Let us all gather together and go up onto the roof.'

'The roof?' said Dina.

'That is what I said, little Adina. We have a visitor up there waiting for us.'

The pirate leader stood, and clapped his hands together. The loggia quietened, apart from one raucous young sailor who was serenading a young serving woman, oblivious to everything else going on. Topaz groaned as he saw who it was.

'Ryan!' he shouted. 'Shut up, you dozy pillock!'

The crew of the *Gull* burst into laughter as Ryan glanced around.

Olo'osso smiled. 'Thank you for that intervention, Master Oto. It pleases me to see the senior crew of the *Giddy Gull* enjoying themselves; after all, that's what parties are for. However, there is a little business we need to attend to before the dancing begins, and so I would like you all to make your way up the steps onto the roof. You may all take a drink with you, but be respectful to our guest, who is waiting for us patiently.'

He raised his arms, and the officers and petty officers of the *Gull* got to their feet, and began to make their way to the stairs.

Topaz started to walk towards Ryan and Vitz, but Lara pulled at his elbow.

'A little advice,' she whispered. 'When my sisters and father are debating tactics, keep your big mouth shut. I thought father was going to hit you when you went on about me teaming up with Ann in the Eastern Rim. When you're at his table, you speak when you're spoken to; got it?'

'Sure. Sorry.'

She shook her head at him. 'Have you been smoking something? You're acting weird.'

'Uhh...'

'Please don't embarrass me in front of the others, Topaz; and keep that idiot Ryan under control. I can't believe it; the one time you're all invited to the castle, and you and Ryan turn up completely out of your faces.'

He nodded as they approached the steps. 'You and Sable, eh? I thought as much.'

'Do you want me to slap you?' she said. 'Me and Sable are none of your damn business. And, what do you mean, you thought as much?'

He shrugged. 'I saw the way you were looking at her when she rescued us from jail. It reminded me of the way Ryan looks at pretty much every young woman, like you were going to pounce.'

'You're sailing in very shallow water, Topaz,' she growled. 'I will punch you in front of everyone else; don't think I won't.'

He frowned. 'You asked.'

They ascended the steps and came out onto a wide, flat roof, with a panoramic view of the town of Langbeg and the bay. Topaz's glance was not on the view, however. Sitting in the corner of the roof was an enormous dragon, its red and silver scales shining in the afternoon sunlight. The senior crew of the *Giddy Gull* were keeping their distance from the great beast, but Olo'osso walked right up to the dragon, and they started talking.

'Holy crap,' muttered Topaz.

'It's just Redblade,' said Lara.

'You know it? Him? Her? Whatever it is?'

'I know him well, Topaz. Redblade's been a friend of the Five Sisters for decades. Now, shut up.'

Olo'osso turned to face the assembled crew on the roof.

'Our great allies, the dragons of Skythorn,' he began, 'have some news for us, and my old friend Redblade is here to deliver it. But first, I have a rather unpleasant duty to get out of the way.' His expression hardened. 'The takings from the *Gull's* last foray were pathetic. There is no other way to describe it.' He stared at the crew as they stood around in an awkward silence. 'I'm disappointed in you. The *Giddy Gull* is the finest vessel that flies the flag of the Five Sisters, and is meant for better things than harassing insignificant merchant vessels. When the costs are tallied against profits, you actually made a loss on your last trip, and I cannot allow this to continue. Therefore, I am removing Alara from her command.'

Lara stared at her father, her eyes wide with shock.

'Whether this is temporary or not,' Olo'osso went on, 'I have yet to decide. For the *Gull's* next operation, I will take command, personally. Alara will serve as my first lieutenant, and my nephew Udaxa will assume the duties of a second lieutenant.'

Topaz gasped. The legendary Olo'osso was going to captain the *Gull*? He glanced at the rest of the crew, who seemed as taken aback as he was, apart from Ryan, who was swaying, his attention distracted by a young woman who was handing out drinks from a tray.

Olo'osso turned to the dragon. 'My apologies for forcing you to listen to our trivial human concerns, my friend. I would be obliged if you addressed my daughters and the crew now. Tell them what you have to report.'

The dragon tilted his head. 'Thank you, Olo'osso of Befallen. Our alliance remains as strong as ever, and that pleases me greatly. It also pleases me to see four of your daughters here among us. The news I bear concerns the fifth sister, Atili'osso.'

'You've seen Tilly?' said Dina.

'I have,' said the dragon. 'Her vessel, the *Little Sneak*, was spotted by one of my kin yesterday evening, and I flew out this morning to confirm it. They were sailing for Luckenbay, and should be entering the Skerries this evening. However, all is not well. The vessel was limping along, battered and under-crewed. I counted the sailors on board, and deemed there to be less than half than is normally required for a ship of that size. Furthermore, the health of those remaining seemed poor. It is clear to me that Captain Tilly's ship and crew have both suffered greatly from their voyage. Worse, several Sea Banner vessels were also observed. They have been watching the approach of the *Little Sneak*, and I fear that they will attack this night, before the sloop has a chance to disappear among the Skerries. As you know, we dragons will defend any ship that makes it to Langbeg, but we cannot risk an attack so far from Skythorn. This is what I have come to tell you – if aid is to be given to the *Little Sneak*, it must come from the humans.'

'Thank you for your words, old friend,' said Olo'osso. 'I understand that you cannot attack the Sea Banner vessels so far from Langbeg, but might I ask if you or your kin would be prepared to carry one or two humans to my daughter's ship?'

'We can do this,' said the dragon.

'Excellent, thank you,' said Olo'osso. He glanced at his four daughters. 'What Atili needs now is a sensible hand to guide her in her moment of peril. Ani, will you go?'

Ann bowed her head. 'Of course, father.'

'Good girl. The *Little Sneak* has a decent master, but I imagine that he will be utterly exhausted by now. Therefore, I shall also send Master Oto to lend a hand. He is, as Alara never ceases to remind me, the best in the business.'

Topaz's mouth fell open.

'Be ready to leave in ten minutes, Ani and Oto. Redblade will carry you to the sloop, while the rest of us go back downstairs to enjoy the dancing.'

The crowd began to disperse. Vitz caught Topaz's eye for a moment, and the younger man shrugged.

'You alright?' said Lara.

'No. Are you?' said Topaz.

'I'm pissed off about losing the captaincy of the *Gull*, but at least I'll have a chance to show father what I can do. Make sure you don't get killed tonight, alright?'

She slapped him on the back and strode away towards the stairs.

Ryan staggered over to him.

'This is a great party, mate,' he slurred. 'You coming back downstairs? There are so many gorgeous women here that even you have a chance.'

Topaz stared at him. 'Did you not hear a word of what the dragon and Olo'osso said?'

'I wasn't really paying attention, to be honest. Was it important?'

'I have to go with Captain Ann...'

'You and Ann, eh?' Ryan said, grinning. 'Nice one, mate.'

Topaz sighed. 'Never mind. I'll see you in the morning, I hope.'

Ryan winked at him, then swayed, and headed for the stairs. Topaz glanced over towards the corner of the roof, and saw Olo'osso and Captain Ann speaking to the dragon. He tried to clear his mind, but it was still spinning from the keenweed and alcohol. He muttered a silent curse, and walked over to join them.

CHAPTER 17

LIMPING HOME

L uckenbay, Olkis, Western Rim – 30th Essinch 5254 (18th Gylean Year 5)

Maddie unfolded the large chart, and held it out for Tilly. The captain of the *Little Sneak* stared at it, her hands resting on the ship's wheel.

'There are an awful lot of rocks depicted on this chart,' said Maddie.

'Shut up; I'm trying to concentrate.'

'But the ship isn't moving.'

'I am aware of that, Miss Jackdaw. We'll be sailing as soon as it gets dark, if the Sea Banner don't find us lurking in this cove first; and then we'll be heading straight into Luckenbay.'

'What will happen if we hit any of these little rocks?'

'They're called Skerries, and we'll sink and drown. Shit. This is a bleeding nightmare.' She lowered her voice. 'Don't tell the crew, but I've never piloted a ship through Luckenbay.'

'Is that bad? Should I wake up the master?'

'The master's still sick from drinking that batch of bad water. He can't even stand up, never mind take the damn wheel. No, I'm the captain; it's my responsibility.'

'Can I help?'

'Yes. You can hold up that chart when it's time to leave, and you can keep your mouth shut. Whatever you do, don't distract me while I'm trying to guide us through the Skerries. One more night, Miss Jackdaw; we've just got to get through one more night. In the morning, we'll either be heroes, or we'll be dead.'

'Will I be a hero too?'

'Well, except for you. I'll be a damn hero; you'll still be a prisoner. Look, I'm sorry about dragging you half way across the world; you seem like a decent woman, apart from the fact that you talk too much, but when we get to Langbeg, your future will be out of my hands. My father will decide what's to be done with you.'

'Is Langbeg civilised?'

'Eh?'

'Is it a civilised place? Does it have nice houses, and shops, and hot water and baths, and comfy clothes? The refugee camp on Tunkatta was miserable and overcrowded – is it like that?'

'No, it's a proper town. It has all of those things you mentioned, along with about fifty taverns; not that you'll be seeing any of them. If we make it into harbour, I'll be sending you straight up the cliff to Befallen.'

'Is that the castle where your father lives?'

'Ah, so you do listen occasionally.'

'Be honest with me, Tilly – are my prospects good? How will your father treat me?'

'I don't know. I'm the one who's going to be in trouble. I mean, you can't go around kidnapping the riders of dragons, especially ones who also happen to be queens. Add to that the fact that I've lost half my crew, and I imagine that things might get ugly. My father will probably be very angry. Let me deal with his temper; try and look demure and helpless, and don't talk his ear off. You'll be all right; well, I hope so.'

'Those aren't very comforting words.'

'Just wait until he sees how much gold I've brought him; that will cheer the old bastard up. You may be a right hassle, Miss Jackdaw, but you were highly profitable.'

Maddie scowled. 'At least I'm good for something.'

'Put the chart away for now, but keep it somewhere safe, and close by.'

'Yes, Captain.'

Tilly smiled. 'It sounds weird, but I think I'm going to miss you, Miss Jackdaw. It's been grand to have another woman on board, even one who talks as much as you do.'

Maddie shrugged as she folded up the chart. 'I'm going to escape, Tilly; you should know that. If Blackrose can't get to me, then I'll have to go to her.'

'As long as you're no longer under my charge when it happens, then I couldn't give a shit.'

Tilly glanced out to sea. The cove where they were hiding from the Sea Banner was narrow, and high cliffs rose up on either side of the little sloop. At the end of the cove, the entrance to Luckenbay was visible in the fading daylight, while, above, the first stars were shining in the sky. Tilly rubbed her chin.

'Let's give it another hour,' she said. 'Come on; we'll make coffee.'

'I thought we'd run out.'

'I've been keeping a small tin of the stuff aside, for precisely this moment,' Tilly said. She winked. 'Another thing not to tell the rest of the crew.'

They were about to leave the quarter deck, when a shout came from the mast.

'Something is approaching from the south!'

Tilly's face drained of colour. She lifted her hands to her mouth. 'Sea Banner?'

'No, Captain,' the sailor shouted; 'a dragon.'

'Praise the gods,' said Tilly.

She ran down the steps onto the main deck, then hurried up to the bow, Maddie following. They reached the front of the ship, and stared out to sea. In the distance, a black speck was travelling towards them, keeping low over the surface of the water.

'Is it Blackrose?' said Maddie.

'I highly doubt it,' said Tilly. 'If we're in luck, they've come from Skythorn.'

'What's that?'

'It's a big dragon colony a few miles from Langbeg. The dragons there are allied to the folk in the town; we protect each other. You don't usually see one of them this far north, though; they tend to stick close to their lairs.' She squinted into the gloom. 'It looks like the dragon is carrying something.'

'Yes,' said Maddie; 'two people, I think; in their forelimbs.'

Tilly turned to a sailor. 'Launch the rowboat. Take it out in front of the *Little Sneak*; let's say about fifty yards or so. I think the dragon is bringing us someone.'

The weary-looking sailor saluted. 'Yes, ma'am.'

Tilly frowned as she watched the crew prepare the small rowing boat.

'Poor guys,' she muttered. 'Every single one of them is ill and exhausted. They'll be needing a long rest in Langbeg, but at least I have enough to pay them all.'

The dragon got closer. It soared up, and swooped over the sloop, as if looking for somewhere to deposit its human cargo. It seemed to realise what was happening with the rowing boat, and circled overhead as the small vessel was lowered over the side.

'It's Redblade,' said Tilly, peering upwards with a smile on her lips. 'Good lad.'

The dragon continued to circle as the rowing boat was steered along the cove. When it was far enough from the sloop, Redblade lowered his body until he was directly over the little boat, then he dropped the two humans. The sailors caught them, and the dragon soared away again, heading back towards the south.

'A man and a woman, I think,' said Maddie. 'Could they not have brought a dozen dragons and just lifted the *Little Sneak* out of the water and carried it to Langbeg?'

'You wouldn't say that if you knew how many dragons have been killed by death-powered gods in Olkis,' said Tilly. 'Even coming this far north was a risk. The gods here kill dragons on sight.' She glanced down as the rowing boat crossed back to the sloop. 'Holy shit; it's Ann.'

'Your sister? I've met her.'

'I know. What's she doing here? Does my father not trust me to navigate the *Little Sneak* on my own?'

'But you said that you'd never piloted a ship through Luckenbay before.'

'That's not the point! Damn him. If Ann thinks she's here to take over, then she has another thing coming.'

Tilly strode off towards the middle of the ship, where the rowing boat was being lifted by the sloop's crane. The two sailors stepped out of the vessel as soon as it landed on the main deck, then Captain Ann did the same, followed by a man, who was staggering as if drunk. Ann glanced around, then walked towards Tilly.

'What a mess,' said Ann. 'What in the names of the gods have you done to the *Little Sneak*, Tilly? And where's the rest of your crew?'

Tilly frowned. 'Nice to see you too, Ann.'

'I'm here to make sure we get this ship into Langbeg safely,' said Ann, 'we can exchange pleasantries later. How many sailors have you got left?'

'Forty-three.'

'Shit, Tilly – you lost over half of your people? What officers are remaining?'

'The purser and the sailmaker are around somewhere. That's about it. The master's alive, but he's sick in his hammock, along with about ten others.'

'Don't worry about that; father has sent you a replacement master to navigate us through Luckenbay.'

Tilly pointed at the drunk man, who looked as though he was about to throw up. 'Who, this guy?'

'This is Oto'pazzi, sister,' said Ann, 'though he prefers to be called Topaz. He might not look it, but he's a fine master. He works for Lara.'

'He's drunk.'

Ann nodded. 'It certainly appears so.'

Topaz glanced around, as if suddenly aware that he was being spoken about. He stared at Tilly, then his eyes roved over Maddie.

His mouth opened. 'Holy shit,' he slurred; 'who's that?' He blinked. 'She's beautiful.'

Ann glanced at Maddie, her eyes narrowing. 'I recognise you from somewhere. Have we met?'

'Yes,' said Maddie; 'in Seabound Palace, a couple of years ago.'

Ann's face went pale. 'No. You can't be. Not even Tilly is that stupid. Lara, maybe, but not Tilly.'

'I didn't know who she was when we set sail from Ulna, honest,' said Tilly. 'I would never have knowingly abducted a dragon rider.'

'She's Blackrose's rider, you bleeding idiot!' cried Ann. 'Oh, Tilly – what have you done?'

'I told you I didn't know!' Tilly shouted. 'I took the money, and we bolted. Was I supposed to take her back once I'd found out? Blackrose would have killed us all.'

'So, instead, you brought her home – to Langbeg? Father's head is going to explode. And what about me? I was due to sail to the Eastern Rim as soon as the winds change; I can't bleeding well go now, can I? Any Five Sisters ship that goes near Ulna will be incinerated.'

Tilly lowered her gaze. 'Sorry.'

'It's a little late for sorry, sister,' Ann went on. 'Holy, holy shit. Of all the stupid things to do, I never thought...'

'I got four thousand in gold for her.'

Ann paused, and glanced up at Tilly. 'Four thousand, eh? That might just save your ass. I advise you to lead with that fact when you next speak to father. Gold first, dragon rider second.'

'She's a dragon rider, eh?' said Topaz, then he threw up all over the deck. 'Oops.'

Maddie, Ann and Tilly watched him for a moment.

'I think our new master might require some strong coffee,' said Ann. 'You got any?'

'In my cabin,' said Tilly.

She led the way, and the others followed her up onto the quarter deck. She opened the door to her cabin, then held a hand up to bar Topaz from entering.

'Not you,' she said. 'I'm not having you dripping vomit all over my stuff. Get yourself cleaned up, and come back, then knock. Got it, sailor?'

Topaz nodded, then Tilly closed the door in his face.

'It's not his fault,' said Ann, as she sat at a round table. 'Father got everyone drunk at a party in Befallen, then announced that we were coming here to help you.'

'You seem sober enough,' said Maddie, as Tilly lit the stove and began to prepare a pot of coffee.

'I never drink in front of father,' said Ann. 'I don't want to risk saying something I'll regret. What was your name, girl?'

'Maddie Jackdaw.'

'That's right; the foreigner. You were Sable's friend, weren't you?'

'Yes.'

'Have you heard from her recently?'

'No. Have you?'

Ann shook her head. 'Nothing. Lara said that she thinks Sable might be dead, but it's just as likely that she's been lying low.'

'She was badly wounded in the battle for Seabound.'

'Was she? That might explain her silence.' She glanced at her sister. 'What's the plan?'

Tilly stirred some coffee into the pot. 'I was intending on pulling up the anchor and heading into Luckenbay as soon as it's dark.'

'Alright; we'll stick to that. The nearest Sea Banner vessels are over ten miles from here, so we should be able to slip past them.'

'It's the Skerries that I'm worried about.'

Ann nodded. 'Hang on. If the master's ill, then who was going to take the wheel? Is there a master's mate?'

'He got himself killed in Alef,' said Tilly. 'I was going to steer us through to Langbeg.'

Ann laughed. 'You? Holy shit, sister. No offence, but I'll take a drunken Topaz over you any day.'

'Piss off,' muttered Tilly. 'I've captained this ship all the way from Ulna, via Rigga and Alef; you can't speak to me like that.'

'You went to Rigga?'

'We had to, to avoid dragon patrols.'

'No wonder it's taken so long for you to get back. Rigga, eh? That took guts.'

'Yes, it did, so you can stop with the little digs at me. I realise that I'm not the best pilot around, but I was willing to take the wheel tonight. I still might, if Topaz is too drunk.'

A knock came at the cabin door.

'Enter,' yelled Tilly, and Topaz walked in, wearing a threadbare but clean set of clothes.

Maddie glanced at him. His eyes were bleary, and he looked exhausted as well as drunk.

'Take a seat,' said Tilly.

He fell into a chair. 'Can I smoke?'

Tilly nodded, then poured him a mug of black coffee. 'Drink this.'

'I don't know if my stomach can take it.'

'I don't give a shit,' said Tilly. 'Drink it.'

He fumbled in his pockets, and took out a battered packet of cigarettes. He tried to light one, but dropped the matches on the rug. Ann shook her head, and retrieved them for him, then struck a match and lit his cigarette.

He inhaled deeply.

'If you're going to be sick again,' said Tilly, as she sat down, 'run back out onto the quarter deck. If you do it in here, I'll beat you senseless.'

Maddie eyed the man. 'How much did you have to drink?'

He stared at her for a moment, until Maddie snapped her fingers under his nose.

He jumped. 'What?'

'I said, how much did you have to drink?'

'Oh. I can't remember. Some wine, I think, but it's all a bit hazy. I should never have smoked that keenweed, but I was so tired from piloting the *Giddy Gull* through Luckenbay last night, that I needed something to keep me awake.'

'You came this way last night?'

He nodded. 'Yup.' He slurped at his coffee. 'I have to do it again tonight, don't I?'

'Do you think you'll manage?'

'Yeah. I'll manage. The *Little Sneak* is much smaller than the *Gull* and has a shallower draft. If I wasn't feeling so rough, I'd even say that it'd be easy.' He glanced at Tilly. 'How is the ship? The sails alright? Everything still working? The rudder?'

'The sails have been patched up a dozen times,' said Tilly, 'but everything's in working order. The biggest problem is lack of crew. The lads have been toiling away on double shifts ever since Alef, and they're all completely knackered. I have them resting just now, so they can all be on duty tonight.'

Topaz nodded, then seemed to drift away for a moment. He blinked, and took another large gulp of coffee.

'You know what I need?' he said.

'A slap in the face?' said Tilly.

'I need someone who will talk to me all night. I have a guy on the *Gull* who does that for me. He brings me coffee and cigarettes, and keeps talking to me. It helps a lot.'

Tilly laughed. 'You need someone who will chatter to you for hours on end? I think I know someone who would be perfect.'

'Yeah, who?'

'Master Topaz,' she said, 'meet Maddie Jackdaw.'

Maddie walked out from Tilly's cabin, and closed the door quietly so she wouldn't wake up the dozing captain. Ann was standing on the dark quarter deck, her eyes peering out into the night sky, as Topaz steered the sloop through the Skerries. Maddie strode up to the wheel, and handed him his fifth mug of coffee.

He grunted. To Maddie's eyes, he looked as if he were about to topple over at any moment, but he had been standing by the wheel for eight straight hours. Every few minutes, a young sailor would sprint up onto the quarter deck, listen to Topaz's orders, and run away again to relay them to the exhausted crew. Adjust this, change that – it was all meaningless to Maddie, but, so far, the ship hadn't hit any of the rocks in Luckenbay.

'You were talking about your sister,' he said.

'So I was,' said Maddie. 'She was a cheeky little toerag while I was growing up, but she was always more clever than I was. She built her first ballista when she was fourteen, from spare parts she found on a rubbish dump; and then she used it to kill greenhides when they breached the walls. After that, she became friends with Corthie Holdfast, of all people...'

'Is he related to Sable?'

'Yes. He's her nephew, I think. I also met two more of that family – Karalyn, who wasn't very nice to me at all, and Kelsey, who was slightly less horrible, but still difficult to get along with. I knew Corthie when I was a soldier. I used to watch him going out beyond the walls to slaughter the greenhides; he always put on a good show. Sable's still my favourite Holdfast, though.'

'She messed up my head, more than once.'

'She has a habit of doing that.'

Ann turned, and pointed to their left. 'Sandbar ahead.'

'I see it,' said Topaz.

Ann smiled. 'If you get us to Langbeg in one piece, I might be forced to concede to Lara that you are the best master around.'

'Thank you, Captain Ann,' he said. 'Have someone ready to carry me off the ship when we dock, and then I'll need to sleep for a few days.'

'Understood, Master.'

'You seem to be quite popular,' said Maddie. 'Have you always been a pirate?'

'No,' he said. 'Captain Lara impressed me a couple of years ago.'

'She impressed you so much that you joined the pirates?'

Topaz grunted out a laugh. 'No. She impressed me; in other words, she forced me to join her ship. I had to swear an oath with a crossbow pointed at my head. Before that, I was in the Sea Banner.'

'Oh. You were lucky you weren't in Alg Bay when the big wave destroyed the fleet.'

'I owe Sable for that. If she hadn't made me sail towards Lara and Ann, I would have been in Alg Bay with the rest of the Sea Banner. Funny how stuff turns out.' He glanced at the young sailor who had been relaying his orders. 'We're through,' he said; 'we've passed the last of the Skerries. I want every yard of sail put up; let's see how much speed we can get from the *Little Sneak*.'

'Yes, sir,' said the boy, saluting.

'We're through?' said Ann.

'Yes, ma'am.'

He turned the wheel, and the ship started heading away from the glow on the eastern horizon. Ann slapped him on the back, and he slipped and fell onto the deck.

'Shit,' said Ann. 'Topaz, are you alright?'

The sound of heavy snoring rose up from the prone sailor. Ann gave him a gentle kick with a boot, but he carried on sleeping.

'Bollocks,' muttered Ann. 'I suppose I'd better take the wheel.'

Maddie helped her drag Topaz to the side, then Ann placed her hands onto the wheel.

She laughed. 'He did his job, though; you can't argue with that.'

Maddie regarded the woman. 'What's going to happen to me when we land?'

'That will be up to my father.'

Maddie frowned. 'That's what Tilly said.'

'It's true. He's the head of the Osso family. It'll be a tricky decision. In some ways, the easiest solution would be to kill you and then dump your body in the ocean, weighted, of course, so that you'd sink to the bottom. But, that would seriously displease the dragons who live on Skythorn. Redblade would have noticed your presence on board, and it will be impossible to keep your identity hidden from them for long. There are no easy answers.'

They sailed on for a further twenty minutes, and then the sun rose above the horizon, and Maddie smiled as she glanced around. To their left, she could see a castle on top of a ridge of high cliffs, and beyond that, a town with brightly-coloured houses. Ann handled the wheel with ease, and aimed the sloop towards the welcoming breakwaters by the large harbour.

Tilly came out from her cabin, and she did a double take when she saw her sister at the wheel.

'Who said you could pilot my ship?'

Ann smiled. 'What choice did I have? Check the state of Topaz.'

Tilly glanced down, and saw the unconscious sailor lying on the quarter deck. Maddie had placed a blanket over him, and he was snoring loudly.

'He toppled over as soon as we cleared the last Skerries,' said Ann.

'That's a bleeding relief,' said Tilly. 'For a moment, I thought that you'd done it.' She smirked at her sister. 'Take us in, Master Ann.'

'Don't push your luck, Tilly. I ain't your master.'

The sloop passed the breakwaters and entered the calm harbour basin. Ann shouted out a few orders to the crew, and the ship began to slow.

Tilly stared at a long, sleek vessel tied up by a pier. 'Holy crap. Is that...?'

'The *Giddy Gull*?' said Ann. 'It certainly is. It's quite something, isn't it?'

'It's... it's beautiful. Gods, I hate Lara sometimes.'

'Then, you'll find this funny,' said Ann. 'Father's removed her from command, and he's going to captain it, personally. He's made Lara his lieutenant.'

The two sisters roared with laughter, while Maddie listened, not really grasping what they were talking about.

'That's cheered me right up,' said Tilly, wiping a tear from her eye. 'Stay here. I'm going to speak to the crew. Time to tell them about their landing bonus.'

A few moments later, a great cheer rose up from the main deck, where Tilly had assembled what remained of her crew.

'I'm guessing Tilly has chosen to be generous,' said Ann, as she guided the sloop toward a space next to a pier. The craft bumped against the side, and the sailors got to work, tying ropes to either end, and pulling down the patched-up sails. A small crowd of locals had gathered on the pier, and were gazing down at the battered ship.

'Well, we made it,' said Tilly, striding back up onto the quarter deck. She glanced at Maddie. 'Now for the hard part. Let's pay father a visit.'

They loaded up a wagon with chests, then Maddie, Tilly and Ann climbed onto the back. Two sailors lifted the sleeping form of Topaz up, and laid him down by the women's feet. Tilly rested her boots on his stomach, then took them off again after Ann gave her a sharp glance.

The wagon got underway, and started climbing a road that led away from the town. Maddie stared at Langbeg, her curiosity piqued. The houses were shining in the clear sunlight, and she could see lots of people by the quayside. There was a fish market, and another selling fruit and vegetables, while a third had racks of clothes for sale. She looked down at her own clothes. They were falling apart, and she wished she could go back down the hill and buy something new to wear. At the top of the cliff, the wagon turned for the castle, and her nerves began to build. She had made no attempt to run away, even when they had passed through the crowd of onlookers by the pier. Where could she run to? She just had to hope that Olo'osso wasn't a savage.

The wagon stopped in front of a gatehouse. Ann jumped down and spoke to a few armed guards, and the gates were opened. The wagon pulled through, and came to a halt in a large, square courtyard, with three high towers. A middle-aged man was waiting for them by the entrance to the largest tower, along with three young women, one of whom Maddie recognised as Lara.

The man stepped down from the entrance, and Tilly ran to him. They embraced, and the man held her tightly for a moment, then kissed her on the forehead.

'Good work, my dear Ani,' the man called out to the wagon. 'Where is Oto of the Sea Banner?'

'He's unconscious, father,' said Ann.

Olo'osso's face went red with rage. 'How dare he? I'll have the little bastard strung up by his ankles...'

'Wait, father,' said Ann. 'He did his job to perfection; he guided us through Luckenbay. It was only once we were safe that he collapsed.'

'Oh. I see,' said Olo'osso, calming in an instant. 'In that case, I shall reward him.'

'I told you he was good,' said Lara, smirking.

Her father eyed the chests on the back of the wagon. 'And what have you brought me from your long voyage, little Atili?'

Tilly smiled. 'Gold, father. Four thousand sovereigns.'

Olo'osso's eyes nearly popped out of his head. Tilly strode over to the wagon, and opened one of the chests. 'This one contains a thousand, and there are three more like it.'

Her father and sisters gathered round, and Maddie watched as they each slapped Tilly on the back. Lara looked a little put out, then she noticed Maddie, who was still sitting on the back of the wagon.

'Hello,' said Maddie.

'Do I know you?' said Lara.

Olo'osso seemed to see Maddie for the first time. 'Who is this? A passenger?' He laughed. 'Are the Five Sisters taking passengers these days? She can't stay here, I'm afraid. She will...'

'She's not a passenger, father,' said Ann. 'Tilly, tell him.'

'Tell me what?' said Olo'osso.

'Oh, crap,' said Lara. 'I recognise her.' She started to laugh manically. 'Tilly, you're in deep shit now.'

'Would someone please tell me who this woman is?' cried Olo'osso.

Tilly's face flushed. 'Well, you see... she, um...'

Maddie stood up on the back on the wagon. 'My name is Maddie Jackdaw. The Unk Tannic stole me from my home, and gave Tilly four thousand gold sovereigns to carry me away.'

Olo'osso frowned. 'The Unk Tannic? But, why would they do that?'

'Because,' said Maddie, 'I'm Queen Blackrose's rider.'

CHAPTER 18

COMMITTED TO THE CAUSE

Na Sun Ka, Western Rim – 31st Essinch 5254 (18th Gylean Year 5)
Lava oozed out of the side of the mountain, its progress slow but inexorable. Clouds of grey smoke lingered over the rocky wasteland, obscuring the view of the rest of the island, while waves crashed against the base of the cliffs to the west. Sable looked out over the ocean. Somewhere, hundreds of miles away, was Gyle. If she used her vision, she would probably be able to see it, but chose to conserve her energy.

Next to her, Meader lit a cigarette and sat down on the black rocks, his back leaning against a jagged boulder. He placed the palm of a hand onto the ground, and closed his eyes.

'I can feel the volcano under us,' he said. 'All that molten rock, swirling about, wanting to burst free; the pressure building in cycles, ebbing and flowing... I wish you could feel it too.'

'I just want to get to Gyle,' she said.

'Staring out into the ocean isn't going to bring it any closer, Sable,' he said. 'We'll have to be patient for a little longer.'

Sable turned her glance towards the caves on their left. Blackrose's head was poking out of one entrance, but there was no sign of the other three dragons.

'It's not Badblood's fault,' Meader said.

'I know that,' she snapped. 'Back in the Catacombs on Lostwell, which reminds me of this place, I had to help him fly, twice, after he had sustained injuries. I know how he's feeling. It's partly my fault. I should have been encouraging him to do longer flights, but I had no idea that the journey here would nearly kill him. If only he'd practised.'

'The two Haurn dragons were in much the same state,' said Meader. 'Only Blackrose got through the journey without collapsing in exhaustion. Badblood is strong; he'll recover.'

'It was his decades in captivity that I blame. All those years of being chained up in the fighting pits of Alea Tanton, without ever being able to fly. I was stupid not to have realised how much that would have affected him. On the journey from Haurn to Ulna a couple of years ago, we were able to stop every few hours for a rest. What if he can't make it to Gyle? Blackrose estimated that it'll take a twelve hour flight, without a single rocky island along the way. Twelve hours, Meader. It was only seven hours from Haurn to Yearning, and then another seven hours from Yearning to Na Sun Ka. How is he supposed to manage twelve in one go?'

'We had barely an hour's rest on Yearning; the gods in the Sea Banner base saw to that. They would have killed us if we'd stayed any longer. So, really, it was a fourteen hour flight. Think of it that way. If he can manage fourteen hours, then he can manage twelve.'

The mountain rumbled behind them, and a plume of smoke rose up from its summit. A cascade of small rocks started to slide down the slope a hundred yards to their right. They rolled off the side of the cliff and plummeted down into the raging waves below.

'I hate this place,' muttered Sable.

'Na Sun Ka is a beautiful island; well, it is on the eastern side. Not so much out here. But, I do love a volcano.'

'So you've said.'

'For someone with stone powers, there's nothing else like it. To feel the molten rocks move beneath you – it's an amazing feeling.'

'I'm glad someone's happy.'

'Do you want a cigarette?'

Sable hesitated. She had been forced to give up tobacco months before, while injured on Haurn, but her nerves were strained, and maybe a cigarette would help.

She shook her head. 'I'll resist, thank you.'

'Suit yourself.'

'Pass me the water.'

Meader pulled the skin from over a shoulder, and handed it to her. She pulled out the stopper and took a long drink. The water was luke-warm, but it soothed her parched throat.

'It's just as well that Deepblue didn't attempt the flight,' said Meader. 'I wonder how Millen's doing.'

'Never mind Millen; where's your damn brother with the Quadrant? That's what would make the difference right now.'

'I'm sure Austin is doing the best he can.'

'Yeah, right. He's probably back in Implacatus right now, living it up in a damn palace. I should have gone back for the Quadrant; we were fools to trust him.'

'Hey! That's enough. Austin is a decent guy; he doesn't break his promises. I'm more worried that something bad has happened to him, and Ashfall. Anyway, that's immaterial to our current situation. We've come this far, and the only thing we can do now is press on.'

'There will be Quadrants in Gyle, yes?'

'There will be one. The only problem is that it'll be in the posses-sion of Lord Horace, and I hardly think he's going to be happy to let us borrow it. It'll be locked up somewhere inside the Winter Palace in Port Edmond. If we already had a Quadrant, it might be easy to steal it, but without one, we have no chance.'

Sable felt like screaming, her frustration feeling like shackles weighing her down.

'I'm going to see Blackrose,' she said; 'see if there's any progress.'

'Fine. I'll stay here. I already know what she's going to say.'

Sable turned away, and trudged down the steep path towards the caves. It was a dangerous route that wound by the edge of a sheer precipice, with nothing but the waves crashing against the rocks down to her right. One slip, and she would be sent over the side, to drown in the dark waters of the ocean. She reached the entrance to the first cave, and Blackrose turned to regard her.

'I hope you aren't here to ask if we are ready to leave, witch,' the black dragon said. 'If you are, then my answer remains the same.'

Sable slumped down, and sat a few yards from Blackrose's head.

'You must be patient,' said the black dragon. 'Badblood requires more time to rest.'

'Maybe I should speak to him.'

'No. I forbid it. He needs to sleep. I know that he is your dragon, and that you love him, but waking him up will not help. I, too, long to be on our way; do not forget this. I understand the frustration you are feeling.'

'We should have practised.'

'I know, but it is too late for that. The young dragon that Evensward brought along is barely better off than Badblood. He also should have practised long-distance flying before we set off from Haurn. The truth is, we all thought that we would be able to rest for longer on Yearning. None of us appreciated how difficult it would be to find shelter on that island. It is not as I remember it once was – the entire island is now one large Sea Banner base. When we rescue Maddie, we shall burn Yearning on our way back.'

'If I had a Quadrant, I could do it now.'

'Indeed, but we don't, witch. Go for a walk, or take a nap; occupy yourself in some way, for we shall be here for a while longer.'

'Give me your best estimate.'

Blackrose tilted her head. 'Four more days.'

'You've got to be joking.'

'Do I have a reputation for making jokes? Once Badblood has recovered, he will need to eat his whole body-weight in food, to have the strength for the next stage.'

'You could do it now though, couldn't you? You could fly to Gyle today if you wanted to.'

'Yes. I am stronger than the others. There are very few dragons as mighty as I am.'

'But you spent twenty years in captivity.'

'I am aware of that. My wings were in a terrible condition when Maddie first helped me fly again, and my muscles had almost wasted away. Those days are long gone, however, and I am back to my peak. I am probably the greatest dragon on this, or any other world. Now, off with you, Sable, and leave me in peace.'

Sable pulled herself to her feet, and went back up the path. Meader was where she had left him, pressing his palms onto the ground with his eyes closed, and she crept round him and continued along the path. She veered inland, and walked up over a large, barren spur of rock. Ahead of her, she could see a whole complex of volcanoes. Rivers of slow-moving lava were seeping out from the sides of several mountains, and the summits were hidden in wreaths of smoke. She still had the water skin, so she decided to take a walk down the valley to the spring where they collected fresh water. It would only take a couple of hours, but it was better than sitting next to Meader and listening to him talk about how wonderful it was to sense molten rock with his powers.

She set off down into a valley between two volcanic peaks, her boots crunching on the soft, grey rock. Ash was billowing around, and she narrowed her eyes as she made her way down the slope. The location made her think of the Catacombs, and the time she had spent there. The smell was similar, as well as the heat, and the choking clouds of vapours and smoke. On Lostwell, the Catacombs were taken as a sign of the decay and lingering death of that world, whereas, on Dragon Eyre, the volcanoes were seen as harbingers of new life. Blackrose had told her that many of the archipelagos had been formed by volcanoes, and that new islands would suddenly appear in the aftermath of massive eruptions at sea. They also made the soil fertile, and were responsible for the forests that covered most island chains.

The sound of the ocean faded away as she walked along the floor of the valley. There was no wind, and the air was stifling. She carried on for an hour, making for the place where the spring was located, and was so wrapped up in her thoughts, that she almost didn't notice the three men ahead of her, walking in the same direction.

She froze. What were they doing in the middle of a volcanic wasteland? She ducked behind a rock, and watched the three men for a moment. They were armed, and dressed in grey clothing that camouflaged them against the background. They passed out of sight, and she followed them, keeping her footsteps silent as she crept along. They came back into view by the spring. Sable hid in the shadows, and observed them crouching by the fresh water gushing from the side of a cliff. They drank, then began filling a multitude of skins that they had been carrying.

She went into one of their minds, and had a look around.

Unk Tannic rebels. They were operating from a series of hidden tunnels carved out of a mountain, a few miles to the east of the coast. Sable hesitated. She loathed the Unk Tannic, but weren't they fighting against the same enemy as she was? Besides, she was bored with waiting for the dragons to recover. She stepped out of the shadows and approached them.

She was only a few yards away when one of them noticed her. He grabbed his crossbow and aimed it at her, while his two companions turned.

'Good morning,' she said.

'Keep your hands away from the sword,' said the one pointing the crossbow at her.

She lifted her cloak to show that the scabbard was empty. 'I don't have one,' she said. 'I lost it in the ocean. Do you have one I could buy?'

The three men glanced at each other.

'Are you out here on your own?' said one.

'Do you see anyone with me?'

'You're coming with us, little lady,' said the first.

'Where? To buy a sword?'

The men laughed. 'Our camp could do with a woman; someone to cook and clean, and look after the lads.'

'No, thanks.'

'It wasn't a request,' said another one, standing. 'How did you get here?'

'I walked.'

'Past the guard pickets? I don't think so.'

'You have a sword,' she said. 'Can I have it?'

One of the men threw a coil of rope to the others. 'Tie her hands.'

'If you touch me, you will regret it,' she said. 'Give me your sword, and I'll allow you all to walk away.'

'You're an unarmed woman wandering about on her own. How exactly do you plan on over-powering us?'

She glanced at one. *Sleep.*

The man toppled over onto the ground, his eyes closed.

'Like that, I guess,' she said.

The two others stared at her.

'She's a god!' cried one, pulling his crossbow over his shoulder.

Sleep.

He fell before his fingers could reach the trigger of the crossbow, and crashed to the rocky ground.

'Just you and me left,' she said to the last one. 'Now, how about that sword?'

'You Implacatus bitch!' he cried. 'I'm not scared of you.'

'I'm not from Implacatus, and I'm not a god. It's an easy mistake to make, though. Pass me a sword, and I'll tell you my name.'

Drop your crossbow and throw me a sword. Now.

The man's eyes went hazy for a second, then he let go of his crossbow as if it were on fire. He unbuckled his belt, and threw the sword and scabbard at her feet.

'Excellent. Alright, my name is Sable Holdfast. I want you to start spreading the rumour that I'm back. Tell the rest of the Unk Tannic, and any Banner soldiers that you come across. It's been a while since they would have heard my name, and I want them to fear me again. Got it?'

The man nodded.

Sleep.

The last man fell forwards, and collapsed in front of her. She stepped over him, and crouched by the spring. She plunged her hands into the water, then splashed the dust and ash from her face. She frowned, wondering if she should kill the men and hide their bodies. If the Unk Tannic rebels were in the habit of using that particular spring, then there was a good chance they would meet again, especially if the dragons needed another four days to regain their fitness. She glanced at the three unconscious men as she filled her water skin. When they awoke, they would most likely run back to their base, and report what had happened. Then, they might send out patrols to look for her, and they might discover Badblood and the other dragons.

She considered wiping their memories, but her ego objected. She wanted the men to pass her name around; she wanted them to know who had done it. It was a risk, though, and she knew that Blackrose would be angry if she discovered what she had done. She sighed; she needed to wipe their minds. That way, the three men would remember nothing, and wonder how they had lost a sword.

Sable frowned, then entered the mind of the nearest rebel. She found his recent memories, then looked back a little further, seeing images from their life in the underground base where they lived. The rebels were holding a handful of Banner soldiers prisoner, who were being kept in horrendous conditions – chained, beaten and starved in an airless and lightless pit in the ground. She searched back further, and saw the rebels plan the bombing of a tavern where Sea Banner personnel drank. They had used a young woman to carry the explosives into the tavern, somehow managing to persuade her to give her own life for the cause. Then she saw the rebels celebrating afterwards, cheering and laughing at their achievement. Over fifty sailors had been blown to pieces, along with the young woman, and a dozen staff who had worked in the tavern.

Were these monsters her allies? A nauseous feeling of guilt surfaced within her. Hadn't she also planned suicide killings? Hadn't she sent naive young Army of Pyre volunteers into markets in Plateau City, with orders to kill everyone in sight until they themselves were cut down? If she had been able to possess explosives on her home world, wouldn't she have leapt at the chance to blow up places where the imperial soldiers congregated? Of course she would have. That had been her job. So sure was she in the righteousness of her cause, that she would have stooped to the lowest level to achieve her aims. The Unk Tannic were monsters, but they were the same as she had once been.

But, she had changed, hadn't she? And not just because her cause had collapsed into lies and deceit. When she had discovered the truth about the Creator, that he wasn't any kind of real god, but that he was merely a highly-powered man with an extended lifespan, her entire life had seemed ruined beyond repair. Yet, the Holdfasts had given her another chance. First Kelsey, who had stood up for her in front of the Empress, then Daphne, who had spared her life. Even Karalyn, who had more reason to hate Sable than most, had taken pity on her and dragged her along to Lostwell to see if she could be redeemed.

It was a debt that bore down upon her shoulders. Would she ever be able to repay her newfound family for what they had done for her? No. She was cut off from them, on another world, and she would probably never see any of them again. But that didn't mean she couldn't strive to be better, not just for their sake, but for her own. Helping to rescue Maddie was all very well, but there was so much more that she could do. She could fight for the people of Dragon Eyre; all of the people, to free them from the occupying forces, the Unk Tannic, and even from the oppression of the dragons. She stared at the three men. The Unk Tannic weren't her allies, they were her enemies, just as the Banner soldiers were, and she would start to treat them as such.

She leaned over, and grabbed the first rebel by his collar, then dragged him towards the pool next to the spring. She glanced at his face, then she pushed his head under the surface of the pool, a hand gripping the back of his brown hair. He didn't struggle. Her sleep spell had rendered him completely unconscious, and she was pleased that he didn't suffer as his lungs filled with water. She marvelled at how easy she found it to take another's life. Just another one to the list. When he was dead, she dragged the other two men over to the pool, and drowned them both at the same time, keeping a hand on each head to make sure their faces remained submerged. Kelsey and Karalyn would probably be sickened if they could see what she was doing, but she had a feeling that Daphne would approve of the concept of removing three sadistic bastards from the world.

She rifled their pockets once all three had drowned, but found nothing of any value. One of the men had a battered old prayer book lodged in his tunic, and she flicked through its yellowed pages briefly before putting it back. They had a few coins, which she pocketed, and she selected the best-looking sword out of the three on offer, and strapped it to her waist.

It took the best part of an hour to carry the three bodies up a slope to where she could drop them into a fiery pit of lava. The vapours and intense heat made her sweat, and she slipped on the loose rocks several times, skinning a knee in the process. When she had hauled each one to the top of the ridge, she rolled them off, and they plunged down into the red-hot mass of molten rock, their bodies swallowed up in seconds, their clothes and hair bursting into flames as they sank into the pit. She then returned to the pool, and cleaned away any sign that the three men had ever been there, disposing of the water skins in the lava pit, and sweeping away the footprints.

The Unk Tannic rebels in the nearby base would have a little mystery to solve, she thought, as she stood and admired her patient handiwork. They would search and search, but they would never discover what had happened to the three men sent out to get water. Part of her wanted to go to the base, and kill everyone hiding within the tunnels, but that would attract too much attention to their little corner of Na Sun Ka. Perhaps once Maddie was safely back with Blackrose, then Sable could launch her own deadly offensive on behalf of the downtrodden masses of Dragon Eyre.

She shouldered her water skin, and set off back towards the coast. It was after noon by the time she got back to the cliffs where Meader was still sitting, a cigarette hanging from his lips. She threw the water skin at him, and he caught it.

'Nice walk?' he said.

She shrugged. 'Fine.'

She sat down next to him as he drank.

He glanced at the blood on her knee. 'You fall over or something?'

'Yeah, I slipped on some rocks. Clumsy.'

He chuckled. 'You need to be more careful. You feeble mortals are always hurting yourselves. If you'd broken your leg, or even twisted your ankle, then we'd be screwed.'

She gazed out at the ocean. 'I'll try to be more careful.'

He offered her a cigarette, but she shook her head.

'Meader,' she said, 'once we rescue Maddie, what are we going to do next?'

'I don't know. To be honest, I still think it's unlikely that we'll make it as far as Olkis. Even if the dragons are fully revived, they'll be utterly exhausted again when we arrive in Gyle, and we'll need to hide there for a while until they recover.'

'Forget all that for a moment,' she said. 'That's not what I was getting at. What are your aims? You say that you want to be a part of a rebellion against the ruling gods, but what does that mean?'

'I see. Well, if I had my way, I'd tell you to stay on Gyle, and make a start from there. We could free thousands of slaves, and lead them in an uprising against the Banner forces. You and I could take care of the gods, and the dragons could attack the Sea Banner ships. Gyle depends on slave labour; without it, the settler economy would collapse. Of course, to be successful, we would have to prevent the opening of a portal, to stop thousands of reinforcements arriving. That means stealing the Quadrant from Horace.'

She smiled. 'I thought you said that would be futile?'

'That was when we were discussing the rescue of Maddie. If Maddie is our objective, then any attempt to get our hands on the Quadrant would only hinder us. However, if you're talking about a full-scale rebellion, then that's where I'd start.'

'Alright. So, once we've rescued Maddie, we can go back to Gyle, and put our scheme into action.'

'Are you serious? What about your plans to go back to Haurn and live in peace? Have you changed your mind?'

'How can I live in peace, when there's so much suffering? All over Dragon Eyre, innocent men, women and children are living in misery, because of the gods, and the Banner soldiers, and the Unk Tannic.'

'I know, Sable. This is exactly what I've been trying to tell you. You are the most powerful mortal on Dragon Eyre; it's your duty to help those unable to defend themselves.'

'And we'll kill them all, yeah? Every last Banner soldier, and every single member of the Unk Tannic?'

'And every god; don't forget them.'

'*Every* god?'

He laughed. 'Alright; not me or Austin. Every bad god.'

She frowned at his logic. 'Let's do it. As soon as Maddie's safe, let's go on a rampage.'

'What made you change your mind?'

She shrugged. 'I had a chance to think on my little walk.' She leaned back against the cliff. 'Tell me more about how the molten rock feels. We still have three and a half days to get through.'

CHAPTER 19

PEELING AWAY THE LAYERS

Desert Wasteland – 3rd Beldinch 5255

Austin staggered through the sandstorm, his eyes almost closed as he focussed on keeping his legs moving. He was weakening, and he knew it. His self-healing was barely able to keep up with the punishment his body was undergoing, and no food or water had passed his lips in twelve days, ever since the Quadrant had transported him to the midst of the wasteland in which he found himself.

It was daytime, or so he presumed. Night and day had lost most of their meaning to him, as the dense clouds of dust and sand blotted out the light. A dull glow was present, but there was no sign of the sun. His feet were blistered and aching, and the rash on his skin was getting worse.

He was the son of an Ancient, he told himself, trying to bolster his diminishing resolve. Sons of Ancients did not give up; they endured. He tried to imagine that his father was watching him, and silently urging him onwards. He couldn't falter, not after having suffered for twelve days. There had to be an end to the desert, and he would find it.

He stumbled into a giant rock, and nearly fell over. He lifted his rash-covered hands to the face of the stone, and began to feel his way along. It wasn't a rock, he realised; it was the side of a solid cliff-face that stood directly in his path. A sharp edge of stone cut the flesh on his left hand and he cursed as the pain bit. What would have been a trivial injury, insignificant, even, on Dragon Eyre was transformed in the wastes into a source of agony, as his self-healing struggled to deal with this latest setback. He watched as the blistered skin tried to repair itself, and felt a wave of exhaustion ripple over him. He needed to find somewhere to shelter – anywhere out of the incessant, howling winds.

He tore a strip of cloth from his tunic and wrapped it round his left hand, then carried on, following the side of the cliff. For another hour, he trudged on, perhaps travelling a mile, maybe less, but there was no end to the cliff. He kept his bandaged left hand on the rocks as he struggled forwards, then his hand felt nothing, and he fell into a dark opening in the rockface, his knees cracking against some jagged stones. He grimaced as he lay on the ground, then noticed that the opening stretched away into a dark cave.

Shelter, he thought, his spirits lifting a little. He got onto his hands and knees and crawled ten yards into the cave, the wind dying down. He raised his hand, but could see nothing but darkness ahead of him. If he could manage to go a little further, then he would be out of the wind completely, and then he would be able to rest for a while. Slowly, carefully, he inched his way deeper into the cave. The ceiling grew lower, and the sides narrower, then the cave turned to the right. He pulled his exhausted body round the corner, and collapsed. For the first time in twelve days, there was no wind battering against him, and he fell asleep as soon as he closed his eyes.

When he awoke, he had no idea how much time had passed. He peered round the corner, and saw a dull glow at the end of the cave where he had entered, so he reckoned it must still be daytime. He pulled his head back out of the wind and sat up, leaning against the wall of the cave.

He tried to think over his options, but it was hard to drive the thirst he felt from his mind, or the pain coming from the rash that now covered his entire body. The skin on his hands was red and angry-looking, and was bleeding from dozens of tiny cuts and sores. He wondered what his face looked like. He touched his hair, and some of it came away in his hands, and the sight made him want to weep. Some of his teeth were loose, and his tongue had swollen and cracked. Was he dying? It seemed like a ludicrous suggestion, but the signs were undeniable. Slowly, piece by piece, his body was breaking down. How could that be possible? He wondered how long a mortal would survive in the wasteland, if a demigod had been reduced to such a condition in a dozen days.

Keep going, he imagined his father saying to him. Don't give up. He glanced into the darkness to his right, where the cave continued. Maybe there would be water somewhere, deep within an underground cavern. Anything would be better than going back out into the wind. He took a breath of the foul air, then began crawling deeper into the cave. The noise coming from the wind outside began to fade into the background, then disappeared as he made his way further into the side of the cliff. At one point, he had to squeeze his body between the rocks as the cave narrowed, but it opened out on the other side, and he could feel nothing on his left or right. In pitch darkness, he crawled forwards, then his hands went over a void, and he tumbled through the air, falling. He raised his arms to protect his face, then landed with a crash onto something solid.

He groaned, and rolled onto his back. For a moment, he wasn't sure if his eyes were open or not, such was the darkness surrounding him. He needed a source of light. There could be other holes and voids close by, and he could easily fall again if he couldn't see where he was going. He patted down his pockets, but they had been emptied by Unk Tannic guards when he had been arrested with Ashfall in Udall. All he had were the clothes he was wearing, and the Quadrant.

The Quadrant.

The memory of a lesson he had received at school came back to him, and he pulled the Quadrant out from under his clothes. The surface seemed sticky, and he realised that it had been spattered in blood from the rash covering his chest. He concentrated, trying to remember what their teacher had told them. It had been after he had demonstrated the device's two most basic functions, and had been presented to the class as a mere afterthought; a silly party trick. He found one of the jewels embedded into the rim of the Quadrant, and pressed his thumb against it. Nothing happened. He felt for the jewel at the corner of the device, and tried there. At once, a dim glow came from the other four jewels. It was nothing special, but in the pitch darkness of the cavern, it seemed to Austin like a minor miracle.

He held the Quadrant up, and glanced around. The light it gave off was weak, and coloured in the hues of the various jewels, but he saw enough to ensure that he wasn't about to fall through another crack in the ground. He looked up, but the light didn't extend to the cave he had fallen from, and the ceiling of the cavern was lost in the gloom. He turned his gaze to the ground, and saw that it was fairly level. A few boulders were scattered around, and everything was coated in a layer of sand. Austin stood, and grunted from the pain. His skin had worsened in the fall, and the backs of his hands were bleeding again. Shining the dim light around, he became aware of a few shadowy shapes in the distance. He set off towards one, and realised that it wasn't a shape, it was a doorway, complete with an arch at the top. Was he inside some ancient building, long buried by the sandstorms? If so, then perhaps the cliff he had stumbled into was actually the remains of a wall.

He limped through the entrance, and soon became lost in the gloom. He shone the Quadrant around, but could see nothing apart from the ground. He coughed up some blood, and noticed the sound echo off a wall. He was in a vast space, a hall, maybe. After a few more faltering steps, he saw another shadowy shape ahead of him. Getting closer, it looked like an enormous, square chunk of masonry, made of yellow granite. On top of it was something else, and as he approached, he could make out a pair of colossal sandaled feet carved from marble, with ankles that disappeared into the gloom above him. It was a statue, and the huge block, its pedestal. On the pedestal, some words had been inscribed, and his heart raced with excitement.

Lifting the Quadrant high above his head, he limped forwards, until he was close enough to read the inscription.

Lord Simon – the Blessed and Holy Tenth Ascendant – Lord of the Plains – Praise be to His Name

Austin sunk to his knees. How was this possible? Lord Simon had disappeared over four millennia before, but Austin had been taught that, thousands of years prior to his disappearance, the Tenth Ascendant had once ruled a gargantuan city on the plains a hundred miles from the mountain that later became Serene.

He bowed his head and wept. He was on Implacatus. He was home, and it was a desolate wasteland. Was this the reason why no one ever left the safety of the mountain tops; why no one ever descended the slopes down from Serene or Cumulus? The teachers at school had lied to him; they had lied to everyone in his class. They had told them that the plains were fertile and teeming with happy mortals, who tilled the fields and worshipped the Ascendants. He wondered how many gods knew the truth. Every Ascendant and Ancient possessed vision powers; they would be able to see through the thick clouds that always surrounded the lower slopes of Serene – so too would any god or demigod with the same powers. Were they all sworn to secrecy? No one in his class had vision powers, and he had often wondered why. Now, he knew.

It was over. He would never be able to walk as far as the base of the mountain, let alone scale its heights all the way to Serene. He was barely able to stand, and would surely collapse from thirst and exhaustion long before he could reach the city of the gods. He glanced at the Quadrant. It was covered in little bloody smudges from his wrecked hands. He stared at the low light coming from the jewels. If only he knew how to operate the device properly, he could go to Serene, and then commence the search for his mother. Instead, he was going to have to return to Dragon Eyre.

It was several hours before he could summon the courage to do what was needed. He had toyed with the idea of randomly swiping his bloody fingers over the surface of the device, but that would probably result in his immediate death. His teachers at school had drummed into them never to do that. The chances were that he would appear inside the heart of a mountain, or deep under the waves of an ocean, or somewhere else equally inhospitable.

For the rest of the time, he had sat in silence, staring at the enormous statue of Lord Simon, the creator of Dragon Eyre. He wondered if the Quadrant had once been owned by the Tenth Ascendant. The legend of his disappearance told of an accident that had occurred while he was trying to flee from the wrath of Lord Edmond, the Second Ascendant. Simon had vanished, but his Quadrant had been left behind. If the Quadrant in Austin's hands had once been Simon's, then that would explain why the device had taken him to the middle of a desert. The desert had once been Simon's city, a shining metropolis from a long ago era of Implacatus, now reduced to a vast, arid wasteland.

His fingers hovered over the device, then he took a breath and triggered the Quadrant. The air around him wavered, and he found himself sitting on the floor of Ata'nix's bedroom. The room was empty, but sound and light were seeping under the doorway leading to the sitting room. Though he was still in considerable pain, he felt his self-healing start to recover a little, and his breathing eased. Austin tried to pull himself to his feet, but his legs gave way, and he fell onto the bed, then rolled off it onto the floor with a thud. The sounds from the next room quietened.

Austin raised one bloody hand, but his flow powers had diminished to such an extent that he could barely feel them. The door burst open, and two men with crossbows charged in. Behind them, Austin could see Ata'nix standing, his guards surrounding him. In the light from the doorway, the two men stared at Austin, and one of them gagged in disgust.

'By the sacred spirits,' the other one gasped; 'look at him.'

Ata'nix approached, still shielded by several guards.

'This proves what I have said all along,' the leader of the Unk

Tannic said, 'the gods of Implacatus are not real gods. Under their young-looking skin lies the soul of a demon! A foul, decayed beast. Shoot him, then restrain him, but do not kill him. I want him to be displayed to the people of Udall.'

One of the guards loosed his bow, and a bolt struck Austin's chest. He cried out in agony, and slumped to the floor. His arms were yanked behind his back, and the heavy gauntlets were strapped onto his bloody hands, the metal scraping off more of his loose and peeling skin.

'Take him up to the audience chamber,' said Ata'nix. 'Let us show this demon to Lord Splendoursun and the other blessed dragons.'

'Yes, sir,' said a guard, and Austin was hauled up to his feet, his head lolling.

Ata'nix stared at him, his face twisted with loathing and disgust, then he reached down and snatched the Quadrant from where it lay on the floor. He walked from his rooms, and the guards followed, with two holding on to Austin's arms. Austin didn't try to resist. His energy and strength were utterly spent, and his spirits as low as they had ever been. Once his rotten flesh had been shown to the humans and dragons of Ulna, the Unk Tannic would probably put him out of his misery, but he no longer cared. What he had seen on Implacatus was burned into his mind; everything else seemed trivial.

The guards dragged him up the steps to the huge caverns and hall-ways that sat above the human areas of the bridge palace, and they entered a great hall, with Ata'nix leading the way. Sunlight was shining down through the apertures in the ceiling, and the glare hurt Austin's eyes.

'My humble apologies for interrupting your meeting, most gracious dragons,' Ata'nix said, bowing low.

The dragons turned their necks to look down at the group of humans.

'I hope this is important, Ata'nix,' said Splendoursun. 'We were in the middle of an urgent discussion.'

The Unk Tannic leader gestured to the guards, and they pulled

Austin forward, then threw him onto the ground in front of the dragons.

Splendoursun backed away a little, his head tilted. 'What is this disgusting creature?'

'It is the demigod who escaped twelve days ago, my most noble lord,' said Ata'nix.

'How can that be?' said the gold and white dragon. 'His face looks like it is rotting; as if the skin has fallen off.'

'Now we can see their true nature, my noble lord,' Ata'nix went on. 'Behold; this is what a god of Implacatus looks like, with their false flesh laid bare. They are demons, just as our religion has always stated.' He reached within his black robes, and held up the bloody Quadrant. 'We have also recovered the device he used to flee.'

'Destroy it!' cried Splendoursun.

Ata'nix hesitated. 'My lord?'

'That... thing is pure evil,' said Splendoursun. 'Its sole purpose is to allow our enemies to travel to Dragon Eyre. If none existed, then our world would be free at last. Is that not correct?'

'You... you speak the truth, my lord; however, I recommend that...'

'Destroy it at once,' Splendoursun cried. 'I will not tell you again, Ata'nix. Break it in two; that is an order.'

The dragons stared at Ata'nix, waiting for him to comply. The Unk Tannic leader gazed at the Quadrant in his hands for a moment, as a mixture of emotions passed over his features, then he laid the Quadrant down at an angle, with one part resting against the edge of the stone platform where the dragons were standing. He swallowed, then he stamped down onto it with the heel of his boot, cracking the Quadrant down the middle. He brought his boot down again, and the Quadrant broke apart. He leaned over, picked up the pieces, and then raised them so that the dragons could see.

'Thank you, Ata'nix,' said Splendoursun. 'Now, no gods or Banner soldiers will be able to use it to travel here; we are one step closer to safety.'

'Indeed, my lord,' said Ata'nix, his voice low.

'Now, tell me – what do you intend to do with the ruined body of this demigod?'

'I want to hang him in a cage, my lord,' said Ata'nix, 'for the people of Udall to see him. To show them what the false gods of Implacatus are really like. Many of the humans fear these false gods, and I want them to take heart from witnessing one in his condition.'

'Do so,' said Splendoursun. 'But, before you go, I shall tell you the news that my inner council and I were discussing before you entered the hall.'

'I would be honoured, my lord.'

'The news is not good, Ata'nix. We have discovered where the traitor Shadowblaze has gone, and he is not alone. As if freeing this demigod was not bad enough, the fool has decided to openly declare his opposition to our legitimate rule here in Udall, and he has gathered a band of other disaffected and feeble-minded dragons, including several failed suitors.'

'Where is he, my lord?'

'My scouts have seen him in Seabound Palace. They tried to approach, but Shadowblaze and his pathetic minions drove them away. Moreover, the Queen's uncle was also seen in the traitor's company.'

Ata'nix blinked. 'Lord Greysteel is with Shadowblaze in Seabound, my lord?'

'He is. Clearly, neither of them understands the laws of Ulna. As the sole remaining suitor, I am the only true and lawful source of authority in Ulna, as long as the Queen herself is not present. Therefore, I have declared both Shadowblaze and Greysteel to be traitors, who must be killed on sight.'

'How many dragons have they assembled, my lord?'

'Several dozen, it seems. However, they will be no match for my kinfolk from Gyle. I intend to crush this show of defiance, and annihilate the dragons and humans who prefer the company of traitors. Your Unk Tannic soldiers will be involved in the assault we are planning; I shall need them to root out the humans skulking in places where dragons cannot reach.'

'Of course, my lord. My men are at your service. Upon which day is the attack planned?'

'It will be soon. It is imperative that the resistance is dealt with before I am formally anointed as the Queen's mate, in twenty-one days' time. Gather your forces, and ready them for battle.'

Ata'nix bowed. 'As you will, my blessed lord.'

'Leave us,' said Splendoursun, 'and be sure to take that foul creature with you.'

Two guards stepped forwards, and hauled Austin up by his shoulders, leaving a bloody mark on the ground where he had been lying. The Unk Tannic bowed their heads towards the dragons, then they turned and left the chamber.

Once they were out in a vast hallway, Ata'nix turned to his men. 'Take the demigod down to the town. There is a cage by the harbour, designed to hold captured pirates that would be a suitable location for him. Ensure the gauntlets are securely fastened, and lock him inside. Then hoist the cage up and hang it from the crane that sits by the quayside. I want at least four men to stand guard there at all times. If he expires from his injuries, leave him there to rot; but, if he shows any signs of recovering, inform me immediately. I shall leave you now, to begin planning the capture of Seabound from the traitors.'

'Is he to receive food or water, sir?' said one of the guards.

'No. Allow the locals to throw stones at him if they so desire, but no sustenance must reach him. If anyone displays overt signs of sympathy for his plight, arrest them.'

'Yes, sir.'

Ata'nix turned, and strode away.

'You heard him,' said one of the guards. 'Let's go.'

A crowd had gathered by the base of the crane to watch, as Austin was placed inside the steel-framed cage. It was large enough for the demigod to stand up in, but his legs were too weak to try, so he lay on the bars of the floor of the cage, curled up into a ball. The flicker he had felt from his self-healing when he had returned from Implacatus was fading again, over-powered by the injuries he had sustained. The guards had not been gentle with him, and had kicked and punched him over and over on the way from the palace to the harbour, their boots and fists smeared with blood.

The gauntlets had been double-checked, and then the guards had bound them together behind Austin's back, twisting his arms until the demigod had screamed.

Some in the crowd laughed when the Unk Tannic told them who they were placing inside the cage, but many stood around with grim expressions on their faces, and several parents shielded their children's eyes from the sight of Austin. One older woman had started weeping when Austin had cried out in pain, only to be mocked by the Unk Tannic guards and chased away from the quayside. Once Austin's gauntlets had been bound, the cage door was closed and locked, and then the harbour crane's hook was attached to the top of the steel frame. The cage jerked as it was raised into the air, and Austin looked down at the upturned faces lining the quay.

Despite the pain, Austin felt as though it was all happening to someone else. He had already forgotten much of what Ata'nix and Splendoursun had been discussing in the palace, his mind unable to rid itself of what he had witnessed on Implacatus. He wished he could see Meader one last time before he died, so that he could tell him that he had finally solved the mystery that his brother had been obsessing about. Austin knew the dirty secret of Implacatus, and it was now obvious to him why the Ascendants wanted Dragon Eyre for themselves. They had ruined their own world, and needed another. That was why they had refrained from utterly destroying Dragon Eyre, for what use would yet another desolate wasteland be to them? They craved the beauty and clean, fresh air of Dragon Eyre, and Austin realised that they would stop at nothing until it was in their grasp, even if that meant the complete annihilation of every native and dragon who lived there.

Was this the cause that Austin had been fighting for? He felt ashamed, and finally understood what Meader had been trying to tell him.

He began to sob, and his tears dripped down through the bars of the cage onto the quayside below, mixing with the blood from his ruined flesh.

CHAPTER 20

EVALUATION

West of Olkis, Western Rim – 8th Beldinch 5255 (18th Gylean Year 6)

Topaz knocked on the door of the carpenter's workshop and entered. Ryan glanced up from where he was hunched over a bench filled with wood and tools.

'Morning, mate,' he said. 'How can I help the Master?'

'Morning, Ryan,' said Topaz. He wiped some sawdust from a chair and sat.

'Take a seat, mate,' said Ryan. 'I hope you ain't here to annoy me; I'm busy.'

'I needed somewhere to go; I've been kicked off the quarter deck.'

Ryan stared at him. 'What?'

'Only temporarily, mate,' said Topaz. 'Captain Olo'osso wants to put Vitz through his paces. He's got the lad on the wheel, and he told me to bugger off, so that he could judge him without me standing over his shoulder.'

Ryan turned back to his work. 'Well, you can sit there, but don't distract me. The bosun's been nagging me to get this finished today. And remember, you can't smoke in here.'

'I wasn't going to.'

'Good.'

'Has the captain been round here yet, to watch you at work?'

Ryan sighed. 'What did I just bleeding well say, mate? I need to concentrate. What I do is a bit more delicate compared to turning a big wheel.'

'I could always order you to speak to me.'

'Fine. First, write a note to the bosun, telling him that his urgent job wasn't finished because you were bored and wanted a chat. Pass me the half-inch chisel.'

'The what?'

'The thing with the red handle that's sitting in the tray.'

Topaz glanced around. 'What tray?'

Ryan sighed, leaned over Topaz, and picked up a tool. He took it back to his workbench, picked up a hammer, and started to cut away tiny slivers of wood from a thin beam in front of him. Topaz watched him work for a moment, and wondered how Vitz was getting on. The *Giddy Gull* was still sailing in a straight line, so nothing too disastrous had occurred.

'You know,' said Topaz. 'I always imagined that you were constantly dozing in this workshop, sleeping off a hangover or something. It never occurred to me that you might actually be working.'

'You're hilarious, mate. You do realise that the ship is mostly made of wood, yeah? And Captain Lara is just as ship-proud as any captain in the Sea Banner; she wants to keep her beloved vessel looking shiny and new. I ain't worked so hard since we were patching the *Winsome* back together.'

'It's Olo'osso's ship now.'

'That it is, mate. He was round earlier, just like you said. He paid the workshop a visit yesterday evening, and sat right where you're sitting. He didn't let me work, either. Just kept peppering me with questions. He seemed to think that I was a drunken layabout.'

Topaz laughed. 'I wonder where he got that idea?'

'Shore leave is shore leave, mate. What I get up to in the taverns of Langbeg has no bearing on my job.' He gazed into the middle distance.

'Still, I'm looking forward to our next night out in the *Bo'sun's Droop*; but for now, kindly bugger off and leave me to work in peace.'

Topaz frowned, then got to his feet and left the workshop. He strode through the lower deck, where the sailors from the night watch were catching up on some sleep, then climbed the stairs to the main deck. The sun was out, though there were some heavy rain clouds off to the west. He glanced up at the wind pennant, and judged that the weather might hit them in an hour or so. He resisted the urge to look up at the quarter deck, and instead leaned on the side railings and gazed at the clouds. They were sailing fifty miles to the west of Olkis, and it was strange to think that there was nothing else out there, just the endless Outer Ocean. Any vessel heading more than a hundred miles into the vastness of the Outer Ocean was liable to meet a storm; something to be risked only if you were being chased by the Sea Banner. The *Gull* began to turn to the east, and Topaz tensed, hoping that Vitz was doing alright. He lit a cigarette to calm his nerves, then noticed Lara join him by the railing.

'Did you get booted off the quarter deck as well, ma'am?' he said.

She frowned at him, then nodded. 'Father's switched me and Dax around for a couple of hours. Said he wants to test Dax's abilities as a first lieutenant, so he told me to make myself scarce. Can you believe it? Me and you are the best team in the Western Rim, and here we are, thrown off the bleeding quarter deck, while my idiot cousin is giving out the orders.' She lowered her voice. 'We should have got rid of him when he had the chance.'

'I guess your father needs to evaluate everyone.'

'You know, Topaz, I had this stupid notion that, once father was back on board a ship, he'd hate it, and go back to Befallen. But no. He bleeding loves it. He loves the *Giddy Gull*; he loves being a captain again, and he loves being back at sea.' She sighed. 'I should have bought that small sloop, instead of the *Gull*. It might have been a piece of crap, but at least it would still be mine. I don't think father is ever going to relinquish control of the *Gull*, not now that he's been out on it.'

Topaz frowned. 'Eh, ma'am; there's something I've been meaning to ask you.'

'Yeah; what?'

'Has your father, eh, decided what to do about that woman Tilly brought in?'

'He's refusing to discuss it. I tried bringing it up with him a few days ago, just before we left Langbeg, and so did Ann, but he told us to shut up.' She glanced at him. 'Why do you want to know?'

He shrugged. 'Just curious.'

She laughed. 'I'm surprised you even remember that night, you were so wasted. You certainly impressed Ann, though; she went on about your performance for days. Watch that she doesn't try to snatch you for her own ship.'

'I can remember a lot of it,' he said. 'I remember being sick, and I remember drinking so much coffee that I almost pissed myself. I also remember Maddie; she spoke to me for eight solid hours. I know her whole bleeding life story. I could tell you the names of a dozen other Jackdaws, and every unit she was attached to in the Blades, and every type of food that she likes and hates. She doesn't eat meat; did you know that? I've never met anyone who doesn't eat meat.'

'Got a thing for her, have you?'

His cheeks flushed.

'I wouldn't get your hopes up, Topaz. There's a good chance that father will decide that it's too dangerous to keep her in Langbeg. It's a sure bet that the dragons of Skythorn will want to speak to him once we return to Befallen; who knows what they'll recommend? There's also a good chance that Tilly will lose the *Little Sneak*.'

'But she brought your father four thousand gold sovereigns.'

'Yes, but if the dragons object to what she did, which they will, then they might threaten to withdraw support from the Five Sisters unless Tilly is punished. Don't ever tell her I said this, but I almost feel sorry for her. She shouldn't have abducted a dragon rider, but she did a damn fine job of getting her back here in one piece, and she shouldn't have to lose her ship over it. Besides, Blackrose is an idiot, and I told her as much when I last saw her.'

'Was that wise, ma'am?'

'Who gives a shit? Someone needed to say it. That was right before you delivered the *Winsome* to me.'

'Now, there's a night I'd rather forget.'

'What did it feel like? When did you realise that Sable had made you do it?'

'Not until you'd captured us. Right up to that point, I was totally convinced that I was doing the right thing.' He shook his head. 'Sable made a complete fool out of me.'

'Don't take it personally. She also saved your life. If you'd sailed the *Winsome* to Alg Bay, you'd be dead along with the rest of the Eastern Fleet. And look at you now – the master of the finest vessel in Olkian waters. My position is looking shaky, but you're secure enough.'

'Listen. If your father removes you from the *Gull*, then I'm going with you. You were right about us making a good team, ma'am. I'd rather pilot a rowing boat if you were the captain, than sail anywhere under someone else.'

She stared at him, and for a tiny moment, he thought he saw a crack in her tough outer shell.

She glanced away. 'Thanks,' she muttered. 'You'd be a dozy bastard for giving up the *Gull*, but thanks.'

A midshipman appeared at their back. 'Ma'am, sir – the captain wants you both on the quarter deck.'

Lara nodded, then she and Topaz followed the young officer to the rear of the brigantine. They climbed the steps to the quarter deck, and waited for Captain Olo'osso to address them. Lara's father was talking to Dax, while both were keeping an eye on Vitz, who was grasping onto the wheel, a look of near panic in his eyes. Ann was also there, standing a little back from her father, a miserable expression on her face.

Olo'osso turned to greet Lara and Topaz. 'There you are. Right, I think it's time we had a little chat about the *Giddy Gull*. Let's go into my cabin. Ani, you come too. Lieutenant Udaxa can keep an eye on things for a while.'

Dax saluted. 'Yes, sir.'

Topaz, Lara and Ann followed the captain into what used to be Lara's cabin. He gestured to them to take a seat, then he grinned down at them.

'The *Giddy Gull* is a marvellous vessel. Alara, you did well to buy it, despite your lack of funds. I hope you've learned your lesson, my little princess – never bite off more than you can swallow.' He began to pace up and down, while the others sat in silence. 'I'm also very happy with the crew you have assembled, Alara; they're a tight-knit bunch, who have nothing but good things to say about your captaincy. If anything, you might have been too generous to the lads; and they all expect me to be just as generous now that I am the captain. I have a few concerns about some of the petty officers, including your little protégé, Oto of the Sea Banner.'

'Did Vitz make any mistakes, sir?' said Topaz.

'No. He did everything I asked of him, and he can read and understand a chart at a glance. He's actually not bad, for a damn settler. It's his nerves that worry me. He had this anxious look on his face the entire time. I'm not sure how he'd deal with pressure, say, if the ship came under attack. However, you are the master, and I'll allow him to remain in his position for now. He deserves a few more months to prove himself.'

'Thank you, sir.'

'Ani,' said Olo'osso, 'what are your thoughts? I respect your opinion, but you have been awfully quiet these past few days at sea.'

'I'm still pissed off, father,' said Ann. 'My entire expedition to the Eastern Rim has been cancelled, and my ship and crew are rotting away in Langbeg harbour.'

Olo'osso frowned. 'Yes. I know. That fact irritates me also. The consequences of dear little Atili's voyage to Ulna are still making themselves felt. That's one reason I brought you along, to try to take your mind off it. All the same, you must have come to a few conclusions about the running of the *Gull*.'

'Alright. Dax is utterly incompetent, father. If I were you, I'd keep him on dry land. Give him a job as a goatherd in the mountains – somewhere he can't cause any trouble.'

Olo'osso glared at her.

Ann shrugged. 'You asked.'

Lara smirked, then flattened her expression as her father gave her a look.

'I'm very disappointed in you both, girls. Udaxa is family. You know how important it is for family to stick together. We are but one family among several in Langbeg with ships and influence, and we have to look out for each other.' He narrowed his eyes at Ann. 'Do you have any further advice, my dear?'

'Yes. You should go back to Befallen, and leave ship operations to us, father. You're too old for this shit.'

Olo'osso's face went red with anger. 'I own the *Giddy Gull*!'

'I know that, father, but you should leave it to Lara to captain. Take your share of the takings, of course, but let her sail the *Gull*.'

Lara blinked in surprise. 'Are you coming to my defence, sister?'

'Don't get too used to it,' said Ann. 'I still think you're an irresponsible fool at times, but you've grown up a lot in the last couple of years. You're a far cry from the brat I took to the Eastern Rim.'

'Thank you, I think,' said Lara.

'I have a solution,' said Olo'osso. 'I'm going to ignore Ana's sly comments about my age; I have fallen in love with the *Gull*, and intend to be its captain for some time to come. After ten years on land, you have no idea how good it feels to be back out at sea, and I am not going to give that up. So, here's my solution. Alara, how would you feel if I transferred the *Little Sneak* into your full ownership? All paperwork would be signed over to you – you would own it in its entirety, with nothing to owe. I would even let you keep one hundred per cent of the takings, for the first year – after that we would settle into the usual arrangement. In return, you would sign over to me your share of thirty per cent of the *Gull*.'

'Are you serious, father?' said Lara.

Olo'osso beamed. 'Yes. I can be generous too.'

Lara snorted. 'No chance. Do you think that I'd swap the *Gull* for that piece of crap?'

'I see you want to drive a hard bargain, my little petal. Alright; what if I also pay for the full refit of the *Little Sneak*? I would hand the vessel over to you in perfect condition.'

'Do I get to keep Topaz?'

Olo'osso chuckled. 'No, dear. He will be staying with the *Gull*.'

'Then, my answer is no.'

'You'd rather be a lieutenant on the *Gull* than the captain of the *Sneak*? I thought you had a little more ambition than that.'

'What about Tilly?' said Ann. 'Is she aware that you're trying to negotiate away her ship, father?'

'No, but she knows that the dragons of Skythorn will probably demand some sort of punishment for what she did. I don't think she'd be shocked to discover that she'd lost the *Sneak*. At least she will still have her life.'

Topaz fidgeted. He wanted to ask about Maddie's fate, but he remembered Lara's advice about never interrupting the family when they were in the middle of a discussion.

Olo'osso turned back to his youngest daughter. 'State your price, Alara; tell me what you want for your thirty per cent.'

'Alright,' she said. 'I want the *Little Sneak*, fully refitted at your expense; I want my pick of the *Gull's* crew to man the *Sneak*, including Topaz, and anyone else I choose; and I want you to swear that Dax will never set foot onto another Five Sisters vessel. I also want Ann to accompany me in her ship to the Eastern Rim, where we will return the dragon rider to her home. Finally, I want you to promise us that Tilly will get another ship within a year.'

Olo'osso raised an eyebrow. 'I see. You realise, of course, that I cannot possibly make those kinds of promises. The dragons of Skythorn will want to say their piece, and I am obliged to listen to their words, and act upon them if I wish to remain in the alliance. As for the crew, I suppose I could allow you to choose some of them, but not the master. He stays where he is.'

Lara smiled. 'No Topaz, no deal.'

'And what does Master Oto of the Sea Banner have to say about this, eh?' said Olo'osso. 'I'm sure he'd prefer to remain on this splendid brigantine.'

'Why don't you ask him, father?'

'I shall. Oto, please disabuse my daughter of the notion that you would rather depart the *Gull*.'

Topaz swallowed. 'I swore an oath to Captain Lara, sir, not to any particular ship. If she leaves, then I leave too.'

Ann started to laugh. 'You see, father? This is what happens if you try to interfere with our ships. You should stick to sitting in Befallen, and leave the sailing to us.'

'Don't be awkward, Oto,' said Olo'osso, glaring at him. 'I could make your life very difficult on board.'

'That's exactly what more than a few Sea Banner officers used to say to me, sir,' he said. 'If I could survive their threats, then I can survive yours.'

'I could make you swear an oath to me, boy!'

'Yes, sir, if you were to hold a crossbow to my head.'

'I might just do that. Or, I might strike you back down to master's mate, for your insolence.'

'You can't do that, sir. I own ten per cent of the *Gull*, and I know my rights.'

'Damn your rights!' cried the old pirate.

'Steady on,' said Ann. 'Let's not bandy threats around. We should keep things just as they are, for the time being. Lara's made it quite clear what she wants; and, if I'm being honest, her list of demands is a reasonable one, but we need to see what the dragons say about that rider first. Why don't we wait until we've spoken to them, and then decide?'

Olo'osso's expression calmed. 'You always were the sensible one, dear. That is what we shall do. Alara, and Oto, I want you both to think deeply about your futures. If you continue to defy me after we have spoken to the dragons, then I will have no choice but to take certain steps that you may not like. Am I clear?'

'Yes, father,' said Lara.

'Oto?' said Olo'osso.

Topaz frowned, then nodded. 'Yes, sir.'

'Excellent. I am going back out onto the quarter deck, to ensure that we avoid the storm clouds coming in from the west. Feel free to complain about me in my absence.'

He strode out of the cabin, and slammed the door behind him.

Ann narrowed her eyes at Lara. 'You shouldn't have bought this damned ship. If you hadn't, father would still be in Befallen, instead of thinking he's a sailor again.'

'That doesn't make any sense,' said Lara, lighting a cigarette. 'All I needed was one decent haul from a big ship, and none of this would be happening.' She banged her fist on the table. 'I'm not giving up the *Gull* without a fight.'

'What about all those conditions you gave father? If he grants everything you asked for, then you'll have to give it up.'

'He'll never agree to them; that was the whole point. Shit, you're clueless at times.'

Ann glared at her, then turned to Topaz. 'And you shouldn't have argued with him.'

'Don't blame him,' said Lara; 'he was just being loyal.'

'He compared father to a Sea Banner officer!'

'So? Father was being a dipshit.'

'You can't say that in front of someone who isn't family, Lara – you know that.'

'Oops. I forgot. What a shame.'

'You're making me sorry that I defended you.'

'Why did you?'

'Because, Lara, believe it or not, I agree with most, well, some, of what you said. I especially liked the bit about us taking that rider back to Ulna together; that might be the only way to assuage the anger of the dragons. We need to get rid of that woman as quickly as possible.'

'Her name's Maddie,' said Topaz. 'Maddie Jackdaw.'

Ann raised an eyebrow. 'I know what her name is, Topaz.'

'Where is she?'

'What? She's locked up in Befallen; where else do you think she would be?'

'I wasn't sure; that's why I asked.'

Ann glanced back at Lara, and the younger woman laughed.

'I think my master has taken a shine to Maddie Jackdaw.'

'Is that so?' said Ann, laughing. 'You know, when we boarded the *Little Sneak*, the first thing he said was how beautiful he thought Maddie was, but he was pissed out of his mind at the time, and then he threw up all over himself a moment later.'

Lara shrugged. 'He's a sailor. He thinks every young woman is beautiful. His mate Ryan is even worse.'

'I am nothing like Ryan,' said Topaz. 'And, I haven't "taken a shine" to Maddie. She just seems like a decent person, and I don't want her to be killed for something that wasn't her fault.'

'But, you do think she's beautiful?' said Lara.

Topaz's cheeks flushed. 'I... well, um...'

The two sisters laughed.

'Go to a brothel or something,' said Lara. 'Get it out of your system, boy.'

Ann pulled a face at her. 'How romantic, Lara. Poor Topaz is in love, and you're telling him to go to a brothel? What would Maddie think?'

Topaz jumped to his feet. 'Stop laughing at me! I am not in love with Maddie!'

He stormed out of the cabin, the sound of the two sisters' laughter echoing behind him. Olo'osso was standing next to Dax on the quarter deck, and he glanced in his direction.

'Had enough of my daughters' company, eh, lad?' he said. 'Never mind. Take a break; you'll be back on the wheel in thirty minutes.'

Topaz calmed down enough to salute, then he hurried off the quarter deck. He paused by the railings, lit a cigarette, and gazed out into the ocean as the wind swept through his hair.

What was wrong with him? If it had been Ryan or Vitz who had been teasing him about Maddie, then he would have brushed it off with ease; after all, the three of them were always swapping good-natured insults. It was different when it was women doing the teasing, he thought. That somehow made it more real. It was ridiculous, though – of course he wasn't in love with Maddie Jackdaw. He barely knew her. Well, that wasn't true; he did, in fact, know quite a lot about her, after their eight-hour stint at the wheel of the *Little Sneak*. Still, all he was feeling was a humane compassion for someone who had been dragged across the ocean to the other side of the world against her will, and who was now languishing in a cell within the walls of Befallen Castle. He was feeling what any decent person would feel. He thought about Lara's suggestion – that they should take Maddie back to Ulna, to be reunited with her dragon. That did seem the most reasonable thing to do. Return her to Ulna, and hope that Queen Blackrose was in a forgiving mood. He had heard stories about dragons who had been driven mad when their riders were killed, or went missing and couldn't be found. The dragons of Skythorn were extremely possessive about the riders they selected from among the young men and women of Langbeg. They were particularly fond of choosing orphans or only-children, so that their riders would have few ties to the human community that lived a few miles from their colony. And, once they had been selected, they usually never returned to Langbeg; their lives forever bound to the dragon with whom they shared a bond.

He had asked Maddie about her life as a rider, but she was a foreigner, from another world altogether, and understood little about Dragon Eyre customs and traditions. That was part of why he had liked her. Her opinions, of which she had many, were fresh-sounding, and she didn't talk like any of the snobbish and stuck-up riders that he had previously met. Usually, dragon riders thought that they were better than everyone else, but Maddie hadn't been like that.

And, she was beautiful. In fact, to his mind, she was the most beautiful woman he had ever seen.

A weird, dull ache formed within his chest, and he cursed. No. He would not allow it. He was the finest master among the Five Sisters fleet, with a long and prosperous career ahead of him; and he would not allow himself to be distracted. Maddie's fate was out of his hands, and what happened to her was none of his business. If Captain Olo'osso ordered him to tie her up, weigh her down, and toss her overboard, he would salute and say 'yes, sir.'

He threw the cigarette butt into the sea. Who was he kidding?

CHAPTER 21

THE DRAGONS OF SKYTHORN

L angbeg, Olkis, Western Rim – 13th Beldinch 5255 (18th Gylean Year 6)

Maddie sat on her balcony with a glass of wine in her hand, and gazed down at the town of Langbeg. The sun was shining in the western sky, and it was another warm day. It had rained the day before, but the wind had blown the clouds away, and the sky was a perfect blue.

For a prison, she thought, it wasn't all bad.

True, she wasn't allowed to leave her rooms, which were locked from the outside, but she had been well supplied with food, drink, toiletries and a fresh set of clothes, not to mention the fully-furnished apartment. Her guards referred to her as a 'guest', never as a prisoner, and even bowed when they brought her meals to the front door.

She very much doubted that all 'guests' lived in such luxury while incarcerated within the walls of Befallen Castle, and she reckoned that Olo'osso was worried about the reaction of the dragons, so had ordered that she be treated with all courtesy, amid plenty of home comforts. Whatever the reason, it was far better than being on the *Little Sneak*. Her favourite place was the balcony, with its great views of the town and the bay. It was completely enclosed by steel bars to prevent any escape, not that Maddie would have tried to scale the walls of the tower. There was a sheer drop of a hundred feet to the rocky ground below, and she had never been much of a climber.

She heard the sound of a key turning in the door of her main room, and frowned. It wasn't time for dinner. She glanced over her shoulder, and saw a guard escort Tilly into the apartment. Maddie smiled. She had missed the young pirate captain, and had been a little concerned about what had happened to her after they had arrived at the castle.

'Afternoon, Maddie,' said Tilly, as she walked out onto the balcony. 'I like your dress.'

'Thanks. It was a gift from your father, along with a whole bunch of other clothes. He even gave me six pairs of shoes, although one of them has heels that are too high for me. I tried them on and nearly broke my ankle.' She lifted the hem of her dress. 'I like these sandals the best, especially in this weather.'

Tilly nodded, and sat down on one of the free chairs.

'You look glum, Tilly,' said Maddie. 'Tell me your woes.'

'Father has returned from his little trip out on the *Giddy Gull.*'

'Yes. I saw that fancy-looking ship come into the harbour yesterday evening. Did he have a nice time?'

Tilly shrugged. 'I guess so. I don't know. I didn't ask.' She sighed. 'Look, now that he's back, a meeting has been planned, and some dragons are going to be coming here, to question me about what happened. They'll probably want to question you as well. And then, they'll make a decision. Father doesn't have to agree with the dragons, but he's going to. He can't afford to lose his place in the alliance.'

Maddie sipped her wine. 'Oops, sorry. Do you want something to drink?'

Tilly shook her head. 'Dragons can smell alcohol, and they'll think less of me if I turn up to the meeting with wine on my breath.'

'Really? I never knew that. So, what do you think the dragons will decide?'

'They'll probably demand that father punishes me for abducting you from Ulna. I asked father outright about it, but he wouldn't tell me anything. Lara, on the other hand, kept dropping hints that I can expect to lose the *Little Sneak*. I worked so hard to get that boat, and they're probably going to take it away from me, and give it to someone else, along with my crew.' Her voice tailed away. 'It's not fair.'

'It sounds better than some of the things that they could do. They could throw you in jail, or even execute you. Not that I think they should; I'm just trying to put it into perspective. I imagine that the dragons will think that snatching a rider is quite a serious crime.'

'Lara said something similar. She said I would be lucky if all they did was take my little sloop.'

'Now, I don't want to sound insensitive, but what do you think the dragons will decide to do with me?'

'I reckon they'll demand that we return you immediately to Ulna, but that's only a guess. There's a fair bit of tension between the dragons of the Western and Eastern Rims. They used to squabble a lot in the past, before the invasion; there were even a few wars between the two sides. All the same, they'll probably not want to risk Blackrose turning up here and wreaking havoc.'

'They might decide to carry me back to Ulna.'

Tilly shook her head. 'The Olkian dragons never stray far from their homes. The ones at Skythorn rarely leave this part of Luckenbay, which is why I was so surprised to see Redblade bring Ann and that master guy out to our ship. That's risky behaviour for them. They'll protect us if the Sea Banner ever attack Langbeg, but they're desperate not to attract the attention of the gods.' She paused, and glanced at Maddie for a moment. 'I treated you well on board, didn't I? I mean, you weren't harmed in any way?'

'Don't worry,' said Maddie. 'I'm not going to make up any stories about how you tortured or starved me or anything. If I'm asked, I'll tell the truth. Does that sound fair?'

Tilly stood. 'I guess so. Well, I'll see you at the hearing.'

Maddie watched as Tilly trudged from the balcony, her head lowered. She felt a twinge of sympathy for the young pirate captain, despite the fact that she had abducted her from her home, and separated her from Blackrose. Maddie tried to summon some anger towards

Tilly and the Five Sisters, but found that, no matter how much she missed Blackrose, she lacked any hatred towards them.

She lifted the wine glass to her lips, and gazed back out to sea.

Two hours later, Maddie was escorted through the winding corridors of the tower, a couple of Olo'osso's burly guards leading the way. She was still wearing her new dress, and her hands hadn't been bound, but she made no attempt to escape. They descended a narrow spiral staircase, and emerged out into the central courtyard that sat in the middle of the castle's three high towers. A small crowd had gathered there, and she saw a line of chairs in the shade by the edge of the square yard. Olo'osso was seated, while his five daughters were standing close by. Ann was speaking earnestly to Tilly, who was wearing an anxious expression on her face. Lara and Dina were bickering, while Ellie stood alone in the background, her eyes on the sky above them. Also present were a few men from the ships run by the Five Sisters, and Maddie saw the master who had steered the *Lucky Sneak* through Luckenbay. Their eyes met for a moment, and the man half-smiled, then glanced away.

The two guards led Maddie up to the line of chairs, and Olo'osso rose to his feet.

'Our honoured guest,' he said; 'thank you for coming down to the yard. The dragons from Skythorn shouldn't be too much longer.'

Maddie nodded. 'How many are coming?'

'Only three can fit into the courtyard, young lady,' he said, 'so I imagine it won't be more than that. They usually send three for these sorts of meetings.'

Maddie raised an eyebrow. 'Are your daughters in the habit of kidnapping dragon riders?'

'Eh? No, no. This is the first, and last, time.'

'Will they be bringing their own riders with them?'

'I imagine so, though they rarely descend from their dragons' shoulders. Has your stay been comfortable?'

'Yeah, it's been fine. A little boring, but fine. Thanks for the new clothes. Do you have any books? If I'm going to be locked up here for any longer, I'll need something to read. Or, maybe I could go for walks along the cliffs, with an escort, of course. I like looking at the flowers that grow by the edge of the cliffs. I can see them from my balcony, and I thought that maybe I could pick some and put them in a vase in my room? That would brighten the place up, don't you think?'

'I'm sure we could work something out,' he said. 'We shall have to wait and see what the dragons advise.'

Maddie frowned. Olo'osso seemed a little nervous in her presence. She glanced at his daughters, and they were also looking at her with worried expressions, except for Lara, who was wearing the same cocky smile that Maddie remembered from Seabound. She realised that she held some power over them. As a queen's rider, if she chose to report to the dragons of Skythorn that the pirates had been wicked and cruel, then they could be in serious trouble. She smiled, then caught the *Gull's* master looking at her again. She needed someone to talk to while they waited, so she walked up to him.

'Hello,' she said. 'Are you feeling sober today?'

His face went red.

'Were you out sailing with Olo'osso?' Maddie went on. 'I was watching the ships from my rooms up in the tower, and saw the *Giddy Gull* sail into the harbour yesterday evening. Were you on board?'

'Uh... yes.'

She nodded. 'Did you plunder any innocent merchant ships? I hope you didn't kill anyone. Life seems to be a little cheap on Dragon Eyre, and that upsets me, if I'm honest. Why does there need to be so much killing? I mean, Tilly seems nice, well, she is nice, but even she had no problem ordering her sailors to slaughter a whole bunch of natives on Rigga. Have you ever killed anyone?'

He blinked. 'No.'

'Good. So, why are you here? I thought this was family business.'

'I, um... Olo'osso requested that every master and officer from the Five Sisters' fleet attend, as a sign of respect towards the dragons.'

'Really? I don't see the master from the *Little Sneak*.'

'He's still sick in bed.'

'Is he? I didn't know that. I should go and visit him, but I'm not allowed out of my rooms. They're very comfortable, and I have a balcony from where I can see the entire bay; but it's still a prison, if you know what I mean. You should come up and take a look; I hardly get any visitors, and I spend most of each day by myself, which can be a bit tedious, if I'm honest.'

The man glanced away again, and she wondered if he didn't like her.

'You're not very talkative,' she said. 'When we were on the *Little Sneak*, I must have said a thousand words to your every one. At the time, I thought that was because you were so unbelievably drunk, but maybe you're quiet all of the time. Am I annoying you?'

'No! No. I like listening to you speak.'

She raised an eyebrow. Clearly, he was just being polite, and would rather she stopped talking. Once again, her big mouth had pushed someone away.

'The dragons are coming!' yelled a guard, his arm pointing upwards.

Maddie turned, and glanced up, a hand shielding her eyes from the mid-morning sun. She had stopped drinking wine an hour before, and had then eaten, and hoped that the dragons wouldn't smell any alcohol on her breath.

'Over here, Miss Jackdaw, if you please,' said Ann, gesturing for Maddie to sit between her and Olo'osso.

Maddie gave a weak smile to Topaz, then she went and sat down.

Ann nudged her. 'Remember; don't speak unless the dragons address you.'

'I know how to deal with dragons, thank you very much.'

Ann frowned. 'Of course. Sorry.'

Maddie saw Lara smirk from the corner of her eye, then she looked up, and spotted the three dragons approaching. They circled over the castle a few times, then landed in the courtyard, one by one. She recognised the large red and silver dragon as the one who had carried Ann and Topaz out to the *Little Sneak*, but the other two were strangers to her. Upon the shoulders of each dragon sat a rider, but they made no attempt to dismount.

Olo'osso stood, and opened his arms. 'Welcome, friends, and thank you for gracing Befallen with your presence.'

'This is not a social call, Lord Osso,' said a lime-green dragon.

'Of course not, Leafscale,' said the old pirate. 'My apologies.'

'Where is the dragon rider?' said a white dragon.

'I see her,' said Redblade. 'I noticed her presence on the deck of the *Little Sneak*, although I was unaware of her identity at the time. She is seated to Lord Osso's right.'

The white dragon extended her long neck, and her dark eyes stared down at Blackrose's rider.

'Hello,' said Maddie. 'My name's Maddie Jackdaw. How are you today?'

'I am well, thank you,' said the white dragon.

'I didn't catch your name,' Maddie went on.

'Indeed,' said the white dragon. 'Lord Osso has been remiss to have neglected a formal introduction. I am known to the humans as Starbright, and I am one of the leaders of the Skythorn colony. My colleagues are Redblade and Leafscale, who also sit upon the colony's governing council. I have some questions for you, Maddie Jackdaw.'

'I thought you might. Should I begin, or do you want to speak to Captain Tilly first?'

Starbright tilted her head. 'We shall commence this hearing by interrogating the one who abducted you. Atili'osso, please stand up.'

Tilly got to her feet, her head bowed.

'Speak,' said Starbright. 'We wish to know how it came about that you stole the Queen of Ulna's rider.'

Tilly took a breath. 'Let me start by saying sorry.'

'We are not interested in your apologies, girl; we want to know what happened.'

'Of course, yes. Alright, I was docked at Udall in Ulna, and someone from the Unk Tannic approached me and offered me a lot of gold to take someone. They had already kidnapped her from her home, and they didn't tell me that she was a dragon rider.'

'Did you not think to ask?' said Leafscale.

'No. I assumed that she was an enemy of the Unk Tannic.'

The dragons glanced at each other, and Leafscale made a guttural mocking sound.

'You assumed?' he said, his lime-green scales glimmering in the sunlight. 'Let me guess – you were too busy thinking about gold to make any inquiries?'

Tilly nodded. 'I thought it better not to ask any questions.'

'When did you learn that the girl you had abducted was the queen's rider?' said Redblade.

'The day after we had sailed from Ulna.'

'What?' cried Leafscale. 'But, if you were only a day away from Ulna, then why did you not return immediately?'

'I was... I was too scared of what Blackrose might do to my crew.'

'Lies!' roared Leafscale. 'It was pure greed that made you continue, wasn't it? You knew that if you went back to Udall, you would have to return the gold.'

'No,' said Tilly; 'it was fear.'

'Yes, fear of losing your profit. Lord Osso, your daughter must be punished. She has committed a heinous crime; she should be executed.'

'Let us not be hasty, Leafscale,' said Starbright. 'While I agree that Atili'osso seems to have broken one of the most ancient laws of Dragon Eyre, I wish to hear from the rider before we pronounce any judgement.'

The lime-green dragon tilted his head. 'I bow to your authority, noble Starbright.'

'Is it my turn?' said Maddie.

'Yes,' said the white dragon. 'First, do you perceive Atili'osso to have told any untruths in her version of events?'

Maddie stood. 'I don't think so. It was the Unk Tannic who

kidnapped me, from the palace in Udall, while Blackrose was away in Geist, speaking to the dragons there. The next thing I knew, I woke up on the *Little Sneak*. That's when I told Tilly who I was. She and the crew seemed terrified by what they had done. And shocked. They treated me well, though, and I wasn't hurt or anything. I really do think that execution is a little harsh as a punishment. Maybe if she'd killed me, then it would be deserved, but Captain Tilly made sure I was well looked after.'

'I have a question,' said Redblade. 'Your name is Maddie Jackdaw, yes?'

'Eh, yes.'

'That is not a name that sounds like it belongs to a native of Dragon Eyre, and your accent is also a little strange. Are you not from this world?'

'No. I came to Dragon Eyre with Blackrose from my own world, via Lostwell. I met Blackrose when she was a prisoner in the City where I lived.'

'And when was this?'

'When did I meet Blackrose, you mean? Oh, about three years ago. I didn't have the traditional rider training or anything like that, but my bond with Blackrose is genuine.'

Redblade turned to Starbright. 'Perhaps we are wasting our time. This girl is not a proper rider. She is a foreigner.'

Maddie's temper started to bubble away. 'That's what some of the Ulnan dragons also said. They were wrong, and now you're wrong too. Blackrose chose me, and that's all that matters.'

The dragons ignored her.

'According to the strict application of the law,' said Starbright, 'Atili'osso has committed no crime, as this Maddie Jackdaw is clearly not a rider in the traditional sense. However, Queen Blackrose may feel differently. We must tread carefully.'

'She is an imposter,' said Redblade. 'We only have her word that she even knows Queen Blackrose.'

'Hey!' said Maddie. 'I'm still standing here.'

Redblade regarded her with contempt. 'We know that. Tell me, what is the third law in the rider's code of conduct?'

'Uh... I don't know.'

'And what are the six sacred duties of a rider?'

'Nope; no idea.'

'See?' said Redblade to the other dragons. 'This case is none of our business. We should leave Lord Osso to deal with it in whichever way he desires.'

'I concur,' said Leafscale. 'This girl, whoever she is, is obviously not the rider of a queen. No queen on Dragon Eyre would ever dream of bonding with a foreigner. She is a liar.'

'I am not a liar!' cried Maddie. 'You pompous, tradition-bound oafs. You must send me back to Ulna.'

'We are under no obligation to do any such thing, Maddie Jackdaw,' said Starbright. 'Lord Osso, we shall now leave you in peace. Our alliance remains intact. Deal with this girl in any way you see fit. Furthermore, there will be no punishment required for your daughter, as she has committed no crime against the dragons of this world. Good day to you all.'

The three dragons extended their wings, and ascended back into the air. They circled once, then sped off into the west. Down in the courtyard, no one spoke for a moment, then the pirates roared out a cheer. Ann embraced Tilly, while Olo'osso grinned from ear to ear. Maddie was completely ignored, as backs were slapped, and fists were raised into the air.

Maddie glanced around, feeling more alone than ever. What had just happened? She had gone from holding a position of power to being an expendable prisoner in the blink of an eye. The faces around her were laughing and grinning, but she noticed a frown on the lips of the *Gull's* master. He really must hate her, she thought. She glanced over at Tilly, but the young woman was being hugged by her father, and seemed oblivious to Maddie's presence.

'Settle down, everyone,' said Olo'osso, his left arm over Tilly's shoulder. 'A mere ten minutes ago, we were all nervously praying for a good outcome, and I think I speak for us all, when I say how relieved I am that my daughter will not have to face any punishment. This calls for a celebration. I, for one, need a stiff drink, or maybe two! All duties are suspended for the rest of the day, and I would be honoured if you would join me and my daughters for a little party.' He glanced at a servant. 'Bring food and drink, plenty of drink, up to my loggia.'

The servant bowed. 'Yes, my lord.'

Tilly caught Maddie's eye, and her grin faded. She broke away from her father, as the others started to troop into the largest tower, and walked towards Maddie.

'Well,' she said, 'that was unexpected.'

Maddie glared at her. 'I suppose you get to keep your ship now.'

'I suppose so.'

Dina joined her sister. 'So, you were lying all this time, eh? And you thought you'd get away with it? You've no idea how much worry you've put us through, you silly bitch.'

'I am not a liar,' said Maddie, grinding the words out. 'I am Blackrose's rider.'

Dina shrugged. 'So you say. The dragons didn't believe you, though, did they? And that's all that really matters.'

'You don't know what you're talking about, Dina,' said Lara, approaching. 'Me and Ann saw Maddie in Seabound Palace.'

Dina scowled at her sister. 'And did Blackrose say, "Hey, everybody, this is my rider"?'

'Not exactly,' said Lara, 'but...'

'But nothing,' said Dina. 'We all know that dragons are good at telling the truth from lies, and it's obvious that her story is a load of bullshit. There's no way a queen of one of the realms would even consider taking on a clueless foreigner as their rider – no way. She'll be lucky if father doesn't sell her as a slave.'

Dina turned and walked away, leaving Tilly and Lara with Maddie. Maddie's two guards were also still in the courtyard, but everyone else had entered the tower.

'Will your father really sell me into slavery?' said Maddie, after an awkward silence.

Tilly shrugged. 'I don't know. Maybe.'

'Whatever happens,' said Lara, looking Maddie in the eye, 'you should know that I believe you. I know what I saw inside Seabound, and I don't care what that cow Dina says. But, you should probably prepare for the worst.'

'What shall we do with the prisoner?' said one of the guards.

'Take her back to her rooms in the tower,' said Tilly.

'Are her living conditions to change, ma'am, or is she still to be treated like royalty?'

'Leave everything as it is for now,' Tilly said. 'We'll speak to father, and see what he wants to do next.'

'Right you are, ma'am,' said the guard. He gestured to Maddie. 'This way, miss.'

Maddie felt like crying, but she refused to be humiliated in front of two of Olo'osso's daughters. She kept her mouth closed, and allowed the guards to escort her into the tower, while Lara and Tilly followed in silence. The two young pirate captains left them after they had ascended a flight of stairs, and headed in the direction of Olo'osso's grand loggia, from where raucous sounds of celebrations were already emanating. The guards led Maddie up to her corner apartment, and locked her inside.

Maddie glanced around, her head spinning. Not for a single moment had she imagined that the dragons of Skythorn wouldn't believe her, but she thought back to Shadowblaze's first reaction, and it started to make sense. She walked out onto her balcony, the steel bars making it seem like a cage. The noise coming from the open loggia above and to her left rang out, and she heard a great cheer that signified Tilly's arrival at the party.

Maddie slumped down into a chair, the sounds of the celebrating pirates making her feel sick and angry at the same time. She leaned over and picked up a half-full bottle of wine. She glanced around for a glass, then gave up, and swigged it down straight from the bottle.

CHAPTER 22
FLAGGING

Western Gyle, Western Rim – 17th Beldinch 5255 (18th Gylean Year 6)

Badblood soared over the high cliffs, then surged down to the ocean, his wings barely above the waves crashing against the rocks. A light had appeared in the east, and it would soon be time to return to where they had been hiding, before the sun came up. It was too dangerous for a dragon to fly in the vicinity of Gyle in daylight, a fact that Meader had constantly repeated to them, ever since they had landed on the island a few days before.

'Talk to me, Badblood,' said Sable, as he skimmed over the waves. 'I don't like it when you're this quiet.'

'I am too ashamed, rider,' the dark red dragon said. 'My weak body has let us all down.'

'Come on, Badblood. Apart from Blackrose, you're the strongest dragon I know.'

'I am not. Just getting to Gyle nearly killed me. For the last hundred miles of the journey from Na Sun Ka, I thought I was going to crash into the sea.'

'But you didn't. You're getting stronger, my love. Look at you now –

you're already back in the air, after only a few days' rest. Not many dragons can fly that distance; you should be proud.'

'I am flying – yes, but I am in no condition for the next stage of our journey. It will be days before I am ready to attempt the flight to Ectus.'

'Stop putting yourself down. Oh, Badblood, for all the time I've known you, you have always felt yourself to be lesser than other dragons, and it's simply not true. You think other dragons are faster, stronger, and fitter, and you forget how amazing you are. You destroyed the gates of Old Alea, my love; do you not remember? Without you, the Ascendants would have taken the Sextant, and, more importantly, we would be dead. It makes me sad that you have such a low opinion of yourself.'

'Except for you, my rider, my memories of Lostwell are tainted with shame. My long years of captivity, when I was nothing more than a dumb brute, expected to fight for the amusement of crowds, are seared into my mind. I lived those decades in a dream, believing myself to be the mighty Sanguino. How wrong I was. Do you not recall how Frostback and Halfclaw ripped me to shreds? Mere children, yet they utterly humiliated me in front of Blackrose and the Catacombs dragons. And then, when I lost my eye, and was unable to fly – again because I was attacked and beaten by dragons far younger than me. I longed to come to Dragon Eyre, so that I could make a fresh start, and put those days of shame behind me, but the shame has followed me here. I was powerless to stop Shadowblaze from throwing you to the greenhides, and now I have embarrassed you again, by almost dying from exhaustion from a few flights that Blackrose was able to easily manage. I am a failure, Sable; you should find a dragon more worthy of your love.'

'Don't you ever say that. I mean it, Badblood – I never want to hear you say those words again; do you understand? Do you have any conception of how much I love you? Listening to you speak like that tears at my heart. I will never find another dragon like you, nor would I ever want to. You and I are both maimed, both incomplete, but together, we can accomplish anything we set our minds to.'

'I don't deserve you, Sable.'

'Many think I don't deserve you, Badblood. Blackrose, for instance. She might tolerate me at the moment, because we're helping her get to Olkis to look for Maddie, but her feelings for me haven't changed. She still thinks I'm a lying, devious witch who cannot be trusted.' She shrugged. 'I am a lying, devious witch. You understand me, and yet you accept me for who I am, and that means more to me than any words can convey. I've made a lot of mistakes, and you have always been there for me; always ready to forgive, always ready to give me another chance. I know you disapprove of some of the things I've done – some of my more... rash decisions, but you've never let me down.'

'I have learned that there is no point in trying to change you, Sable. You are who you are. Your relationship with the truth, in particular, can make me uneasy; but I would never leave you. I am more scared that you would leave me, and find someone strong and beautiful, like Ashfall, for example, or Evensward. I feel like a lumbering oaf next to them.'

'That's Sanguino talking, my love. You are Badblood, and I would never choose another dragon over you. Come on; the sun is about to rise. We should head back before it gets too light.'

Badblood banked, and turned in a wide arc, his forelimbs almost brushing the top of the ocean swell. He straightened out when the light on the horizon was directly in front of them, and they began to fly east, back towards the coast of western Gyle. As they sped over the waves, Sable tried not to think too deeply about the dark red dragon's lack of confidence; their minds were connected, as they always were when they were flying together, and he would be able to perceive her thoughts if she focussed on them.

'Do you ever lie to me?' he said.

'No.'

'Why not?'

'I respect you too much.'

'Do you not respect Blackrose or Meader? I know you lied to them about the three men you killed on Na Sun Ka.'

'They didn't need to know about that. They would have only worried.'

'I worry too, my rider, but not about a few Unk Tannic rebels; I worry that you sometimes forget the difference between the truth and your fabrications.'

Sable smiled. 'It can be hard work being a good liar. You need a great memory.'

She saw the cliffs of Gyle ahead in the distance. The sky in front of them was getting lighter, and she could make out the deep greens of the forests that covered the mountains in the western half of Gyle. No ships were visible, but gods could be watching, as Meader continually reminded them, and Badblood kept low. It took more energy to fly at that altitude, and Sable could sense the dragon tiring. It was good that he was flying again, but he needed more practice before they could carry onwards to Ectus, their next stepping stone on the way to Olkis.

The cliffs reared up out of the ocean, and Badblood soared upwards, clearing them with only a yard to spare. He skimmed over the tops of the trees, then plunged down into a narrow valley, and followed the course of a river for a few miles. They turned a corner, and the abandoned dragon palace came into view. It had been almost swallowed up by the thick vegetation, and only a few glimpses of marble could be seen through the tangled undergrowth. The river ran by its side, and Badblood aimed for an arched opening that sat just a few yards from the banks of the swiftly-flowing waterway. Sitting at the entrance was Boldspark, the young blue and red dragon that Evensward had brought along with them from Haurn. He moved aside to allow Badblood to land just as the sun breached the horizon.

'A few more minutes,' said the young dragon, laughing, 'and Meader would have given you a telling off for flying in daylight, Badblood.'

The dark red dragon tilted his head, but was too tired to laugh.

'Did you have a good flight?' said Boldspark. 'I was watching your approach; you were very low.'

'We went out over the ocean,' said Badblood.

'You look exhausted. I guess this means that we'll be here for a few more days. There's food in the old throne room, if you want some. I caught a few deer during the night; the mountains are full of them.'

'Thank you,' said Badblood, then he strode past the younger dragon and made his way into the shadowy depths of the ancient palace. Vines and ivy had encroached through every opening, and snaked their way along the cavernous hallways, clinging to the weather-beaten marble surfaces. The throne room was at the head of a ramp that ascended from the ground level, and Badblood forced his tired limbs up it, and entered the vast hall. On the side facing the river, there were over a dozen large openings, but most had been covered by the invading plant-life, and the sunlight had a green hue to it. Blackrose and Evensward were gazing out of the one opening that they had cleared, and Meader was sitting cross-legged on the ground next to them, a cigarette in his fingers. Over in the far corner, a pile of deer carcasses was leaking blood onto the stone floor, and Badblood glanced over at the sight.

'I will eat,' he said.

Sable unbuckled the straps holding her to the harness. 'You do that,' she said. 'Get your strength back.'

She slid down to the ground, and Badblood walked towards the raw meat. Sable watched him for a moment, then severed the connection to his mind, and strolled over to the others.

'You were cutting it fine,' said Meader. 'I was getting worried.'

'We timed it to perfection,' she said, sitting next to him, her legs dangling over the edge.

'It was a needless risk,' he said. 'I keep telling you – the gods begin their vision scans of the skies over Gyle at dawn every day. If they see us, we're finished.'

'Not necessarily,' she said. 'Even if they spotted us, we could still get away in plenty of time before any gods or Banner soldiers could get all the way here. There are miles and miles of mountains between us and Port Edmond.'

'You're not thinking ahead, Sable. Say that, despite the odds, we are successful in locating and rescuing Maddie, we'll have to return to

Haurn by the same route. If the gods in Port Edmond see us, then they'll be on high alert for days.'

Sable sighed. 'Stop nagging, Meader.'

'You're only saying that because you know I'm right.'

'Shut up.'

Blackrose turned to them. 'You should listen to Meader, Sable. Perhaps you should try to get back a little earlier from your practice flights.'

Sable rolled her eyes.

Evensward glanced down at her. 'Is Badblood ready to attempt to fly to Ectus?'

'No,' she said. 'Not yet.'

'Then, please do as Queen Blackrose suggests. If we are to be here for a few more days, then we should make all efforts to be discreet.'

'Fine. If it'll make you all happy, then...' Her voice tailed away as she felt a faint presence trying to probe her mind. She leapt to her feet. 'Shit!'

'What is it?' said Meader, his eyes wide.

'Quiet,' she said. She dived into Meader's mind, and immediately sensed that a god was already inside the head of the demigod, looking out at her from his eyes. She cut the link anchoring the god to Meader's mind.

'I don't understand,' she said. 'We were back before dawn.'

'What's wrong?' said Blackrose.

'A god was just reading Meader's mind – they know we're here.'

'A god was in my head?' cried Meader. 'I didn't feel anything; are you sure?'

'Of course I'm sure,' said Sable. 'Whoever it was, they tried to get inside my head first, but failed, and moved on to you.'

'What has happened?' said Badblood, walking over from the far corner.

'We have been discovered,' said Blackrose. 'We shall have to leave right away. How far do you think you can fly, son?'

Sable saw the dark red dragon's exhaustion etched onto his features.

'I can fly for as long as we need to,' he said.

'Could you tell which god was in my mind, Sable?' said Meader. 'Male? Female?'

'I cut the connection before checking,' she said. 'Does it matter?'

'Where should we go?' said Evensward.

'Perhaps one of the smaller islands that flank Gyle?' said Blackrose. 'Such as Mastino, for example. I estimate that it would take us about three and a half hours to fly there.'

Badblood lowered his gaze. 'I cannot fly for three and a half hours. I am sorry.'

'Then you should have answered my previous question with more precision,' said Blackrose. 'Now is not the time for false bravado, son. So, I ask again – how far do you think you could fly?'

'I could manage an hour,' the dark red dragon said, his voice low as he burned with shame.

'Meader,' said Blackrose, 'where could we hide that is within fifty miles of here?'

'Nowhere,' said the demigod. 'I mean, there are a few other abandoned palaces in the mountains, but whoever was in my head will be watching us, right now. They'll see where we go.'

Blackrose's eyes tightened. 'Sable, it is time for some of your witch tricks. Send your vision out to Port Edmond, and find the god who has discovered us. Can you immobilise them from here?'

'I can try,' she said.

'Do so.'

Meader offered her a cigarette, but she shook her head and took a deep breath. She relaxed her body, and sent her vision out of herself. If she had been Daphne, then it would have been easy to track the god who was watching them, as her half-sister possessed the power to sense when others used vision. Karalyn could do it too, but Sable was blind to that aspect of dream powers. She had no choice but to do it the hard way, and travel all the way to Port Edmond to look for them. Her vision shot out over the green-clad mountains, racing at high speed towards the lowlands that spread out over the eastern half of Gyle. Port Edmond was almost two hundred miles from the abandoned dragon palace, and it took her a few minutes to reach the enormous city. She homed in on the tallest building, and powered her vision in through a window of the Winter Palace, the place from where she had abducted Meader two years before.

She went up a few floors, to the level where Meader had lived, thinking it the most likely place for gods to reside. She found a Banner sergeant patrolling a hallway, and stole into his mind. She raided his memories, looking for mentions of the gods who lived in the palace, and where they might be. Lord Horace was holding a meeting, she discovered – the Governor's usual morning briefing. Sable darted out from the soldier's head, and raced off again, heading towards a large conference room on the floor above. The doors of the room were closed, but Sable forced her vision through a keyhole, and scanned the large chamber. A long, oval table dominated the room. Horace was seated, but not at the head of the table, where she had imagined he would be. Another man sat there, in the governor's place. Sable peered at his features. She recognised him, but from where? A scattering of demigods were also seated, and many had their eyes glazed over. She went into the mind of the first as quickly as she was able, and saw that the demigod was scanning the seas to the east of Gyle, on the other side of the island from the abandoned palace.

Sable cursed. She was about to pull out, and go into the mind of the next in line, when a demigod sitting further along came out of his trance.

'I have found them, my lords,' the demigod said. 'Three dragons and two humans. One of the humans is Lord Meader, and the other is Sable Holdfast.'

The man at the end of the table glanced up, and Sable read his name from the mind of the demigod where she was hiding – Lord Bastion.

'Well done,' said Horace. 'Did you get inside the mind of the Hold-fast freak?'

'Of course he didn't,' said Bastion. 'The minds of the Holdfasts are sealed, even to the Ascendants.'

'Apologies, Lord Bastion; of course.' Horace turned back to the demigod. 'Where are they?'

'I've already read the location out of his mind,' said Bastion, an irritated expression on his face, as if he would rather be elsewhere. 'They are hiding in one of the ruined palaces in the west of Gyle. Send an entire regiment of Banner soldiers there immediately, along with two death-power-wielding demigods.'

Horace frowned. 'My lord, wouldn't it be far more efficient to use a Quadrant to send soldiers there?'

'It would, but we cannot spare a Quadrant for now. There are two portals being opened to allow reinforcements to enter Dragon Eyre, and I will not order their delay.'

'The Blessed Lord Edmond told me that the Holdfasts were a priority, and...'

'Yes, yes,' said Bastion. 'I know what the sacred Second Ascendant said. However, I am in command of all operational matters, and it is imperative that the portals are opened on time, so that I can return to Implacatus.'

Horace nodded. 'As you wish, my lord. We shall dispatch a full regiment of Banner soldiers, along with a couple of demigods or gods with death powers to accompany them, and also one with vision powers, in order for them to keep in contact.'

'My lords,' said the demigod who had found the abandoned palace; 'I fear that the rebels have discovered that I have seen them. I was inside Lord Meader's head, reading his memories, when I felt something sever the connection, and I had to start again from scratch.'

'That will be the Holdfast witch,' said Bastion. 'Sable has a strange set of powers, different from Kelsey's. Sable can read minds.' His lips formed into a cold smile. 'In fact, if she's as clever as I think she is, then there's a good chance that she's inside one of our heads as we speak.'

Several of the demigods looked anxious, and they glanced at each other with nervous eyes.

'Don't panic,' said Bastion. 'There is nothing she can do to us from here.'

We'll see about that, thought Sable. She dug down deep into the mind of the demigod where she was hiding, and drew on all of her strength. They had been eating breakfast, and the surface of the table was littered with plates, glasses and cutlery. Let's start with something simple.

Pick up a fork, nice and quietly.

The demigod reached out, and his fingers grasped onto a metal fork. No one paid any attention. Lord Horace was giving out some orders to a Banner officer, while Bastion was sipping coffee from a tiny cup.

Now, stab the fork into the eye of the demigod sitting to your right.

The demigod's hand trembled for a moment, then it lashed out towards the man to his right. He jabbed the end of the fork into his neighbour's left eye, then let go of the handle, and blinked, as the struck demigod screamed in surprise and agony.

Now, repeat the following – Sable can see you, Bastion, you dumb piece of shit. Point at him while you say it.

The demigod raised a finger, as the others stared at him with wide eyes.

'Sable can see you, Bastion, you dumb piece of shit!'

Sable cut the connection. She opened her eyes, and coughed.

'Well?' said Blackrose. 'Did you find them?'

'I did. They're going to send a regiment of Banner soldiers, on foot.' She turned to Meader. 'Remind me, who's Bastion?'

Meader's face paled. 'Why do you ask?'

'Because he's sitting in Port Edmond.'

Meader staggered backwards, and almost fell off the window ledge. 'Holy shit!' he cried. 'We have to leave. Now!'

'Did you incapacitate them, Sable?' said Blackrose.

'There were too many of them,' she said; 'but I did manage to distract them for a while.'

'Bastion will have a Quadrant,' said Meader.

'I know,' said Sable. 'Should we try to steal it?'

'That's not what I meant. He could use it to come here, in person, to kill us all. We have to go.'

'He's using it to open portals,' said Sable; 'to bring in reinforcements. We'll be fine here, for a while.'

'I agree,' said Evensward. 'However, perhaps it's worth trying to find a new place to hide, before the soldiers get here.'

'Meader,' said Blackrose; 'climb up onto my harness. We shall leave immediately.'

Sable clambered up onto Badblood's shoulder, while Meader pulled himself up onto Blackrose's harness. Evensward led the way down the ramp, and they reached Boldspark, who was still on guard at the main entrance to the palace.

'We're leaving,' said Evensward to the young red and blue dragon. 'Stay low, and follow Queen Blackrose.'

'Yes, my lady,' said Boldspark, tilting his head.

Blackrose launched herself into the air, and the other dragons did the same. They formed a single column, and the black dragon led them through a succession of tight ravines, keeping only yards from the ground.

'Where are we going?' said Badblood.

'I don't know, my love,' said Sable. 'I imagine Meader will be telling Blackrose about other places to hide.'

'Did you really see Lord Bastion in Port Edmond?'

'Of course; I wouldn't lie about something like that. Meader seemed quite worried about him, didn't he? I've seen Bastion before; I remember him now. He was with Edmond in Old Alea. He must be important, I guess. He was ordering Governor Horace about as if he were in charge.'

Ahead, Blackrose increased her speed, and Badblood fell silent as he tried to keep up. The tip of his left wing brushed through the upper branches of a tree, and Sable could feel him struggle with the intense pace as they hurtled through the narrow ravines.

You're doing great, Sable said in his mind; *you can do this.*

They flew for an hour, traversing countless tree-filled valleys, and skirting the higher mountain peaks. Blackrose kept low the entire way, her underside only a few feet above the ground, while Badblood toiled in her wake. Sable's spirits fell the further they travelled, and her heart was breaking from how much Badblood was suffering. Several times, he struck something along their path, and once sheared the top of a tree off, sending branches flying, before managing to gain a little altitude.

Eventually, when he was about to collapse from exhaustion, Blackrose slowed, and glided down to the bottom of a steep ravine. She folded her wings in, and waited for the others to join her. Evensward and Boldspark both landed without any problem, but Badblood's limbs gave way as soon as he came into contact with the rough ground; and he lay still for a moment, panting, his eyes closed.

You did it, my love. Well done.

Blackrose regarded Badblood for a moment, then turned to the others.

'Meader has guided us to another abandoned structure; what was it called?'

'It's an ancient hunting lodge,' said Meader, from up on Blackrose's shoulders. 'It's where royal dragons used to occasionally stay, when they were hunting for the local wildlife. I chose it because it's not one of the more obvious palaces, and it's not marked on many maps of the area. If we're lucky, then Bastion might not be aware of it; that is, if he wasn't watching us.'

Sable quickly entered the heads of everyone there, to ensure that no one had penetrated their minds.

Blackrose turned to her. 'What are you doing, witch?'

She shrugged. 'Just checking that there aren't any gods hiding inside your minds.'

'Don't do it again, witch. I would know if a god was trying to read my mind; I don't need you to tell me. If I catch you inside my mind again, without my express permission...'

'Leave her alone,' gasped Badblood. 'She was only trying to help.'

'Come on,' said Meader, pointing down the ravine. 'The entrance to the hunting lodge isn't far.'

He jumped off Blackrose's shoulders and landed on the rocky ground. Sable unbuckled herself from Badblood's harness, and joined him, as the four dragons began striding along the bottom of the ravine. Badblood followed at the rear, his body trembling with exhaustion.

Sable glanced at him, then turned to Meader. 'What's so special about Bastion? I remember you telling me that he was in Gyle a while ago, to arrest your father. When I saw him in Port Edmond, he was giving orders to Governor Horace. How can that be, when they are both Ancients?'

'Lord Bastion is the oldest Ancient in existence,' said Meader, as they walked through the shadows of the narrow ravine, 'and his powers are equal to, or better than, those possessed by most Ascendants. I think only Edmond, Theodora, Belinda, and maybe Nathaniel were more powerful than him. Edmond uses him to carry out his dirty work. He's a sadistic bastard, but then, he learned from the best – his father.'

They reached a large, dark opening to a cave that stretched back into the side of the mountain.

'Is this it?' said Evensward. 'It doesn't look very comfortable.'

'I don't think it's been used for a very long time,' said Meader, 'but we should be able to hide in it until we're ready to travel to Ectus.'

The dragons filed into the dark interior, while Meader stood outside and lit a cigarette.

'Well?' said Sable.

'Well, what?'

'Who is Bastion's father?'

Meader smiled, but his eyes were tinged with fear. 'Lord Bastion is the son of the two most powerful Ascendants that have ever lived – Edmond and Theodora.'

CHAPTER 23

DANGLING BY A THREAD

U dall, Ulna, Eastern Rim – 21ˢᵗ Beldinch 5255 (18ᵗʰ Gylean Year 6)
Austin had never been so grateful for a rain shower. He lay
on the bottom of the cage, his eyes closed, and his mouth open, as the
raindrops hit his face. Each one that hit his parched and swollen tongue
felt like bliss.

For eighteen days and nights, he had been confined in the cage
down by the harbour of Udall. For the first few days, large groups of
onlookers had gathered twenty feet below him to gaze upon the ragged
and bloody remains of the demigod, but as his self-healing had slowly
recovered from his ordeal on Implacatus, the numbers attending had
thinned out, until, on most days, only his four guards were there to keep
watch on him. Ata'nix himself had come down from the bridge palace
to peer up at him, and had seemed disappointed that Austin hadn't
expired from his wounds, but had made no changes to the conditions of
his captivity.

The rash that had covered Austin's skin had gone, and his flow
powers had returned; not that he could do anything about them with
the metal gauntlets strapped to his wrists. Were it not for the lack of
food and water, his recovery would have been complete.

The rain stopped, and Austin sat up. He opened his eyes and gazed at the clouds as they drifted by, willing them to release more water onto him. Instead, the wind broke them up, and the sun shone down upon Udall again, bathing the harbour in light. The workers by the fish market at the head of the main quay pulled off the tarpaulin sheets that they had used to keep their produce dry, and re-opened for business. Austin stared at the fish and crabs on sale, his stomach growling in discomfort. He had never liked fish much, but in his half-starved state, he would have leapt at the chance to eat whatever the market was selling. He pulled his eyes away, and turned to look out over the sea. From his elevated position, he could make out every vessel in the harbour, from the small fishing boats, to the larger merchant ships that plied the waters between Enna and Ulna. Black-robed militia from the Unk Tannic were patrolling the quayside, making themselves unpopular by insisting that every vessel landing at Udall was thoroughly searched and then heavily taxed. It was clear to Austin that most of the ordinary folk of Udall hated the Unk Tannic, but they were the only armed force in the city, and there was little the civilians could do to oppose them.

Austin frowned. Two hundred well-armed Banner soldiers would be able to take and hold Udall without any considerable difficulties, he reckoned. If they played it right, they might even be welcomed as liberators by the bullied population. Of course, he hadn't taken into account the presence of the dragons within the palace, but he saw them so rarely that several days could go by without a sighting. Of Splendoursun himself, there had been no sign. The daily business of the humans in the city seemed to be of no interest to the dragons who had usurped control of Udall, and if it weren't for the considerable amounts of food that were loaded onto wagons and sent up to the palace every day, Austin might have forgotten that they were even there. He wondered how Ashfall was being treated. The slender grey dragon had been another to have trusted Austin, only to be let down. He tried to put her out of his mind, but a nagging guilt remained.

The wind blew the last of the clouds away, and the day warmed up. The streets were starting to dry out below him, and he gazed with longing at the last few puddles. He tried to ignore his raging thirst, but it was impossible. The rain had been wonderful, but it had tantalised him, rather than satisfying his needs, and his tongue was parched again. A group of children ran out from the stalls of the fish market, and began jumping in the puddles, and Austin nearly wept from the waste of water.

One of the children turned, and peered up into the sky to the east, then pointed. His companions stopped playing and glanced in the same direction. Austin couldn't make out what they were saying, so he looked up, staring into the distance. Was that another cloud on the horizon? Whatever it was, it was moving towards the harbour, crossing the ocean at speed. No, it wasn't a cloud. Perhaps it was a flock of seabirds. Did seabirds migrate on Dragon Eyre? Austin had no idea. He turned his body round to watch, making the cage sway under the crane from which it was suspended. A few sailors and dockworkers had also seen the strange dark patch in the sky, and several stopped working to stare. Two Unk Tannic agents were among them, then they broke away from the crowd of civilians, and began running along the quayside, in the direction of the bridge palace. Austin's heart began to race. He knew what he wanted the dark smudge to represent, but couldn't allow his hopes to rise. A nervous anxiety rippled through the crowds down in the harbour, and a few others began to run away from the quayside. Someone ushered the children away, then, as if an unspoken signal had passed among the civilians, a panic broke out. Someone screamed, while others pushed and shoved their way off the quay. An old man fell to the ground, and was nearly trampled before being pulled to safety. Austin glanced down. His guards were staring up into the sky, frozen to their posts, their crossbows slung over their shoulders.

'Dragons!' cried a voice above the roar of panic and confusion.

Austin tensed. His eyes picked out the individual shapes of the numerous flying beasts heading straight towards Udall, while his brain tried to work out how to turn any attack to his advantage. He was under no illusions that any dragons would come to his assistance. If Shadowblaze was leading them, there was a chance that they would try to kill him, for disappearing with the Quadrant rather than taking it to Blackrose as he had promised. Still, anything was better than staying in the cage.

The two dozen approaching dragons moved into a wide diamond formation just as the bells of Udall were rung. Groups of armed Unk Tannic were racing through the streets, ordering the civilians to return to their homes, but they had no ballistae, or anything that could counter a dragon attack. Austin glanced over his shoulder, and saw several dragons emerging from the bridge palace. Some took to the air, and circled over the giant structure, as more appeared on the high rooftop platforms. He turned back to face the harbour, and watched as the lead dragons soared over the ships berthed along the quayside. He spotted Shadowblaze – the huge grey and red dragon was at the tip of the diamond formation. The attacking dragons ignored the chaos in the streets of the city, and the front rank passed over the crane from where Austin's cage dangled. Austin's eyes followed them, and he gasped as Shadowblaze collided with a dragon that had flown out from the palace.

Within seconds, the air over Udall was filled with duelling dragons. More were emerging from the palace with every second that passed, and the attacking dragons under Shadowblaze's leadership were soon out-numbered. Austin stared as claws lashed out, and flames enveloped the battling dragons. He could no longer tell which dragons were on either side; all was lost within the confusion of wings and fire above the town. Two huge dragons attacked a smaller beast, and while one gripped its wings with its talons, the other ripped out its throat with fiery jaws. The dead dragon plummeted from the sky, and struck the waters of the harbour, shattering a fishing vessel that had been sailing away from the quayside. Shadowblaze was winning his own duel, against a large blue dragon. His claws were rending its left flank, as his jaws clamped down on the base of a wing. The blue dragon cried out in agony, and Shadowblaze was attacked by two others from the rear. Flames bathed them as the four dragons became entwined in a mass of claws and teeth. Another dragon fell, its neck broken, and crashed into the marketplace, gouging a path through the stalls where the children had been playing only minutes before. A red dragon swooped in low over the harbour, opened its jaws, and incinerated a group of black-robed Unk Tannic agents who had been pointing their crossbows into the air. An enormous white and gold dragon flashed past, hurtling downwards towards the red. Austin gasped. It was Splendoursun. The Queen's suitor lashed out, and his claws ripped through the red dragon's wings, tearing them into tattered shreds. Splendoursun's long tail swung past as he went in for the kill, and the crane holding up the cage was struck. The wooden beams of the crane snapped like twigs, and the cage went spinning through the air. Austin was bounced off the bars as the cage fell, then it struck the side of a building. The bars bent and buckled, and Austin was thrown clear. He skidded down the paved surface of the quayside, tumbling over and over, then rolled to a halt next to a pile of rubble.

Austin opened his eyes, but his vision was blurry, and he could feel pain coming from every part of his body. Flames erupted a few yards to his left, and another dragon fell, smashing into the roof of a harbour building. Shattered tiles flew in every direction, and Austin was showered in fragments.

This was his chance, he thought. Udall had descended into utter chaos as dozens of dragons battled overhead. If he dived into the water of the harbour, he might be able to swim away before anyone noticed what had happened to his cage. He powered his self-healing, weakened though it was, and his pains faded. Two dragons passed over his head, their claws and teeth locked onto each other. The moment they had moved away, Austin readied himself, preparing to sprint across the short gap towards the edge of the quay. He was just about to start running, when he heard a soft cry coming from the rubble next to him. He glanced over, and saw one of the children from before. The young boy was cowering behind the twisted remains of a market stall, shaking with terror.

Austin hesitated. His brain screamed at him to ignore the mortal child – what was his short life worth compared to that of a demigod? He told himself to harden his heart and run, but his legs refused to move.

Above them, a green dragon howled in agony, and began to fall from the sky. Without thinking, Austin turned back, and ran towards the market stalls as the dragon plunged downwards. The young boy was staring up at the falling beast, paralysed with fear. Austin reached him, and scooped him up in his arms, then charged as the green dragon crashed down into the street. Austin was thrown forwards by the force of the impact, but his arms kept a firm grip of the child as they landed onto the cobbles and slid to a halt.

The boy stared at him, his eyes wild with panic, and Austin released him from his grasp.

'Go home,' Austin said. 'Go home and hide.'

The boy wriggled free.

'Wait!' cried Austin. He held out the gauntlets covering his hands. 'Please,' he said. 'Undo one of the buckles first.'

The boy hesitated, then reached forwards, his hands trembling. He unfastened a strap on Austin's left gauntlet, then turned and fled through the piles of debris, disappearing amid the wreckage of the harbour buildings. Austin squeezed his hand out of the gauntlet, then unfastened the straps on the other one.

Free. Austin flexed his fingers, feeling for his flow powers, then got to his feet. It would be much easier to swim without the gauntlets. Above, the battle was starting to ebb, and a few of the attacking dragons were retreating, soaring away back over the harbour to safety. He couldn't see Shadowblaze anywhere, but Splendoursun was rallying his kinfolk, and urging them to drive the invaders away. Austin ran towards the quayside, then his eyes went to the body of a dead Unk Tannic guard. His corpse had been ripped in two by dragon claws, but attached to his belt was a water bottle. All thoughts of escape dwindled as Austin's savage thirst took over. He pulled the water bottle from the body, tossed away the lid, and drank, oblivious to the flames and destruction all around him. The water was tepid and stale, but it still felt like the best thing he had ever tasted in his life. He drained the last drops from the bottle and dropped it, then fell to his knees, panting in relief.

He still had time to escape, he told himself, but another thought entered his head. Shadowblaze's assault on Udall had failed, that much was clear, but Ashfall was still imprisoned within the bridge palace. So? That was nothing to do with Austin. Many dragons were lying dead all over Udall – what was one more to him? Hadn't he already saved the life of a mortal child? It wasn't the time for pointless heroics; it was time to flee. All the same, the thought of Ashfall in chains in a lightless dungeon gnawed at his heart. He knew what it felt like to be isolated within the confines of a cell – for nearly two years he had been a prisoner – and the grey dragon had trusted him. She would have heard the sounds of the battle, and would have wondered if her rescue was imminent; how could he leave her?

'Damn it,' he muttered. 'Stupid dragons.'

He turned back to the bodies of the Unk Tannic lying on the street, then crouched down and took one of their black robes. He pulled it on, then picked up a crossbow. He had never loosed one in his life, but, if he was going to get far, he would need to look as convincing as possible. He glanced up as he stood. Splendoursun and his dragons were circling over the harbour, their voices roaring out in triumph, as the last of Shadowblaze's allies fled back towards the ocean.

Austin covered his head with the hood of the black robes, and started running towards the palace.

———

Getting into the palace had been easy. It seemed that every Unk Tannic guard had gone out to begin clearing up the devastation by the harbour, and the human riders of Splendoursun's kinfolk were all still on the shoulders of their dragons as they soared and wheeled over the town, basking in their victory.

Finding Ashfall, on the other hand, was proving more difficult. Not for the first time, Austin wished he possessed vision powers. He ran along deserted hallways, passing the cells where he had spent so many days and nights. He remembered Splendoursun saying that Ashfall was being interned within a dungeon directly below the vast audience chamber, but there seemed to be no way to get there. Again and again, he had been forced to turn back, to search for another way, and his frustration was growing. The Unk Tannic would have discovered the shattered cage, and would know that he had escaped. They might have also found the discarded metal gauntlets, and he wished he had thrown them into the waters of the harbour. They would be searching for him, and his heart was beating ever faster with mounting panic.

He came across a ramp that he hadn't seen before, and sprinted down it, heading into the gloom of the lower levels of the palace. At the bottom of the ramp, a long hallway stretched out, with dragon-sized doors on either side. The doors were all framed with thick strips of iron, and barred on the outside. Austin ran to the first entrance. The bar was too high for him to reach, so he pressed his ear to the wooden door and listened. Nothing.

'Ashfall!' he cried, his voice echoing down the hallway. He knew he shouldn't shout, but he was becoming desperate. 'Ashfall!'

'Austin?' came a low voice.

He froze, trying to work out where the voice had come from.

'Austin; is that you?'

He ran up the hallway. 'Where are you?'

'I'm in here,' said the dragon's voice.

Austin stared around, then approached one of the huge doorways. He banged his fist onto the iron frame.

'Yes,' said Ashfall. 'I am trapped within this cell. Are you here to get me out?'

'I am, but I don't know how to. The door isn't locked, but the bar is too high.'

He found a narrow gap in the doorframe, and peered through into the shadows. Inside, he caught a glimpse of a dark form moving, then he saw Ashfall's eyes gleam.

'You came for me, human?'

'I did,' he said, 'but it's a waste of time. I can't get you out. I need a dragon to reach up and move the bar that's keeping the door closed.'

'Did you not come with Shadowblaze? I heard the sounds of a battle raging outside.'

'Shadowblaze lost. His allies have all fled; maybe a dozen or so were killed. The harbour area is wrecked, but Splendoursun and the others will be returning soon.'

'I see.'

'I'm sorry, Ashfall; I don't know what to do.'

'Perhaps you should run, Austin,' said the dragon.

'I can't leave you here. Are you chained up?'

'No. I have a muzzle that stops me from emitting flames, but there are no other shackles binding me.'

'Can you break the door down?'

'I am not strong enough. I would need to be as mighty as Blackrose or Shadowblaze to destroy this door. If only I were stronger, then...'

The dragon's voice tailed off.

'What is it?' said Austin.

'There might be a way. Blackrose once told me a story about how she was able to destroy a greenhide nest, entirely on her own, without any other dragon to help her. Austin, are you prepared to risk yourself for me again?'

'Yes. Tell me what to do.'

'Listen carefully,' said the dragon, 'and do exactly as I say.'

Austin raced through the corridors of the palace. The Unk Tannic were starting to return from the town, and Austin had heard several of Splendoursun's dragons landing back onto the platforms, the battle over.

He burst out into a large hallway, and sprinted past a few Unk Tannic guards. They glanced in his direction, but his black robes seemed to fool them, and, although they gave him a strange look, they didn't try to stop him. He turned a corner, and reached Ashfall's old lair. Another dragon had moved in, but no one was present as Austin charged through the entrance. He ran to the rear of the vast cavern, to an abandoned heap of Ashfall's belongings – her old bedding, her rider's harness, and a large, open chest. He reached into the chest, and pulled out various objects made of gold and silver. He had been told that dragons loved the sight of gold, and had even heard stories that some liked to sleep on top of their accumulated hoards, which seemed ridiculous. At the bottom of the chest, he found what he had come for. He shoved it deep into a pocket, then turned, and raced for the entrance, just as a black and white dragon appeared in the doorway.

The dragon's eyes tightened as he saw Austin.

'What are you doing in my lair, Unk Tannic insect?'

Without hesitating, Austin raised his right arm, and unleashed his full flow powers at the dragon's head. The dragon groaned, his eyes going bloodshot. Blood seeped from his ears, and he tried to reach out with his claws to rip Austin to pieces, but crashed down instead, his head hitting the stone slabs covering the ground. The dragon writhed in torment, then his eyes burst from their sockets, spraying Austin with blood, and he lay still.

Austin stared at the enormous body, staggered by what he had done. Blood was dripping from his black robes, so he threw them off, and left them in a pile on the ground.

He had slain a dragon. For some reason, all he could think about was what his old school friends would think.

A scream of horror shook him from his stupor. The dragon's rider was standing in the huge doorway, his eyes wide as he stared at the dead beast lying on the cold ground. Austin raised his hand, and the rider's head exploded. After killing a dragon, one weak human mortal was nothing.

Austin walked past the two corpses and left the lair. He felt nothing – no fear, and no shame at his actions. He was a demigod, the son of a powerful Ancient, and he wasn't afraid. He strode down the empty hallway, his flow powers tingling through his fingers. He reached the hallway where the group of Unk Tannic guards had been earlier, and didn't wait for them to challenge him. He swept his right hand from left to right, and the walls darkened with blood, and fragments of their skulls. The four headless men slumped to the ground, and Austin gave no more thought to them.

Alarms were sounding within the palace by the time he reached Ashfall's cell. Dragons and more Unk Tannic would be coming for him soon, but he wasn't scared. He smiled at the image of Splendoursun's rage when he discovered that one of his dragons had been killed, and hoped that the gold and white dragon would come for him in person.

'Were you successful?' said Ashfall.

'I was,' said Austin. He reached into his pocket and took out the ceramic jug that he had taken from the lair. He pushed it through the gap in the doorframe, and saw Ashfall take it, her giant forelimbs making the jug seem tiny.

'Stand well back,' said Ashfall. 'I'm not sure what effect Sable's salve will have on me. Blackrose told me that it temporarily increased her strength. If it does the same to me, then I shall rip the muzzle off and burn down the door. Make sure you are not standing outside when that happens.'

Austin retreated to the end of the hallway. From inside the cell, he heard a low roar of pain, then his attention was distracted by the sound of footsteps hurrying down the ramp. Austin rolled his shoulders, and lifted his arm.

A dozen Unk Tannic agents appeared at the bottom of the ramp, their crossbows grasped in their hands.

'He's down here!' one of them yelled. 'The demigod is...'

The man's head blew apart before he could finish the sentence. Several of the Unk Tannic began to panic, while others aimed their bows at Austin. The demigod pointed to each in turn. His powers had weakened after slaying the dragon, but he still had more than enough to stop the hearts of the men arrayed against him. It wasn't quite as dramatic and satisfying as disintegrating their heads, but it killed them all the same. As the last one fell, there was an enormous explosion behind him that knocked him off his feet. He turned, dazed, and saw huge fragments of burning wood scattered across the hallway. Ashfall emerged from her cell. Her eyes were wild with aggression, and she had deep, bloody scores down her face from where the muzzle had been ripped off. She glanced at the bodies of the Unk Tannic, then reached out and grasped Austin with a forelimb.

For the first time since he had been freed from the cage, Austin was afraid. Ashfall's eyes were burning with pure rage, and she seemed like a wild and savage beast. Foam flecked her jaws, along with the roiling sparks, and her breath was ragged. She pulled Austin close to her chest, and squeezed him, then strode up the ramp, her rear limbs flattening the corpses of the Unk Tannic that he had killed. More guards were sprinting down from the upper level, and Ashfall opened her jaws. Flames leapt out from her mouth, and the men were reduced to smouldering, blackened corpses in seconds.

'Kill them all,' Ashfall grunted, her voice twisted by the salve.

'No,' cried Austin; 'there are too many for us. Fly to Seabound, Ashfall; get us out of here.'

Ashfall stared at him, and for a split second, he thought she was going to rip his head off.

'I need to rest,' he said. 'I killed a dragon; my powers need time to recover. Ashfall, please!'

The slender grey dragon reached the top of the ramp. Three other dragons were approaching, and they stared at Ashfall in shock. Before they could react, Ashfall opened her jaws and bathed them in flames, then she turned for the huge entrance. She extended her wings, and pushed herself up into the open air. A green dragon dived down at her from above, but Ashfall surged to the side, and blasted her with flames as she passed. The green dragon howled in pain, then Ashfall ascended. She banked for the south-west, and sped off, the salve powering her wings until she was flying faster than any dragon Austin had ever seen. The landscape below them passed in a blur – the town, then the farms, then the abandoned defensive line of towers that Blackrose had erected to protect the humans from the greenhides. After that, the plains of central Ulna stretched away into the distance. Austin tried to move, but the dragon's grasp on him was too tight, as she soared like an arrow away from Udall.

When they reached Seabound, Ashfall's energy was almost spent, and she crash-landed onto one of the platforms that extended out over the dark waters of Alg Bay. She unclenched her forelimb, and Austin rolled out, bruised and winded. He glanced up, and saw two dragon riders looking down at him, crossbows aimed at his face.

'Don't shoot him,' gasped Ashfall. 'The demigod saved me.'

'Get Ahi'edo,' one of the men shouted, and the other ran away into the interior of the old palace.

Austin lay still for a moment, letting his self-healing repair the damage caused by Ashfall's grip. He sorely needed rest, food and water, but his first priority was Ashfall. He reached out with a hand, and touched the grey dragon's scales, sending a soothing surge of healing into her exhausted body.

Shadowblaze appeared at the arched entrance to the platform.

'Ashfall!' he cried. 'I am overjoyed to see you. I tried to reach the palace in Udall to rescue you, but we were driven off. How did you...' His voice fell away as he noticed Austin lying next to her. 'You? I was told that you had betrayed my trust, demigod. Is it true? Tell me that you delivered the Quadrant to Queen Blackrose.'

'I did not,' Austin said.

Shadowblaze's eyes erupted with rage.

'I told you he would abandon us, master,' said Ahi'edo, appearing next to him. 'What did I say? He did exactly as I predicted.'

'Then, why is he back here, rider?' said Shadowblaze. 'If he truly fled, why would he return?'

'I've been hanging in a cage in the harbour of Udall for eighteen days,' said Austin.

'That was you I saw in there?' said Shadowblaze.

'Yes. I managed to escape in the battle.'

Ashfall lifted her head. 'Austin said you were defeated, my lord.'

'It is true,' said the giant grey and red dragon. 'We failed to evict the usurpers from Udall. Splendoursun has won. In three days time, the

Queen's two-year courtship period will be at an end, and Splendoursun will become the master of Ulna, his rule unchecked.'

'We should kill this demigod,' said Ahi'edo, 'before he betrays us again, my lord.'

'Do not touch him!' roared Ashfall. 'He is mine. He saved me.' She turned her fiery eyes to Shadowblaze. 'Do not despair. There is still time.'

'Time for what?' said Shadowblaze. 'The Queen will not be returning; we are too late.'

'No,' said Ashfall. 'You can save Ulna, Shadowblaze. We must return to Udall; you must register your claim – it is the only way.'

'My claim?' said Shadowblaze. 'I don't understand – my claim for what?'

'Your claim as suitor to the Queen. If there are two suitors alive in three day's time, then Splendoursun's authority will be meaningless.'

'We already tried to breach the palace, Ashfall. We failed.'

The slender grey dragon reached out, and pulled Austin towards her in a protective embrace.

'This time will be different,' she said. 'This time, we shall have a demigod on our side.'

CHAPTER 24

TOEING THE LINE

K oleti Isles, Olkis, Western Rim – 21st Beldinch 5255 (18th Gylean Year 6)

'The merchant ship's main mast has been disabled, Captain,' said Lieutenant Dax. 'There's no way they'll be able to follow us, or sail off for help.'

Olo'osso nodded. 'Good work, Udaxa. And the haul? What are my takings?'

'Oil, food, and weapons, sir. I estimate the value to be in the region of eight hundred gold sovereigns.'

Olo'osso glanced at Lara. 'That's how it's done, daughter. I hope you have been watching closely. You girls think you're experts, but this old pirate still has a few tricks left to teach you.'

Lara said nothing, the glare on her face rendering words unnecessary.

Olo'osso turned to Ann, who was also on the quarter deck of the *Giddy Gull*. 'Ani, be a dear, and signal the men to disengage from the merchantman. It's time to head back to Langbeg. Master Oto of the Sea Banner, steer us east once we're free of the other ship. We shall travel via Pangba this time.'

'Yes, Captain,' said Topaz, his hands on the wheel.

He waited while Ann walked down to the main deck. She raised her hand as soon as the last ropes connecting the *Gull* to the merchant vessel had been loosened, and Topaz turned the wheel. He shouted out a few orders to Vitz, who was acting as his midshipman, and the sails filled. Olo'osso turned for his cabin, then grimaced, a hand going to his back.

'Oh, these old bones,' he muttered.

Lara rolled her eyes, but kept her mouth shut. Her father limped a little as he strode into his cabin, then he closed the door.

Lara sidled up to Topaz. 'Did you see that?' she said, her voice low. 'Father's too old for this. He's spent so long feasting and getting drunk in Befallen, that he's out of shape. He thinks he can just step back onto a ship, and it'll be like the old days. I blame the divorce. If he was still with Opina, then she would have talked him out of it.'

'I'm not sure what to say to that,' said Topaz.

Lara shrugged. 'I wasn't expecting a response. I know that you have to serve my father, but I need someone I can unload my complaints onto; and, guess what – it's you.'

Dax glanced over at them. 'What are you two whispering about?'

'None of your damn business, asswipe,' said Lara.

'Shut your mouth, Second Lieutenant, and remember that I am your superior officer. If you don't start showing me some respect, I'll make sure you stay in Langbeg the next time we sail.'

'Kiss my ass. I ain't never calling you "sir".'

Dax glowered at her, then strode to the captain's cabin and went in.

'He's away to complain about you to father again,' said Ann, who was back on the quarter deck.

'So?' said Lara. 'I own thirty per cent of the *Gull*. That prick can't tell me what to do.'

'You don't get it,' said Ann, shaking her head. 'This is a test. Father wants to see if you can take orders as well as dish them out. Insulting Dax isn't helping your case.'

'Come on; you hate him as much as I do.'

'Yeah, but we're working. If father thinks you haven't got any discipline, he might well leave you behind next time.'

Lara glanced at Topaz. 'If I ever show any respect to Dax, you have permission to slap me.'

'Make her see sense, Master,' said Ann. 'She listens to you.'

'I ain't getting involved in family matters, ma'am,' he said.

Ann sighed. 'Shit. I wished I'd stayed in Langbeg. This voyage has been nothing but misery. Between father's aches and pains, and Lara always squabbling with Dax, I would have been better off getting drunk in Befallen with Tilly. My entire year's been screwed up; I should be halfway to the Eastern Rim by now.'

'You can still go,' said Lara. 'After all, Maddie Jackdaw was a fraud.'

'We three know that isn't true,' said Ann. 'We might be the only three who understand, but I doubt very much that Blackrose will be forgiving. Regardless of what the dragons of Skythorn decided, it ain't safe for a Five Sisters vessel to go anywhere near Ulna.'

'I still don't understand what happened,' said Topaz. 'Why would Maddie being foreign make any difference? It was bullshit, that's what it was.'

Lara raised an eyebrow. 'You seem a little emotional about poor old Maddie. It was obvious to me what happened – the dragons were grateful not to have to take any responsibility. They've been hiding in Skythorn for so long that the thought of having to take any action terrifies them. They leapt at the first chance to dispose of the problem.'

'They're risking the anger of Blackrose,' said Topaz. 'She's not just any dragon – she's a queen.'

'The dragons think the exact same as father,' said Ann. 'They all believe that the chances of Blackrose ever making it to Olkis are negligible. Lara's right. Starbright and the others were desperate to find a way not to get involved. I could see it in their eyes the moment that Redblade began questioning Maddie about where she came from.'

'But I know she was telling the truth!' cried Topaz. 'She spilled out her entire life story to me that night when we sailed the *Little Sneak* through the Skerries. You were there, ma'am; you must have heard her.'

Ann nodded. 'I heard her. Look, Topaz, we agree with you. Lara and I saw Maddie with our own eyes in Ulna – there's no doubt that she really is, or was, Blackrose's rider. But, there's nothing we can do about it.'

'I can't just sit back while she's sold off as a slave in the markets of Pangba,' said Topaz. 'It ain't fair.'

'Life ain't fair,' said Lara. 'If it was, then I'd still be captain of this damn ship. Hey, why don't you buy her? I'm sure father would come to a deal with you.'

'What?' said Topaz. 'Are you saying I should buy Maddie, as a personal slave? No way; that's totally degrading.'

'You could always free her.'

Ann shook her head. 'That won't work. Father wants Maddie as far away from Langbeg as possible. He won't be happy if she's shacked up with Topaz in Langbeg.'

Lara shrugged. 'It's worth a shot.'

'Are you actually smitten with the girl?' said Ann. 'You could try speaking to father, but only if you're serious about Maddie. Do you think she likes you?'

'She thinks I'm a drunken idiot,' said Topaz.

'Did she tell you that?'

'Not exactly, but I could see it in her eyes.'

Ann and Lara glanced at each other. Lieutenant Dax appeared at that moment, striding out of the captain's cabin.

He smirked at Lara. 'Your father wants to see you, Second Lieutenant.'

Lara scowled at him.

'Keep calm in there,' said Ann, as Lara strode towards the cabin. She walked in, and slammed the door behind her, as Dax laughed.

'Ann,' said Dax; 'make me a coffee.'

'No,' she said. 'I'm not on board to be ordered around by you. I'm a guest.'

'You're an idler,' he said. 'I haven't seen you do a stroke of work since we set sail. Everyone's got to pull their weight on this ship; even you.'

Ann sighed. 'Fine; I'll do it – but only so I don't have to stand here and listen to you.'

She walked from the quarter deck, leaving Topaz and Dax alone. Vitz ran up the steps from the main deck, and Dax shooed him away.

'I wanted to get you by yourself, Master,' said Dax. 'We both know that Lara will never be back in command of the *Giddy Gull*.'

'Do we, sir?'

'Yes, Master; we do. Her old man's had it up to here with her constant insubordination. She can't take orders – that's her problem, well, one of them. She has several. Ann and the rest of the sisters all have their own ships, so none of them will be captain of the *Gull* neither. Do you get where this conversation is headed?'

'You'll have to enlighten me, sir.'

Dax stared at him. 'You think you're something special, eh? You're a decent master, but you're an idiot when it comes to thinking about your future. My dear old uncle is not as fit as he thought he was, and I don't reckon he'll want to carry on playing at captain for all that much longer. That's why this voyage was so crucial; he wanted to test us, to see which one has what it takes to captain the *Gull* in his name. Now, who could that be, eh? I'll give you a clue – it's me.'

The sound of raised voices echoed through from the captain's cabin, and Dax sniggered. Topaz kept his eyes on the bow of the ship. One of the small Koleti Isles was off to their right as they sailed east, and a strong breeze was filling the sails. Ideal sailing conditions, he thought, were it not for Dax hovering by his shoulder.

'I want to make you an offer, Master,' the lieutenant said. 'Don't answer right away; think about it. When we get back to Langbeg, Captain Olo'osso is going to make a few announcements. The thing is, he told me that you'd foolishly pledged your loyalty to Lara. That's fine, if you want to spend the next few months sitting on your ass in a tavern, touting for work with one of the other families, but it doesn't have to be that way. The Five Sisters are about to become four – the question is, do you want to become unemployed, or do you want to be the foremost master serving under our family? That's the choice: poverty and shame, or fame and riches. Break with Lara, and sail with me, Topaz, and I will make sure you'll end up the most celebrated master to ever work for the Osso family. Is she really worth throwing away your prospects? The other families won't hire you, not if you make the wrong decision – none of them will want to cross my uncle, no matter how good you are. Lara is finished, but it's not too late for you. Right; that's all I wanted to say. Carry on.'

'Thank you, sir.'

Dax wandered away to the far side of the quarter deck and lit a cigarette. Topaz smothered a sigh. Had it really come to that? He knew there was some truth in what Dax had said. Lara was terrible at being second or third in the chain of command; she hated being told what to do, but she was still the best captain Topaz had ever sailed under, despite the manner in which he had been pressed into her service. He remembered the day well. The settler crew of the *Winsome* had been massacred, and he had been forced to swear an oath of allegiance to a woman he hated. And yet, in the two years in which he had served as her master, he had seen what she was capable of achieving.

Vitz appeared on the steps leading up from the main deck, and Topaz gestured for him to approach. The tall, well-built young man bounded up on to the quarter deck and strode over to the wheel. Before Topaz could open his mouth to speak, Lara stormed out of the captain's cabin, her face red with rage. She glared at Dax, then ran past him, and disappeared down the aft hatch.

Vitz raised an eyebrow. 'Anything I should be worried about, sir?'

Topaz shook his head. 'No. It's family business.'

———

Topaz came off watch when the ship's bell rang at sunset. Vitz was standing next to him, ready to take over, and Topaz stepped away from the wheel, relieved to be able to get off the quarter deck for a while. Vitz took over, while Dax lurked in the background, keeping a watchful eye on the young settler.

'Any questions before I head down the hatch?' said Topaz.

'No, sir,' said Vitz. 'I have the course in my head. I'll see you at dawn.'

'Fair enough. Don't be afraid to send someone to wake me up if you need anything; alright?'

'Yes, sir. Thank you, sir.'

Topaz turned to go, then noticed Olo'osso stick his head out from his cabin. 'Master,' he said. 'I'd like a quick word, if you please.'

Topaz nodded, then walked back towards the cabin.

'You too, Lieutenant,' Olo'osso said to Dax. 'Ani, please keep an eye on things here for me.'

'Yes, father,' said Ann.

Topaz and Dax went into the captain's cabin, and Olo'osso closed the door. He gestured to the chairs that sat round his table. A few lamps had been lit, and a bottle of wine was sitting in the centre of the table.

They sat, and Olo'osso gripped his back as he slid into his chair.

'The sea air ain't doing much for my old bones,' he said. 'If only I was twenty years younger, eh, lads?'

Dax laughed, but it sounded forced to Topaz's ears.

'Right, then,' Olo'osso went on. 'I had a little word with Ani earlier, and she told me of a few concerns that you have, Master.'

'What about, sir?'

'About that fake dragon rider,' he said. He lifted a hand. 'Don't say anything, not yet. Ani told me that she and Lara had seen Miss Jackdaw in Ulna, and I've heard that you are also of the opinion that this girl is really the rider of Queen Blackrose. However, I don't want to get into a debate about this. As far as I'm concerned, the judgement of the dragons of Skythorn is the final word on the subject. They pronounced her as false, and that's exactly how I'm going to treat her. So, I have decided to inform you of my plans for the girl. As soon as we return to Langbeg, I'm going to put her on board one of our vessels, and have her taken straight to Pangba, where she will be sold to the slave market. I reckon a pretty young thing like that should fetch at least a few hundred, but that's beside the point.' He lifted the wine bottle, and filled three glasses. 'Here's the thing. Ani also told me that you might be interested in purchasing this girl, Master.'

Dax laughed again. 'Looking for a slave girl, are you, Topaz? You should have told me; I have excellent contacts in the slave auction houses of Pangba. I could have found you someone.'

Olo'osso looked Topaz in the eye. 'I'm sorry to disappoint you, lad, but I can't sell her to you. It's clearly not in my interests to keep a false dragon rider anywhere near Langbeg, just in case.'

Topaz's temper started to rise. 'Just in case what, sir?'

Olo'osso took a sip of wine. 'Well, just in case Blackrose does actually turn up in Olkis, lad. I mean, I think it's highly unlikely. No dragon has managed to fly from Ulna all the way to Olkis since the invasion started. They'd have to go via Na Sun Ka, then Gyle, and then Ectus; it's a virtual impossibility. Still, I ain't taking any chances.'

'What if I was to travel to Pangba and buy her anyway, sir?'

'Well, if you were to do something that rash, Oto of the Sea Banner, then there would be consequences. For starters, I would confiscate your ten per cent holding of the *Giddy Gull*, as a punishment for disobeying a direct order. Secondly, you'd no longer be welcome in Langbeg. I'd have a quiet word with the other families, and make sure that no one went near you. This would be a tragedy, in my opinion. You're a fine sailor – reliable, and skilled, and you don't seem to harbour any ambition of ever becoming a captain, which just about makes you the perfect master. I don't want to lose you, which is why I thought this little chat was necessary, so that we all know where we stand.'

Dax lifted his glass. 'I don't think Topaz is stupid enough to wreck his life over a slave girl, uncle. If I were you, I'd be more worried about his loyalty to Lara.'

'His loyalty to my daughter is commendable,' said Olo'osso. 'However, it needs to evolve into a loyalty to the overall family, not just to one member of that family.' He put down his glass. 'You should know, lad, that when we return to Langbeg, I intend to temporarily relieve Lara of her sea-going duties. That lass needs to learn how to be a part of a team; she needs to prove to me that she can slot into a chain of command. Perhaps I was too indulgent of her; perhaps I should have waited before giving her a command. The other girls all had to serve as first or second lieutenants for a few years before they became captains. Lara's only experience of obeying orders was on a solitary trip to the Eastern Rim with Ani as her captain, and from what Ani's told me, she hated taking orders.'

Topaz glanced down at the table. 'If you free Maddie, sir, I will agree to serve on any of the Five Sisters' vessels, no matter who the captain is.'

'What?' cried Olo'osso. 'Are you mad, Oto of the Sea Banner? Do you seriously believe I would allow Miss Jackdaw the freedom to run around Langbeg, telling all and sundry her wicked lies, that she's the rider of a dragon queen? Not a chance, lad. She needs to go far away from Langbeg.'

'We could take her back to the Eastern Rim, sir.'

'Oh yes, what a great idea. Wonderful. I imagine that Blackrose will be thrilled to discover that it was one of my daughters who abducted her in the first place.' He sighed. 'I don't understand, lad. Have you fallen for this girl?'

'No, sir.'

'It sounds like you have. If you want a slave girl, let Udaxa buy you one. Damn it, I'll even pay the bill; but Maddie Jackdaw will be sent to Pangba, and that's the end of it. Tell me, lad – are you going to accept my orders, or do we have a problem?'

'I will accept your orders, sir.'

Olo'osso stared at him for a few moments, then nodded. 'Very well. Dismissed. Udaxa, stay here a little longer.'

Topaz got to his feet, saluted, then strode from the cabin. He caught Ann's eyes when he emerged onto the quarter deck, but said nothing, keeping his face expressionless, despite the turmoil roiling through him. He walked down the steps to the main deck, then climbed down the aft hatch, where his tiny cabin lay. Ryan was playing his guitar in front of a few sailors, and he glanced up as Topaz approached.

'Any requests, mate?' Ryan grinned.

Topaz shook his head, and slumped down onto a chest.

'Alright, lads,' said Ryan, putting the guitar down. 'Show's over. Beat it.'

The sailors grumbled as they dispersed, then Ryan turned to Topaz.

'What's up, mate? You look like you caught a rat pissing in your ale.'

Topaz said nothing. He glanced around the lower deck, counting how many sailors were within hearing distance. Back in the Sea Banner, he had been happy to voice his complaints among the rest of the crew, but as a master, he had responsibilities. Besides, he knew that whatever he said would make it back to Dax and Olo'osso.

He got back to his feet, and nodded towards his cabin. Ryan made no response, but Topaz could see that he understood. They walked to the rear of the deck, and entered the small space. Topaz closed the door, and Ryan sat on one of the two seats. Topaz pushed his chest under his hammock, and sat on the other.

'Right then, mate,' said Ryan, lighting a cigarette. 'Let's hear it.'

'They're going to sell Maddie as a slave.'

Ryan nodded. 'And this has upset you?'

'Of course it upsets me, mate.'

'Why?'

'Well, for starters, she ain't done nothing wrong. She *is* a dragon rider, despite the bullshit that the dragons of Skythorn said. Because she's a foreigner, they think that it's impossible for her to be a rider – do you know what that reminds me of? Me and you in the Sea Banner. The damn settlers would tell us that we didn't belong, just because of where we were born, and now the dragons and the Five Sisters are doing the same thing to Maddie.'

'But you know how much the dragons love their rituals and traditions, mate. Every rider I've met has gone through at least a decade of training, and they have to learn all about the customs and so on. You and I were trained sailors when the Sea Banner picked us up. From what I've heard, this Maddie knows bugger all about being a rider. Didn't the dragons ask her some basic questions that she couldn't answer? She's not the same as us.'

'Fine – so she can't recite the ancient laws of being a rider. Does it matter? She told me all about how Blackrose chose her. She even told her what her true dragon names were; would she have done that if they didn't have a proper bond?'

'You only have her word for that, mate. I've known plenty of scam artists who knew how to spin a good tale.'

'What about Ann and Lara? They both say that they saw Maddie in Ulna, standing next to Blackrose.'

'And did they hear Blackrose say – "this is my rider"? Blackrose also brought that Sable woman from Lostwell, but she's not the queen's rider.'

Topaz frowned. 'Are you saying that you think she's a liar; that she was bullshitting me the whole time?'

'I don't know, mate, but I do think it's possible. Look, I know you've got a thing for this girl, but it seems that the captain has made his decision, and that's that. And, let's face it, even if she is telling the truth, there's no chance that Blackrose is going to turn up here looking for her. You're going to have to accept it and move on.'

'She's going to be sold into slavery, Ryan; how am I supposed to get that out of my head? Someone will buy her, and turn her into their house slave, or worse.'

'It's rough, and no mistake; but what can we do? I assume you've thought about buying the girl? You've got the money, eh? How much do you think she'll go for?'

'The captain has forbidden me from buying her. He doesn't want her in Langbeg, and he told me I'd be exiled if I went ahead and did it anyway.'

Ryan puffed out his cheeks.

'You know, mate,' Topaz said, 'I can still remember the day my mother sold me to a group of merchants in Nankiss. I was only seven, but it still feels like it was yesterday. Seeing all those faces staring at you when you're standing in the slave auction house, like you're nothing but a piece of meat, and listening to them haggling over your price. Folk prodding you, and checking your teeth, while all the time you're praying that you don't get bought by the sleazy old guy who's leering at you. My heart breaks when I think of Maddie going through all that. Why do we still put up with slavery, mate? We complain when the settlers enslave native islanders, and yet we allow it to happen on Olkis? If it's wrong for them to do it, it's wrong for us to do it, too.'

'I hear you, mate, but what can we do? Best to put her out of your mind. Find a nice girl in Langbeg; I can introduce you to a few who would jump at the chance to get to know a Five Sisters master. If you're heart's set on marriage and settling down, then let's face it – you're one of the most eligible bachelors in Langbeg. You'll have no problem finding a wife.'

'I don't want just any wife, mate.'

'You can't tell me that you're in love with this Maddie, mate. You barely know her. You've got a kind heart, and you feel sorry for her – but that ain't love.'

Topaz said nothing. Ryan offered him a cigarette, and he took it.

'Listen,' Ryan went on; 'in a few days, we'll be back in Langbeg, and Maddie will be shipped off to Pangba, or wherever she's being sent, and that'll be it over and done with. In a few months, you will have forgotten all about her. In the meantime, don't do anything stupid, eh?'

'I won't.'

'Good. How did you leave it with the captain?'

'I told him I would obey his orders.'

'Praise the gods for that. That's all you can do, mate. Obey orders, work hard, and then we can cut loose when we hit the taverns in Langbeg.'

'Easy to say, mate. How am I supposed to forget about her?'

Ryan shrugged. 'Got any gin?'

CHAPTER 25

A PLAN OF SORTS

L angbeg, Olkis, Western Rim – 24th Beldinch 5255 (18th Gylean Year 6)

Maddie yawned and stretched her arms. Her bed in her room in Befallen was so comfortable that she didn't want to get up, but she had been told that the *Giddy Gull* was due to return to Langbeg that morning, and wanted to see if it was true. She grabbed her dressing gown and pulled it over her shoulders, then slid out of bed and opened the door to her balcony. The sky was a deep shade of blue, with just a few specks of white cloud, while the bay below was glistening in the dawn light. The palm trees down by the harbour were swaying in the mild breeze, and Maddie savoured the sea air for a moment. The smell of it reminded her of the Warm Sea back home and, if she closed her eyes, she could almost be in Tara.

She glanced down at the piers extending out from the long quay-side, and had no trouble identifying the *Giddy Gull*. Even to someone as inexperienced with boats as she was, its sleek lines were unmistakable.

Her heart sank. Tilly had told her that a decision would be made about her future once the *Gull* had returned from its latest voyage, and she had hoped for a few more days of peace before that happened. It was a day for decisions, she thought. On the other side of the world, in

Ulna, it was also the day when Blackrose's courtship period would formally end. Maddie found it hard to believe that two years had passed since the first suitor had staked his claim, and she wished she was there to see what happened. Would Blackrose choose someone, or would she reject them all? Whichever way it went, Maddie was heartbroken that she wouldn't be there to support her dragon. She gazed down at the *Giddy Gull*, watching as two cranes unloaded cargo from its deck. A line of wagons was waiting by the end of the pier, and she could see people striding towards them, ready to make the short journey up the face of the cliff to Befallen Castle. Maybe they had decided to send her back to Ulna. That would be the sensible thing to do. Take her back, and explain to Blackrose that it had all been a terrible misunderstanding. Maddie would make sure that the pirates weren't punished; she would tell Blackrose that it had been the Unk Tannic who had spirited her away, and then everything would be sorted out.

The lead wagons by the pier started to move, then they disappeared out of view as they headed around a spur of rock. The next time she would see the wagons would be when they were approaching the castle's mighty gatehouse, where the bulk of Olo'osso's militia guards were based. Maddie walked back into her bedroom, and decided to get ready. She washed herself, and cleaned her hair by dunking her head into a basin of water, then rinsed it with a jug. She wrapped a towel round her head and looked through her clothes. She needed something practical, just in case, she thought, so she pushed the flowery dresses to one side, and selected an outfit that looked like the kind of thing that Tilly had worn on the *Little Sneak*. Next, she examined her small collection of shoes. She ignored the high heels, and swithered over sandals or boots, eventually choosing the tough-looking leather boots. She laced them up, then glanced at her reflection in the mirror. She looked like a sailor, she thought. She sat on the bed and brushed her hair, then tied it back into a ponytail. It was only then that she noticed that no one had brought her any breakfast that morning, and her stomach rumbled. Was it a sign?

A key turned in the lock, and her front door opened. A guard poked his head through the gap. He glanced at Maddie, then opened the door fully, and allowed Tilly to enter. As soon as she had crossed the threshold, the guard swung the door closed again and locked it.

Maddie put down the brush and stood. 'Morning, Tilly.'

Tilly kept her eyes lowered. 'I have some news,' she said, her voice almost a whisper.

'Oh yeah?' said Maddie. 'Well, tell me.'

'My father has made a decision, about what to do with you.'

'Did he send you to tell me?'

'No. He doesn't know I'm here, but I thought that you deserved to know.' Tilly glanced up at her, and Maddie could see the pain in the young woman's eyes. 'I'm so sorry, Maddie, but you are going to be sold into slavery.'

Maddie's knees buckled, and she sat back down on the bed.

'You will be placed on board the *Giddy Gull*,' Tilly went on, 'and taken to the slave auction houses in Pangba.'

'I don't understand,' said Maddie. 'No one can sell me. I'm not a thing; I'm a person.'

'I captured you, and handed you over to father, so under Olkian law, you now belong to him.'

'No,' said Maddie. 'I don't accept that.'

'It doesn't matter if you accept it or not, Maddie. It's what's going to happen.'

'Will someone buy me?'

'I imagine so. If you're lucky, some kindly old woman will purchase you to help around her house or farm. If she likes you, she might even free you after a while.'

'A farm? I don't know how to farm. What if I'm unlucky?'

Tilly glanced away, and shrugged.

'This can't be happening.'

'I'm sorry. I tried to argue with father about it, but his mind's made up. He wouldn't even allow me to buy you.'

Maddie narrowed her eyes. 'Why would you buy me?'

'So I could free you, of course. Topaz wanted to buy you too, but father's answer was the same.'

'Topaz wanted to buy me? Eww. He wants me to be his slave? That's disgusting.'

'What? No, you misunderstand. Topaz feels sorry for you too. Like me, he thinks it's unfair. He likes you.'

'Does he? That's a strange way to show it.'

'Topaz wouldn't hurt a fly, Maddie. But anyway, it doesn't matter. Father has forbidden any of us here in Langbeg to buy you. He wants you to be sent far away. After today, we'll never see each other again.'

'Today? It's happening today?'

Tilly nodded. 'Father wants it over with as soon as possible. The *Giddy Gull* is already being re-supplied to make the short trip to Pangba. You'll be there by dawn, on the second day from now. I need to prepare you, Maddie. I've seen the slave auction houses in Pangba; I know what they're like. You'll be poked and prodded, and... and...' Tilly's words ceased, and she started to cry.

Maddie stared at her. This couldn't be happening. It was a mistake. Tilly had made a mistake. Olo'osso was a pirate, but he was also a civilised man, and civilised men didn't sell young women into slavery. That was what bad people did.

'Maybe I should speak to your father,' she said, as Tilly continued to weep. 'I'll offer to leave Langbeg of my own accord, and make my way back to Ulna. I could work on a ship. I know that there aren't many women sailors, but I don't have any money to pay to travel as a passenger. Maybe your father could lend me some out of the four thousand the Unk Tannic gave you; after all, it was partly my money. Blackrose, Sable and I brought it all the way from Lostwell, and now your father has a big chunk of it. Sable robbed a lot of people for that gold, and it seems a pity that the Unk Tannic control the rest of it.' She glanced at Tilly. 'Did you know that Blackrose is due to pick a suitor today? She'll probably reject them all, to be honest; I don't think she fancied a single one of them. Hey, why are none of the Five Sisters married? Are you all just too picky?'

'What's wrong with you?' cried Tilly. 'How can you be so calm?'

'Do I look calm? Strange. I don't feel very calm. I actually feel quite cross. Your family is powerful – why haven't you put a stop to slavery? Before I came to Olkis, I was under the impression that only the settlers from Implacatus enslaved people, and by people, I mean natives, of course. There was slavery on Lostwell too, so it seemed like an Implacatus thing.'

'Please, shut up,' said Tilly; 'I'm trying to think.'

Maddie frowned, then she got up and walked out onto her balcony. She glanced at the steel bars enclosing the sides and the top, and the sight of them almost made her break down. If only Blackrose would come flying over the horizon to her rescue. She lowered her head. It was a foolish hope.

'I have an idea,' said Tilly, coming onto the balcony.

'Yeah? Are you going to let me speak to your father?'

'No, that would be pointless. I'm going to help you escape.'

Maddie blinked. 'What?'

'This is all my fault, Maddie. I was the one who took you from Ulna, so I owe it to you to set things right. I'm going to need help, though.'

'Are you going to ask that Topaz guy?'

'No. Unfortunately, he's still down in Langbeg. He's probably in a tavern with his mates from the *Gull*, getting drunk. It'll have to be one of my sisters, but who? Ann's too obedient to father; Ellie's too cautious; and Dina's too much of a cow. Shit. It'll have to be Lara. Damn it. I can't believe I'm going to have to ask Lara for help.'

'Can we trust her?'

'I don't know, but she's incredibly pissed off with father right now, and that's more important. I don't need to tell her exactly what I'm doing – I just need her to distract the guards, so I can smuggle you out of Befallen. Right, stay here...'

Maddie laughed. 'Alright. I promise I won't leave my prison cell.'

Tilly gave her a look. 'You know what I mean. I'll be back soon. Be ready.'

A long, slow hour passed, and Tilly had yet to re-appear at Maddie's front door. The young pirate captain had rushed off, leaving Maddie to pace the floor of her bedroom. Tiring of that, she had gone out to sit on her balcony, her stomach continuing to rumble as she grew ever hungrier. Voices were coming down from Olo'osso's loggia above her, and she began to wonder if Tilly had had second thoughts. Loyalty to the Osso family seemed to be highly prized, and it was difficult to believe that any of the sisters would go against their father. Lara, maybe. Maddie could remember the youngest of the sisters coming to Seabound Palace, just before the battle in Alg Bay. She had torn into Blackrose that day, insulting the great black dragon to her face over her treatment of Sable, so Maddie knew she didn't lack any courage. Common sense, perhaps; but not courage.

Maddie leapt from her seat as she heard her door open. She rushed back through into her bedroom, and saw Tilly and Lara enter.

'Hello,' said Maddie, once the door had been closed again.

Tilly rubbed her face. 'I think I've got everything ready, but Lara insisted on coming in here to speak to you first.'

'I sure did,' said Lara, a smirk on her lips. 'I want to ask you a question.'

'Alright,' said Maddie. 'Ask away.'

'I need to know what you'll do if you ever make it back to Ulna,' said Lara. 'Are you going to blame it all on us? The thing is, me and Ann want to sail over to the Eastern Rim again, but we can't do that if Blackrose will roast us the moment we land at Udall. So, what are you going to tell her?'

'I'll tell her that two of the Five Sisters helped me escape.'

Lara nodded, then glanced at Tilly. 'Maybe I should take her back myself.'

'In the *Giddy Gull*?' said Maddie.

'No,' said Lara. 'I doubt I'll be setting foot back on my beloved brigantine at any time in the near future. I meant on the *Little Sneak*.'

'You want me to lend you my sloop?' said Tilly. 'No chance.'

Lara sighed. 'Then tell me, Tilly, how exactly is she supposed to make it all the way back to Ulna? Are you expecting the girl to swim?'

'I was going to put her on a merchant ship bound for Nankiss,' said Tilly. 'She can take a ship from there to Gyle, and then another across to the Eastern Rim.'

'Are you out of your mind? She'll never make it back to Ulna that way; the Banner soldiers will pick her up in Gyle, if not before. Have you ever actually planned anything in your life? She'd be safer as a slave. Well, probably. Maybe.'

'We can't use any of our ships,' said Tilly. 'Father's going to be angry enough when he discovers we helped her get out of Langbeg.'

Lara shrugged. 'I thought the whole point of this was to piss off father?'

'Is that why you're helping me?' said Maddie.

'Yup. No offence, but I don't particularly care what happens to you. All I want is the chance to plunder some ships in the Eastern Rim, and get a new boat of my own; and to annoy the living shit out of dear old papa. Plus, it'll earn me lots of points with Topaz, and I need him not to desert me.' She shrugged. 'I never said I was a hero.'

'We stick to my plan,' said Tilly.

'Your shit plan,' said Lara.

Tilly glared at her sister. 'Are you going to help us or not?'

Lara rolled her eyes. 'Fine. What do you need me to do?'

'I have a wagon ready by the gatehouse,' Tilly said. 'Father's up in his loggia, telling everyone how much money he made from his latest voyage, so he'll be distracted for a while. I want you to lure the guards away from outside this room, and clear them from the stairs. I'll handle the rest.'

'What about the guards in the gatehouse?'

'I was thinking that I'll pretend that she's my prisoner, and that I'm escorting her down to the harbour, just as father has ordered. I mean, that's exactly what father has ordered, so they should believe it.'

Lara frowned. 'It'll never work.'

'I knew I shouldn't have asked you!' cried Tilly. 'Could you not just be helpful and supportive for the first time in your life?'

'I resent that,' said Lara. 'I don't remember you being very supportive of me when I got my first ship.'

'That was because you didn't have to spend years as a lieutenant first, like the rest of us did. Father's always spoiled you.'

'Spoiled me? Are you joking? Out of the two of us, which one is being stripped of her captaincy, eh? Answer me that.'

'That's got nothing to do...'

'Both of you, stop it,' said Maddie.

Tilly and Lara turned to stare at her.

'Thank you,' said Maddie. 'Now, I don't want to seem like a pest, but can we just get on with it?'

'Fine,' muttered Lara. 'I'll be ten minutes.'

She knocked on the front door, and a guard opened it and let her out. The door closed again, and Maddie shook her head.

'Those guards will have heard every word,' she said. 'Even if this does work, you and Lara are going to be caught.'

'I know,' said Tilly. 'Part of me wants to get caught. I want father to know why I did it. You were right before, our family is powerful, and we shouldn't be selling folk into slavery; well, not unless they're criminals or something. You're innocent. Right, now pay attention; I've a lot to go over.'

Tilly spent the next few minutes rattling off a list of things that Maddie should do when she arrived at Nankiss. It was a huge city, she said, and a dangerous one, so Maddie shouldn't linger. Instead, she should use the money that Tilly was going to give her to buy a place on a ship heading south, to Ectus or Gyle, or even Na Sun Ka, if she was lucky. Tilly's father wouldn't waste time and gold looking for her; he would be angry, but not so angry that he'd bother to hunt Maddie down.

Tilly was in full flow, describing the layout of the harbour at Nankiss, when the door opened. Lara leaned against the doorframe, a hand on her hip.

'Ta-dah!' she said.

'Have the guards all gone?' said Tilly.

'Just like you requested, dear sister.'

'What did you tell them?'

'An artist never reveals their secrets,' said Lara. 'I'd estimate that you've got about five minutes to get Maddie out of the castle before they come back.'

'Thank you,' said Maddie.

Lara shrugged. 'I can tell Topaz that I helped you escape; that'll cheer up the miserable sod.'

Maddie frowned. 'Why?'

'Why what?'

'Why will it cheer him up?'

Lara laughed. 'The lad's besotted with you. I don't know what you said to him on the *Little Sneak*, but he ain't shut up about you since. Now, piss off; quickly.'

Maddie's cheeks flushed. Topaz was besotted with her? That sounded highly unlikely. She thought about asking Lara some more questions, but Tilly was shoving her out of the room. Once they were in the hallway, Lara re-locked the door, then tossed the keys out of a window.

'Good luck!' she beamed.

Tilly led Maddie down the deserted stairwell. They came to a landing, and Tilly peered around, but no one was there.

'The cow actually did it,' she muttered. 'The guards have gone.'

'What did she mean "besotted"?' said Maddie.

'Never mind that; come on.'

They raced down another flight of stairs, then Tilly slowed as they reached the main entrance to the tower.

'Act depressed and sullen,' said Tilly. 'Remember, you're my prisoner, and I'm leading you off into slavery.'

'Shouldn't you be armed? I mean, couldn't I just run away?'

'Good point,' said Tilly. 'Hang on.'

Tilly disappeared into a side room, and came out brandishing a crossbow. She pointed it at Maddie.

'Do you have to do that?'

'It's not loaded,' said Tilly. 'Walk in front of me. Eyes on the ground.'

Maddie stepped out into the bright sunshine, and blinked. The sun was directly overhead, and she could feel the warmth touch her skin. She glanced around the courtyard, then remembered that she was supposed to be dejected, so she planted a disconsolate look on her face and trudged forward. Behind her, Tilly was pointing the crossbow at her back.

'Move,' Tilly growled.

Maddie headed towards the large gatehouse, where several guards were stationed. They glanced up as Maddie and Tilly approached the closed gates, and their officer raised a hand.

'Miss Atili,' he said. 'What are you doing?'

'I'm taking the prisoner down to the harbour,' Tilly said. 'She is to be loaded onto the *Giddy Gull*. Father's orders.'

The officer frowned. 'I was told, ma'am, that Udaxa'osso would be escorting the prisoner to the *Gull*.'

'Yeah?' said Tilly. 'Well, he's, uh, busy. Father told me to do it.'

The officer nodded. 'Alright, ma'am. I'll just need to check, and then you can be on your way.'

'Check?' cried Tilly. 'Do you know who you're speaking to? I'm not a damn servant; I'm Captain Tilly of the *Little Sneak*. You don't need to check.'

'Sorry, ma'am, but your father insists that we follow correct procedure. If there's been a change in our orders, then I'll need it confirmed.'

'The orders haven't changed,' said Tilly. 'They're exactly the same, except that it's me doing the escorting. Open the gates, or I'll make sure you never work for this family again.'

The officer frowned for a moment, then he nodded to a couple of the other guards. 'Do as she says.'

The barred gates were hauled open, their hinges squealing like a hurt animal. Beyond, a wagon was parked on the road that led down to

Langbeg. A driver was waiting by the ponies, smoking a cigarette. Tilly shoved Maddie in the back, and urged her on. As they were passing through the arched opening, from the corner of her eye Maddie noticed the officer signal to one of his men, who sprinted off into the tower.

Tilly and Maddie reached the wagon.

'Just the one passenger, ma'am?' said the driver, stubbing out his cigarette into the dusty ground.

'She ain't a passenger,' said Tilly; 'she's my prisoner, and we're both going.'

'Right you are, ma'am. Climb aboard.'

He helped Tilly and Maddie clamber up onto the back of the wagon, then strolled round to the front. He checked the harnesses, and patted the side of one of the ponies.

'Old Gertrude's got a sore foot,' he said, as he crouched down to examine one of the ponies.

'Get a move on!' cried Tilly, her voice edged with panic.

'Sorry, ma'am,' said the driver, 'but the health of my ponies is important to me. Up and down the cliff they go, a dozen times a day, and...'

'We haven't got time for this shit,' said Tilly. 'Please.'

The driver scowled, muttered something under his breath, then climbed up onto the front bench.

'Where to, ma'am?' he said, his lips set into a deep frown.

'The quayside,' snapped Tilly. 'Dear gods, man; I already told you this.'

'There's no need to be rude. I'm just doing my job.'

'Try to do it a little faster.'

The driver pulled on the reins, and the wagon started moving. They had barely covered a yard, when a whistle blew from the gatehouse, and a dozen guards raced out.

'Stop that wagon!' cried the officer.

The driver halted the ponies, and turned round. 'What is it now?' His eyes widened as he saw a dozen crossbows pointed towards the wagon. He raised his hands. 'Am I in trouble?'

The guards ignored him.

'Atili'osso,' the officer cried, 'drop the crossbow and step down from the wagon.'

'How dare you?' shouted Tilly. 'On whose authority...'

'Mine,' said Olo'osso, striding out from the archway. He approached the wagon, and glared up at Tilly. 'What are you playing at, girl? Why are you defying my orders?'

Tilly's face paled. 'Father, I was, um... I was carrying out your orders. I was taking Maddie Jackdaw down to the harbour, you know, like you said, and...'

'Don't you lie to me, Atili. You know very well that I ordered you to stay away from the prisoner. It breaks my heart to discover how little you think of me. After all I've done for you, this is how you repay me? And to think that you dragged Alara into your devious plans as well; frankly, it beggars belief. Get down from the wagon. Now.'

Tilly swallowed, then climbed back down to the ground.

Olo'osso gestured to the driver. 'You – remain where you are. My nephew will be escorting the prisoner to the harbour.'

The driver nodded. 'Yes, sir.'

Dax walked out from the gatehouse, along with a sheepish-looking Lara and several more guards.

Lara glanced at Tilly. 'I told you it was a shit plan.'

'Silence,' said Olo'osso. 'Udaxa, I am placing you in charge of the prisoner, as of this moment. Take her to the *Gull*, and assume the captaincy. I shall send down one of my more reliable daughters to act as your first lieutenant – Adina, most likely.'

'You making him captain of the *Gull*?' cried Lara. 'That's my damn ship!'

'Not any more, Alara, dear,' said her father. 'As of this moment, I am stripping both you and Atili of your captaincies. The *Gull* shall go to Udaxa, and I'll probably scrap the *Little Sneak*, as a punishment for Atili's gross disobedience.'

'No!' said Tilly. 'You can't!'

'I am sorry, daughter, but my mind is made up. It may seem harsh, but if it teaches you both a lesson, then it shall be worth the pain it causes.'

'I'll take the prisoner down to the harbour right away, sir,' said Dax. 'Thank you for your faith in me. I'll have a midshipman and some of the master-at-arms' lads go through the taverns to collect the crew as soon as I get to the *Gull*.'

Olo'osso chewed his lip for a moment. 'Wait,' he said, after a while. 'I think it might be a good idea to use the *Sneak's* master for this voyage. It's a short journey to Pangba and back, and it'll give him some experience of handling the *Gull*. Also, it'll mean that Oto of the Sea Banner is not involved in the operation. I know he's fond of the prisoner, and I'd like to spare him the pain of seeing her sold into slavery.'

Maddie stared at the old pirate. 'Are you really going to sell me, as if I were a pig or a cow? Even if you think I'm a liar, which I'm not, can you really believe it's right to sell a person into slavery? I've never done anything to hurt you, or any of your family – Tilly and Lara were only being kind; they didn't want me to become a slave. Do you? The person who buys me could hurt or even kill me – don't you care? Does my life mean nothing? Am I worth nothing?'

Dax laughed. 'I wouldn't say that, girl; you'll probably fetch a few hundred coins!'

Maddie ignored him, her stare fixed on Olo'osso's face. He hesitated for a moment, his eyes troubled, then he glanced away.

'I don't have time for this nonsense,' he muttered. 'Girls, get back into the castle; I haven't quite finished with either of you yet.'

'This is bullshit,' said Lara, as Tilly sobbed.

'You should have thought of that before you went against my orders,' said their father. 'Get inside. Now.'

Olo'osso turned towards the wagon, as the two sisters walked back through the archway in the gatehouse, escorted by guards.

'You know what to do, Captain Udaxa,' said the old pirate. 'Get her out of here.'

CHAPTER 26

DEAD WEIGHT

South of Ectus, Western Rim – 24th Beldinch 5255 (18th Gylean Year 6)

The four dragons soared over the ocean swell as the sun split the horizon to their right. For eight hours, they had kept in a tight formation, staying low over the water, while, ahead of them, the dark, forested slopes of the mountains of southern Ectus could be seen looming up out of the sea. Sable yawned as she gripped onto the leather handle of the dragon harness. Beneath her, she could sense Badblood tiring, but his improvement since their first long flight from Haurn to Yearning was considerable. Hours of resting and eating, interspersed with extended practise flights over the ocean, had toughened him up.

The rising sun transformed the ocean, dispelling the gloom into a glistening swell of blues and reflected light that dazzled Sable's eyes. Above them, a few rain clouds were nestling around the upper peaks of Ectus, as fields of steam rose from the lower forests. The sun also signified that they were late. They had intended to reach the cliffs of southern Ectus before dawn, but Blackrose had set a steady pace, to ensure that they had some energy in reserve in case they encountered any Sea Banner vessels along the way. To Sable's surprise, they had seen nothing move on the waters between Mastino and Ectus, despite it being one of the busiest shipping lanes on Dragon Eyre. Meader had assured them that the sea traffic was continuous, with ships bearing oil and timber heading south, and others carrying supplies for the Banner garrisons on Olkis and Alef sailing north, all with plentiful Sea Banner escorts to protect them. Instead, there had been nothing.

Sable longed to use her powers to check ahead, but she had needed to focus everything on keeping Badblood aloft. As soon as they landed, she promised herself, she would sweep the island.

To their left, Blackrose moved closer to Badblood, until their wingtips were almost touching. Upon her shoulders, Meader waved over to Sable, and she waved back.

'Badblood,' said the great black dragon, 'I have decided to make for the western cape of Ectus. Meader has told me that the entire northern coast of the island is infested with Banner and Sea Banner bases, while multitudes of native slaves work in the forests on the southern side. We would do well to avoid both regions. Can you fly for another hour? I estimate that the western cape is some forty or fifty miles from here.'

'I can fly that distance,' he said.

'Good, my son. I am pleased to see how much your strength has improved on this journey. Now, follow my course.'

Blackrose veered away, and banked a little, adjusting her bearing until she was soaring in a north-westerly direction. On their right, Evensward and Boldspark also turned. The wind was against them, as it had been for the entire journey from Mastino, but Sable could feel Badblood's powerful wings surge through the air.

'You're doing great,' she said. 'Blackrose is right – your improvement has been very impressive.'

'Thank you, my rider,' he said. 'As always, I couldn't have done it without you.'

She scanned the ocean to either side. Nothing. Should she be worried? The Sea Banner base on the northern coast of Ectus was the largest on Dragon Eyre, and the Banner garrisons held tens of thousands of soldiers. If Lord Bastion had read the thoughts of Meader, or any of the dragons, then he would be aware of where they were going.

Blackrose had insisted that the dragons would have sensed any attempt to invade their minds, but Sable wasn't so sure. Even if it were true, there was always Meader. A mere demigod had managed to read his mind on Gyle without him knowing, so Bastion would have had no problem.

The cliffs of southern Ectus moved round to their right as they approached the far western corner of the island. Along the slopes of the mountains, vast squares of forest had been cut down, while other areas were covered in young saplings – testament to the labour of thousands of slaves who toiled to bring in the timber necessary to keep the Sea Banner afloat. In comparison, the western cape was rocky and barren, with only a few trees dotted here and there amid the high cliffs and gullies. At the westernmost tip of the island stood a tall lighthouse and observation tower that rose up to a height of over a hundred feet. Sable couldn't yet see it, but she guessed that the occupation forces would have posted a god to that location, to watch out for pirates approaching from Olkis, and it was imperative that they avoided it.

Blackrose turned again when the coastline was a mile away, and headed due north, towards a waterfall that was spilling its contents down the cliffs and into the ocean below. The dragons ascended to the height of the ridgeline, and circled once, before alighting onto the scrubby ground by the stream that ended in the waterfall.

Badblood landed next to the great black dragon, and lowered his head down to the river to drink, his tiredness seeping through every muscle.

'That was a lot quieter than I had expected,' said Evensward, as her eyes roamed around the barren cliff top.

'Perhaps the Sea Banner are busy elsewhere,' said Boldspark, looking fresh and alert.

'Perhaps,' said Blackrose. 'However, I think it would be prudent if we pushed on quickly from this place. There are a number of small, uninhabited isles to the north of Ectus, and I deem those more suitable as a location where we could rest for a few days. Meader, you are more familiar with this region than I – what are your thoughts?'

Meader slid down to the ground and stretched his legs. 'I agree,' he said. 'Ectus is armed to the teeth; it's not a place to linger.'

Sable unbuckled the straps of the harness and joined him on the rocky ground, as Badblood continued to drink from the stream.

'We shall need food before we set off again,' said Evensward. 'Boldspark and I will hunt. If the forests of Ectus are as rich in wildlife as those in Gyle, it shouldn't take too long to bring back enough meat for all of us.'

'Very well,' said Blackrose. 'Remember to stay low, and to remain out of sight of the lighthouse on the edge of the cape. If you spot any trouble, return immediately.'

Evensward's eyes flashed, and Sable could sense that it rankled for the leader of the Haurn colony to take orders from the Queen of Ulna. Nevertheless, she tilted her head, and then she and Boldspark extended their wings and soared into the air, before swooping away to the east.

Meader glanced at Sable. 'Do you fancy using your vision to take a look? I'm a little concerned that we didn't see any ships along the entire journey. I'll prepare some breakfast from our rations.'

'Sure,' she said. She yawned again, and looked for a comfortable place to sit. There was a gnarly old tree by the banks of the stream, and she walked over to it and sat down in the shade of its branches. She crossed her legs, and took a deep breath to clear her mind. Eight hours of constantly being linked to Badblood's thoughts had tired her out, and she was looking forward to breakfast.

She sent her vision out, and forgot about how tired she was feeling. She took a moment to gaze down at their corner of the island, marvelling in its beauty, then turned towards the east. She saw Boldspark down by a forested slope, his forelimbs gripping onto the body of a mountain deer, while Evensward was keeping a lookout above. Sable continued past them, and came to the region where the slaves worked. She saw a large encampment, nestled within a valley, where dozens of low timber structures lay, surrounded by a high palisade wall. Banner soldiers were organising the captive work force for another day's labour, and the slaves were lining up outside each of the timber buildings.

A spine of mountains cut across the island, running east to west, dividing Ectus into two separate regions. There were no towns on the southern flank, just endless forests sprinkled with slave labour camps, so Sable headed north. She crossed the high peaks, where rain was falling from thick, dark clouds, and her vision caught its first glimpse of the northern half of the island as it emerged from the gloom. She paused for a moment to take in the view. The entire northern coast was built-up, with mile after mile of settlements. In its centre was Sabat City – a huge, sprawling town of stone buildings and fortifications. On either side were shanty settlements, filled with the native slaves, and enormous, walled-off Banner compounds. Sable counted five separate harbours, only two of which were open to merchant shipping. The others were Sea Banner bases, their harbours bristling with masts, while the largest contained a set of enormous ship-building dockyards, where over two dozen vessels were in various stages of construction. Sable stared at it all, amazed at the scale and power of the colonial authorities. The whole of Ectus seemed to be one massive military camp – the buffer that protected Gyle, and an offensive base from which to conduct operations against the rebels in Olkis.

Sable blinked, and her vision returned to her body. Meader was kneeling next to her, a cigarette hanging from his lips as he prepared their breakfast.

He glanced at her. 'Well?'

'I've never seen anything like it,' she said. 'The northern coast seems to consist of nothing but base after base. There's enough room for tens of thousands of soldiers in the garrison areas – why do they need so many troops here?'

'It's a rest area for those who are rotated out of Olkis,' he said. 'Every few months, the soldiers there are swapped out, and given time to recover on Ectus. It also houses the main training facilities for both the Banner and Sea Banner; every new recruit does his initial training here. It's the first place that many soldiers arriving from Implacatus see, before they're shipped off to the nightmare that is Olkis.'

'Are things bad up there?'

'What, on Olkis?' Meader puffed out his cheeks. 'Yes, is the short answer. The northern half of Olkis is heavily garrisoned, but even thousands of Banner soldiers are barely enough to keep a lid on things. Bombs go off in Nankiss and Yafra every day, and soldiers return to Ectus maimed and broken.'

'What about the southern half?' said Sable.

'The Banner have got the south-eastern corner under control, though Pangba and Vipara are still dangerous places to be. As for the south-western corner, no Banner forces can penetrate the interior. It's shielded by vast marshlands, and then impassable mountains. That's where the majority of the surviving Olkian dragons live, along with a multitude of pirates and rebels.'

'Why don't the Sea Banner attack from the ocean?'

'The south-western corner is protected from that direction too. There's a huge bay, filled with thousands of rocky islets, where more Sea Banner ships have sunk than anywhere else on Dragon Eyre. Any that do make it through are incinerated by dragon fire. It's one of the only safe havens for rebels left on this world. Each governor in turn has tried to subdue the area, but my father gave up a long time ago. The casualty rates were too high for him to stomach. There are still greenhides roaming certain areas, left over from Governor Sabat's attempts to conquer the island. Between them, disease, and the rebels, Olkis is the worst possible place for a Banner soldier to be based; that's why they need to be rotated back to Ectus so often.'

'So, if Maddie is on Olkis, she'll most likely be in the south-western corner of the island?'

'Yes. If she was abducted by Five Sisters pirates, then that's where they will have taken her. Those bastards have the skills needed to get through Luckenbay, where all those islets are located.'

Blackrose lowered her head towards them. 'How many dragons remain on Olkis?'

'Several thousand,' said Meader. 'It's the largest population of your kinsfolk outside Wyst. Most of them are on the shores of Luckenbay, hiding from the Banner soldiers, though there are also a few colonies up by the volcanoes in the far north.'

'Once we have departed Ectus,' said Blackrose, 'we shall make for the south-west of Olkis, and approach the dragons who dwell there. No dragon would refuse to offer assistance in the search for a missing rider, not even the strange dragons of the Western Rim. Sable, is our route to the north clear?'

'I was so busy investigating the Banner bases that I didn't look.' She sighed. 'I'll do it now.'

For the second time that morning, she took a deep breath and let her vision come free from her body. This time, she headed north-west, away from the crowded shores that housed the shipyards and bases. She crossed the tail-end of the mountainous spine, and saw the lighthouse, perched atop the very edge of the island. Waves were crashing against its stone foundations, but the structure was wide and solid, built to withstand anything nature could throw at it. Sable sped her vision to the top of the tower, which was flat and ringed with battlements. Standing up there was a squad of Banner soldiers, their eyes on the seas to the north and west. Olkis was too far away to see, but Sable saw the few scattered islands to the north of Ectus that Blackrose had mentioned. The ocean was empty of ships in that direction, so she turned a little to the north-west, then stopped. Sailing towards the western cape of Ectus was an enormous fleet, barely a few miles from the waterfall where Sable's body was sitting cross-legged on the ground. Their sails were full, and they were sailing at top speed towards them. She counted four huge battleships, and over two dozen smaller frigates. The decks of the ships were bustling with activity. Ballistae were being prepared, and ceramic explosive devices were lined up next to huge catapults.

Sable pulled her vision back to herself. Blackrose, Badblood and Meader were all gazing at her.

'We have to leave,' she gasped. 'We have to leave now.'

'Calm yourself, witch,' said Blackrose. 'Tell us what you have seen.'

'At any moment, an enormous fleet will pass the cape to our west,' she said; 'armed and ready. They knew we were coming; they were just waiting to see where we landed before striking.'

Blackrose's eyes burned. 'Wait here,' she said, then launched herself into the air, sending a wave of dust over the others from the wash of her great wings.

Sable stared at the black dragon as she sped off to the west. 'Does she not believe me? What does she think she's going to see? Damn it; we need to be moving, before those ships come into range.'

She jumped to her feet, then hesitated. She needed to recall Evensward and Boldspark. She sat again, cursing, and sent her vision out for a third time, feeling her energy start to wane. She found Evensward after a few moments, still circling over Boldspark as he foraged through the forest.

Come back, Evensward. Ships are approaching; we have to go.

We need to gather more food, Sable, came the dragon's response.

There's no time. The ships will be in ballista range in just a few minutes.

Evensward growled. *Very well.*

Sable snapped her vision back, and stood again, her legs wobbly.

'Badblood,' she said. 'Sorry about this, but we need to fly again. Can you manage?'

'If I must,' said the dark red dragon.

'Here they come!' cried Meader, pointing to the west. 'Holy shit! They've brought half the Western Fleet against us.'

'They've been watching us this entire time,' said Sable, 'luring us into a trap.'

A yard-long steel ballista bolt whistled past, missing Badblood's flank by a couple of feet.

'That didn't come from the sea,' yelled Meader, his eyes on the forests to their east.

Sable stared at the treeline in the distance, and saw movement amid the scrubby undergrowth. Banner soldiers were manning ballistae from the back of wheeled carts at the edge of the forest. Over a dozen machines had been lined up, and were pointing in their direction.

'They've surrounded us!' cried Meader. 'Where's Blackrose?'

'Never mind about Blackrose, said Sable. 'Get up onto Badblood's shoulder before those bastards knock us off the cliff.'

At that moment, Evensward and Boldspark soared up from where they had been hunting, and flew directly in front of the line of ballistae. Within seconds, a hail of yard-long bolts was hurled in their direction. Evensward swerved, missing most, though a bolt passed through the tip of her right wing as she banked. Boldspark attempted to follow her, but was struck in the chest, and then in the left flank. He screamed in pain, his wings failing, then crashed down into the ground between Badblood and the Banner soldiers. He skidded on for several yards along the rocks and dusty thorn bushes, then lay still.

Sable stared in disbelief, then pulled herself up into Badblood's harness as the Banner squads reloaded the ballistae. Evensward wheeled about again, then unleashed a blast of flames down onto the Banner positions. One of the ballistae burst into flames, and then another, their crews aflame. The nearby trees caught fire, and smoke belched up from the edge of the forest.

'Stop gawking and get up here!' Sable cried to Meader, as Badblood prepared to take off.

Meader ran towards the dark red dragon and threw himself up onto the harness straps, then scrambled into a seat. Evensward swooped down for another attack run on the Banner soldiers, but she was met with a barrage of ballista bolts, and she had to pull back. A bolt grazed a forelimb, and she ascended out of range. Badblood extended his wings, and had just cleared the ground, when a deafening explosion shook the cliffside. Fragments of stone burst out amid a cloud of dust and a flash of white light. Rubble rained down upon them, and Badblood was flung backwards by the force of the impact. He collided with a rocky outcrop, sending more stones flying, and his legs gave way under him as he tried to regain his balance.

'You can do it!' Sable cried. 'Badblood, listen to me. You can do it!'

A ballista bolt glanced off his dark red scales, its angle too acute to penetrate his thick skin, but its razor sharp tip left a long score down the dragon's flank. Badblood grunted, then hurled himself off the cliff.

A ceramic canister soared through the air just above them, and another explosion ripped a chunk out of the ridge where they had been just moments before. Badblood plummeted through the air, falling towards the ocean, but, at the last moment, he managed to pull up from the dive. Ahead of them, just a hundred yards offshore, were three frigates. Ballista bolts cut through the air, aimed horizontally from the bows of the ships, as more explosions impacted off the side of the cliff, showering the dark red dragon in blisteringly hot fragments of rock.

'We need to climb!' Meader yelled. 'We have to get out of range.'

Blackrose appeared above them in the sky – a black smear of movement as she dived down at the frigates. She opened her jaws and emitted a great funnel of flames at the first ship, scorching the main deck and the sails. The ballista station at the bow erupted into an inferno, and burning sailors fell off the sides into the deep waters of the ocean. Blackrose turned, then cried out in agony. She fell twenty feet, then righted herself.

'They have a god!' she screamed at Badblood. 'Get out of here, son.'

Badblood soared upwards, then, ignoring Blackrose's command, paused to unleash a wave of fire over the bows of the other two frigates. Behind them, more ships were fast approaching, including the battleships that had been hurling the pisspots at the cliffside. As soon as the two bow ballista stations on the frigates were burning, Badblood soared away, dodging more bolts coming from the other ships in the fleet.

'We're going to make it!' cried Meader, and then a yard-long bolt ripped his head clean from his shoulders.

Sable stared as the headless demigod strapped into the harness next to her. Meader's fingers were still clutching onto the handle bar, as a stream of blood whipped through the air from the severed neck on his shoulders. Badblood seemed oblivious to Meader's fate, and he climbed higher and higher into the sky. He joined Blackrose and Evensward, both of whom were carrying injuries as bad as he had taken, and they circled for a moment over the ships of the Western Fleet.

Sable paid no attention to anything that was going on, unable to pull her eyes away from the corpse of Meader sitting a foot to her left. Silent tears sprang from her eyes and rolled down her cheeks.

'Meader,' she whispered, her thoughts frozen in shock.

A small part of her conscious mind realised that the three surviving dragons were fleeing back over the ocean, away from the western cape of Ectus. When they had moved far out of range of the ships, they circled, keeping close together.

'We can't keep going south,' said Blackrose. 'We will never make it back to Mastino. We have no choice but to attempt to break through the lines of the fleet and escape to the north.'

'Do you not care about the death of young Boldspark, Queen of Ulna?' said Evensward.

'I care deeply,' said the black dragon, 'but in order to mourn him, we have to survive this day. Meader, where do...'

Blackrose's voice fell away into silence as she gazed at the remains of the demigod strapped onto Badblood's harness.

'What is it?' said Badblood.

'The demigod is dead,' said Evensward. 'You are carrying a corpse upon your shoulders.'

'My rider,' cried Badblood, 'are you alright? Speak to me!'

Sable closed her eyes, but could still see the image of Meader's decapitated body next to her.

'I'm uninjured,' she said, her voice barely above a whisper.

'Unstrap the body and let it fall, Sable,' said Evensward. 'Badblood does not need to carry dead weight.'

'Give her a moment,' said Blackrose. 'The witch is clearly in shock.'

'I can bear Meader,' said Badblood; 'but we should make a decision and go.'

'I agree,' said Blackrose. 'We shall fly east, and try to get round Ectus from the other side. Follow me.'

She sped off, her great wings out, and the two other dragons chased after her. Sable said nothing, her eyes closed, and her heart filled with despair.

Badblood was shaking with exhaustion as the dragons landed upon the steep slopes of a high mountain near the eastern edge of Ectus. Below them, and to the north-east, cordons of Sea Banner vessels were covering the sea lanes, ready to strike if the dragons tried to fly north via the eastern end of the island. Sable remained sitting on Badblood's harness as he collapsed onto the rocky ground. For nearly three hours, she had sat in silence next to the body of Meader as the dragons had swung out over the ocean, before doubling back towards the southern coastline of Ectus.

'It is time, Sable,' said Blackrose. 'Unfasten the straps keeping Meader to the harness, and climb down.'

She stared at the black dragon.

'Are you not a Holdfast, witch?' said Blackrose. 'Where is the indomitable spirit that I am told lies within the hearts of each of your kin? I know Meader was your friend; let us honour his passing. Unbuckle his body from the harness.'

Sable moved her hands towards the body, her fingers shaking. She fumbled with a clasp, then released its catch. Blackrose reached out with a forelimb, and plucked the body from Badblood's shoulders, then set it down onto the barren ground. Sable undid her own straps and slid down from Badblood. She placed a hand onto the dark red dragon's flank to support her, feeling his scales under her fingertips.

'What killed the demigod?' said Evensward, sniffing the headless body.

'A ballista bolt,' said Sable.

'It looks as though he had a quick death, at least,' said the dark green dragon. She glanced at Blackrose. 'What shall we do now? The way north appears blocked, unless we wish to pass over the mountaintops.'

'If we go that way,' said Sable, her own words sounding strange to her, 'we'll have to fly over the Banner bases.'

She crouched down by Meader, and took a cold hand in hers. Something in her mind seemed to snap as she gazed at the body. She was utterly exhausted, and her nerves were shattered. Boldspark and Meader had been killed in a few moments of horrific violence, and Sable struggled to see how the rest of them could survive another attack by the Sea Banner. Flying over the fleet would only get them all killed. Whatever they did would get them all killed. If that was the case, then perhaps it was time to raise the stakes, and risk everything on one, final throw of the dice. An idea emerged from the turmoil in her mind.

'Meader tried to warn us about Ectus,' she said. 'We won't be able to get to Olkis this way.'

'I haven't come this far to give up,' said Blackrose. 'My rider is north, and so I must go north. I refuse to turn back.'

'I wasn't suggesting that we turn back,' said Sable.

'No? Then tell me, witch – what were you suggesting?'

Her eyes glinted. 'We should attack the shipyards on the northern coast and reduce them to ashes.'

'That would be suicide,' said Evensward. 'Didn't you once tell me that there was no such thing as a noble death? Have you changed your mind? Are two deaths from our company not enough for you?'

'Let her speak,' said Blackrose. 'Sable, why should we do as you suggest?'

'If we incinerate the dockyards, and burn up as many soldiers and ships as possible, then either Horace or Bastion will have to come to Sabat City to deal with us.'

'That's if the gods and ballistae of Ectus do not kill us first,' said Evensward. 'Sable, your plan is born of desperation and grief. We must think clearly.'

'The witch might have a point,' said Blackrose. 'A direct attack will be the last thing our enemy is expecting. If we slip over the mountains at nightfall, the vision gods will most likely lose us in the clouds. We could appear at dawn, and wreak destruction upon the Banner forces gathered around Sabat City. We may be able to break out to the north, and fly onwards to Olkis that way.'

'No,' said Sable. 'Between us and Olkis will be more ships, and more gods, and they'll be waiting for us there, just as they were waiting for us here.'

'Enlighten me, witch,' said the black dragon. 'What do you wish this attack to achieve?'

'There's only one way we're getting to Olkis,' Sable said, standing and looking out to sea. 'With a Quadrant.'

'But, Sable,' said Evensward; 'we have no Quadrant.'

'I'm aware of that,' she said. 'That's why we wait for Horace or Bastion to show up. As soon as they do, we kill them, and take theirs. That's how we get to Olkis.'

'This is madness!' cried Evensward.

'I am forced to agree,' said Blackrose. 'A breakout seems feasible, but to await those with the power to kill us from four hundred yards away would surely invite only disaster.'

Badblood lifted his head from the stony ground. 'We shall do as my rider says.'

'Why?' said Evensward.

'Because I love her, and I trust her,' said the dark red dragon; 'and she has never once let me down.'

Blackrose gazed out into the thick clouds for a long time, her features still. 'So be it,' she said. 'We are safe up here at this altitude. We shall rest, and prepare for the morrow – and whatever it brings.'

CHAPTER 27

FOR BETTER OR WORSE

S eabound, Ulna, Eastern Rim – 24th Beldinch 5255 (18th Gylean
Year 6)

Austin had sat through many lessons in his school on Implacatus,
but one in particular had been repeated so often, it had come to feel
like a cliché – the more a god or demigod used their powers, the easier
they became to control. If you practised, you became better. You needed
to rest less, and your powers arrived at your fingertips almost without a
conscious thought behind them. Like the rest of his classmates, Austin
had nodded along at the teachers' words, his mind rarely on his school-
work; but sitting on a wide balcony overlooking Alg Bay, with the
palace of Seabound behind him, he realised that this simple, core
lesson had been true. He had healed over a dozen dragons in the
previous few days, using his powers to repair the damage inflicted by
Splendoursun and his allies, and yet he had never felt stronger. His flow
powers, too, had been stretched. He had been exhausted when he had
killed the dragon in Udall, but it had only taken a single day of good
food and plentiful rest for his powers to have returned in full. The
torment his body had gone through in the desert wastes of Implacatus
seemed like a distant memory, but he knew that the experience had

toughened him – after all, if he could get through that, he could get through anything.

'There you are, demigod,' said Ashfall, poking her head out from the interior of the palace. 'I had wondered where you had wandered off to. What are you doing?'

Austin glanced at the beautiful grey dragon. 'I was testing my flow powers; trying to make them reach the waters of the bay.'

'I see. Were you successful?'

Austin smiled. 'Yes. I can create little eddies and whirlpools. I know that doesn't sound very impressive, but it's more than I was ever able to do before. I'm getting stronger.'

'Good. You will need your powers today, if, that is, we can persuade Shadowblaze to go through with it.'

'Is he having second thoughts?'

'He is. He fears that more dragons will die. He is correct – more dragons will die. It is weighing heavily on his conscience. However, I do not despise him for this. It is not a weakness - on the contrary, it shows that he has a good heart, and that he loves those who serve under him. Nevertheless, today is the day when we must act. Will you come with me, to help assuage his fears?'

'What good will I do?'

'Austin,' she said, 'you are the difference between the last, failed, attack, and the attack that we are planning for this day. Shadowblaze needs to see that you are committed to our cause.' She tilted her head. 'You are committed, are you not?'

Austin turned back to gaze at the dark waters of the bay, then nodded. 'I am. Splendoursun cares about nothing but himself, and his rule means that the Unk Tannic will be in control of Ulna. If we're going to save Dragon Eyre, then we need to get rid of the Unk Tannic, permanently.'

Ashfall's nose nudged Austin's shoulder. 'Save Dragon Eyre? Austin, thank you for saying those words. I had my doubts about you, but you have changed. You are turning into a good man. Come; let us speak to Shadowblaze.'

Austin pulled himself to his feet, then accompanied the dragon into the palace. The caverns and giant hallways of Seabound were bustling with activity, with dragons and their riders preparing for what was to come. Ashfall led Austin into the great banqueting hall, where Shadow-blaze, Greysteel, and several other dragons were talking. Ahi'edo and a handful of other riders were also there, clustered in a small group by the edge of the hall.

'Greetings,' said Ashfall. 'I have brought Austin. The demigod is ready to help us.'

Greysteel glanced down at him. 'Our secret weapon? It is good to know that we have a powerful demigod on our side, although it is also a little strange. Never have I imagined that a god from Implacatus would lend us his aid.'

'But will he?' said Shadowblaze. 'Might he not betray us again? I cannot risk the lives of more of my kinsfolk on such shaky foundations.'

'I will help you,' said Austin.

'Really? And what do you wish in return this time? I recall that each time you have aided us in the past, it was only so you could receive something in exchange.'

'That's true,' said Austin. 'But this time, defeating the Unk Tannic will be reward enough. If Queen Blackrose is to drive the Banner forces out of Dragon Eyre, her realm will need to remain intact. Splendoursun and his Unk Tannic forces are doing nothing but bringing Ulna to its knees.'

'I believe him,' said a purple dragon. 'He healed me and my brother a few days ago, and asked for nothing in return.'

'I do not believe him,' said another dragon. 'Why would a god from Implacatus turn against his own people in this manner? He wants dragons to slay other dragons – to make it easier for the Banner soldiers to destroy us once the dust has settled.'

'That's what worries me,' said Shadowblaze. 'I trusted him before, and was proved a fool. Why should I trust him again?'

'I have changed,' said Austin. 'You may find it hard to believe, and I understand why you harbour doubts.'

'Why have you changed?' said Greysteel. 'Explain this to us, demigod.'

'I admit that I lied to you, Shadowblaze, when I told you that I knew how to use a Quadrant. In truth, all I knew was how to make the device take me back to Implacatus, so that is where I went.'

Several dragons cried out at his words, and the group of riders strode over.

'I knew it!' cried Ahi'edo. 'I told you that he would do this, master, and you didn't listen to me. This vile creature fled to Implacatus at the first opportunity. We would be insane to trust him again.'

'Wait,' said Ashfall. 'I want to know why Austin returned from Implacatus. He must have known that the Unk Tannic would imprison him if he came back, and yet he did so.'

Austin swallowed, then took a breath. 'I didn't go to Implacatus in order to bring back Banner reinforcements, or to do anything to hurt you. I went to find my mother. I learned from my brother that my father sold her into slavery, and I went back to find her. I still want to find her. One day, I shall.'

'Could you not locate her, demigod?' said Greysteel.

'No. Instead, what I discovered was something else altogether – the reason why the Ascendants wish to conquer this world. This knowledge is what changed my opinion. I realised that what my brother has been trying to tell me all along is correct, that the occupation of this world is wrong. For my entire life, I have believed what the Ascendants have told me, that they are a force for good, for civilisation; but I was wrong. They will not stop until every dragon is dead, and every native either slaughtered or enslaved. It shamed me, to know this. All the evidence was before my eyes, but I refused to accept it. I accept it now. I will help you, because it is the right thing to do, and then, one day, I hope to return home and find my mother. Until that day comes, I will do everything in my power to help you defeat the colonial forces. The first step is to prevent Splendoursun from taking over Ulna.'

Ashfall's eyes gleamed. 'Well said, Austin.'

'Mere words,' said Ahi'edo; 'designed to trick us.'

'I am content with his explanation,' said Greysteel. 'Austin is a young god, and is still learning. I am prepared to trust him.'

'I too,' said the purple dragon.

'And what of the plan?' said Shadowblaze. 'My heart remains full of doubts about that, even if the demigod is telling us the truth. Me? A suitor to the Queen? I am not worthy of such an honour.'

'Of course you are,' cried Greysteel. 'You are Blackrose's oldest and closest friend. What is it that you fear?'

Shadowblaze lowered his head. 'Her inevitable rejection. Even if we are successful, and stop Splendoursun from assuming full authority over Ulna, when Queen Blackrose returns, she will reject me, and my life will collapse into unthinkable shame.'

'It is a tactical ploy, Shadowblaze,' said Greysteel. 'The Queen will not shame you for intervening in this matter to save her realm – she will thank you for it. It would be different if you wanted to be her mate, but you neglected to put forward your name during the two years of the courtship period. The Queen will understand.'

'You are wrong,' said the great grey and red dragon, his voice low. 'I have loved Blackrose with all my heart since we were children. It is not merely a tactical ploy to me; it is everything. I have dreamed about Blackrose and I being together, but have always felt myself to be unworthy as a consort to such a mighty queen. To have her reject me would destroy my soul.'

The hall fell still. Austin glanced at the dragons, each of whom seemed dumbfounded by Shadowblaze's admission. Even Ahi'edo looked shocked.

'My boy,' said Greysteel; 'I had no idea you felt this way.'

'This is the first time I have ever uttered the words aloud,' said Shadowblaze. 'My duty to my queen has always outweighed my own feelings. I sought to serve her as well as I was able, and to admit such a thing would have only divided us; for Blackrose does not feel the same way as I do.'

'Do you know this for a fact?' said Ashfall.

'I do not, but I sense the truth of it.'

'There is nothing to debate here,' said Austin. 'If you love Blackrose, then the way ahead is clear – you must stop Splendoursun becoming the only suitor before the sun sets today. What better proof of your love could you offer the Queen? Even if she decides to reject you, everyone will know that your love saved her realm. There is no shame in that. It is noble, and honourable, just as you are, Shadowblaze.'

The grey and red dragon closed his eyes for a moment, as everyone waited in silence.

'So be it,' he said. 'I will do the right thing, even if it means the annihilation of my dreams. Dragons, collect your riders, and make ready to fly to Udall.'

The forty-three dragons loyal to Shadowblaze soared into the sky above Seabound, circling, and gathering into their formations. Shadowblaze himself was to lead the main contingent of thirty, while Greysteel and Ashfall would each command a smaller group. A rider had found a spare harness for Ashfall to wear, and Austin was strapped onto her shoulders, his eyes taking in the view as the slender grey dragon banked and wheeled over the dark bay.

'Are you ready?' she said.

'Yes. Are you?'

'I do not fear death, Austin.'

'Do you believe in the dragon spirits?'

'No. I believe that death is the end. What we do in this life is what defines each of us, and that is why we must act. What the Unk Tannic would have us believe, that my soul is immortal, and that I will join the other dragon spirits after death, serves only to prevent us from living our lives as we should. Perhaps I am wrong, but if I am, then at least I will meet the spirits with a clear conscience.'

'Spoken like a queen,' said Austin.

Ashfall signalled to her group, and the dragons moved off, soaring over the eastern edge of the bay, the smoking volcano to their right. The three groups held together until they had passed the ruined remains of the southern greenhide nest. A few beasts were aimlessly wandering the slopes, but scattered at the sight of the approaching dragons, scuttling back into their hiding places. When they reached the lowlands, the groups split. Shadowblaze led the bulk of the dragons to the east, in order to repeat the same tactics that he had employed on the first attack on Udall. They were going to approach the town from the sea, while Ashfall and Greysteel's smaller groups were to fly over the desolate plains of central Ulna.

Ten miles over the plains, Greysteel's band of six dragons separated from the others, and soared away to the north, while Ashfall's group continued in a north-easterly direction. Austin gazed down at the muddy ruins of the lowlands. Solitary greenhides were still roaming the land, the sunlight of Dragon Eyre sustaining them despite the lack of food. The dragons in Ashfall's group reached one of the abandoned watchtowers, and landed close to its base, while Ashfall herself soared up to the high platform and alighted there.

Austin squinted in the direction of Udall. 'Will you be able to see Shadowblaze begin his attack?'

'No,' said Ashfall, 'but I will hear it.' She glanced around the tower. 'This is criminal negligence. To have abandoned the defences of Udall while greenhides still wander the lowlands is proof enough for me that Splendoursun does not deserve to rule. He cares not if his human subjects are killed and eaten; all he cares about is power. Imagine the horror if even one greenhide was to reach a farmstead or village. It makes me very angry.'

'If we win today,' said Austin, 'then I shall destroy the last of the greenhides on Ulna.'

'And I will help you. This land was once green and fertile; we shall make it so again.'

'I like the sound of that.'

The dragons waited. Shadowblaze's route would take him out over the ocean, and they would have to cover twice the distance that Ashfall and her group had crossed. Austin could feel his nerves tighten as they waited, but what surprised him was his lack of fear. He trusted Ashfall, and was content with the decisions he had made. He thought about his brother, and how proud and taken aback he would be to learn how much Austin had grown. He missed Meader, and couldn't wait to tell him about what he had discovered on Implacatus. Meader would understand the implications in an instant.

When the moment to leave arrived, Austin had heard nothing, but every dragon had pricked up their ears and gazed over the plains towards Udall.

'Make haste!' cried Ashfall, as she extended her grey wings. 'To Shadowblaze!'

The seven dragons in Ashfall's group launched themselves into the air, their riders clinging on to the harnesses. Ashfall moved out in front, with three on either flank, and they soared off towards Udall, the ground passing beneath them in a blur of brown. Above, the morning sun was shining down upon them amid a perfect blue sky, and Austin revelled in the warm breeze. They crossed over the wide band of farmland on the outskirts of the town, and a few people glanced up from the fields where they were working.

'Ashfall,' said Austin, 'please remember that I still find it difficult to tell some of the dragons apart. Will you point out to me the ones to attack?'

'I shall,' said the grey dragon. 'I will call out their colour and direction for you.'

'Thanks. You're not offended that I can't tell them apart, are you?'

'Demigod, I struggle to distinguish humans – most of you look extremely alike to my eyes; so, no – I am not offended.'

They reached the first buildings of Udall, and soared low over the dilapidated roofs of the areas that were still uninhabited. Ahead, the bridge palace was visible, towering over every other structure. From it, a few dragons were emerging, but Austin could see that most had already left the palace, and were engaging Shadowblaze and his allies.

The plan was working, he thought. Splendoursun had assumed that Shadowblaze was merely repeating his earlier tactics, and so he had decided to respond in the same manner as before, by emptying the palace of his kinsfolk to join the battle. As Ashfall's band grew closer, it was clear that Splendoursun's dragons were winning. A green dragon that Austin recognised from Seabound was plummeting through the air, his wings in tatters. He struck the quayside and smashed into one of the harbour buildings, sending a cloud of dust into the sky.

The distance between Ashfall and the battle narrowed, and, all at once, they had entered the fray, attacking Splendoursun and his allies from behind.

The gold and white dragon turned his long, graceful neck to stare at the new arrivals.

'Ashfall!' Splendoursun cried. 'Do you think your measly band of seven will make the slightest difference to the outcome of this battle? You fool.'

Ashfall ignored him as she drove into the heart of the conflict. 'Red dragon, on our right,' she called out.

Austin raised his hand, located the dragon, and unleashed a massive stream of flow powers. The red dragon pulled up, then his eyes exploded from his face, and he dropped from the sky like a stone, his rider screaming.

'Black and green,' cried Ashfall; 'above us.'

Austin glanced up, his hand still raised, and concentrated on the dragon's heart, stopping it. The black and green dragon made a choking noise, then almost collided with Ashfall as he fell. Ashfall darted to the left, and the dead dragon missed her by inches. The already chaotic battle disintegrated into pandemonium. At Ashfall's direction, Austin brought down a riderless lavender dragon three times her size, and she crashed into the waters of the harbour, capsizing many of the fishing vessels tied up by the pier. Some of Splendoursun's kinsfolk were starting to pull back, desperate to avoid Ashfall and the god she was carrying on her shoulders.

'Silver and blue; below and to our left,' Ashfall called out, as she swerved out of range of an orange dragon's claws.

Again Austin sent out his powers, and again the targeted dragon fell, his eye sockets streaming blood. The dying beast struck another dragon on the way down, their limbs and wings entwined, and they crashed into the middle of the main road that led to the palace, gouging out a long furrow through the paving slabs.

'A prize to whoever brings down Ashfall!' cried Splendoursun. 'Kill her!'

Three dragons peeled off from the Gylean's side, and charged down through the air towards the grey dragon. Austin swept his hand from left to right, feeling his powers surge through him like never before, and all three dragons screamed at once, their death howls ripping through the air as they plummeted from the sky, blood trailing in their wake.

Ashfall banked, and headed towards the harbour basin, where Shadowblaze was being attacked by two dragons the same size as he was. Blood was pouring from a long wound down the grey and red dragon's flank, as he tried to fend off the attacks. Austin didn't need any words from Ashfall – he extended his arm, and pointed at one of Shadowblaze's attackers. The dragon's head exploded in a crescendo of gore, showering the clear water of the basin below them with blood. Shadowblaze opened his jaws, and closed them like a vice around the neck of the other dragon who had been attacking him. There was a snap and crunch of bones, and the dragon's eyes stared lifelessly as it fell.

'Thank you,' said Shadowblaze, as Ashfall approached. From his shoulders, Ahi'edo was staring at Austin with terror in his eyes.

Dead dragons were lying scattered all over the harbour, while black-robed Unk Tannic guards stared helplessly upwards, their feeble cross-bows useless. On one side, Splendoursun's allies were beginning to retreat, despite the gold and white's dragon's exhortations to stay and fight to the end, while the dragons of Shadowblaze were pressing home their advantage. The purple dragon who had stood up for Austin in Seabound was being chased by a pair of green dragons, who were closing in on her. Austin saw them, and pointed at each in turn, stopping their hearts as easily as extinguishing a lamp. The two green dragons dropped from the sky, their corpses adding to the piles of dead on the streets of Udall.

Shadowblaze glanced at Ashfall, then surveyed the scene of carnage.

'To the palace,' he said. 'Is Greysteel in position?'

'We shall soon see,' said Ashfall.

'Follow me!' Shadowblaze cried to his followers, and, as one, the dragons of Seabound turned for the palace.

Austin brought down a black dragon blocking their path, and then the way was clear. Splendoursun's allies were scattering in every direction, panic hastening their flight as they rushed to escape the slaughter. Of Splendoursun himself, there was no sign. Ashfall and Shadowblaze reached the high platform that led to the palace's main hall, and saw two of Greysteel's band guarding the ramp, their riders gripping onto crossbows as they sat on their shoulders.

'Is Lord Greysteel inside?' said Shadowblaze, as he landed.

'Yes, my lord,' said one of the dragons. 'It was exactly as the demigod said – every dragon under Splendoursun's command left to join the battle. There was no one here when we arrived.'

Shadowblaze nodded his great head, then turned back to look at the town. More of his allies were approaching the palace, and landing on each of the platforms in turn.

'Do not hesitate,' said Ashfall. 'This is your moment, Shadowblaze. Do what you came here to do.'

Shadowblaze closed his eyes for a moment, then walked down the ramp. Ashfall followed him, leaving the two dragons to guard the entrance to the palace. They descended into the vast hallways of the upper floors, and strode through the deserted palace until they reached the great reception hall.

Waiting inside were Greysteel and two of his dragons. Austin unbuckled the harness straps and leapt down to the ground, his eyes scanning the doorways for Unk Tannic guards, willing them to appear so that he could kill them. Ahi'edo slid down from Shadowblaze's shoulders, but kept his distance from Austin as the dragons gathered in the centre of the hall.

'My lord,' said Greysteel, tilting his head towards Shadowblaze. 'Is there something you wish to say?'

Shadowblaze strode across the stone floor. 'Yes,' he said. 'There is something I need to say.'

Greysteel and the others waited.

Shadowblaze stood tall. 'I wish to be accepted as a suitor to the Queen.'

'Granted,' said Greysteel. 'By the authority vested in me by her Majesty as her agent in these matters, I hereby declare that your claim has been duly registered, in front of witnesses.'

'Stop this farce!' cried a dragon's voice from an entranceway.

They turned, and saw Splendoursun stride into the hall, flanked by four of his kinsfolk from Gyle.

'You are too late,' said the gold and white dragon; 'I am the only suitor.'

'No,' said Greysteel. 'The deadline is sunset today. Shadowblaze's claim is valid.'

'You are a shamed exile, Greysteel,' said Splendoursun. 'You do not have the authority to accept any new suitors.'

'The Queen sent me away,' said Greysteel, 'but she did not rescind my authority as her agent. You are the one who is mistaken – and I thought you knew all about the laws of Ulna, o great one? I declare, that with two suitors both vying for the Queen, neither of you shall hold sovereignty over Ulna in the Queen's absence.'

'This is the law,' said Shadowblaze, 'and I accept it.'

'I do not!' cried Splendoursun. 'This is nothing but a bad joke. Ulna is mine, and no one shall take it from me.'

'Your supporters will melt away, if you flagrantly flout our laws, my lord,' said Greysteel. 'That is, of course, if you have any supporters remaining. I hear most have fled.'

Splendoursun halted in his tracks. 'I still have until sunset, do I not? I drove away the other suitors; I can drive away this unworthy pretender. Fight me, Shadowblaze. That wound in your flank looks painful. Submit, and withdraw your claim, or I will rip you to shreds.'

Austin stepped forward and raised his hand towards the gold and white dragon.

'No,' said Ashfall. 'You must not intervene, Austin. This is dragon business.'

Splendoursun gazed down at Austin. 'So, this is how you defeated my kinfolk in the skies over Udall – by employing a filthy god to aid you? Shame! You have truly dredged the depths of dishonour by using our enemy against us dragons.'

'There is no dishonour,' said Shadowblaze. 'Austin fights by our side. However, I shall not need his powers to defeat you, Splendoursun. I will do that on my own. The mere thought of you as Queen Black-rose's mate will give me the strength and courage that I require.'

'I am the last living relative of the Eighteenth Gylean!' Splendoursun cried. 'What are you? A simple, rustic dragon from the peasant villages of Ulna. You possess no noble blood – you are nothing.'

'I may be nothing,' said Shadowblaze, 'but while you were hiding in a mountain cave on Throscala for years, I stayed here, fighting for my people, both dragons and humans. Did I ever desert them? Did I ever crawl off to skulk in the darkness? You are a coward, Splendoursun, despite your royal heritage; and I would rather be nothing than a coward.'

Splendoursun roared in rage and sprang at Shadowblaze, his talons flashing out. Flames leapt from the gold and white dragon's jaws, bathing Shadowblaze in fire, as the other dragons pulled back from the centre of the hall to watch.

Austin stared, his mouth open. Splendoursun's claws ripped a new gouge down Shadowblaze's flank, and he clamped his jaws round the base of the grey and red dragon's neck. Ahi'edo let out a cry of despair, his hands on his face as he watched. Up until that point, it hadn't occurred to Austin that their plan might fail at the final stage. His powers twitched along his fingertips, and he struggled to restrain himself.

'I sense what you are thinking, Austin,' said Ashfall, 'but you must resist. I too wish to help, but we cannot; we must not.'

Splendoursun raked his hind claws down Shadowblaze's chest as the two dragons writhed in the centre of the hall. Shadowblaze turned his head and bit down into Splendoursun's left wing, then pulled his head back, ripping the wing to pieces. Splendoursun cried out in pain, and released his grip on Shadowblaze's neck for a split second. It was enough. Shadowblaze reared up, using his weight to push the other dragon down. He rammed a forelimb down onto Splendoursun's head and tore out his throat with his jaws. The mighty gold and white dragon struggled for a moment, his limbs thrashing around, then Shadowblaze ripped his neck in two. He picked up the severed head of Splendoursun, and bathed it in flames, then, blood streaming from a dozen wounds, he crashed to the ground, shuddered, then lay still.

Austin bolted towards him, passing Ahi'edo, who was standing frozen, his eyes wide. He vaulted a golden forelimb of the corpse of Splendoursun, and pressed his palms onto Shadowblaze's flank, sending a great surge of healing powers into the grey and red dragon's body. The ragged wounds on the dragon's flanks and chest closed up. Shadowblaze vomited a torrent of blood on the floor of the hall, then opened his eyes.

'I declare,' shouted Greysteel, 'that Lord Shadowblaze is the sole suitor to the Queen! At sunset, he shall assume sovereignty over Ulna, as dictated by the law, until our beloved Queen returns to us. Arise, Shadowblaze; you are triumphant!'

The grey and red dragon got to his feet. He gazed down at his rider, then stared at the ripped and torn body of Splendoursun.

'So ends the heir to the Gylean throne,' he said. 'I did not seek this outcome, but I accept the words of Lord Greysteel.' He glanced at the four Gyle dragons who were standing to one side, their heads lowered. 'The conflict is at an end, my brethren. I shall not hold a single one of your kinsfolk, or your riders, responsible for what has happened here today. Go, and tell the others from Gyle that I now rule Ulna in the Queen's name. After that, those who choose to remain here under my authority shall be welcomed. For too long, we have fought among ourselves; but the time is fast approaching when every dragon will have to bind together to resist the forces of Implacatus.'

The four dragons backed away, keeping their gazes low. They reached the entrance, then turned and hurried away.

Shadowblaze glanced down at Austin. 'Thank you, demigod.'

'No,' said Austin, 'it is I who must thank you, Shadowblaze. I betrayed you before, but you gave me another chance, and I'm grateful.'

'You have Ashfall to thank for that, along with the wise counsel of Greysteel. My rider, my kin, my allies – I thank you all.'

Greysteel tilted his head. 'What are your orders, my lord?'

'First,' said Shadowblaze, 'we must clear the town of the fallen, and then I want the greenhide towers re-occupied, to protect the humans under our authority. Lastly, I want the head of Ata'nix. Where is he?'

'I have not seen any of the Unk Tannic since we arrived in the palace, my lord,' said Greysteel.

'I witnessed many of them down by the harbour,' said Ashfall. 'The news of Splendoursun's defeat will reach them soon. Shall we send out patrols to destroy them, my lord?'

'Yes, but first we shall go up onto the highest platform of the palace, so that everyone knows what has happened. Ahi'edo, climb up onto my shoulders.'

The rider ran forward, and clambered up onto Shadowblaze's harness. The dragons processed out of the hall, with Greysteel carrying the charred head of Splendoursun in his jaws. They strode up the ramp, and Shadowblaze went to the front of the platform, with Ahi'edo sitting tall upon his harness. Ashfall and Austin stood to his left, and Greysteel was on his right. Above them, dozens of dragons were wheeling and circling, while the humans were starting to emerge from their homes all over the town.

Greysteel dropped the head he had been carrying. 'The reign of Splendoursun and the Unk Tannic is over!' he cried, his powerful voice booming out. 'Behold our saviour – Lord Shadowblaze the mighty, slayer of Splendoursun, and the sole suitor of our Queen, the great and beloved Blackrose!'

Austin glanced up at Ashfall as the dragons cheered. She gazed back down at him, then extended a forelimb, and pulled him close to her.

'I think I am growing quite fond of you, Austin,' she said. 'You're not too bad, for a human.'

CHAPTER 28
REPLACED

Langbeg, Olkis, Western Rim – 24th Beldinch 5255 (18th Gylean Year 6)

Topaz stared at his untouched tankard of ale. Surrounding the table where he was sitting with Vitz and Ryan, a few dozen members of the *Gull's* crew were drinking and laughing in the packed-out tavern. Ryan was singing and playing his guitar, but he could barely be heard over the background noise of so many sailors who seemed determined to get drunk as quickly as possible.

'Not drinking, sir?' said Vitz.

Topaz eyed him. 'Don't call me "sir" in here, lad. We're off duty. And no, clearly, I'm not bleeding well drinking. Well done for having eyes in your head.'

Vitz puffed out his cheeks and glanced away.

Topaz frowned. 'Sorry, mate; I didn't mean to bite your head off. I'm just not in the mood today.'

'When do you think we'll be heading back out of the harbour?' Vitz said. 'The dockers were loading fresh supplies onto the *Gull* as we were disembarking, so I reckon it'll be soon – maybe as early as dawn tomorrow.'

Topaz shrugged. 'I guess that's up to our new captain.'

'I still can't believe that Olo'osso is actually on board our ship, Topaz,' said Vitz. 'Growing up in Gyle, I always thought he was nothing but an old legend – a story to scare the children. One of the old slaves on the estate used to tell us stories about him, and...'

'How did your family treat the slaves who worked for you?' said Topaz.

Vitz's cheeks flushed, and he glanced around, to make sure no one was listening.

'Well,' he said, keeping his voice down, 'my father could be pretty strict, but if they behaved and worked hard, then their lives were tough, but not terrible. If any of them ever tried to escape, though, or gave trouble to the guards, then things could get a little ugly.'

'Define "not terrible" for me, please.'

'They had enough to eat,' said Vitz, who was shifting uncomfortably in his seat. 'They lived in these long shacks – a bit like army barracks, I guess, with the men separated from the women and children, except when, you know, my father wanted them to breed.'

Topaz lowered his eyes.

'Can we change the subject?' said Vitz. 'I don't like talking about this, especially not in a crowded tavern.'

'I want to know more,' said Topaz.

'Why?'

Ryan glanced over. 'He's thinking about that girl again, lad. He should just get drunk and forget about her.'

'What girl?' said Vitz. 'Oh, the fake rider?'

Topaz clenched his fists under the table. 'She ain't a fake. Can folk stop saying that?'

Vitz shrugged. 'It's what everyone believes. That's what the dragons said.'

'I know what those grizzled old lizards said,' snapped Topaz. 'The bastards are full of shit. They're damned cowards – pathetic, selfish cowards.'

Vitz and Ryan glanced at each other.

'I know what you're thinking,' said Topaz. '"Poor old Topaz, he's losing his mind over a girl he's met once", but I don't give a shit what you think. What Olo'osso is planning to do is plain wrong, and I'm sick of it.'

'I agree, mate,' said Ryan, putting down his guitar and picking up his ale, 'but there's sod all we can do about it. It's rough luck for that girl, and no mistake; even if she is a liar, which I'm not saying she is. You know, mate, maybe you should stay off the booze today. The mood you're in, it might only make it worse.'

The front doors of the *Bo'sun's Droop* swung open, and several men walked in.

'Close the bar!' a midshipman yelled towards the owner.

A chorus of shouts and angry comments rose up as the sailors turned towards the entrance.

'All crew of the *Giddy Gull*,' cried the midshipman, 'report immediately to the ship. Shore leave has been cancelled.'

Boos and jeers drowned out all other noise in the tavern, and a tankard of ale was flung towards the midshipman, who stepped to the side.

'Any more of that,' he shouted, 'and every man in this tavern will lose their next landing bonus.' He smiled as the place quietened. 'I see that got your attention. Finish the ales in your hands, then make your way to the *Gull*. We're casting off this afternoon.'

Ryan groaned. 'But, Middie, we only just got here.'

'I could not give one flying shit, Petty Officer Ryan,' said the midshipman. 'Orders are orders. Get your asses outside.'

Several sailors downed their pints, while a few tried to flee by the back door, but one of the master-at-arms' men appeared there, wielding a long baton. For a moment the atmosphere tensed, then there was a collective sigh of resignation, and most of the sailors began trooping out of the tavern, each casting evil glances at the midshipman.

'I had bleeding plans for tonight,' said Ryan, as he stood. He picked up his guitar and slung the strap over his shoulder. 'Plans that involved...'

'I don't need to hear the details, Petty Officer,' said the midshipman.

'We should be back in six days or so; I'm afraid you'll have to keep your pants on until then.'

Vitz and Topaz also stood, as the tavern emptied.

The midshipman raised a hand. 'Not you, Master.'

Topaz blinked. 'What?'

'Your services aren't required for this voyage, sir.'

'Are you joking, Middie? Is Vitz expected to pilot the damn *Gull* through Luckenbay?'

The midshipman shook his head. 'We've already picked up the master from the *Little Sneak*, sir. He'll be leading us out to sea.'

'On whose orders?'

'The orders came from Captain Dax, sir.'

'*Captain* Dax? Holy crap.'

'This is bullshit, Middie,' said Ryan. 'Topaz is the master of the *Gull*. Why has Captain Dax decided to leave him in Langbeg?'

The midshipman raised an eyebrow. 'The captain didn't deign to provide me with that information, Petty Officer; and I didn't think to ask. As of this moment, you are back on duty. Petty Officer Vitz, you will be assisting the *Sneak's* master, so report to the *Gull's* quarter deck in quick time. Me and the boys still have four taverns to hit in the next half hour.'

They walked outside into the scorching sunshine. Angry and fed-up sailors were milling around the quayside, making their way towards the *Giddy Gull* in small groups, as the midshipman headed along the water front towards the next tavern.

'You might as well stay here and get well and truly drunk, mate,' said Ryan, glancing at Topaz.

'No way,' he said. 'I need to find out what's going on. Olo'osso told me that I'd be staying with the *Gull*. If he's changed his damn mind, then I need to know why.'

Topaz accompanied the other crew members towards the long pier where the *Giddy Gull* was tied up. Cranes were still loading supplies onto the main deck, and sailors were up in the tall rigging, preparing the sails for departure. The master-at-arms was standing by the main gang-plank, keeping a close eye on the crew as they re-embarked upon the ship. He allowed Ryan and Vitz to board, then moved to block Topaz.

'And just what do you think you're doing, sir? Didn't the middies tell you that you ain't sailing with us today?'

'They told me alright, but I need to know why. I've been the master of this ship ever since the Five Sisters bought it, and I deserve an explanation.'

The master-at-arms narrowed his eyes, then nodded. 'Right you are, sir. Wait here.' He gestured to a young lad. 'Fetch the captain, boy. Tell him that Master Topaz is out here.'

'Yes, sir,' said the lad, then he ran up onto the deck and disappeared among the bustle.

The master-at-arms glanced at Topaz. 'It does seem a bit rough that they didn't tell you why, sir.'

'Rough? It's like being kicked in the knackers. Where is the *Gull* headed?'

'Pangba, I think, sir. A prisoner was brought on board a short time ago, and I think our job is to ferry her to the slave market. That's between me and you, sir – nothing official's been announced.'

Topaz put a hand to his eyes. It was Maddie; it had to be. For some reason, Olo'osso had decided not to wait any longer. An image of her chained and shackled in a filthy slave auction house passed through his mind, and he felt sick.

'Master Topaz?' said a voice. 'What are you doing here?'

He glanced up, and saw Dax smirking down at him from the side of the deck. Standing next to him was Dina, dressed in the uniform of a lieutenant.

Topaz glared at them. 'I'd like to know why I've been taken off duty, sir.'

'Oh, you would, would you?' said Dax. 'Can't you guess? Go on, guess.'

'My mind is blank, sir.'

Dax's smirk changed to a gaze of contempt. 'My uncle has decided that you can't be trusted on this particular voyage.'

Topaz blinked, and even the stern-faced master-at-arms raised an eyebrow.

'But, sir,' said Topaz; 'have I ever given any indication that I can't be trusted? I don't understand.'

'It's quite simple, Topaz,' said Dina. 'My father thinks that your personal feelings towards our prisoner have got in the way of your duty. Now, kindly piss off and leave us to work.'

'Is Maddie Jackdaw on board, ma'am?'

Dina shrugged, then she and Dax turned and strode away.

'Assholes,' muttered Topaz.

'I'll pretend I never heard that, sir,' said the master-at-arms. 'You'd best do as they say, sir; nothing good will come from making a scene.'

Topaz stared at the side of the ship for a moment, then turned and trudged away. He got to the end of the pier, then glanced over his shoulder at the *Giddy Gull*, his stomach churning. How could they do this to him? Then he thought about what he would have done had he been on board while Maddie was sitting in chains in the hold. Would he have carried out his orders without question? What if Dax or Dina had commanded him to ensure Maddie was taken to the slave market? Would he have done it?

He turned back towards the quayside, where the last of the *Gull's* crew were hurrying away from the taverns. The master-at-arms' men were watching them, to make sure none tried to flee.

Perhaps he should take Ryan's advice and head back to *Bo'sun's Droop*, where he could drown his woes in a welter of alcohol. No. He was already angry and frustrated, and getting drunk would be highly unlikely to improve his mood. He glanced up at the steep cliffside. Befallen Castle was out of sight, but he knew that Olo'osso and his four other daughters would be up there. He turned for the path that led to the castle, and lit a cigarette. He had no idea what he was going to say when he got to Befallen, but the alternative – sitting alone in a tavern while Maddie was borne away from Langbeg – was unthinkable. He passed the wagons that carried passengers up the hillside, and kept going. Perhaps a long walk would give him time to calm down.

He was out of breath by the time he reached the summit of the ridge, and the underarms of his uniform were damp with sweat from the heat of the sun. He stopped for a moment, and glanced back down at the harbour. The *Giddy Gull* was still tied up alongside the pier, but the cranes had been wheeled away, and the ship looked ready to depart. He realised that he no longer cared about another man acting as the *Gull's* master. He had no desire to serve under Captain Dax, though he hoped that Vitz would be alright. Ryan would be fine; he was adaptable to almost any set of circumstances, but he worried that, without his protection, Vitz would be vulnerable. He pulled his gaze away from the ship, and turned back towards the castle. The path wound along the top of the ridge, and it took another ten minutes of walking to get near the gatehouse. There was a bend in the road ahead of him, and he could see the side of the castle that overlooked the bay. His eyes went up to the loggia on the top floor, and his anger produced images of Olo'osso laughing and drinking while Maddie sat in misery aboard the *Gull*. It wasn't fair; none of it was. How was he supposed to respect a man who acted in such a way?

He was about to carry on along the path, when he noticed something. He frowned. Two figures were clambering down the sheer side of the castle, swinging from block to block, with nothing below them but the long drop down to the waves crashing against the base of the cliffs. Who was stupid enough to scale the walls of the castle? He glanced at the gatehouse, then turned off the path and sat by the edge of the cliff, watching as the two figures gradually lowered themselves further down. He winced as one of them nearly slipped and fell, but, eventually, both made it to the bottom of the wall, and began to edge round towards the path. Topaz silently cheered them on. Whoever it was, they had guts. When they reached the side of the cliff, they scampered down again, through the shadows, and disappeared from Topaz's view. He leaned over the ridge, and saw them approach where he was sitting, their faces now visible to him.

Holy crap. It was Lara and Tilly. They were laughing as they climbed back up the slope, then Lara nudged Tilly with an elbow, and pointed towards Topaz.

'You watching us, eh?' said Lara, as she reached the ledge where he was sitting.

'I was,' he said. 'It was a damn miracle that you didn't fall.'

'Nah,' said Lara; 'it's a piece of piss; though, to be fair, I ain't done it since I was fourteen.'

'I was shitting myself,' said Tilly. 'It was a terrible idea.'

'Shut up,' said Lara, as she sat down next to Topaz. 'It was better than your shit plan. You never even made it out of the gatehouse.'

'You tried to get out of Befallen before?' said Topaz.

Lara thumbed at Tilly, who looked exhausted. 'She did. She was trying to help Maddie escape, but they were rumbled by the guards. Father then locked us in a room together, but I refuse to be caged.' She belched. 'So, Topaz; why are you here?'

'I came to speak to your father, about why the *Gull's* leaving without me.'

'That's a bad idea,' said Tilly. 'Father's in a right temper.'

'Yeah, because of you,' said Lara.

'Why were you trying to help Maddie escape?' said Topaz.

'Why do you think, dumbass?' said Lara. 'You ain't the only one around here with a damn conscience, laddo. The big question is, what are we going to do about it now?'

Tilly glanced at Topaz. 'Father's going to go crazy when he finds out that me and Lara have sneaked away. Will you help us?'

Topaz nodded. 'Sure.'

Lara grinned. 'I told you he would. Got a cigarette? My fingers and calves are bleeding aching after that climb. Let's smoke for a minute while we tell you the next stage of our, no, *my* plan.'

Topaz handed them both a cigarette, and took one for himself. 'Let's hear it, then.'

'Tilly has been stripped of her captaincy of the *Little Sneak*,' said Lara.

'Yeah? Shit. I assume it was because she tried to help Maddie escape?'

Lara lit her cigarette. 'You assume correctly.'

'Can you believe it?' said Tilly. 'My ship, gone; just like that.'

'Your sister Dina told me that I'd been removed from my post because I couldn't be trusted,' said Topaz, 'so I think I know how you feel, ma'am.'

Lara frowned. 'Why does she warrant a "ma'am"? I'm your damn captain, lad.'

'Not any more, you ain't,' said Tilly. 'You lost the *Gull*, just like I lost the *Sneak*.'

'Do you have to bleeding remind me of that?' snapped Lara.

'You mentioned a plan?' said Topaz.

'Oh yeah,' said Lara. 'It's obvious, really. Father ain't sent word down to Langbeg yet, to tell the crew of the *Little Sneak* that Tilly ain't the captain no more, so we're going to sail it out of the harbour, chase down the *Gull*, free Maddie, kill Dax, maroon Dina, and then me and Tilly will both have our ships back.'

Topaz's mouth opened, but no words came out.

Lara laughed. 'We're going to be outlaws.'

'It's insanity,' said Tilly, shaking her head. 'Father will never forgive us.'

'So? I'll never forgive him for handing over my beautiful brigantine to Dax and Dina. We'll sail to the Eastern Rim, and lay low for a couple of years, until it's all blown over.'

Tilly put her head in her hands. 'Why did I let you persuade me to do this?'

'You got any better ideas?' said Lara. 'If you do, then let's hear them. No? Thought not.' She stubbed her cigarette out. 'Right. We should get moving. Topaz, I assume that you're coming with us?'

'I... uh...'

Lara glared at him. 'You swore an oath to me – not to my father. You'd better not be thinking about deserting me; we need you to guide us through the Skerries. Just think of the prize: we'll get the *Gull* back, and you can have your wicked way with Maddie.'

'We'll never be able to return to Langbeg,' he said.

She shrugged. 'Probably. So what? I ain't staying somewhere that doesn't show me any respect. And think of your position. If they can remove you from your post once, then they'll do it again. Don't you want to rescue Maddie?'

'Of course I do, but...'

'But nothing,' she said, standing. 'Move your ass, and that's a damn order.'

She climbed up onto the path and strode away in the direction of town. Tilly and Topaz shared a glance. Both shrugged, then scrambled up after Lara.

When they reached the end of the ridge, they looked down into the harbour. The *Giddy Gull* was manoeuvring past the other ships in the basin, its forward sails filled with the warm breeze.

'My *Gull*,' said Lara, her voice pained. 'Those bastards. I'm going to string Dax up by his ankles, then cut bits off his body and feed them to the fish.'

'Or,' said Tilly, 'we take him to Pangba, and leave him there.'

Lara frowned. 'You mean sell him to the slave market, instead of Maddie? I like your thinking, sister.'

'Eh, that wasn't what...'

'Too late,' said Lara, setting off again. 'It's a fine idea; your first for a while, I might add.'

They hurried down the path that led towards the town, and approached the quayside. The markets and taverns were busy, and the harbour front was swarming with activity. A few dockworkers nodded to them as they tried to stroll casually towards where the *Little Sneak* was berthed. They walked up a long wooden pier, and came to the sloop.

'Good afternoon, ma'am,' said a sailor from the deck.

'Afternoon, Bosun,' said Tilly. 'How many of the crew are ready to leave?'

The sailor narrowed his eyes. 'Um, why, ma'am?'

'My father wants me to take the *Sneak* out for a few hours, to see how the sloop performs after its refit.'

'But the refit ain't complete, ma'am,' he said. 'We're expecting a bunch of carpenters and sailmakers on board later today.'

Tilly shrugged. 'You know what my father's like – he won't take no for an answer. Let's humour him, and we'll be quick. Just once or twice round the closest Skerrie, and then we'll head back. Is the sloop up to it?'

'I guess so, ma'am. The crew are on board, helping out with the repairs. Did you hear about the master, though? He's been transferred to the *Giddy Gull*, which just left twenty minutes ago.'

'Don't worry about that, Bosun,' said Tilly. 'Father's letting us borrow Topaz for a few hours.'

The bosun raised an eyebrow. Tilly led Lara and Topaz up the gangplank, and they stepped down onto the main deck. Sailors were painting and scrubbing, while others were fixing new rigging to the mast.

'My sister's going to act as my lieutenant,' said Tilly to the bosun.

Lara looked like she wanted to say something, but managed to keep her mouth closed.

'Tell the crew to cast off right away,' said Tilly. 'Let's get this over with.'

The bosun edged in closer to them. 'Ma'am, you should know that a rumour's being making the rounds.'

'What rumour?' said Tilly.

'When the midshipman from the *Gull* turned up to take the master, we heard that you, eh, had been removed as captain of the *Little Sneak*.'

Tilly laughed out loud, and slapped her thigh. 'Dear gods, sailors are so damn gullible at times. Me – removed as captain? That'll be the day.'

'So, you are still the captain, ma'am?'

'Of course I bleeding well am, Bosun. Who else would want to take on my little sloop, eh? Go on, get to work. I want us leaving the harbour in the next ten minutes.'

The bosun glanced around, while chewing his lip, then he saluted, and turned to the crew.

'We're taking the *Sneak* out, lads,' he shouted. 'Stop what you're doing and get to your stations!'

Tilly strode towards the quarter deck, and Lara and Topaz followed her. Topaz went straight to the wheel, and exhaled, his nerves building. He glanced up at the ridge top, but there was no sign of movement coming from the castle.

'Your lieutenant?' said Lara. 'I think I'm about to die of shame.'

'Shut your mouth,' said Tilly. 'What else was I supposed to say? And, we're missing a lieutenant, as my last one was killed by the Sea Banner off Alef. Now, most of my crew think you're a right bitch, so start acting like one, and give out some orders.'

'I don't know any of your crew,' said Lara. 'Why do they think I'm a bitch?'

Tilly shrugged. 'Because I told them you were.'

Lara rolled her eyes, then she strode down the steps to the main deck.

'Get a move on, assholes,' she cried, 'or I'll rip your dicks off!' She glanced over her shoulder at Tilly. 'Is that the kind of thing you meant?'

Tilly sighed, then turned to Topaz. 'Right, Master, do you think we can catch the *Gull*?'

'Yes, ma'am,' he said, trying to focus on the job at hand. 'The *Sneak's* keel is much shallower than the *Gull's*, and we'll be able to cut a few corners through the Skerries. We'll have to catch up with them before we leave Luckenbay, though; otherwise the brigantine's speed will leave us behind in the open sea.'

'But we can do it, though?'

'We'll be cutting it fine, ma'am, but I think so.'

Lara was striding along the main deck, cajoling the crew as they rushed around getting the sloop ready. The gangplank was pulled in, and the first ropes connecting them to the pier were being loosened, when a bell pealed behind them in the town.

'Stop that boat!' cried a loud voice from the quayside.

The crew glanced round. A large group of armed men were running along the quayside towards the pier.

'Ignore those bastards!' cried Lara. 'Get us moving; now!'

'I need a midshipman,' said Topaz. 'Who have you got?'

Tilly whistled, and a young boy ran up onto the quarter deck.

'Congratulations, lad,' said Tilly, 'you just made midshipman. Do exactly what Master Topaz tells you – no hesitation, and don't mess it up.'

The boy stared at her, his mouth open, then Topaz rattled out a long list of instructions as he turned the wheel. The sloop had yet to move, but the last ropes had been thrown back onto the deck. The boy sprinted away, and began relaying Topaz's orders. The mainsail was hoisted, and the wind filled it. On the pier, the first of the men were fast approaching the *Sneak* just as it edged away from its moorings. One of them jumped, trying to leap across the gap, but splashed into the water of the harbour.

Lara pointed at the floundering man and laughed. 'Get it right up you, asswipe!'

Four men dropped to one knee on the pier, and aimed crossbows at the deck of the departing sloop, but Ann appeared behind them.

'No shooting!' she cried. 'Those are my damn sisters on board.' She stared onto the quarter deck of the *Little Sneak*, and locked eyes with Tilly. 'Get back here, Tilly. Father will forgive you, if you stop now.'

'Sorry, Ann,' said Tilly, 'but no one's stealing the *Sneak* from me, no one.'

Ann ran up the pier, keeping pace with the sloop as it began to move forward. 'You're making a terrible mistake! And you, Topaz – think about what you're doing. If you betray father, you will never be able to return here. This is your last chance.'

'Screw you!' yelled Lara from the main deck. 'You're not in charge of me.'

Ann reached the end of the pier, her eyes narrowing as she watched the fleeing ship. She shook her head, then turned her back to them, and strode away.

'Never mind about her,' said Lara, as she jumped up the steps onto the quarter deck. She turned towards the main deck. 'Keep working, dipshits!' she shouted down to the crew.

'Dear gods,' said Tilly; 'this is a catastrophe of epic proportions.'

Topaz glanced at her, as he guided the *Little Sneak* through the breakwaters at the mouth of the harbour.

'It's too late for doubts now, ma'am,' he said. 'We'll have to make the best of it.'

Lara grinned, a manic gleam in her eyes. 'Well said, Master. Now, let's catch ourselves a brigantine.'

CHAPTER 29

RUDDERLESS

Luckenbay, Olkis, Western Rim – 24th Beldinch 5255 (18th Gylean Year 6)

Maddie sat in the darkness, listening to the sounds of the *Giddy Gull* as it sailed through the bay. Wooden boards squeaked and groaned, while countless footsteps thumped overhead, going up and down the steep steps that lay outside the small, locked cabin where she had been placed. The heat was stifling in the airless compartment, and Maddie had been thirsty since the moment the ship had left the harbour of Langbeg. They had been sailing for hours, though Maddie had lost track of how many. From the warmth, she guessed it must still be daytime, which meant that there were three days and nights remaining on the voyage to Pangba. Part of her wanted the journey to be over with as soon as possible, while the rest of her wanted to drag it out, to delay the moment when she would be handed over to a slave auction house. Tilly had told her about them, and they sounded like Maddie's worst nightmare.

Poor Tilly. Maddie felt sorry for the young pirate captain; she had looked heartbroken at the prospect of losing her little sloop, and she had tried her best to help Maddie escape, which had partly made up for the fact that she had abducted the dragon rider in the first place.

She remembered Tilly saying that the strange sickness caused by the motion of the ship was eased if you could glimpse the horizon. It was true. A tight ball of nausea had sat in the pit of her stomach since the brigantine had left the calm waters of the harbour basin. She longed for the movement to stop, but it never did, and twice she had been sure she was about to vomit. Maybe it was better that she had eaten nothing since the previous afternoon; otherwise it might have come back up, stinking out the tiny cabin in the process.

More steps thumped down the stairs, then paused outside her door. A key sounded in the lock, and a sailor opened the door and peered through, as if imagining that Maddie might be ready to leap up and attack. He glanced at her sitting on the low bench.

'Hello,' she said. 'Are we there yet?'

The sailor didn't respond. Maybe he had been told not to speak to her, or perhaps the crew were already treating her as a slave.

'I'm very thirsty,' she said. 'Could I have some water?'

'Do you need a slash?' he said.

'A what?'

'Do you need to pee?'

'Eh, no. I've had nothing to drink since yesterday. That's why I'm so thirsty.'

'Come on, then; time to visit the captain.'

'Why?'

The sailor narrowed his eyes. 'Because he said so. Are you going to cause me trouble?'

'Are you my guard?'

'I work for the master-at-arms, so, yes; I guess I am.'

'The master-at-arms? That sounds important. What's your name?'

'If I tell you, will you shut up and do as I say?'

'That depends. You might ask me to do something I'm unable to do, and then I would break my word. Is it sunny outside?'

'I'm Bennie,' said the sailor.

'My name's Maddie Jackdaw.'

'Yes. I know. Am I going to have to come in and drag you out of there?'

Maddie stood, then swayed as the ship rolled up and down. She gagged, a hand to her mouth, then staggered through the door. The sailor gripped her arm, and led her towards the stairs.

'Up you go,' he said.

She clambered up the steep steps, and a warm breeze brushed against her face as she emerged into the strong sunlight of the main deck, with the quarter deck in front of her. Over to her right, the sun was getting low in the sky, but the heat was still fierce. She felt Bennie nudge her, and she carried on, stepping out onto the busy deck. Several sailors glanced in her direction, and she heard someone mutter something about 'Topaz's girl'.

She frowned, then glanced at Bennie.

'Did you hear that? Why would someone call me "Topaz's girl"? I'm not anyone's girl, thank you very much.'

Bennie eyed her, then shrugged. 'This way.'

'I know the way to the quarter deck,' she said.

They walked up the steps onto the crowded quarter deck. The old master from the *Little Sneak* was standing with both hands on the wheel at the rear of the deck. Maddie waved at him, but he kept his eyes averted from her. Next to him were Dax and Dina, who broke off their conversation when they saw Maddie approach.

'I've brought the prisoner, Captain,' said Bennie.

'I can see that,' said Dax, his eyes roving over Maddie. He turned to Dina. 'You stay here and look after things, Lieutenant.'

'But we're only halfway through the Skerries, Captain,' said Dina.

'I know that; do you think I'm stupid? You and the master can take care of getting us through the rest of Luckenbay. I want to interview our prisoner.'

Dina gave him a look of contempt.

'Do you have a problem, Lieutenant?'

'No, Captain,' she said. 'Enjoy your... interview.'

He grinned. 'I will.' He glanced at Maddie. 'Follow me.'

He strode off towards the door to the captain's cabin, and Bennie nudged Maddie in the back. She tried to catch the master's eye, but he was steadfastly ignoring her, so she made her way across the deck and entered the cabin after Dax. Bennie closed the door, remaining outside, and Dax strode over to a table and poured himself a drink.

'Can I have some water?' said Maddie.

'Speak only if I ask you a question,' said Dax. 'Sit down. No, remain standing.'

He took his full glass and sat on a comfortable chair at the head of the table.

'Right, then,' he said, his eyes on her again. 'Do you understand what's going to happen to you?'

'You're going to sell me to a slave place.'

'Yes. Well done.'

'Are you ashamed? You should be.'

He took a sip from the glass, then put it down onto the table. 'That was your last chance. If you speak unprompted again, I will hit you. Don't think for a second that, just because you're a woman, I would hesitate to beat the crap out of you.'

She tightened her eyes, but said nothing.

'That's better,' he said. 'Now, if you're good to me, then I can arrange for you to be sold to one of the... less disreputable dealers in Pangba. You might be under the impression that each slave auction house is much the same, but, believe me, they're not. There are some pretty nasty establishments in Pangba – places that would chew up a young girl like you. I could spare you from the worst of them, if you cooperate.'

Maddie bit her tongue. He hadn't asked her a question, so she remained silent.

He leered at her. 'Are you a virgin?'

'That's none of your damn business.'

He laughed. 'Actually, it is my business. I'm going to sell you, and I need to know the details. I'll get a lot more for you if you ain't never been tampered with. Take your clothes off; I want to inspect the goods.'

Maddie folded her arms across her chest. 'No.'

Dax's expression darkened. 'Are you one of those bitches who think they're better than everyone else? You might think you're beautiful, but I've seen better. You're nothing special; just another whore, and right now, I'm the only guy who has the power to make your life bearable. If you piss me off, which you're starting to do, then I can make the next few days a living nightmare; do you hear me?'

'I can hear you,' she said.

'And?'

'My dragon is going to kill you, and I'm going to watch.'

Dax banged his fist on the table, his face twisted with anger; then he calmed himself, and smiled.

'I see I'm going to have to do this the hard way,' he said, getting to his feet. 'I gave you a chance to be friendly, and you've thrown it back in my face. What happens next will be your fault.'

She took a step back as he approached. He spread his arms out, as if ready to spring at her, and she glanced around for anything she could use as a weapon.

'There's no escape,' he said, smirking; 'and no one will come to your assistance, so feel free to scream your lungs out.'

'If you touch me...'

'I'm going to do more than touch you, you little bitch.'

He lunged at her, and she dodged away out of his reach, putting the table between Dax and herself.

'Bennie!' she shouted. 'Help me!'

The door to the cabin opened. Dax turned, his eyes narrow with rage.

'Get out!' he cried, then his expression changed as he realised it was Dina.

The pirate sister raised an eyebrow. 'You need to see this, Captain.'

Dax scowled at her. 'Can't you see I'm busy? It'll have to wait.'

'It can't wait, Captain. The *Little Sneak* is directly ahead of us, on an interception course.'

'What? Impossible.'

He ran to the window overlooking the quarter deck, and opened the shutters. Maddie blinked as the bright sunlight entered the cabin, then squinted out at the view. Rocky Skerries were dotted around on their left and right, while a tiny mast was visible ahead and to the left.

'I don't understand,' said Dax. 'They were in harbour when we left Langbeg; how could they be ahead of us?'

Dina shrugged. 'Topaz is on the wheel,' she said, 'with Lara and Tilly standing next to him, sir. I saw them through the eyeglass.'

'Bastards!' Dax cried, then he stormed out of the cabin. Dina signalled to Bennie, who entered, then she left and closed the door.

Maddie walked up to the window. A moment later, Bennie wandered over to stand next to her, and they stared out into the bay. The tiny mast in the distance was growing larger, and she suppressed a grin. What if the *Little Sneak* was coming to rescue her? She tried to calm her racing thoughts, her heart still pounding from being chased around the cabin by Dax.

'I thought this ship was fast,' she said. 'How could they have caught up with us?'

'On the open seas,' the sailor said, his gaze fixed on the horizon, 'nothing can catch us; but we're in the middle of Luckenbay. In these waters, the *Sneak* is more nimble, and can sail up channels that are too shallow for the *Gull*. Still, it's some feat all the same.'

'Maybe Olo'osso's changed his mind,' she said. 'Maybe he's sent them to recall us back to Langbeg.'

Bennie shrugged his shoulders.

'Did you hear me shouting for help?' she said.

'I heard.'

'Would you have come?'

'No.'

'Dax is a horrible sleazy beast,' she said; 'don't you care? He could have hurt me.'

'He's the captain.'

'And that makes it all right? Captain Tilly treated me with kindness, and led me to believe that the crews of the Five Sisters ships were the good guys; and yet you would have done nothing if he'd...'

'Be quiet,' he hissed. 'Look – the lads are getting the pisspot catapult ready.'

'What does that mean?'

'What do you think it means? Holy shit. He can't be thinking of loosing one on the *Sneak*. Surely?'

'Dax is going to blow up the *Little Sneak*? But...'

'Shut up. It's probably just a precaution; you know – just in case.'

Maddie stared towards the bow of the *Gull*. A huge tarpaulin sheet had been dragged off the large catapult that sat at the very front of the ship, and sailors were turning cranks and raising its long throwing arm. Ahead of them, the *Little Sneak* was speeding towards the *Gull*, and the distance between the two ships was narrowing quickly. Maddie's attention snapped back to the quarter deck as a row broke out. She couldn't hear what words were being exchanged, but the tone was unmistakable. Dax was pointing a finger in the old master's face and screaming at him, while Dina was standing back, her eyes tight. The master said something, and Dax punched him in the face. Bennie flinched, then swallowed.

'What are they fighting about?' said Maddie.

'The new master just refused an order,' whispered the sailor, his knuckles white as he gripped the window frame.

Dax's hands went to the wheel, and he tried to turn it, but the master was having none of it. He hunched over the wheel, keeping it steady. Dax roared in frustration, then drew his sword and plunged it into the master's back, the point appearing through the man's chest. The old master staggered, his hands releasing the wheel, then he slumped to the deck in a pool of blood.

'No,' gasped Bennie.

Dax shouted out some orders, and a tall young man ran up onto the quarter deck. Dax held the tip of the sword up to the young man's throat, and ordered him to take the wheel. The young man stared down at the body of the old master, then did as he was told.

'Shit. He's put Vitz on the wheel,' whispered Bennie.

'Who's Vitz – the young guy?'

'Yeah. Topaz's mate.'

'Why did that sailor call me "Topaz's girl"?'

'Eh, what? That's all we know about you. Ryan's told everyone on board about it. Topaz tried to buy you, but Captain Osso said no. That's why he was left behind.' He glanced at the approaching sloop. 'Seems as though he didn't take the news lying down. Topaz will sail rings round us in the Skerries. Dear gods, he must have it bad for you, just like Ryan said.'

Maddie frowned. Had Topaz stolen a ship to rescue her? That couldn't be right. No man had ever acted like that because of her. She couldn't remember the last time a guy had done anything nice for her. For Sable, yes. Men were always trying to impress her, but never Maddie. She felt a strange feeling in her chest as she pictured Topaz at the wheel of the *Little Sneak*, sailing into danger for her.

'Either that,' said Bennie, 'or Lara really wants her ship back.'

She punched Bennie on the arm.

He frowned at her. 'What was that for?'

'Nothing,' she snapped.

Out on the quarter deck, another row was brewing; this time between Dax and Dina. Maddie made out Dax shouting the words 'I am the damn captain!', then he sprinted towards the main deck and disappeared from sight. Dina stamped her foot in anger, her eyes staring at the *Little Sneak*. The sloop was less than a hundred yards away, its course seeming as if it was going to collide with the *Giddy Gull*. Maddie silently urged it on. She could see a cluster of people on the *Sneak's* small quarter deck, including two women, one of whom was waving her arms at the *Gull*.

The throwing arm of the bow catapult leapt forward, and something flashed through the air towards the *Little Sneak*.

'Shit!' cried Bennie, his hands going to his head as he stared.

The projectile arced through the blue sky, then dropped, smashing into the bow of the sloop. For a moment, nothing happened, then a flash of white light exploded, followed by an ear-splitting roar. The bow of the *Little Sneak* disintegrated into a thousand pieces, and the craft lifted from the water, then slammed back down, the bow sinking beneath the waves. The stern rose high, and sailors jumped from the railings, or fell from the mast screaming. A ring of debris settled on the surface of the sea around the stricken sloop, and the stern began to follow the bow into the dark depths.

Maddie felt her hopes vanish as she watched the sloop sink. Tilly had been on board, as well as Topaz and Lara, and her guts churned at the thought that they were all dead.

Dax reappeared on the quarter deck. Dina was standing off to the side, her face turned away from Maddie as she stared at the sinking sloop. Vitz turned the wheel, and the *Gull* started to change course towards the wreckage, where dozens of the *Sneak's* crew were bobbing about in the waves, their arms in the air as they cried out for help. Dax drew his sword again, and pointed it at the young man's throat, but Vitz ignored him. For a moment, Maddie was certain that Dax was going to kill Vitz, but he clubbed him with the hilt of the sword instead of stabbing him, then shoved him to the side. Dax turned the wheel, but the course of the *Gull* didn't change, and it continued heading towards the survivors. The stern of the *Little Sneak* was still floating, and was surrounded by desperate sailors, who were clinging on to anything they could grab.

Dina opened the door to the captain's cabin, her face ashen.

'Get Maddie back below deck,' she whispered.

Bennie didn't move, his eyes wide as he continued to stare at the wreckage of the sloop.

'I gave you an order!' cried Dina.

'Are you still going to obey Dax?' said Maddie, her eyes welling. 'Look what he did to Topaz and your sisters, and all those sailors…'

'Shut her up,' said Dina, 'or I will. Leading Hand Bennie, take her below.'

Bennie pulled his gaze away from the sloop. He glanced at Maddie, then gestured towards the door, his face stricken with fear and doubt. Maddie walked out onto the quarter deck. To her left, the old master that she had sailed with from Ulna to Olkis was lying dead, and next to him, Vitz was groaning in pain, the side of his head bloody. Dax was still turning the wheel, but the *Gull* wasn't responding.

'Get me the bosun,' he cried. 'Something's wrong with the rudder.'

Bennie shoved Maddie across the quarter deck. On the main deck, almost every sailor had stopped working. Several were talking in low voices, and no one obeyed Dax's command.

The captain pointed at a young midshipman. 'You! Boy, fetch me the bosun, now, or I'll have you strung up by your ankles.'

The lad turned to hurry away, but before he could reach the steps leading to the main deck, four men bounded up them, dragging a fifth. One of the men nodded to Bennie, who halted, a hand gripping Maddie's arm.

Dax turned to the new arrivals. 'Yes?'

The four men flung the fifth to the deck in front of the wheel.

'We caught this man sabotaging the rudder, Captain,' said the men's leader.

Dax stared down at the man sprawled on the deck. 'Who is he, Master-at-Arms?'

'Petty Officer Ryan, Captain; one of the carpenter's mates.'

'And it was sabotage – deliberate?'

'Yes, Captain. He cut through the control rods with a saw. The *Giddy Gull's* steering mechanism is no longer operational.'

Dax's eyes widened. 'Halt the ship!' he bellowed. 'Sails down; get the anchors ready!'

Several sailors ran off to carry out his orders, but most remained where they were, staring at the quarter deck with angry and sullen expressions. Maddie noticed blood, both on Ryan's fists, and on the face of one of the men working for the master-at-arms. A low murmur of discontent reverberated around the deck.

Dax kicked Ryan, then stamped on his back. 'You filthy little traitor!' he cried. 'Are you trying to sink us? You'll die for this! Do you know what happens if a ship tries to go through the Skerries when it can't steer?'

'I do indeed, sir,' gasped Ryan.

'You mean you wanted us to flounder on the rocks?'

'No,' said Ryan; 'I knew you'd have to stop the *Gull*, sir.'

A fight broke out on the main deck. Two men were attacked by a mob of sailors as they were trying to make their way to the quarter deck. The master-at-arms clicked his fingers, and his four men pulled their crossbows from their shoulders, and aimed them down into the main deck.

'Loose a few bolts over their heads,' said the master-at-arms, his eyes tight.

His men obeyed, and four bolts thrummed from the bows, narrowly missed the fighting sailors, who scattered. The two beaten men ran onto the quarter deck, panting, their faces bleeding.

'Get behind me, lads,' said the master-at-arms.

'We've lost control of the lower deck, sir,' said one of the men.

'You've gone too far, Dax,' said Dina. 'You're pushing the crew into a mutiny.'

Dax released the wheel and slapped Dina across the face. 'You will address me as captain,' he screamed at her. 'Master-at-arms, send your men through the ship, and kill anyone who resists.'

'I have only seven men under my command, Captain,' said the master-at-arms; 'two of them have been beaten, and one's guarding the prisoner.'

A shrieking sound of chains rattled across the deck as the two anchors were dropped. The sails had been taken down, and the *Gull* slowed to a halt, a hundred yards from the floating stern of the *Little Sneak*.

Dax strode up to the burly master-at-arms. 'Are you questioning my authority?'

'No, Captain. I'm merely pointing out the impractical nature of your last order.'

Dax grabbed a crossbow from one of the master-at-arms' men, and aimed it into the crowd of sailors on the main deck. He loosed, and a bolt struck a man in the face, sending him flying back onto the deck.

The sailors took a few steps back from the quarter deck, seething with anger.

'This ends now,' Dax shouted down to them. 'Captain Olo'osso himself placed me in charge of this vessel, and any sailor who refuses to obey my orders will be gutted like a fish. Where's my bosun? I want the rudder repaired within the next ten minutes, or someone else will be getting a bolt through their brains.'

Maddie edged away to the side of the quarter deck, as the atmosphere on the ship chilled. It seemed as if most of the crew were on the main deck, and the quarter deck felt like it was under siege.

'Murderer!' cried one of the sailors.

'It's not too late, Captain,' said the master-at-arms. 'If you order the launch to pick up the survivors of the *Little Sneak*, it'll calm the lads down, and give them a command they'll be happy to carry out.'

'Are you suggesting that I appease a mutinous mob?' cried Dax.

'Listen to him,' said Dina. 'Listen to him, or they'll lynch us.'

'Shut your mouth,' snapped Dax.

'But my sisters might still be...'

'I said shut your mouth! Your sisters will drown, if they haven't already perished. There will be no rescue of the survivors; understand?' He aimed his voice at the crew. 'Those bastards on the *Little Sneak* got what they deserved. This is your final warning – get back to work, or more blood will be shed.'

The crew remained where they were.

Dax spat onto the deck. 'Master-at-arms, order your men to attack. No mercy.'

The master-at-arms gazed down for a moment, then nodded. 'You heard the captain, lads. Follow me.'

He pulled his own crossbow from his shoulder, and charged down the steps onto the main deck, his men running after him. Bennie glanced at Maddie, swallowed, then went after them. The eight men rushed into the massed group of sailors, their crossbows loosing, and chaos erupted across the main deck. Sailors were struck by bolts, and then two of the master-at-arms' men were pulled down by the mob, and disappeared amid a flurry of boots and flung fists. Dax aimed his crossbow, and loosed, the bolt striking a sailor in the arm.

'Look what you've done,' said Dina.

Dax turned, and pointed the bow at her. 'I've had enough of you questioning me. I am the captain of the *Giddy Gull*.'

'You couldn't captain a rowing boat,' said Maddie.

Dax aimed the bow at her. 'This is all your doing, you bitch! We should have hanged you in Langbeg as a liar. I guess we'll have to forego the money you would have brought us as a slave. You wouldn't have fetched much, anyway.'

He raised the bow to his shoulder, and gazed down the sights at Maddie. Behind him, a figure appeared, scrambling up the railings of the quarter deck, her clothes and long hair dripping wet, and a knife in her right hand. Maddie's mouth opened, as Lara leapt from the railings. She collided with Dax as he was loosing the bow at Maddie, and the bolt thumped into the wooden deck a few inches from her feet. Dax fell to his knees, dropping the bow, as Lara tried to bring the knife round to his throat. He grabbed her wrist, and twisted it, then punched her in the face with his free hand. Dina ran towards him, and he shoved her away. Vitz and Ryan got to their feet, and approached the captain, like predators about to pounce.

Dax wrestled the knife from Lara's hand and held it to her throat.

'Stay back,' he cried, 'or I'll kill Lara in front of you. You hear me?'

'Put down the knife,' said Vitz.

'You settler piece of shit,' said Dax, his eyes wide. Lara struggled to get out of his grip, and a thin trace of blood appeared on her throat.

Maddie picked up the crossbow. She glanced down at it, trying to remember how to use the weapon. Her hands began to tremble; what if she hit Lara by mistake? She closed her eyes and got ready to loose.

'You might want to load it first,' said a voice next to her.

She opened her eyes, and saw Topaz standing next to her, his clothes sodden. She passed him the crossbow. He pulled back the loading mechanism until it clicked, aimed it at Dax, and loosed. The bolt sped through the air, then rammed into Dax's left eye. His head lolled back, then he collapsed onto the deck. Lara wriggled free, jumped to her feet, then spat on the body.

Topaz glanced at Maddie. 'Remember you asked if I'd ever killed anyone?' he said. 'Well, I have now.'

The quarter deck fell into a stunned silence as everyone gazed at the body of Dax lying on the wooden boards. Lara was the first to react. She raised her arms and turned to the main deck.

'It's over!' she cried. 'Your old captain's back! Dax is dead!'

The fighting began to peter out as the crew turned to face the quarter deck. At the sight of Lara, they let out a loud cheer.

'The *Giddy Gull* is mine once more, lads!' Lara shouted. 'Launch the rowing boat, and pick up the survivors from the *Little Sneak*. My sister Tilly is still clinging onto the wreckage. Bring her on board – bring them all on board.'

Lara turned as the crew got to work. She eyed Dina, then strode over to Maddie and Topaz. Ryan and Vitz also walked over, and Ryan hugged Topaz.

'I knew you weren't dead, mate,' Ryan said, 'but, by all the gods, I'm glad to see you.'

'Is Tilly alright?' said Maddie.

'Well,' said Lara, 'her feelings are a little hurt on account of the fact that her ship is now in a million pieces, but other than that, she's fine.' She looked Maddie up and down. 'What about you?'

Maddie hesitated. 'I was terrified, for a bit. Dax... he... never mind; he's dead now. Good. I never thought I'd be happy to see anyone die, but I think I'll make an exception in his case. Thank you for coming.'

'It wasn't all about you,' said Lara. 'I wanted the *Gull* back too; but I know someone who will be happy that you're safe; eh, Topaz?'

Topaz looked into Maddie's eyes. 'I... um...'

Lara laughed. 'Check the state of him. He guided the *Little Sneak* through the Skerries like a man possessed, and now he's all shy in front of Maddie. You'd better be good to my master, girl. If you break his heart, I might have to do something unpleasant to you.'

Dina approached. 'Sister, I tried to stop Dax. I...'

'I'm not interested in hearing your excuses, Dina,' said Lara. 'Pack your shit up, because when the rowing boat's finished picking up the survivors, I'm putting you on it. Good luck rowing back to Langbeg.'

Dina lowered her gaze, nodded, then walked into her cabin.

'Petty Officer Ryan,' said Lara, 'get below, and fix the rudder, if you please. Oh, and thank you for disabling it. Quick thinking.'

Ryan grinned, and saluted. 'Yes, ma'am.'

Ryan winked at Topaz, then turned and hurried away. The rowing boat was being hoisted off the side of the long brigantine, while a collection of bodies had been lined up by the main mast. Among them were the master-at-arms and his men. Maddie nearly wept when she saw Bennie next to them, blood pooling under his body.

'We lost a lot of good lads today,' said Lara, shaking her head. 'Petty Officer Vitz,' she went on, 'man the wheel. As soon as the rudder has been repaired, we'll be moving out of here. It's a long way to Ulna.'

'Are we going to Ulna?' said Maddie.

'We sure are,' said Lara. 'It'll be a few years before it'll be safe to come back here. Master Topaz, please escort Maddie into *my* cabin, and make sure she has something to eat and drink; she's our guest, after all.'

'Yes, ma'am.'

Topaz led Maddie back into the captain's cabin, and Maddie shuddered from the memories of the last time she had been there.

'Are you alright?' said Topaz. 'Did that bastard hurt you?'

She shook her head.

He poured her a drink.

'Got any water?' she said.

'Sure.' He lifted a jug from the table, sniffed it, then filled a mug. 'Here you go.'

She sat, her eyes watching him.

'I've, uh, heard a few things,' she said.

'What about?'

'About, um, you.'

He nodded, his gaze on the table. 'They're probably all true. Look, Maddie, what they were going to do to you was wrong, and I want to believe that, even if I didn't like you, I would have acted in the same way. This must be weird for you; I mean, we hardly know each other, and I can't explain why I feel the way I do; but you're all I can think about. Those eight hours we spent together on the *Sneak* mean a lot to me. I know I was drunk, but I remember it all. Everything about you is perfect; you're like a dream to me. But, you know, if you don't feel the same, then I won't hassle you; I promise.'

'Malik's ass,' she said, 'you talk a lot.

He gazed at her. 'Dear gods, you are so beautiful.'

'Now you're just being silly.'

'What? No. Surely, you must hear this kind of thing from men all the time?'

'Surprisingly enough, no. I don't hear it very often.' She took his hand and smiled. 'But you can keep saying it, if you like.'

CHAPTER 30

WHAT YOU WISH FOR

E astern Ectus, Western Rim – 24th Beldinch 5255 (18th Gylean Year 6)

Sable placed a last stone onto the cairn, as Badblood watched from over her shoulder. Around them, the mountain summit was shrouded in thick cloud, lending a brooding quality to the darkness. While the others had rested, Sable had worked, placing Meader's body into a shallow dip in the ground, and then covering him with a yard-high heap of stones. It had taken her all evening, but she had refused to stop, despite Blackrose's admonitions that she also needed to rest. Meader deserved a monument, Sable had thought, and she had not allowed her will to be weakened.

She took a step back, her hands and knees filthy from the damp ground.

'It will stand for a hundred years, my rider,' said Badblood. 'You have honoured your friend deeply.'

Sable wiped her hands on her clothes as she gazed at the cairn. She had prepared herself to cry at that moment, but no tears came. She was too angry to weep.

'Have you finished at last?' said Blackrose, her head looming out of the murk.

'I have,' said Sable.

'Good. It is almost midnight, and we should be leaving soon.'

'Is it too late too try to change your minds?' said Evensward, appearing next to Blackrose. 'This coming day will see our deaths; of that I am convinced.'

'You don't have to come,' said Sable.

'Don't insult me, Holdfast,' said the dark green dragon. 'Do you believe that I would abandon you, after all we have experienced together? When you and Badblood first came to Haurn, was it not I who chose to shelter you? I will not leave you now.'

Sable nodded. She leaned down and picked up a few of Meader's possessions that she had taken from his body – a ring, a packet of cigarettes, and a metal, oil-filled lighter, its outer case engraved with the image of a mountain. She slipped the cigarettes and lighter into an inside pocket, and pushed the ring onto one of her fingers.

'I'll give the ring to Austin,' she said; 'if I ever see him again.'

'The only way that will happen, Sable,' said Evensward, 'is if we turn back now.'

'We are not turning back,' said Blackrose. 'Olkis lies ahead, not behind.'

'Then we should break through the lines of defences and make for Olkis,' said Evensward, 'instead of this madness.'

'We have already discussed this in depth,' said Badblood. 'I would be grateful if you stopped mocking my rider's plan.'

'She has cast a spell on you,' said Evensward.

'I know she has,' said Badblood; 'I wouldn't have it any other way.'

Sable glanced at the three dragons. 'Are you all rested?'

'We are,' said Blackrose.

'We should leave,' Sable said. 'The clouds will hide us from the gods, and we shall descend like lightning, bringing death and fire to our enemies.'

'Spoken like a dragon,' said Blackrose. 'What is our first target?'

'The northern coast of Ectus lies a hundred miles from here,' said Sable. 'Our main target shall be the ship-building areas and the dockyards. They are protected by a garrison of Sea Banner marines, so their compound shall be where we strike first. I'm going to place an image of the coastal layout into each of your minds. Do you have any objections?'

None of the dragons said anything, so she powered her vision, and entered each of their heads in turn.

'That was disconcerting,' said Evensward. 'I felt nothing, and then a large aerial view of the coast appeared in my mind's eye.'

'I felt her do it,' said Blackrose.

'Do you see the three large dockyards?' said Sable 'The marine compound lies between the two on the western side. If we get separated in the clouds, make for that location.'

She walked round to Badblood's flank, and pulled herself up onto the harness. The seat where Meader had been sitting was still smeared in blood, and she frowned, realising that she had forgotten to clean it. She felt her emotions surge, and had to suppress them. Let the blood-stains remind her of what she had to do, she told herself. Don't weaken; you are a Holdfast.

She buckled the straps, and glanced up. 'Let's kill some gods.'

Badblood extended his wings and launched himself off the side of the mountain peak. Within seconds, all traces of the ground had disappeared amid the dark clouds. Thunder rumbled somewhere to the north as Badblood circled. Snatched glimpses of the other two dragons whirled around them, then they set off towards the north.

'Do you think Bastion will come, my rider?' said Badblood, as they flew through the clouds.

'I hope so,' said Sable. 'I want his Quadrant and his head, though I'd take Horace's too. Bastion might be too busy with the reinforcement portals, which is why we have to burn everything – to get his attention. As soon as I have my hands on a Quadrant, I'll transport us all back to Haurn.'

'Haurn? Why not Olkis?'

'Haurn for a day first – to rest, and to check on Millen and Deep-blue. We can give the news about Boldspark to the Haurn dragons as well.' Sable wrapped a blanket over her shoulders. 'I think this is the first time I've felt cold since we got to Dragon Eyre.'

'We are flying at a very high altitude, my rider. You'll warm up once the flames start.'

They flew for a little under two hours, leaving the mountainous spine of Ectus behind them. There were several breaks in the cloud, and every time they passed through one, Sable could see a multitude of tiny lights coming from the land below, while the moon was shining brightly towards the east. They raced across each gap, only to be smothered by the thick clouds again. Before too long, Sable's clothes were soaking wet from the moisture in the clouds, and Badblood's dark red wings were glistening.

The clouds extended over the northern coast of the island, and it was Badblood who told her that they had arrived.

'Are the dockyards below us?' she said.

'I can't say that with complete certainty, my rider, but we have flown for the requisite distance, and in the correct direction. If I have calculated things with precision, we should be above the marine compound.'

Sable smiled. She glanced around, but could see no sign of the other two dragons.

'Circle for a minute or two,' she said. 'Let's see if Blackrose and Evensward are nearby.'

Badblood did as she asked, and banked round in a wide arc. A streak of lightning shot through the sky to their left, followed almost immediately by a long rumble of thunder.

'We shall be attacking in the midst of a storm, it seems,' said Badblood. 'It is comparatively peaceful up here, but the weather may get wild once we start to descend.'

'Good,' said Sable. 'A storm will aid us. It will add to the confusion and panic on the ground.' She glanced around again, but couldn't see

Blackrose or Evensward. 'We'll begin our first dive,' she said. 'Perhaps the flames will attract the other dragons.'

'Hold on tight, my rider,' said Badblood, then he pulled in his wings and soared downwards, plummeting through the clouds at high speed.

Sable narrowed her eyes as the wind whipped against her. Lightning crackled through the clouds to their right, dazzling her with its brightness, then they burst through into the open air. Rain was pouring down from the clouds, and she struggled to get her bearings for a moment. Then she saw the row of three dockyards and, directly below them, the fortified marine compound. It was protected by high walls and multiple ballista batteries, most of which were aimed to the north, to defend the coast from an attack from Olkis. Lines of squat barrack blocks fanned out from a central square in the heart of the compound.

'No mercy, my love,' whispered Sable. 'Burn them all.'

Badblood dived through the torrential rain, his wings in. At the last moment, he opened his powerful jaws and unleashed a flood of fire over the first rows of barracks, then pulled up, keeping the flow of fire going. Despite the heavy rain, the buildings erupted, the flames reaching high into the dark sky. Marines piled out of some of the barracks. Some stared at the flames, while others ran. Badblood circled, and kept low for another pass, never once letting the torrent of flames cease. He turned his head as he soared over the compound, spraying fire in every direction, until the screams reached Sable's ears. Something dark flashed by them, and Sable saw Blackrose join the attack. She flew to the other end of the compound, and incinerated the ballista towers that sat by the perimeter walls. Evensward also appeared, her jaws belching out smoke and flames as she attacked the only structure in the compound that was more than one storey high. The rain was crackling and sizzling, and some of the fires burned low, only to be restarted as the dragons made more passes.

Sable glanced around. The compound was enveloped in flames from end to end, and bells were being rung all over the coastal area. The light from the inferno was illuminating the entire district, and the half-built Sea Banner ships in the three dockyards were visible. Sable wished she could use her powers to investigate, and to look for gods who might be close by, but her connection to Badblood was paramount – he needed her battle-vision in order to see clearly.

I sense your frustration, he said in her mind.

Don't worry about it, she said back to him.

She looked out of his good eye. Linking to his mind had become second nature to her, and she could switch from her own mind to his without any conscious effort. What Badblood was seeing was blurry and confused; the rain, flames and night sky all contributing to his disorientation. There was no way she could afford to sever the link, not even for a moment.

Without meaning to, she pushed her powers out through Badblood's eye. Her vision shot from the dragon, and she gasped.

What are you doing? he said. *I can still feel your connection, but now I can also see more. I see the dockyards, as if they were in front of me, but I can still fly. How are you doing this?*

I don't know, she said; *I didn't mean it; but it's working. Badblood do you realise what this means? If I can use my vision powers while remaining connected to you, we can fly and vision at the same time. Hold on, I can see a tower overlooking the dockyards. A god is inside; she's preparing to strike. Bank!*

Badblood dropped a wing, and soared down to the left.

She missed us! cried Sable, then she heard a terrible cry behind them.

Badblood kept turning. Ahead of them, Evensward was falling, her wings limp, and her eyes lifeless. The dark green dragon had been to their rear when the god had struck, and what had been meant for Sable and Badblood had hit her instead. She came down at an angle, struck the wall of the marine compound, and ploughed straight through it. She smashed into the base of the tower where the god had been standing, and came to a juddering halt. The tower began to sway, then it toppled over, giant stone blocks cascading down with a thunderous roar.

The god is still inside, said Sable. *Burn it.*

Badblood continued his turn, until he was facing the same direction as he had been before the god had struck. He hovered over the collapsed rubble of the tower, angled his head down, and loosed a barrage of fire. The flames covered the ruins, and the stones glowed red hot. Next to the rubble, Evensward's body caught fire, and was consumed in the flames. A ballista bolt sped past Badblood, then another, and he broke off the attack. He soared upwards, while Sable kept her vision powers going through his good eye.

Over to the right, my love, she said. *A ballista platform, getting ready to aim at Blackrose.*

The dark red dragon turned, and incinerated a tall wooden tower, upon which six ballistae were sitting. Their crews screamed and fell from the burning tower, as the machines were reduced to ash. Blackrose joined them.

'I saw Evensward fall,' she said. 'Was it a god?'

'Yes,' said Badblood. 'She was in the tower. We destroyed her.'

'How did you find her?'

'I shall explain later,' said the dark red dragon. 'Now we must attack the shipyards.'

'Blackrose,' cried Sable, as the rain drenched her; 'you take the ships – Badblood and I will deal with the defences.'

The great black dragon soared away without a word, and Badblood followed her. They reached the central dockyard, and Blackrose dived onto a row of ships under construction, burning six in only a few seconds. Their wooden decks erupted in flames, lighting up the sky, the glow of the fires reflecting off the low, brooding clouds. Badblood ignored the ships, and made for a complex of warehouses and defensive towers. He dodged a ballista bolt that grazed his flank, then unleashed flames onto the first tower. He moved his head to the right, and sent more flames onto a massive warehouse that had its own high, perimeter wall. The roof caught fire, then the walls, and Badblood soared off in search of another target.

There was an explosion so powerful that it seemed as though the world had ended. A flash of white light blinded Sable, and the roar that followed was louder than anything she had ever experienced. An immense shock wave rippled out from the location of the warehouse, and Badblood was thrown backwards a hundred feet through the air. He crashed into something, and Sable slumped into the harness, unconscious.

———

When she opened her eyes, the air was filled with fine particles of dust. The rain was starting to clear them, but all around her was nothing but murky grey fog, as if she were back in the clouds that shrouded the mountain peak. Rubble lay everywhere, and her ears were ringing so badly that she could hear nothing else. She glanced down, and saw that she was still attached to Badblood's harness. He turned his head to face her, his scales covered in a film of dust that the rain was streaking.

He said something to her, but she couldn't hear the words.

Are you alright? she said in his mind.

Winded, but uninjured. What happened?

That warehouse, she said, *it must have been storing explosive devices. Can you move?*

Badblood raised himself up, sending rivulets of rainwater and rubble fragments flowing down his wings and flanks. He shook himself, and Sable glanced around. The murk was clearing in places, but the place looked unrecognisable. The central dockyard had gone, replaced by a vast crater that was rapidly filling with seawater. Behind them, the glow from the burning marine compound was giving off some light, but Sable could see nothing move around the ruins of the dockyard.

Sable sent out her vision through the rain and clouds of dust. She rose high into the sky and looked down. Banner soldiers were moving out from a large base a mile south of the dockyards. Dozens of wagons with ballistae mounted on the back were among them, and the soldiers were setting them up as the rain poured down upon them. To the east, the streets of Sabat City were bustling, with more soldiers moving into defensive positions along its perimeter; while off shore to the north, a wide cordon of ships lay at anchor, their catapults and ballistae stations manned and ready. Sable hoped that, somewhere, a god was in communication with Gyle, reporting the attack to Horace and Bastion. Would they take the bait? She glanced around for Blackrose, but saw no sign of the black dragon.

Where next, my rider? said Badblood.

The supply docks, Sable said. *I saw ships loaded, and ready to leave in the morning.*

She pushed an image of the location into his mind, and he lifted into the air. Sable noticed that his underside was covered in blood from several deep abrasions.

You told me that you were uninjured, she said.

It's nothing; just a few scrapes I collected from the crash landing. It will not stop me fighting, my rider.

For a moment, she considered retreating to the south, or even running the gauntlet of Sea Banner ships to the north, but she hardened her will. A Quadrant was worth the risk.

Badblood soared over the burning marine compound. The flames were dying down in the heavy rain, but many of the low barrack blocks were still on fire, and charred bodies lay scattered everywhere Sable looked. To the east of the compound was another dockyard, where ships were being built, but they ignored it, and flew upwards to avoid the yard's defences. They reached the cloud cover and were enveloped within the darkness. A bolt of lightning flashed by them, and Sable shivered from the cold, her clothes soaking.

She tried to use her vision through Badblood again. She pushed out from his good eye, and took a look directly below them. She scanned the harbour front, and found the long pier she had seen earlier. Nine huge supply vessels were tied up, sitting low in the water, each packed with supplies for the Banner forces occupying Olkis. She marvelled at her newfound ability to use her powers while flying on Badblood. This changes everything, she thought.

A roll of thunder rumbled nearby, and Sable heard it, her hearing starting to recover from the explosion. Her left ear was painful, and she wondered if she had ruptured her eardrum. She could worry about it later, she thought.

'The supply ships are below us,' she cried out to Badblood. 'Dive!'

The dark red dragon pulled in his wings and shot down through the sky. They broke through the cloud cover, and saw the harbour beneath them. Moments later, ballista bolts began speeding past them, loosed from Sea Banner vessels anchored by the quayside, as well as the harbour's own defences. Badblood kept his wings in against his body, to offer the smallest target possible. As soon as he was in range of the ships, he opened his jaws. The first giant supply vessel exploded in flames, its masts and deck consumed, then the next in line caught fire. The light of the flames attracted more bolts from the defences, and Badblood weaved, then pulled up away from the thick hail of steel.

'I can't get close enough to burn the other ships,' the dark red dragon said. 'Where is Blackrose?'

'We'll find another target,' said Sable; 'take us back into the clouds.'

Badblood started to ascend, then he cried out in agony as a powerful blast of death powers found them. Sable felt them wash over her, her own defences rebuffing them, but Badblood took the full brunt. Sable felt him weaken, his mind filled with nothing but pain. She urged him on, but he began to fall from the sky. The light from the fires raging on the supply vessels were making him a clear target, and ballista bolts arced through the air. One tore through Badblood's left wing, ripping a hole a yard wide. Sable felt the dragon lose consciousness, then he crashed down into a street that lay next to the intact dockyard, gouging out a furrow of cobblestones as he skidded along the ground.

Sable unbuckled the straps that held her to the harness and leapt down to the street, her boots splashing into a deep puddle. She drew her sword, then ran to Badblood's head. She glanced around, but the street was still quiet. It wouldn't be that way for long, she thought. She placed a hand on Badblood's head. He made a choking noise, and opened his good eye.

'I have failed you, my beloved rider,' he said, his voice a gasp.

'No; don't say that, my love,' said Sable. 'You just need to rest for a moment. I'll defend you.'

'No, my beautiful rider; you don't understand. I am dying. This is the end for me. Run. You can still escape.'

'I don't accept that,' she said, her will wavering. 'You're going to be alright.'

'You were always an optimist,' he said, 'that is one reason why I love you so much. Sable, these last few years with you have been the best of my life. You saved my soul from despair, and gave me a love that I will never regret. Now, please; leave me.'

A tear slipped down Sable's cheek as she stared at the dragon. 'I will never leave you; never. You're going to be alright.'

'Don't cry, Sable,' he said, his eye starting to close; 'I love you.'

Sable fell to her knees in the rain, dropping her sword as she clung onto the dragon's head.

'Wake up,' she said. 'Please… Badblood, don't leave me. Please.'

She thumped her fists against the still form of the dark red dragon, as tears spilled from her eyes. He was fine, he just needed to rest – but she knew it wasn't true. She had lost him. She had lost the only being in the world who meant more to her than her own life; the only one who truly understood and accepted her; the only one she really loved. He had made her better, had given her a purpose; her soulmate. Without him, there was nothing but grief and emptiness. And rage.

She picked up the sword. Someone was going to die for what they had done. They were all going to die. A fierce rage devoured her thoughts, obliterating every other emotion. She took a ragged breath, and forced herself to turn away from the body of her beloved Badblood. The rain was streaking down her face, mixing with her tears, as she set her heart on revenge. She started to walk, then ran, keeping to the shadows of the street. Soldiers were emerging from the dockyards; they would find the dark red dragon, and would treat the body of her beloved as a trophy. She considered staying where she was, to fight to the end defending his body, but her desire for revenge kept her moving.

She would come back for Badblood, once she had taken the head of the god who had struck him down.

She ducked into an alleyway, and sent her vision out, homing in on the location from where the death powers had originated. She found a tower overlooking the supply harbour, and scanned the battlements on the top floor. A small group of soldiers and gods were there, offering congratulations to a man dressed in long robes, who was wearing a smug expression.

Governor Horace.

Sable started to run. She left the alleyway behind, and came to another street, where a wall surrounded the supply harbour. Embedded into the wall was the stone tower, with a gate that opened out onto the street. A dozen Banner soldiers were guarding the entrance, standing out in the rain with their steel armour. Sable didn't hesitate. She ran out into the street, raising her hand.

Sleep.

The soldiers clattered to the ground, spilling their crossbows as they fell. Sable vaulted over the bodies and entered the tower. A soldier glanced up at her from a doorway, and she powered her battle-vision. Her sword swept out in a vicious lunge. It cleaved the man's head off then rammed into the doorframe, the blade lodging itself into the thick wood. She released the hilt, and pulled the sword from the dead soldier's scabbard. She ran up the first flight of stairs, and barged into a group of unarmed clerks and servants. In fifteen seconds, she had killed them all, her stolen sword hacking through unprotected flesh as her rage consumed her. Blood dripped down from the front of her wet clothes, and smeared the blade of her sword as she stalked through the lamplit hallways. She found another flight of stairs, and strode up them, her mind filled with darkness. A god appeared at the top of the stairs, where they led out onto the roof. He stared at her for a moment, his mouth opening, then raised his hand. He blinked, glanced at his hand, then tried to run. Sable leapt up the steps after him, and rammed her sword into his back, then heaved upwards. The blade ripped up through his chest, then his neck, severing his spine at the base of his skull. She pushed the body out of the way, then crept up the last steps. She had to get to Horace before he had time to activate the Quadrant. She took a breath, then walked out onto the roof, the rain pelting down onto her. Horace and the others had their backs to her as they gazed out over the two burning supply ships, and Sable stole towards them.

'There is one dragon remaining, my lord,' said a Banner officer.

'I am aware of that,' said Horace. 'I just need a moment to locate the beast, and then I can go home.'

'Oh, Governor,' said Sable.

Horace and the others turned.

'Who are you?' said an officer, as Horace's eyes widened. His hand shot to his robes, but Sable raised a finger.

Sleep.

The mortals and demigods collapsed onto the roof of the tower, but Horace remained conscious, his hand creeping towards his robes as he struggled to resist Sable's powers.

Don't move; you cannot move.

'How are you doing this?' Horace cried, his hands shaking.

Sable approached, her sword held out, as the rain thundered down. A flash of lightning lit up the sky.

'You killed my dragon,' she said, 'and now you are going to pay.'

'I am an Ancient!' he bellowed, his voice booming amid the thunder. He grunted, and his fingers moved closer to his robes.

She lashed out with the sword, slicing through the wrist of Horace's right hand. He screamed, and sank to his knees. Sable dropped the sword, and picked up a crossbow. She gripped it in both hands, and clubbed Horace with the butt, smashing his nose. He screamed again, then Sable lost all semblance of self-control. She battered the crossbow butt into his head, splitting open his skull. He fell to the ground, and she brought the bow down again. The butt snapped as she rammed it into his brains, which spilled out, merging with the puddles on the flat roof. She threw the broken bow away, and used the heel of her boot to stamp down onto the Ancient's head. Bones cracked and splintered under the force of her attack, and she stamped again, and again, until the bloody mess under her boot had lost any resemblance to a head. She stopped, panting.

Why didn't she feel any better? Horace was dead, but that wouldn't bring Badblood back. Her thoughts went to the image of his body being torn apart by trophy-hunting Banner soldiers, and her rage rekindled. She crouched down, and rifled through the Ancient's bloody robes. She pulled out his Quadrant.

She had done it. She had achieved what she had set out to do. She had a Quadrant again, but the price was more than she could bear. She stared at the device, her fingers smearing it with the blood of the Ancient. Evensward had been right; Sable had brought them all to ruin. Her fingers glided over the surface of the Quadrant, and the air shimmered around her. She re-appeared on the street next to Badblood's body, to find a battle raging. On one side, Banner soldiers were loosing crossbows, while setting up a pair of ballista wagons, while Blackrose was standing guard over the body of the dark red dragon. She opened her jaws, burning a dozen soldiers, their screams lost to the thunder.

'Blackrose,' said Sable.

The black dragon turned her head. 'My son is dead! Badblood has fallen, and my heart is bereft.'

'The Ancient who killed him is dead,' said Sable, 'and I have the Quadrant.'

More wagons were arriving at the end of the street, and soldiers were preparing a line of ballistae.

Sable glanced down at the copper-coloured device in her hands. She loathed it; hated what her desire for it had made her do. She touched the engravings, and she, Blackrose, and the body of Badblood appeared in the courtyard outside the temple on Haurn. Above, the sky was clear, and the stars were shining.

Sable and Blackrose gazed at each other, neither saying a word.

Millen burst out of the door of his quarters, his eyes wide. He stared at Sable, then saw Badblood, and raised a hand to his mouth.

'Where are the others?' he said. 'What happened?'

'We made it as far as Ectus,' said Blackrose. 'We gained a Quadrant, but lost Boldspark, Meader, Evensward, and Badblood. And we didn't find Maddie.'

Sable tucked the Quadrant away, and sank to the cold ground, her back leaning against the body of her dead dragon. She felt something poke into her waist, and reached inside her clothes for Meader's cigarettes and lighter. They were still dry, having been hidden next to her skin. She lit a cigarette, and stared at the stars.

Millen crouched by her. 'Are you alright, Sable? Speak to me.'

She glanced at him. 'No, Millen, I'm not alright.'

'I'm so sorry,' he said. 'What will we do now?'

'We will burn Badblood's body on a pyre,' said Blackrose, 'and honour his life and passing. He was brave, and good, and I wish...' Her voice tailed away, as the black dragon started to weep.

'We will do that,' said Sable, 'and then I'm going to bring this world to its knees.'

AUTHOR'S NOTES

MARCH 2022

Thank you for reading Dragon Eyre Ashfall – I hope you enjoyed it!

Ashfall is up there with the most difficult books I've written. For a variety of reasons, every now and again, I struggle with the drafting of a book, and the difficulties I had completing Ashfall were as bad as Epic Book 6 – Storm Mage, which also gave me no end of trouble! With Storm Mage, I think it was due to the introduction of several characters who were younger than those I had attempted up until that point; whereas with Ashfall I was tearing my hair out and banging my head off the desk for no particular reason that I could discern. Perhaps it was because I knew what would happen at the end, and that knowledge clouded my steps, hovering above me like a dragon-sized shadow. Or, just maybe, Dragon Eyre was never meant to be easy.

RECEIVE A FREE MAGELANDS ETERNAL SIEGE BOOK

Building a relationship with my readers is very important to me.

Join my newsletter for information on new books and deals and you will also receive a Magelands Eternal Siege prequel novella that is currently EXCLUSIVE to my Reader's Group for FREE.

www.ChristopherMitchellBooks.com/join

ABOUT THE AUTHOR

Christopher Mitchell is the author of the Magelands epic fantasy series.

For more information:
www.christophermitchellbooks.com
info@christophermitchellbooks.com

Printed in Great Britain
by Amazon

18701056R00257